Praise for Meg Macy's Shamelessly Adorable Teddy Bear Mystery Series

"A twisty mystery tale with a likable protagonist and a colorful supporting cast. Sure to be a very enjoyable series!" —**Livia J. Washburn, bestselling author of** *Black and Blueberry Die*

"Sasha Silverman is an adorable protagonist you want to root for from beginning to end of this fun small-town mystery." —**Nancy Coco, national bestselling author of the Candy-Coated Mystery series**

"A quaint teddy bear store in a scenic Michigan town with interesting characters make this a cozy mystery that readers will surely want to snuggle up with—and the twists and turns will make it unbearable to put down." —**Barbara Early, author of the Vintage Toy Shop Mysteries**

"Teddy bears, quaint shops, and murder! *Bearly Departed* is stuffed with everything cozy mystery readers crave." —**Leigh Perry, author of A Family Skeleton Mystery series**

"Information on retail business and, in particular, on the manufacturing of teddy bears is woven throughout this satisfying cozy." —*Booklist*

"Readers will get a kick out of reading this cozy." —*The Cozy Review*

"When the summer heat gets too oppressive, grab the second book in Macy's delightful Teddy Bear Mystery series—you'll be transported to small-town Michigan in the fall! The clever use of the teddy bear theme all over town adds to the cozy atmosphere of the book . . . Well plotted and nicely paced."
—*RT Book Reviews*

"From the first line to the finale, I was immersed in all facets of this multi-plot drama." —*Dru's Book Musings*

"I was kept guessing until the final suspenseful reveal. I loved the first adorable book and I was more than delighted with this second installment in the series!" —*Cinnamon and Sugar and a Little Bit of Murder Reviews*

"Those pages were really flying and so much was happening, there was no way I was going to put this book down until I reached the end. By the way, I was wrong and surprised by the ending. I loved it!" —*Dollycas Reviews*

"I would be thrilled to recommend this book to all mystery fans, I say buy it now and read it in the fall! A five-star hit and I can't wait for the next!" —*Bibliophile Reviews*

"Order a pizza, blow off dinner, and get lost in this book."
—*A Cozy Experience*

"I am looking forward to visiting Silver Hollow again, not only because Ms. Macy is such a talented writer, but because I love teddy bears as much as I love cozy mysteries."
—*Melina's Book Blog*

WEDDING BEAR BLUES

Books by Meg Macy

Bearly Departed

Bear Witness to Murder

Have Yourself a Beary Little Murder

Wedding Bear Blues

WEDDING BEAR BLUES

MEG MACY

KENSINGTON
PUBLISHING CORP.
www.kensingtonbooks.com

KENSINGTON BOOKS are published by

Kensington Publishing Corp.
119 West 40th Street
New York, NY 10018

All Kensington titles, imprints, and distributed lines are available at special quantity discounts for bulk purchases for sales promotion, premiums, fund-raising, educational, or institutional use.

Special book excerpts or customized printings can also be created to fit specific needs. For details, write or phone the office of the Kensington Sales Manager: Kensington Publishing Corp., 119 West 40th Street, New York, NY 10018. Attn. Sales Department. Phone: 1-800-221-2647.

The K logo is a trademark of Kensington Publishing Corp.

ISBN-13: 978-1-4967-2916-3 (ebook)
ISBN-10: 1-4967-2916-1 (ebook)

ISBN-13: 978-1-4967-2915-6
ISBN-10: 1-4967-2915-3
First Kensington Trade Paperback Printing: January 2021

10 9 8 7 6 5 4 3 2 1

Printed in the United States of America

To Mom, again, for fostering my love of teddies, and to my dad, who supported me with every book.

ACKNOWLEDGMENTS

Thanks to my wonderful editor, Wendy McCurdy, to the amazing Elizabeth Trout, plus the talented art department and production staff at Kensington. Bear hugs and kisses to daughters El and Nari for their help, and to all my family and friends for their patience. Plus special thanks to all readers and fans of the series!

A room without a Teddy
is like a face without a smile.
—Gill Davies

You don't marry someone you can live with—you
marry someone you can't live without.
—Unknown

Chapter 1

"**P**lease help me. Teddy has a broken leg!" The little boy thrust his fuzzy bear into my hands. "Fix Beary for me, Dr. Sasha."

"Of course I will." I wiggled the toy's leg. "Hmm, it does seem to be hurting him. We'll fix him up, no problem. What's your name?"

"Connor. Do you think he needs an operation?"

I suppressed a laugh, fighting to remain serious. "How about we take his temperature first. Here, put this thermometer on Beary's forehead. Oh, good. He doesn't have a fever," I said. "Now we'll take an X-ray. Be a good patient, Beary."

The little boy followed me, holding his teddy, along with his mother. We'd moved the office printer into one of the Silver Bear Shop's front rooms. Our store, the only one of its kind in southeastern Michigan, sold teddy bears of all sizes and their accessories, produced in the factory behind our renovated Victorian home. Silver Hollow residents were proud of our family business along with the Quick Mix factory, which provided jobs for village residents. And I was proud of our growing success since my dad retired and I agreed to manage the business.

This afternoon we moved the accessory racks and hung sheets over the shelves to avoid distractions for the children who brought their bears in for a "checkup." Once Connor placed his teddy on the printer's glass, I pressed the button. A sheet of paper emerged from the other side. Aunt Eve took it over to the "developer" and swapped it for preprinted "X-rays" that my sister Maddie had produced a few days before our Teddy Bear Care Clinic. I took my time studying the sheet and then handed it to the little boy with a smile.

"Good news, it's not broken. See the leg bone here? It's straight without any break, but it might be sprained. Have you ever been to the hospital for any reason?"

When he shook his head, I retrieved the stethoscope hanging around my neck and then winced. A strand of my long blond hair had gotten caught, so I untangled it. I knew I should have either gotten a haircut or pulled it all back into my usual ponytail. I handed one of the earpieces to him and placed the diaphragm against my T-shirt.

"Everyone needs a few simple tests when they visit a doctor. Take a listen to my heartbeat. It's not scary, is it?"

"Just thump-ity thump."

"Let's listen to your heart. I bet it's the same." Keeping an eye on the boy's mother, who was smiling, I placed the diaphragm against his chest. "Hear that? Good. Now what do you think we should do for your bear's sprained leg?"

"Put a bandage on it?"

"You'd make a great doctor. Okay, Beary, let's bandage that leg so it can heal. It won't hurt." I pulled open the desk drawer. "What color of elastic wrap for Beary?"

Once I wrapped the toy's leg, Connor flung his arms around my neck. "He's all better now! Thank you, Dr. Sasha. Beary says thank you, too."

"You're welcome. Make sure he gets enough rest. And don't miss the nutrition station to learn what foods are best to eat for you and your teddy."

"Thanks, Dr. Sasha. Bye."

The little boy tugged his mother toward the next table, where my sister explained the various fruits and vegetables, meats, and grains to eat. Maddie looked adorable with her dark pixie haircut and blond streaks that brightened her complexion. Her borrowed scrubs looked huge on her petite build. She tied a balloon around the bear's arm and handed a pamphlet to Connor's mother before they joined the others trooping out the door. We'd given out almost a hundred red and white heart balloons plus goodie bags with teddy bear bandages, coupons for vitamins, hygiene tips, and vaccination pamphlets.

Plus a map to the local pediatric and after-hours clinics. I insisted on giving out heart-shaped candy suckers, too. My friend, a hospital nurse, had suggested it. I'd squeezed into the largest-size green cotton scrubs she'd brought, and now wished I hadn't indulged in so many Christmas cookies over the holidays. My downfall, truly. I couldn't resist them.

"Oof. I'm gonna have to freeze the Girl Scout Thin Mints I ordered," I said.

"I'm shocked you didn't order cookies from Fresh Grounds to hand out," my significant other, Jay Kirby, teased me. His gorgeous hazel eyes twinkled. "Or Teddy Grahams, at least."

"I forgot to buy them. I didn't have the heart to ask Mary Kate to make specialty cookies at the last minute. She's on bed rest. Fresh Grounds is swamped enough with baking all their muffins and pastries for daily sales."

He looked around at the crowd of parents and kids taking part in the health clinic. "Gotta admit, for a late Tuesday afternoon, turnout's been fantastic."

"I'm so glad, too. I scheduled this for Valentine's Day, but then ChocoLair—that new shop over on Main Street— wanted a launch party on that Sunday." I sighed. "That means this whole week will be crazy. Maddie and I are standing up in Cissy Davison's wedding on Saturday. Don't forget you're my plus-one guest for the reception."

"I won't. I'm making an ice sculpture for the rehearsal dinner at the hotel."

My mouth dropped open. "You are? How will you manage, plus delivering it—"

"My brother Paul said he'd get it there."

Jay kissed my cheek and headed over to greet one of the last visitors, a fearful little girl clutching her Winnie the Pooh teddy bear. I turned back to chat with two parents who held out flyers for the Chocolate Bear Bar, and explained how we planned to host it at the Silver Bear Factory, how ChocoLair would provide chocolate-themed treats and activities, and that we'd be finished early enough on Sunday afternoon for parents to enjoy their Valentine's Day evening.

I never figured Cissy Davison would object, since her wedding was on the thirteenth of February. She would be long gone on her honeymoon by then, but Cissy complained that the event would upstage her plans. I stood my ground, however. Since her fiancé took my side in the argument, Cissy had to back down. She'd already alienated one friend, who refused to reschedule a long-planned anniversary trip to Hawaii in order to be in the bridal party.

That led Cissy to ask if I'd be a substitute bridesmaid. I felt uncomfortable, however, even though Maddie begged me to accept. She'd been asked from the beginning, being a close friend of Cissy's sister, Debbie, the maid of honor. I couldn't help wondering why Cissy hadn't asked other friends instead of me. Unless the rumors of her acting like a bridezilla were true.

I dreaded wearing a satin strapless dress with four-inch high heels. I was sure to fall flat on my face. Carrying a bouquet of white lilies would certainly kick in my allergies bigtime, too. I liked Cissy despite her dramatics, although I preferred Debbie for her easygoing and friendly personality. Debbie also provided the Silver Bear Shop with jars of honey from her beehives. We sold out of every jar within days.

That honey was amazing for taste and purity. I sighed, wishing I didn't have to bow to pressure to keep the Davisons happy.

I adjusted the fake DR. SASHA tag on the lanyard around my neck. Maddie created the tags to designate our staff personas. Jay insisted on being a nurse, since more men had joined the ranks formerly filled only by women. My aunt and I acted as doctors. Kids were delighted to bring in their teddy bears, accompanied by parents, despite the weather. We had a streak of bitter cold, below zero at night, but no snow since the January thaw.

I was grateful for that. Winter in Michigan could change from frigid to balmy in a heartbeat. A week ago, I only wore a sweater on a sixty-five-degree afternoon. Today I had donned thermal underwear beneath this thin cotton uniform.

"These kids are adorable, aren't they?" Aunt Eve glanced around the room. "The parents seem receptive to the information, too. Especially the importance of vaccines."

"I don't know how many times Mom told us how miserable she was getting both kinds of measles," I said with a laugh. "And the chicken pox."

"I got the mumps at eight months old," my aunt said, "and both measles. Horrible. Kids are lucky they can avoid all that with shots. Guess we'd better start cleaning up."

Almost everyone had departed by now, the kids happily clutching their bears and the treat bags. I sent Aunt Eve over to chat with the last stragglers, who wanted more information about our specially priced Valentine bears wearing denim overalls and red shirts, white dresses with red hearts, or red-and-white pajamas. A few more sales didn't hurt, either. I helped Jay stack chairs and store them.

"One event down for this week," he said, and folded the tables next.

I gathered the tablecloths. "Maddie and I have Cissy's bachelorette party tonight, then the rehearsal and dinner on Friday, the wedding on Saturday, and finally the Chocolate Bear Bar on Valentine's Day. I wish I could come up to see you at that ice-carving festival up north."

"There's always next year," Jay said. "But I thought Cissy wanted you to cancel the chocolate event at the Silver Bear Factory."

"Not a chance, since I promised to host it. Would you skip the Harrison Frostbite Festival if someone pitched a fit at you about participating?"

"No way. And I'm a rank amateur compared to some of the artists," Jay said, half-joking, while he swept the floor. "I've done what, maybe three dozen ice sculptures. The real pros have hundreds if not thousands in their portfolios. I've got to be there all Friday carving to get the piece looking right. Hope I don't freeze my fingers off, too."

"You said you have special gloves, though. How's the new hand saw?"

"The Japanese one? I paid more for it than all my drills, the grinder and sander tools, the brushes, and chisels put together. Worth the money, though."

"It's so cool you're branching out from woodcarving."

"Gotta admit the ice carvings I'm doing for local restaurants pay the bills, since the bigger commissions in wood are hit and miss." Jay collected the last health clinic sign. "I'm doing the same design for the Frostbite Festival as I did for the

Plymouth Ice Festival, except larger. The teapot, teacup, and saucer with a lot more frills."

Aunt Eve walked over. "The kids were a lot of fun," she said. "All those tips from your friend were so helpful about acting like real health professionals."

I hugged her. "Thanks for volunteering."

We all shivered in the cold air that swept into the shop when the last parent and child departed. I so wanted to head up north to Harrison near Houghton Lake on Friday with Jay, but I couldn't get out of the wedding rehearsal and dinner. Cissy would pitch a fit. So would Maddie, since she'd begged me to join her in the bridal party. My sister already had to soothe Debbie's ruffled feathers over the tight-fitting scarlet bridesmaid dresses and matching high heels.

"How about a La Mesa carryout," Jay asked, "or do you have to leave soon?"

"The bachelorette party starts at seven, but we told them we'd be late due to the health fair today. I can't say no to a few Taco Locos, because I'm starving."

He headed for the parking lot while I filed the extra X-rays in a cabinet. I removed and folded all the cotton sheets from the shelves while Maddie and Aunt Eve rolled out the accessory racks. At last the shop looked back to normal. Maddie pulled off her nurse tag and stethoscope, still chatting about the Super Bowl halftime and commercials. Since I hadn't watched any of that, I gathered up the leftover goodie bags and dumped them on the table.

"Help me push the copy machine back," I asked Maddie. "It's heavy."

"Probably could use a new one," she said. "This one is so old."

"Good luck talking your uncle into that," Aunt Eve said with a laugh. "You know Ross keeps expenses at the factory down to the bare minimum, if he can. Ever since your dad asked him to supervise production, my husband acts like ordering thread is a hardship."

I laughed. "Yeah, Uncle Ross is a real character."

The three of us tugged, pulled, and dragged the machine back into place after a few scrapes along the walls. I wished we'd asked Jay to help move it. Too late now. I glanced around the walls and noticed other dings, scratches, and scrapes. Maybe we needed to close the shop on a weekend and hire painters. That would be a great project for spring. We'd scheduled the exterior job, a huge project given the siding and trim on the corner turret, the second floor Rotunda and sunroom above the back porch, plus all the support posts and shutters.

The thought of all that work gave me a huge headache. Along with the expense—both Dad and Uncle Ross fought against the idea until I produced photos of all the peeling paint, scrapes, and necessary repairs. Maybe we could take a vacation during the down-time. My only worry was preventing damage to our extensive flower beds and shrubbery. But I dismissed that for now.

It was only February, after all.

"I'm looking forward to Cissy and Gus's wedding," Maddie said, wiping her damp face, "because I'm tired of all her texts with reminders."

I laughed. "Yeah, I hear ya. How about if we make a brief appearance tonight, and then come home? I'm ready to crash now."

"Me too, but we'll have to see how it goes. Who knows what Cissy has planned, and from what Debbie said, she's ready for a total meltdown."

"Great. I'm gonna enjoy the Taco Locos that Jay's bringing from La Mesa. Who knows what kind of food they'll have at the party. If any."

"I'm sure they'll have some kind of appetizers."

"Maybe. Why is Cissy on edge anyway? Things have gone well, from what I heard. Love makes the world go around, and the wedding's almost here."

"Debbie told me Cissy's gown didn't fit, and the design is so complicated it will be difficult to alter without looking weird," Maddie said. "But whatever."

"Wow. I thought it's easy to take a dress in at the seams."

"I guess Cissy gained ten pounds from all the stress, but she refuses to own up to it. Cost a few grand, so her mom is really upset. You can't add any material to an already tight-fitting creation. Remember, you had the opposite problem."

"Don't remind me," I said. "Ugh."

My own disastrous fitting long ago proved how nervous I'd been before the wedding, unable to eat or sleep. The dress looked like a parachute on me, another red flag against marrying Flynn Hanson. Divorcing him was far easier.

"How many people did Cissy and Gus invite?" I asked.

"Almost four hundred," Maddie said, "and their friends have already arrived to party hearty, starting with last weekend's bachelor party."

"Knock, knock!"

ChocoLair's owner, Joelynn Owens, entered by the office's side door, pulling a handcart loaded with boxes behind her. The door slammed shut, almost upsetting the cart. I caught a glimpse of the falling snow outside, covering the cars, ground, trees—several inches by now. Joelynn batted her overlarge brown eyes, thick with false eyelashes. Her makeup looked flawless on her bronze-hued skin, and her dark hair curled over her shoulders. I'd never seen her in sweats or old clothes, ever. She always dressed like a star.

I was lucky to dab eye shadow and blush on, grab earrings, and brush my wet hair after a morning shower. If only I could jump out of bed every morning like my sister, but that required massive effort. And a gallon of coffee.

Today Joelynn's white coat reminded me of an alpaca with its shaggy fur. Tall black leather boots, black slacks, and a white beret complemented her trendy look, and the tweedy red scarf added a pop of color. When she held up a bag, I inhaled the delicious scents of chocolate and cinnamon.

"Ooh, what is it?" Maddie squealed, peeking inside.

"Chocolate babka. I just baked it, and figured you deserved a treat after today. Plus it's a thanks for hosting the Chocolate Bear Bar on Sunday. Valentine's Day is perfect timing," she said happily. "These are all the supplies for the different stations at the event. I don't have room for storage. My shop is so tiny, so I figured you wouldn't mind finding a spot here."

"Mmm." Maddie had already gobbled a piece of cake and swooned.

"Hey, save me some," I said, and grabbed the bag.

"There's three or four slices," Joelynn said with a laugh. "Plenty to share."

"Heavenly," I mumbled, my mouth full. "What kind of chocolate did you use?"

"A Dutch-processed cocoa powder that I buy online. Makes the best brownies, too." She waved a sheet of paper. "We're full up already in a head count. I want to give the adults room to help their kids, so I'm putting six at a table instead of eight."

"Wow," I said, surprised. "I figured thirty bucks for a parent and their child might be prohibitive, costwise. I guess not."

"They're getting a lot for the price. Chocolate-dipped Oreos and marshmallows, drizzled popcorn and pretzels, plus all the different molded teddy bears. You've helped so much to get our new shop off the ground in Silver Hollow," Joelynn added. "Cheri was so worried, but orders are piling up.

And we haven't opened yet."

"Cheri's been popping antacids since Christmas, from what her sister told me." I knew Joelynn's business partner was due to give birth any day to her first child. "You won't have any problems getting Easter orders, with all your hand-molded chocolate eggs and bunnies. People will swarm your shop for Mother's Day, too. In the fall, your gourmet caramel and chocolate-coated apples will sell like hotcakes."

"Remember we've got to leave soon, Sasha," Maddie warned. "It's almost seven."

"What's going on tonight?" Joelynn asked.

"The bachelorette party for Cissy Davison."

"Oh, the wedding of the season! I heard all about her personal shower."

Maddie snickered. "The naughty-or-nice theme, with an emphasis on the 'naughty.' 'Tushie' cookies, chocolate-dipped bananas, and a cake with a plastic naked guy emerging from it. A 'Pin the Macho on the Man' game, too. I bought her matching silk robes with 'Hers' and 'Mine, Too' embroidery for their Tahitian honeymoon."

"Cissy received enough lingerie to supply a boutique," I added. "I doubt she even noticed the personalized beach towels I gave her, and a bikini with a matching sarong."

"She loved the designer sunglasses her sister gave her," Maddie said, "plus two sets of 'Thong of the Day' in tropical colors."

"Oh, I saw those in Devonna Walsh's catalog," Joelynn said. "And the teddy bear that hides all the fun, intimate little toys—"

I cut her off. "Don't go there, please."

"But teddy bears are for cuddling, right?" Joelynn laughed. "Okay, so where should I put all this stuff? It's mostly the plastic and silicone chocolate molds, plus sprinkles, decorations, heart streamers, a banner, that kind of stuff. I'm bringing the chocolate on Sunday at noon so we can melt it ahead of time."

"Follow me over to the factory. Might as well store it there."

"I'm going up to change," Maddie said. "We need to go by eight."

"Okay, we'll hurry."

Joelynn waited while I zipped up my jacket and grabbed a knit hat. Together we headed out into icy gusts that stung my eyelids and cheeks. I pointed out any slick spots on the winding pathway, and then held the door open while she pushed the handcart inside. Uncle Ross stood there, the cap on his head at the usual jaunty angle, arms crossed over his chest. I caught a quick glimpse of affection in his eyes before his familiar scowl descended on us.

"What the devil is all this, Sasha?"

"We're hosting the Chocolate Bear Bar on Sunday, remember. Perfect for Valentine's Day, from two o'clock until five."

"But it's only Tuesday."

"We're storing these boxes until then. They won't be in your way."

He shook his head. "We don't have room for more junk—"

"I'll find a spot and make sure everything's put back into place after the event. We're here to serve the community, not just make a profit," I said. "Hosting ChocoLair will give residents a chance to learn what the new shop will offer."

Ignoring my uncle's glare, I breezed past him without another word. Too bad his brief second honeymoon with Aunt Eve hadn't relieved his ornery attitude. But I knew the staff had been swamped with producing Valentine's Day accessories for our teddy bears, plus green sweaters and dresses for St. Patrick's Day, and pastel-hued clothing for spring. I was sure he also resented the upcoming spring painting of the shop and factory as well.

Still, that was no excuse to be rude.

"This way, Joelynn." I gestured down the hall to the room that held the huge stuffing machine. Bags of polyester filled the wall of shelves opposite. "I left a note for my aunt to order more shipping boxes and Styrofoam peanuts. Guess I'd better add Poly-fil to the list."

Joelynn pushed the handcart past me. "Cheri told me that someone was murdered here last fall. Is that true?"

"Unfortunately, yes. That's why we walled this machine off from the factory."

I suppressed all the memories of our former sales rep, Will Taylor and the hassles he'd given me last fall. Few if any mourned his death. But Silver Hollow residents had yet to recover from Mayor Bloom's murder in December. No one had expected that. I didn't anticipate coming face-to-face with his killer, either. A shiver raised goose bumps on my arms.

Joelynn brushed dust from her slacks. "That's the last box. Thanks again, Sasha."

"See you Saturday night to set up all the tables and chairs."

"Sure thing. Maybe Cheri will come, too."

I headed back to the shop, waving when Joelynn drove off, and let my dogs outside. Jay had rescued Sugar Bear, a sweet little poodle, and given her to me as a Christmas present. Rosie, a Lhasa Apso and Bichon Frise mix, had yet to adjust to Sugar Bear's domination. Poor baby. She was so used to being the only dog in the family since her puppy days, but Rosie would eventually adjust. I hoped, anyway, since I'd spoiled her for so long.

I wasn't sure which was worse, the dogs' competition for attention or the dog-and-cat wars. Onyx, Maddie's black cat, had lately shown them both who was the real boss—scratching Rosie's nose, and biting Sugar Bear. When we returned inside, Onyx perched on the window seat and stared at both dogs with haughty derision. She hissed when Sugar Bear danced around for a treat. Rosie gobbled her treat and then curled up near the heating duct.

When Jay arrived, he handed me the large brown bag from La Mesa and kicked off his snowy boots. "I swear I'm gonna roast that damned dog."

I stared at him in shock. "You can't mean Sugar Bear? Or Rosie?"

"Nope. Cissy's dog." He ran a hand over his damp light brown hair. "She dumped him on her parents while she's busy with the wedding, remember, but Mr. Clooney's running around everywhere. And haunting the spot behind Silver Moon where I practice my ice carving."

"So?"

"Every day I have to clean my boots and my car's floor mats. Can't we do something? The dog's leaving big piles of poop all over!"

Chapter 2

I fought back laughter at his dismay. "Aren't they more like frozen logs?"

Jay glared at me. I felt bad for making a joke at his expense, but couldn't help it. He looked adorable, with a faint outline of a five o'clock shadow on his jaw, and clad in his usual plaid flannel shirt and rugged cargo pants. Jay's lean build was deceptive. He had powerful arms and shoulders, given his carvings in ice and wood. And he was incredibly talented with both. Maybe I was biased, but I was so proud of him.

"The weather's been up and down lately, cold one day and springlike the next. Some of the piles are frozen, but most have thawed," he said. "Plus we shouldn't have to clean up after Mr. Clooney. That's the Davisons' job."

"Okay, I'll ask Mrs. Davison to see if they can check their fence and gates."

"I doubt she'll do anything. I had to hose off the studio floor today because I tracked that poop all over the place. And I hate to deliver my ice carvings to the hotel with that smell on my boots. Maddie was complaining about it, too."

"She never mentioned anything to me—"

"I never got a chance," Maddie said from the kitchen doorway. She looked swanky in a black sweater with a brown fur collar, jeans, and a chunky necklace. "That fence isn't tall enough for such a big dog. And Mr. Clooney chews things to bits. He keeps ripping chair cushions from what Debbie told me last month."

"Ugh." I was grateful my dogs were house-trained and not destructive. "I doubt if I can bring it up tonight, but I'll see how it goes."

I'd unpacked the bag from La Mesa and devoured a taco before fetching the pets' bowls. Onyx hissed at Sugar Bear, who stood her ground and barked wildly. Maddie drew the cat's attention with the can opener's whizzing sound, and placed her full dish on the highest shelf of the cat tower. Rosie waited patiently for her dinner, and gobbled up what was left after Sugar Bear finished hers. The little sneak. I'd forgotten to retrieve the smaller dog's bowl.

"Girl, that means you need an extra walk. Or maybe I should get a treadmill," I told her and ruffled her curly ears. "It's been so cold, and we've been too busy."

"So where is this bachelorette party?" Jay wolfed a whole taco in two bites.

"In Ann Arbor." Maddie bit into one of my tacos. "Mmm, nothing better than La Mesa's. Except Amato's pizza. Hurry up, Sash. It's half past seven now, we can't be too late."

I bolted upstairs to change and chose black jeans, a red angora sweater, gold earrings and bracelets, plus my sturdy leather boots. I twisted my blond hair up, added mascara, blush, and lip gloss. At the last minute, I drew on eyeliner and added some gold sparkling shadow on my eyelids. Cissy didn't have to be the only diva at the party.

By the time I returned to the kitchen, Maddie was listing the bridal party to Jay. "Debbie, Cissy's sister, is the maid of honor. Two of Cissy's sorority sisters are standing up, and one of their husbands will be a groomsman. The other bridesmaid is paired with one of Gus's college friends, and I'm standing up with Eric Dyer."

"He owns the Silver Claw, right?" Jay asked. "The new microbrewery."

Maddie nodded. "And winery. I had no idea he knew Gus Antonini."

"That's not a bad thing, is it?" I teased her. "I'm stuck with Gus's cousin from Chicago, and his daughter is the flower girl. I hear little Martina is a holy terror."

"I never saw anyone who could best Cissy for drama," Maddie said, "but you're right. Debbie says that kid takes the prize for being out of control."

"Who's the best man?" Jay asked.

"Dylan Campbell, Gus's best friend from college." My sister blew out a breath. "That's gonna be a problem, because he was once engaged to Debbie. She's still steamed over him dumping her, too, even though it's been a while."

"Yeah, that's not like her to keep hanging on to resentment," I said. "And Mr. Clooney is the ring bearer, with a special pouch to hold the wedding bands, so he won't drop them."

"I bet he'll drop a few things on the way up the aisle."

I burst out laughing at Jay's wry remark. "Pastor Lovett would not approve."

Maddie caught my elbow. "By the way, Mom said Uncle Hank and Aunt Marge decided to visit on the spur of the moment. We haven't seen them in years."

"Cool. Hey, I got a text from Cissy—"

"Yeah, I already picked up our bridesmaid dresses and wedding shoes."

I groaned, thinking of those four-inch heels, and turned to Jay. "Can you hang with the dogs for a bit? They're pretty bored since I didn't get them out for a walk."

He unwrapped another taco. "I've got to head up to Harrison around nine—"

Mom burst through the door. "Sasha, Maddie. I want to make sure it's okay if Uncle Hank and Aunt Marge stay here with you. Remember our guest bedroom and bath renovation isn't finished. Our whole condo is a mess, in fact."

"No problem, Mom. We'd love to have them stay."

Dad brushed snow from his coat and then stooped to pet Sugar Bear. She adored my father, and danced around when he produced a treat from his pocket. "Good to see you, Kirby. Do I smell dinner from La Mesa?"

"Plenty of tacos, Mr. Silverman, if you're hungry," Jay said. "Help yourself."

"Maddie, have you got those flyers ready?" Mom asked. "I'm using my new gallery as headquarters for my campaign, but we've got to start promoting our next art show."

"I'm working on them, along with the special election brochures. I'll get them done in a day or two," she added. "I've heard so many people aren't happy with Gil Thompson around here. He's been mayor pro tem for a few months, ever since Cal Bloom's murder, but hasn't gotten much accomplished."

"I think you'll get more done than both of them ever did once you're elected," I told Mom with pride. "Your campaign is going strong, and look at how fast you got Vintage Nouveau up and running. Twice as many artists than you expected want to show their work in the gallery. Signing Jim Perry was a real bonus, given his national reputation."

"True." Mom sounded particularly pleased. "That's why the next show will be huge. I'm certain private collectors will flock into town to see it."

"I heard Mr. Thompson and the council tabled the motion to open Theodore Lane to through traffic. We really need it now, given the Chocolate Bear Bar and a few other events we've planned. Is he really pushing the Main Street repaving project instead?"

"That would benefit Fresh Grounds," Jay pointed out. "His own business."

"A clear conflict of interest," Mom said. Dad nodded, swallowing a bite of taco.

"People aren't happy with that, from what little I've heard."

"Is it true the Davisons' house has a bidding war going on?" Maddie asked. "She just put it up for sale."

"That's what I heard, yes. Two days, and three offers."

"About Mr. Clooney, Mom," I said in my sweetest tone. "He's been jumping their fence and running around the neighborhood, leaving dog droppings everywhere. Can you convince Mrs. Davison to do something? We'd really appreciate it."

"I believe they also installed an electric fence," she said.

Dad snorted in disgust. "That doesn't stop him. I saw that dog zipping right through with just a shake of his head. Either he likes the jolt, or else they forget to turn it on."

"Mr. Clooney jumped our fence," I added. "Good thing I was in the yard to save Sugar Bear. She was eager to meet him at first, being another poodle. He's a standard and she's only a toy, so she ended up cowering in terror. I rescued her and calmed her down, but Mr. Clooney almost knocked me over to nip at her. I know he was only playing, but it wasn't fun."

"I'll talk to Barbara, although she's swamped with helping Cissy with all the wedding details." Mom sighed. "She wanted to host the bachelorette party, but one of the bridesmaids had already offered to have it at her mother's house. Cissy agreed to let her mother order the food, though, to counter all the booze her bridesmaids wanted."

Maddie fetched her coat and purse. "If anyone eats at all, given how Cissy and her friends drink like fish."

"You girls be careful, then. The roads are bad—"

"Don't worry, Mom. We both have to work tomorrow. Are you staying for a bit?"

She nodded. "I'll make a few casseroles for Hank and Marge's visit."

"Bye, Jay," I said, although he still crunched his taco. "Guess you won't have to keep the dogs company after all."

When I kissed him, he hugged me tight. I savored the feel of his warm arms and a whispered promise that we'd spend more time together after the weekend. Mmm. Something to look forward to, all right. Jay followed me and my sister to the snow-covered parking lot and drove off in his truck. I brushed off our car windows and then buckled my seat belt. Maddie punched the heater buttons to full blast.

"Winter can't end soon enough for me," she grumbled.

The roads did prove slicker than Mom's warning, so Maddie drove with extra caution. Although salt trucks had treated the interstate, we watched SUVs and trucks zip by in the left lane. One skidded until the driver regained control. I breathed easier.

It was eight fifteen by the time we arrived at the party's location in Ann Arbor. Maddie stopped the car behind a long line of others in the circular driveway. The house proved to be a lovely French Colonial home. I glimpsed a crystal chandelier and curving wrought-iron staircase inside the brightly lit foyer. Two wreaths with white flowers and red satin ribbons graced the double doors. I rang the bell, wondering if a maid would answer.

Instead a woman with flaming red hair waved us inside. In a white cashmere sweater, black skirt, and leather boots, plus chunky gold jewelry, she reminded me of Barbara Davison, who wore the latest styles. I preferred Aunt Eve's daring fifties uniqueness, however.

"Welcome, ladies!" She took our coats. "Call me Ginger. Vanessa is my daughter, and you're the last of the bridesmaids to arrive. Sasha and Madeline, correct?"

"Sorry we were delayed," I said automatically, but she waved a hand.

"No need to apologize. Come along."

We followed her past the cream-and-gold living room, which reminded me of Grandma Silverman's pristine home long ago. The cozy kitchen with its brick fireplace and oak cabinetry was more welcoming; bottles of wine stood open on the table, along with the catering trays of canapés, crackers and cheese, stuffed olives, puff seafood pastry, and other finger foods. All untouched so far, as we expected. Maddie nudged me with a smile.

Shrill voices and laughter floated from the back of the house. The other bridesmaids sat on comfortable sofas or chairs back in the family room, each holding a colorful drink in hand. They ogled trays of nail polish, makeup, and hair products.

"You missed the Botox Lady!" Cissy waved at us, although her cheeks and mouth didn't move. Her long blond hair fell over one eye when she shook her head. "Want me to call and have her come back? The injections don't hurt."

"But there is pain." Debbie giggled, although her face looked half-frozen and she held a blue ice pack in one hand. "I can still feel that needle going in. Too bad you missed out."

Cissy introduced us to the rest of the bridal party. Since I'd missed the personal shower, that helped to pair faces with names. Her college friends, Vanessa Leeson and Kim Goddard, were tall, blond, and blue-eyed like Cissy. Debbie didn't look much like her sister; she was much shorter and dark haired, like her mother. Barbara Davison chatted with Ginger and another older woman near the kitchen doorway. I overheard Kim joking about the Botox injections.

"I'm glad I got the extra shots," she said, "although we can't exercise or bend over for what, at least six hours? Anything to hide the bags under my eyes for photos."

I glanced sideways at Maddie, grateful we'd arrived late. No way was I interested in letting anyone inject me with a poisonous toxin. My sister didn't seem disappointed, either.

"We brought wine." Maddie handed the bottle to Debbie. "Eric Dyer recommended this Brut Rosé with strawberry tones. He makes it at his winery and brewery."

"Ooh, everyone loves strawberries. Thanks a lot."

Debbie headed to the kitchen with the bottle while Maddie surveyed the dining table. Ginger set out croissant sandwiches and silver platters of bite-size desserts next to the bottles of gin, vodka, and whiskey, plus a tray of Jell-O shots.

"All that food going to waste, since they can't open their mouths," I said with a grin.

Maddie agreed. "I'm starving. Let's dig in."

We filled plates and then joined the other bridesmaids in the family room. Tiny crystals of ice pitter-pattered against the huge picture window. Vanessa handed me a mimosa in a tulip-shaped glass. I sat on the farthest sofa and took a sip. Whoa, way too strong for my taste.

Kim slid a plastic cup chock-full of ice across the coffee table. "Better if you water it down. It's all about booze and Botox tonight."

"Oh?" I rubbed my forehead. "I could use an ice pack without the injections."

Maddie dropped on the sofa. "Chill. These spinach pies are amazing."

I slumped against the cushions, wishing I'd snagged a few aspirin before leaving home. My sister was right about the spinach phyllo-dough triangles, though. The tiny ham-and-cheese pinwheels were good, too, and the chicken salad croissant. I'd added a pile of salty cashews, which helped balance the boozy and sweet mimosa. Vanessa plopped between me and my sister on the sofa. She pushed a strand of blond hair away and tapped her long acrylic fingernails on her glass. Then she leaned close, her voice a whisper.

"I refused a Botox injection, so now Cissy's mad at me."

"Why would she be angry?" I asked.

"She paid for a specific number," Vanessa said. "Kim volunteered to take mine, plus the ones reserved for you and Maddie. I think she's crazy—"

"This is Gus's aunt," Cissy interrupted, two hands on a plump and petite woman's shoulders. "Zia Noemi is hosting the rehearsal dinner Friday, and the cookie table at the wedding reception. She made cannoli for tonight, too."

"Wow," I said, truly impressed. "I'll definitely check them out."

Zia Noemi beamed, patting her beehive-styled dark hair. She resembled my late Aunt Marie who always dressed to the nines, wore thick pancake makeup, false eyelashes, and bright fire-engine red lipstick, but had a sweet disposition. Ten years gone, I still missed her.

On her tiptoes, Zia Noemi kissed Cissy's cheek. "I make

cannoli for Christmas, every year, and I put amaretto in the filling. I make over a hundred for my family."

"That sounds amazing," I said.

"Gus is like a son to me," she continued, smiling wide. "I'd do anything for him, he's such a dear boy. I baked five hundred wedding cookies for the reception, too! With three icing flavors—lemon, orange, and vanilla."

"Five hundred? Wow."

"Sasha is a cookie fiend," Maddie said. "She'll be in heaven Saturday night."

"No joke," I said, a little shame-faced. "I can't help it."

"—but he's a total jerk." Debbie's loud voice caught my attention. "Gus doesn't really know him, if he thinks he's such a great guy," she added. "Dylan promised to help with my beehives, but refused. They weigh forty to fifty pounds, way too heavy for me. Good thing Kim helped me with them instead."

"You told me Dylan got stung a few times, and that's why he didn't want to help you anymore," Cissy said. "Can't say I blame him."

"Kim got stung, but she didn't whine about it."

"Not to you, anyway," Kim said with a laugh.

"Well, do you remember how Dylan called me on the phone to break our engagement? The jerk couldn't tell me in person!" Debbie's voice shook with fury, and her habit of giving an eye roll whenever someone disagreed with her was almost comical. She always wore jewelry adorned with her beloved bees, like the honeycomb gold brooch pinned to her dress. "I can't believe he did that to me. 'Sorry, honey, but I can't marry you after all.'"

"You're better off without him," Cissy said, and waved her left hand. Her fat diamond engagement ring sent sparkles around the room to compete with the glowing lamps.

"I'm gonna get even with the creep, wait and see. I even asked Gus if he'd get rid of Dylan," Debbie said, "but he flat-out refused."

"He's the most stubborn Italian I know."

Zia Noemi shook a finger at the bride-to-be. "My Gus, stubborn? No, no. He loves you so much, and will always listen to you, Cissy."

Debbie frowned. "Too bad he won't listen to me. I once put ipecac syrup in Dylan's orange juice, so maybe I should add a few drops of arsenic in his champagne."

"I hope you're joking," Barbara Davison said sternly. "How can you talk about poison like that, Debbie, with all these recent murders in Silver Hollow?"

"And I don't want anything disrupting my wedding," Cissy said.

"A little prank, that's all it is," Debbie said. "He treated me worse while we dated—"

Weary of listening to rehashed grievances, I tuned her out and surveyed the fieldstone fireplace. A forest stretched beyond the huge picture window, each tree frosted in white. I mused about walking through the meandering path from the house beneath the trees until a whispered exchange between two other women sparked my interest. Gus Antonini's sister, Gisele Vaccaro, had a cap of dark curls, olive skin, and huge chocolate-brown eyes. Her somber navy suit gave her a matronly air. She looked at least ten years older than her brother. Cissy had introduced the second woman earlier as Claudia Antonini, the wife of Gus's cousin.

"Frank is insanely jealous. I can't even talk to the mailman," she said.

"My Bob has no clue that I met Dylan. And man, that man knows exactly how to please," Gisele purred. "Ooh, baby. Those hands, and his kisses. Totally worth a little make-out session on the sly. And he doesn't mind older women, Claudia. Go ahead, flirt a little."

"It's tempting." She pushed her red hair out of her eyes, her cheeks flushing deep pink. "Frank would kill me if he found out."

Gisele caught my eye. "Have you met Dylan Campbell, Sasha?"

"Nope." I gulped from my drink. "Not my type, but my sister met him."

"He's the worst flirt I've ever seen. He came on so strong, I had to slap his hands away." Maddie waved her wineglass. "And Debbie's not kidding about him playing pranks."

"True, too true." Gisele tried to wink but failed. Clearly those Botox injections affected any facial expressions. "On a camping trip, Dylan put a hognose snake in my brother's sleeping bag. Five feet long. Gus didn't think it was funny, not at first."

"Ugh, I'm terrified of snakes." Kim had sidled over to join the group. "I always have my gun handy when I'm out hiking, in case I see one. Did the snake bite him?"

"Nah, they're harmless enough. The guys were all drunk anyway."

Gisele and Claudia both curled over their drinks, laughing and moaning in pain. I turned away and listened to Cissy's complaints about Gus's wild bachelor party last weekend.

"—got so out of hand." She waved her glass in the air. "Gus should never have let Dylan plan the whole thing without asking about the details. Christophe Benoit is ready to strangle both of them. The guys nearly trashed his restaurant."

"How?" I asked.

"The usual antics over a poker game. Men, I tell you."

"That is true," Zia Noemi said sadly. "Boys will be boys."

A totally lame excuse, in my opinion. I returned to the

dining room table and refused to feel guilty over sampling a second cannoli. They were fabulous, with big chunks of chocolate studding the thick custard. I could taste the kick of amaretto, too. Truly amazing.

I'd better order that treadmill after all.

I heard an odd gasp from Cissy, who stood so fast she knocked her drink over. Vanessa shrieked, but not because of the ice and liquid that puddled over the carpet. A tall and devilishly handsome guy, his brown hair flecked with gold, with a thin mustache and a muscular build, stood in the doorway of the family room. He flashed a dazzlingly white smile that reminded me of Bradley Cooper in *The Hangover*. Who was he? And what was going on?

"Hey, ladies! I just wanted to drop by tonight, and a-pal-apologize," he slurred, clearly two sheets to the wind. "Looks like you're all ha-having a good time."

"No men allowed," Cissy said in annoyance. "Go away, Dylan."

"You're not welcome here," Zia Noemi said firmly. "Please leave, Mr. Campbell."

He ignored her. Ginger, Vanessa's mother, mopped ice and alcohol from the rug. She glanced several times at Dylan, clearly livid, and muttered a few choice curses. When Vanessa blocked him from joining the women, Dylan leaned against the door jamb with a hangdog look.

"It wasn't my fault, Vanessa. I swear it."

"Leave," she hissed. "You're ruining the party!"

"Lissen, I didn't do it. It wasn't my fault," he insisted, over and over.

"You lied to me a long time ago. How do I know you're not lying now?"

I wasn't surprised when Debbie marched over to confront Dylan, her ex-fiancé. She pushed against his chest with so much force, he fell against the door and smacked his head. Dazed, he nearly fell on top of Kim in the nearest chair, who shrieked.

Debbie pushed him again. "Get lost, you lousy rat bast—"

"I got this, ladies." Gus Antonini suddenly appeared behind Dylan and gripped his arm. "I tried to tell him this wasn't a good idea."

"Vanessa, ask Nick for the truth. He'll tell you—" Dylan jerked a thumb at a second man who'd appeared and whose eyes widened in surprise.

"What? Quit making a scene, Dylan. Now's not the time for a chat." Nick reminded me of the actor Jack Black, with dark hair that curled at the ends, a scruffy beard, and a barrel-like physique. "Come on, Steve. Help me get him outside."

The third man behind Gus, who sported glasses and looked odd with white streaks in his red hair and beard, glanced at Vanessa as if for permission. "Yes!" She gave an exaggerated sigh. "My husband's worried that Dylan will punch him out like the last time, Gus."

"He's too drunk to fight," Gus said. "Grab his arms, guys." Steve and Nick obeyed and then dragged Dylan, still slurring his words, out of the room. "We'll get him back to the hotel, babe, and under control. I promise."

Scuffling and curses drifted our way until the front door slammed shut. "Dylan's more like a worst man than a best man," Cissy said.

"I'm sorry this happened." Gus kissed her in further apology and then departed.

Debbie stabbed a finger at her sister. "Now do you believe me? Gus should have asked his cousin Frank, because Dylan is nothing but trouble."

"Whatever." Cissy sighed. "It's only a few days before the rehearsal, so let it go." She turned to Vanessa. "Tell Steve I said thanks for helping. Nick, too."

"Sure. But right now I'm gonna pour myself another drink." Vanessa filled two fresh glasses with orange juice and hefty doses of vodka. "Cheers to the future, and remember to leave bad memories in the dust."

"I'll drink to that." Cissy snatched up the second concoction. "To a peaceful wedding this weekend. Valentine's Day is supposed to be a day of love."

Vanessa poured another drink and handed it to Debbie. "Which is why you need to forget about Dylan and move on. You broke up over a year ago."

"He broke my heart," she snapped, "and Dylan hasn't changed one bit."

I noticed Gisele and Claudia giggling together, ignoring the others. "Didn't I tell you," Gisele whispered. "He's so cute!"

"You were right about that." Claudia flushed scarlet, her freckles disappearing.

"Hey, there's more presents to open," Vanessa said in a loud voice. "Come on, let's get back to the real reason for this party."

Cissy opened several, cooing over each one, and then handed out our bridesmaid gifts of silver jewelry. "Wear the red satin garter under your dress, for luck. Plus false eyelashes and nail polish on fingers and toes. You made hair appointments at the Luxe Salon, right?"

We all nodded, although I wasn't happy about having to wear false eyelashes and a silly garter. What was next, a specific style of underwear? Cissy reminded us for the tenth time to come early Friday night for the rehearsal. I was thankful when Maddie made up an excuse to leave at half past eleven, which helped raise my spirits. I was so done with all this drama.

After thanking Ginger, who was gracious enough to fill a take-home box with desserts, Maddie and I escaped. Shivering, I scraped ice off the car's windshield while my sister did the back and side windows. She drove home with clenched fists, the roads icier. I felt too drained to chat, although Maddie grumbled about our bridesmaid duties.

"That dress cost a fortune, and she wants us to have our hair done, too? Meh. Mine is too short to bother."

My mood improved when my dogs greeted me with happy yelps and plenty of kisses. They raced outside, sniffing around, before Sugar Bear followed Rosie back into the house. I had to towel clumps of snow from their undersides and laughed at their wriggling moves. Sugar Bear didn't stop squirming until I dug ice crystals from between her paw pads. She licked my face and then raced up the stairs before Rosie.

In my bedroom, I plopped into a chair in exhaustion while my sister paused by the door. "I'm glad we didn't get stuck with Botox needles."

"I am so sick of hearing Debbie's complaints about Dylan," Maddie said. "Vanessa is right, she ought to forget what happened. Even though the Davisons lost their deposit on the reception hall after he backed out of the wedding. Plus they'd prepaid for all the flower bouquets, the wedding dress, and invitations. But that was a long time ago."

"Forget, even if they can't forgive." I sighed. "Now tell me why Cissy wants us to paint our toenails. We'll be wearing four-inch heels, not sandals."

"And tied on with stupid bows. She's a control freak, that's why."

Maddie headed off to bed. I was grateful to crawl under the covers, the dogs warming my feet. Too bad Jay hadn't stayed for the night. His schedule was as busy as mine, though. After I plumped the pillows, my thoughts wandered back to the bachelorette party. CDylan Campbell shared a few traits with my ex-husband. Charming in person, but far different in action given his juvenile pranks and flirting with married women. Clearly far worse.

I wondered why Dylan had shown up where he wasn't expected. Or wanted. Vanessa's mother seemed angrier than her daughter at his sudden appearance. What was that all about? And Debbie hung on to her rage, even after Dylan broke their engagement over the phone.

What a coward.

I had a feeling there might be another hitch or two before Saturday.

Chapter 3

"You ready, Sash? It's almost half past four," Maddie called from the stairway.

"Coming!"

I added the silver bridesmaid's necklace to complement my black jumpsuit, along with a red bolero, and then checked my hair. I shouldn't have bothered with the curling iron, since my hair looked ironing-board straight again. Grabbing silver earrings from the dressing table, I raced down the steps and almost tripped at the bottom. Dang. Four inches of torture, despite the tight bows. I needed to get used to them, but I'd be wearing them all day tomorrow.

So why torture myself too soon?

I rushed back to my room and grabbed my black ballet flats. I was on my feet all week at the shop, selling teddy bears for the upcoming Valentine's Day weekend. I'd rejected a dress and chose comfort for tonight. Cissy had ordered everyone to wear black and red in her latest text message, so Maddie paired a cute black-and-white-floral skirt with a black top and a wide red belt. I sighed. The sooner this was over, the better.

Given today's nonstop customers, I was glad I'd called in my temp, Renee, to cover for me until closing time along with tomorrow's hours. Aunt Eve promised to help, although she might be called in to the factory. A few of our sewing staff had called in sick with the flu.

My phone pinged with a text from Jay. *Freezing here. Take a pic of my ice sculpture at the hotel tonight. TTU later?* I texted back with *No prob.* I couldn't wait to fill him in on Tuesday night's bachelorette party. And now the wedding rehearsal was upon us.

I snatched up my coat, hat, and clutch purse. Both dogs gazed up at me, their sad eyes breaking my heart. "Aunt Eve will feed you, don't worry," I crooned. They settled back down, nestled together on the cushioned bed by the heat register, but I felt so guilty.

In the car, Maddie glanced at my feet once I'd slid onto the passenger seat. "No way, sister. Get back in there and put on those heels. If you don't break 'em in tonight, you'll be sorry tomorrow."

Cursing to myself, I stalked back to my room, changed shoes, and returned to the car. "Thanks," I grumbled. "Tonight's already gonna be stressful. Uncle Ross has been hassling me all week, and thinks production is slowing down. He may be right. I think we need to follow up the Beary Potter wizard bear with something new."

"How about a pair of wedding bears?" Maddie drove the car to Kermit Street. "Seems like everyone's tying the knot lately. Uncle Ross and Aunt Eve, Cissy and Gus—"

"Even my ex and his latest flame," I cut in. "That's a great idea! I'll call a meeting with the staff. Wanna sketch out a few examples for us?"

"Sure, once I get my latest deadline met. You've got till June to produce them."

"Ha, like that's much time." I checked my phone for any email messages, then changed the subject. "So, I'm still confused over why Dylan showed up the other night. How come he was apologizing to Vanessa?"

"No idea," Maddie said. "But we have to stop Debbie from attacking Dylan again. Did you get that text from Cissy?"

"No, but she's sent so many." I opened my phone to check while she parked on the street. "That won't be easy, keeping Debbie from making trouble."

The brick bell tower rose above us as we walked toward the church's arched double-door entrance. My heels crunched the rock salt scattered over the cement and steps. I stopped halfway up, stooped, and retied one of the bows on my shoes. Too bad I wasn't wearing flats.

Dusk was close at hand, although I enjoyed seeing the sun for a few minutes. A miracle given the gray winter days Michigan residents endured from November to February. I shivered when Maddie pulled open the church's door.

"Hey, you're right on time."

Eric Dyer's blond hair looked almost white in the last rays of dim winter sunshine. The same dark-haired guy, the Jack Black look-alike who'd showed up with Gus at the bachelorette party, waved behind Eric and then motioned us inside.

"Hi, ladies. I'm Nick Rizzo, one of Gus's best friends. You know Eric, right?"

Maddie nodded, her cheeks flushed dark, which intrigued me. I glanced at Eric, whose dazzling smile was focused on my sister. She was so petite, the top of her head barely reached his shoulder. Eric had pale blue eyes and broad shoulders like a Norse Viking, and wore a smart tailored gray suit. I'd been oblivious to anything going on between them. Besides, after last year's fiasco, Maddie insisted she wouldn't date again for a long time.

Hmm.

"This is Bob Vaccaro, who's married to Gus's sister, Gisele," Nick said. Bob was half-bald and more overweight than his wife. Steve Leeson stood beside his wife, Vanessa, who was a few inches taller, and peered through his thick glasses. I wondered if he could see much without them. He wore red sneakers that almost matched his hair color, too.

"Poor Kim," Vanessa said. "Those extra Botox injections backfired. Her eyes are all puffy and bruised, and she has to use tons of makeup. Plus she felt so nauseous, she could hardly get through the work week."

I glanced over to a back pew where Kim Goddard sat doubled over, head in her hands. Her long blond hair hid most of her face. I felt bad for her, but glad we didn't indulge in the Botox treatments. Maddie seemed to share my thoughts, shaking her head over Kim's misery.

"Hey," Steve called out and made a grab for Mr. Clooney, who resembled a lion with his long, curly beige fur. Claws scrabbling on the wood floor, he dodged Bob Vaccaro as well. "Stupid mutt. I already cleaned up after he—"

"He's not a mutt," Cissy protested, one hand on her hip. "Mr. Clooney is purebred."

"Purebred for trouble," Vanessa muttered.

The bride-to-be must not have heard that remark. Cissy's blond hair was styled in an elegant chignon worthy of Grace Kelly. Her white dress had a wide red ribbon at the waist and tiny red hearts. She went over to help Zia Noemi fasten red silk roses beneath huge white tulle bows on the pews' ends along the center aisle. Gus finally arrived, curly dark hair slicked back, wearing his usual black pants and shirt, plus a leather bomber jacket. He smiled and waved, then walked over to his aunt. Zia Noemi gave him a bear hug and pinched his cheek hard.

"My favorite nephew! I'm so excited about your wedding."

"Great, Zietta. Thanks for everything," Gus told her. Then he walked over to kiss his bride-to-be. "Sorry I'm late. Dylan called, he's also running behind."

Cissy's voice rose to a shriek. "Then how can we start the rehearsal—"

"Chill, babe. He was best man last year for his brother. He knows what to do."

Debbie scowled. "Frank will have to stand in as best man since Dylan, the jerk, isn't here yet. Bet he won't show up at all."

"He'll show," Gus said sternly, "and I'm sick of you trashing him."

"But what if he doesn't show," Cissy moaned. "Dylan's gonna ruin my wedding! Look at how he showed up at the bachelorette party, stinking drunk."

"Gus and I talked to him," Nick reassured her. "For a long time, about everything. The poor guy doesn't get it, though. Vanessa and her family haven't forgiven him, even though that accident was so long ago—"

Silver Hollow's local journalist, Dave Fox, held up a camera. "I'm here to get photos for the *Herald*. Your wedding's the biggest event of winter. Show the love!"

I repressed a laugh, since Cissy immediately struck a pose with her biggest smile. Gus snaked an arm around her, one hand in his pocket. Dave had replaced his usual beat-up sneakers with hiking boots, and new horn-rimmed glasses. He still wore his dark hair pulled back, but this time gathered in a man-bun. The *Silver Hollow Herald* had recently changed to an online edition. The murders last year, especially Mayor Bloom's, boosted his subscriber list, but Fox printed a hundred or so copies for the local nursing home.

"Kiss her," someone called out behind me. "A big smooch, Italian-style."

I turned to see a man who resembled a bouncer, with huge arms and shoulders that strained his suit coat. He also had a hooked nose, and thick, dark eyebrows that rivaled a thatch of dark hair spiked up with plenty of gel. His voice was deep and resonant.

"Oh, Frank, cut it out." Gisele pushed past her husband, Bob, with a laugh. "Where's Claudia? Cissy's upset, and nobody can control your daughter. Martina's already ripped a few ruffles off her flower girl dress, and your aunt had to sew them back into place."

Frank cursed. "Claudia promised she'd keep Tina in line."

"So where is she?"

"How do I know? Claudia said she needed a quick shopping trip and swore she'd be here no later than five o'clock," he growled. "If she doesn't show up soon, I'm gonna give her a piece of my mind. Plus a whole lot more."

Uh-oh. That didn't bode well for his wife. I recalled Claudia's interest last night in Dylan, especially given Gisele's sly smile. Gus's sister turned her attention to the bridal couple who continued to pose for Dave Fox. Frank stalked off in disgust, his jealousy obvious. I walked back to the church's entrance, where Nick talked to Eric about his brewery business.

"Have you considered packaging and distribution beyond your kegs?" Nick asked. Eric shook his head. "I've got a few contacts you could check out."

"Too expensive, dude. We ended up wasting a lot of our

beer with not getting an equal amount in each bottle. We do use the sixty-four ounce tins, though, and then sell those to any customers willing to spend at least fifty bucks."

"Just thought you might be interested." Nick handed him a business card. "Keep this, though, in case you ever get to that point. I talked a brewer up in Traverse City into expanding his operation. Kind of dicey at first, but he made it work over time. Not easy, but he had a bit of capital to spare."

"Yeah, that's the key."

Nick launched into an explanation of various marketing strategies, so I watched Dave Fox. He directed Gus and Cissy to stand at the altar, in front of a stained glass window, and then move against a white wall. Zia Noemi rushed over with a bouquet of roses. Dave took shots of Cissy alone, then with her parents, since they'd arrived, and then with Gus and his aunt, before the bride posed with Mr. Clooney. Frank Antonini ended up carrying off his little daughter, who kicked and screamed all the way to the back of the church.

"I wanna have a picture with Mr. Clooney, too! Why can't I?"

Maddie and I exchanged weary smiles while Dave Fox questioned the bride and groom about the reception and honeymoon. He scribbled answers on a scrap of paper while Cissy, simpering, acted coy about her future plans

"I'm going to be a loving wife and mother. Gus wants five boys."

"I never said that," he said, embarrassed. "Maybe three boys and two girls."

"What about your chef job at Flambé?" Dave asked.

"If Gus still has a job," Eric Dyer whispered to Maddie. "His boss was furious about what happened at the bachelor party."

"Was it that bad?" I asked, but Zia Noemi clapped her hands for attention.

"It is time for the rehearsal, right now," the older woman scolded. "We cannot be late for our dinner reservation at the hotel."

Drat. I really wanted to find out what Dylan Campbell did to anger Gus's boss, but Maddie pushed me into place beside the rest of the bridesmaids. Dave Fox lumbered out of the church, apparently satisfied with the photos and answers, while Pastor Lovett explained all the ceremony's particulars. Barbara Davison and Marianne Lovett consulted with Zia Noemi about the candles, the flowers, and other minor details. Cissy groaned when Martina shrieked like a banshee and chased the poodle down the aisle.

"Mr. Clooney! Come here, come here! I wanna hug you—"

"Nick, please rescue my dog," Cissy pleaded. He rushed off.

"Can we get back to the rehearsal?" Pastor Lovett asked, although Gus and Cissy had been laughing at every mistake so far.

"Oh, no."

Maddie had noticed the bows on her shoes had come untied. Martina snuck unseen to Vanessa's shoes next and untied hers, then giggled and darted away. Kim wore flats, the lucky dog. Now I wished I'd ignored my sister's order and bent to retie mine.

"Frank, where is Claudia?" Debbie demanded. "She promised to keep Tina under control. Don't you dare come any closer, stop right there!"

The little girl obeyed but chased Mr. Clooney down the center aisle again. Apparently Frank had given up trying to control his daughter since Nick Rizzo took him aside for a furtive conversation. Zia Noemi's firm commands didn't stop the child from pestering the dog. Martina pulled my sister's bows loose again, but I dodged her little fingers.

Maddie rose from retying her shoes for the second time

and grumbled under her breath. "Next time I'm gonna kick that little brat—"

"Shh. Why would Claudia be so late after a quick shopping trip?"

"I wonder if she hooked up with Dylan," my sister whispered. "He's not here, either, you know. Remember how Gisele encouraged Claudia."

"Hey, there she is. At last."

Maddie flashed a knowing look when Claudia meandered up a side aisle, minus a single shopping bag. Frank stalked over to challenge her, his face red. I felt awkward listening to their heated exchange, but Kim and Gisele giggled together. Martina scampered up and down the aisles with a length of ribbon streaming behind her, oblivious to her parents' arguing. Mr. Clooney barked nonstop. At last Cissy marched over to scold him.

"Didn't Cissy claim that Mr. Clooney won prizes at shows?" Maddie asked. "You'd think he would be trained better to behave."

"I only saw one photo and a ribbon she displayed at the Time Turner," I said. "I think it said something about 'Prettiest Puppy.'"

Mr. Clooney stopped to scratch furiously, hind leg digging into his coat. He'd been doing that every so often and shaking his head as well. I had a suspicion that the dog might have fleas. Curious, I somehow managed to grab his collar. To my surprise, he dropped onto his haunches while I examined the skin under his thick beige coat.

Yep. Tiny black moving dots, not hard to miss.

I also noticed a white satin bag with a red bow attached to his collar. Under my searching fingers, I felt two hard round circles inside. They had to be Cissy and Gus's wedding rings.

After tugging the bag's strings open, I noticed the bands sparkled with diamonds. I tightened the bag and let it dangle from the leather collar. Hopefully, since he was the official ring bearer, Mr. Clooney wouldn't escape from his collar and the attached bag at some point.

"Hate to mention this to Cissy, but the dog's got a major problem," I said to Maddie, my voice low. "Fleas. See how the dog keeps scratching?"

"Oh, no—don't tell her. She'd have a bigger meltdown than over her wedding gown."

"That's true." I winced, seeing the dog lift his leg to piddle near a pew. "Isn't he house-trained? Although we can't blame the dog if no one's paying attention to his signals. Who knows when he was last taken outside."

"From what Debbie said, Mr. Clooney was never fully trained. And he got worse after Cissy dumped him at her parents' house. That dog is more stressed than she is."

"No wonder he's running around the neighborhood."

"Where is Dylan?" Cissy demanded, although Gus shrugged. "Text him, at least! Make sure he is planning on coming tonight."

We stood around in silence while Gus reluctantly fiddled with his phone. After another five minutes, he shrugged. "No answer. What do you want me to do?"

"Frank will have to take his place," Cissy said, looking pleased, but Maddie nudged me when the doors to the narthex banged open.

Dylan Campbell strolled into the church. The best man wore a suit coat but without a tie, his collar open, and walked forward to greet the other guys with a handshake. Except Frank, who stalked off to meet Debbie halfway down the center aisle. Their voices were inaudible.

Dylan clapped Gus on the back. "Hey, man. What did I miss?"

"We're the ones who missed something." Nick grinned. "Where you been?"

"Working late," Gus said, "so let it go."

But Nick flashed the rest of us a knowing wink.

Chapter 4

Eric leaned over to Dylan. "Man, you need to steer clear of married women."

Debbie shook a finger at him. "Steer clear of me, too. I'll never forgive you for what you did, dumping me after everything was planned for our wedding."

"Haven't you gotten over that yet?" Dylan asked. "Ancient history."

"How can I forget? My parents lost so much money—"

"That's because they waited too long. You're to blame, thinking I'd change my mind and we'd get back together. Besides, you sold that diamond engagement ring. That should have made up for all the expenses. Twice over."

"Like that really matters," Debbie spat. "You're such a skank."

Dylan turned away, clearly annoyed. "Yeah, yeah. The struggle is real."

Zia Noemi dragged Debbie away, tut-tutting in disapproval, with help from Kim and Vanessa. Cissy patted her sister on the back, murmuring comfort as well. Maddie and I chose to ignore Dylan and joined the group of women in solidarity.

Frank Antonini returned minus Claudia. He grabbed Martina by the arm and rushed her to the back of the church. "Daddy, no! I don't wanna go—"

The little girl howled so loud, she drowned out Mr. Clooney's barks. Pastor Lovett looked confused, and so did his wife. I wondered if the rehearsal was over. Not that we'd gotten far into it. Dylan huddled with the other groomsmen near the altar railing until Gus, urged on by Cissy, hurried off to fetch his cousin Frank. Claudia crept back into the church, head down, holding Martina's hand. Maddie nudged me with an elbow.

"He gave her a black eye. Did you see it?"

I shook my head. "No—"

"Shh!"

"Everyone please line up again," Barbara Davison called out.

The pastor's wife hurried forward to help. At last the bridal party paired up and then practiced where to stand, processing and recessing up and down the center aisle, but minus the flower girl. She sat beside her mother, sulking, since Richard Davison had taken Mr. Clooney out of the church. If only Frank had left as well. I dreaded dancing with him at the reception. The idea of him touching me, knowing that he'd abused his wife, wasn't pleasant.

"All right, everyone," Zia Noemi said, clearly relieved things had settled down. "We all can make our way over to the hotel for dinner."

Debbie rushed off, giving a lame excuse about changing shoes. Gus and Frank headed outside, and I overheard the groom admonishing his cousin about being more patient with his wife and daughter. Dylan, Cissy, Kim, and Eric trailed behind, followed by Vanessa and Steve Leeson, and Bob and Gisele Vaccaro. Maddie had gone to the bathroom. I waited for her and was surprised when Dylan suddenly returned from outside. Hair tousled by the wind, coat flapping, he clapped Nick on the back.

"Hey, man. Left my car in front of the theater, but someone slashed the tires."

Nick looked startled. "My Jeep's parked right behind yours—"

Dylan waved a hand. "Only mine was hit. Can I bum a ride with you to the hotel?"

"Sure. Always willing to help a friend."

Dylan thanked him with obvious relief, although Nick hadn't sounded that sincere. When Maddie beckoned me from the church's far door, I hurried to join her.

"Whew, I'm glad that's over. Can't we skip the rehearsal dinner tonight?"

"In your dreams. We're all supposed to make a speech, telling everyone how Gus and Cissy's wedding is the highlight of our whole year."

"Maybe yours—"

"I'm kidding! Hope the other bridesmaids hog all the time delegated for that." Maddie clicked the remote to unlock the car. "I saw Claudia Antonini in the ladies' room, and her black eye is starting to look worse."

"Not cool," I said, fuming. "Frank is such a jealous jerk. He didn't have to hit her, even if she didn't go shopping."

"Yeah. I'm sick of how everyone pretends how this wedding is going so well. Come on, or we'll be late to the dinner."

"I hope Zia Noemi brought some cannoli," I said. "That would help a lot."

Maddie snickered. She lucked out finding a parking spot

in front of the Regency Hotel. Given the frigid wind, we scuttled inside the plush lobby with its red carpeting, white pillars, and brass trim. Veering left at the reception desk, I followed the hostess to a side hallway and the private banquet room that Gus and Cissy had reserved. Or maybe Zia Noemi had, since she was clearly in charge of the dinner tonight. I nudged my sister.

"Why aren't Gus's parents here?"

"I think they're deceased. That's why Zia Noemi is like a second mom to him," Maddie said. "I'm not sure what happened—"

"A car accident," Vanessa Leeson piped up, walking behind us. "Poor Gus, he was so young to lose his parents. Drunk driver, like my niece."

"That's horrible," I said.

"Except she didn't die," Vanessa continued, her voice tinged with fury. "And she never recovered from the traumatic brain injury."

"Now, honey, don't get upset." Steve slid an arm around her waist.

"How can I not be upset? Poor thing can barely function, my sister will be taking care of her for the rest of her life! And then what will happen—"

"Shh, it's not private here."

Steve pulled Vanessa into an alcove and tried to calm her. We kept walking, subdued, until Maddie suddenly gasped and grabbed my arm. In a small side room, I spotted my ex-husband, Flynn Hanson. Oh, no.

He sat with his fiancée, Cheryl Cummings, and an older couple. They didn't look pleased. They couldn't be clients since Flynn looked anxious. That wasn't his basic MO even with the most difficult people. Cheryl seemed uneasy as well. Maybe this was a "meet the parents," since they were now engaged. Maddie pushed me forward and out of sight before Flynn could spot us. No way did I want him to think I was spying.

"I thought he was moving his practice to Ann Arbor," my sister muttered.

"He is, yeah. Or so I heard."

"Good. That way he'll finally be out of your hair."

"I sure hope so."

My heels sank so deep into the larger banquet room's thick carpeting, I struggled to keep from falling. Vanessa pushed past us, smiling again, and greeted Kim, Gisele, and Cissy. She waved at a waiter holding a tray of champagne, who rushed over to serve them. I snagged a glass from a different waiter while Maddie joined the group. The first sip proved this was quality stuff. Savoring the delicious flavor, I walked over to the bar's far end.

A gorgeous ice carving sat inside a large container filled with huge chunks of ice. Given its quality, I knew Jay had sculpted it. I studied the cupid with its delicate wings, standing on one foot with his bow outstretched; his bent leg balanced on a nearly transparent shaft of ice. A red heart-shaped cake had been placed near the sculpture, with an arrow piercing its center. The bartender chipped off smaller pieces with a pick and filled two glasses, then added a jigger of whiskey and soda to each. He handed the drinks to Dylan and Gus.

Dylan took a hefty swig. "So tomorrow's the big day. Feeling the love yet?"

"Through my wallet," Gus replied. They both laughed and walked away.

As promised, I took several photos with my cell from various angles. "That cake looks fabulous. Second on my list to cookies," I said to Maddie.

"Hello, you two," Zia Noemi said, beaming. She hugged

us both like we were long-lost children despite seeing everyone at church less than half an hour ago. "I'm so pleased
you're here to celebrate Gus's big day tomorrow. Isn't his
bride lovely?"

We agreed. Cissy simpered with pleasure, her corsage of
white lilies and glossy green leaves pinned on one shoulder of
her white dress with its tiny red hearts. The tight fit empha-
sized her curvy behind. All of Gus's groomsmen near the bar
ogled her, along with the waiters and the bartender. Dylan
must have told a joke, the way his friends laughed uproariously.

"If you think that's funny, wait till you hear the one
about—"

Maddie turned away, shaking her head. "I wish I'd come
down with the flu."

"Aw, come on. It's not so bad." I held up my glass. "And
this is a great perk."

I sipped more champagne and turned to hear Kim's loud
voice. "—naming them like Cissy's dog, Mr. Clooney." She
patted her puffy eyes with her fingers, as if hoping the swelling
had diminished. "We call Vanessa's husband Mr. Redbeard,
which is obvious. Gisele, what's your husband's nickname?"

"Mr. Rocky. Bob loves boxing more than his Cadillac,"
she joked. "I'm third, or fourth behind the kids. And there's
Mr. Sales." Gisele nodded toward Nick Rizzo. "I think he's
either divorced or on the brink of it. Born with a silver spoon
in his mouth, too, and he's a natural salesman. He can talk
anyone into buying anything."

Vanessa laughed. "You're right, a smooth operator. Watch
out. You'll end up with a new garage door, extra insurance, or
a week-long cruise."

"Don't forget Mr. Macho." Gisele pointed in her cousin
Frank Antonini's direction. He'd taken off his suit coat, and

his sculpted muscles rippled beneath his white shirt. "You saw how he acted at the church, right? I didn't think Claudia would act so fast about meeting Dylan."

"But maybe she did go shopping," I said, but Gisele laughed.

"Yeah, and I'm the Queen of Sheba. Just wait. Frank will pay Dylan back."

"Sasha!" Cissy waved me over to her chair. "Thanks for rescheduling that chocolate bar and liquor event. Why would Joelynn Owens disrupt my wedding weekend?"

I blinked, staring at my empty champagne glass. "Um. It's all about chocolate candy, not liquor. Her shop's grand opening is next week, so we're still planning to host the Chocolate Bear Bar on Sunday—"

"But you can't!" Cissy's flushed cheeks matched the red ribbon at her waist. "You heard Dave Fox. My wedding is 'the' event in Silver Hollow for Valentine's Day."

"But you're leaving on your honeymoon Sunday."

"Why should that matter? Oh, never mind. People are just so selfish." Impatient, Cissy turned to Vanessa. "Where's Debbie? I can't let her keep on threatening Dylan. It's bad enough how Frank's acting. Poor Claudia, did you see her black eye?"

"Good thing she's not a bridesmaid. No makeup would hide that."

"Go find Debbie. She must be in the bathroom."

Vanessa quickly obeyed. I limped over to lean on the bar near Jay's sculpture. Maybe Kim would take twenty bucks for her flats. I was willing to offer her fifty, the way I teetered back and forth on these silly heels. I didn't get a chance to approach her, however.

Dylan Campbell held up a beer glass. "A toast to the bride and groom," he called out in a loud voice. "Might as well practice before tomorrow's reception. Here's to my best friend, Gus Antonini, and his sizzling-hot fiancée. May they have the best life together. Cheers!"

We all clinked glasses. Zia Noemi kissed Gus and then hugged Cissy, looking thrilled, until Dylan tossed back his beer and spilled half over his suit coat. She frowned when he laughed and shook drops everywhere. Mr. Clooney licked the carpet, despite Cissy's fury. A waitress darted forward to sponge him off with a towel and then blot the soaked carpet. Still laughing, Dylan aimed his damp coat at a chair but missed. When it slithered to the floor, the dog grabbed a sleeve and shook it with his teeth. Dylan failed to pry his coat loose from Mr. Clooney.

"Everyone, please take your seats," Zia Noemi said firmly. "Dinner is served."

Gisele lowered her voice. "She's a hoot, and we do love her, but Zietta drives the family crazy. Gus never notices, of course, but I've tangled with her a few times. Big mistake."

"She seems very sweet," I said. "And her cannoli are fabulous."

"You would say that," Maddie said with a snort. "But I have to agree."

My sister headed off to join Nick and Kim at a table. Once I'd collected another flute of champagne, Gisele nudged me.

"Question for ya. Is Maddie dating Eric Dyer?"

"I'm not sure. Why?"

"She seems all starry-eyed whenever he smiles at her. We call Eric Mr. Brewmaster since the only thing he ever talks about is his Silver Claw business."

"It's a winery as well as a microbrewery," I said, "and from what Maddie told me, he talks about plenty of other stuff besides beer. But let me ask you something. How wild was that bachelor party held at Flambé?"

"Oh, have I got the dirt." Gisele glanced around to make sure no one was eavesdropping. "Dylan cleaned out everyone at poker. They all started fighting, broke a few tables and chairs. Even Gus lost a bundle, and was he steamed."

"So the restaurant had damage, I take it."

"A few Tiffany light fixtures smashed to pieces, and not cheap to replace." Gisele sighed. "Oh, brother. That dog is such a pain."

She rushed off to rescue a tablecloth that Mr. Clooney had seized between his jaws. Cissy's pampered standard poodle pulled hard enough to dislodge one place setting, although the china bounced on the carpet. Gisele wrestled the dog away, but he twisted out of his collar with the attached satin bag. He raced around the banquet room until she cornered him and restored the collar over his sleek head.

I couldn't help chuckling over his antics and joined my sister. Nick Rizzo waved a brochure. "I hear you're addicted to cookies, Sasha. Let me describe this specialty program. A Cookie of the Month, the most delectable and delicious, delivered right to your door."

I stared at the photos with longing, but Maddie snatched it away. "She's not interested."

"Hey, let her decide. No? Okay, give me a minute—" Nick dug another flyer out of his pocket. "Okay, then. You're a graphics designer, right? I bet you get a ten percent discount on everything you need."

Maddie shrugged. "So?"

"I can get you a twenty percent discount. Just take these. Look 'em over," Nick said, laying the brochures on the table and backing away. "No pressure."

"Ha," she said under her breath.

When Nick walked over to join the rest of the grooms-men at the bar, I grabbed the flyer for the monthly cookies and then stuffed it into my purse. Eric sauntered over to our table and sat beside Maddie. I noticed Debbie Davison over by the bar. She tugged at her red knit dress, since it kept puckering around the waist. She wore three gold necklaces that dripped with tiny honey bees, and a gold honeycomb clip in her hair.

Debbie continued her tirade against Dylan, ignoring Cissy's hissed warnings. "Someone needs to take out that jerk," she said to me, her voice loud, "and I don't care if he hears me! He caused big trouble between Frank and Claudia. Dylan Campbell's a snake in the grass."

I drained my champagne flute and returned to the table. Waiters plunked down baskets of rolls and huge bowls of salad, along with boats of dressing and Parmesan cheese. I snatched a crusty roll, hoping it would soak up the champagne buzz in my head. The salad was fresh, with grape tomatoes, croutons, and black olives, but overloaded with red onions. I plucked them out. An olive flipped out of my plate and onto the carpet, along with an onion ring. Mr. Clooney gobbled the olive but left the onion. He also scarfed a roll that Martina dropped on purpose.

"Look, Mommy—"

"Stop it, Tina. That dog will get sick."

Kim blocked my view of the dog, however. "Pass the cheese, Sasha." She leaned toward me, blue eyes bright, and hooked a loose strand of her blond hair behind one ear. "You heard that Dylan loves to play pranks, right? For April Fool's last year, he crushed a bunch of laxative tablets and put them in a pitcher of beer at some party. Isn't that right, Eric?"

"We were in the bathroom forever," he confirmed. "All night, it seemed."

"Ugh." Maddie shuddered. "Why would he do that?"

Vanessa brushed by our table with her husband, although

Steve veered off toward the bar again. She would have followed, except Kim jumped to her feet and clutched Vanessa's arm. She whispered something, and they rushed to the bathroom. That seemed odd, but I was distracted by Mr. Clooney again, who helped himself to an unattended bread plate.

"That's the second roll the dog managed to get—"

"Fourth or fifth, actually," Maddie interrupted. "I saw Mr. Clooney jump one of the waiters who was carrying a breadbasket to Gus and Cissy's table. He didn't get any, though, since Gus dragged him out of range while the waiter collected them all."

I sniffed. "That dog needs serious training. Even Sugar Bear has better manners."

"Rosie, too," my sister said.

"Watch out!"

I pushed Mr. Clooney away, since the dog had lifted a leg. The stream of urine soaked the carpeting instead. Luckily, a waiter rushed over to take care of the problem, covering the stain with napkins and stepping on them.

"Mr. Clooney! How could you?" Cissy rushed over to hug her dog. "Poor baby. All these people are making you too excited. Where's your collar—oh, drat. Your underside's all wet. Gus, honey? Bring me a napkin or two."

Maddie and I exchanged glances, barely able to suppress disgust. "Come with me to the bathroom," I whispered. She followed me without protest.

Vanessa Leeson stood guard by the door marked LADIES. "You don't wanna go in there, sorry. Kim is sicker than a dog. She's supposed to be second after me in the order of speeches. At least Debbie is first. I doubt if Kim can manage it after this."

I heard violent retching behind the door and winced in sympathy. "Was it the Botox?"

"No, I don't think so." She shuddered. "Kim had a few drinks, but it's not like she hasn't indulged before. She said the last one tasted funny, though."

Maddie sighed and led me back to sit at our banquet table. Vanessa followed, although she ran into Nick, who seemed concerned. He slid an arm around her shoulders and drew her to a corner of the room. She shook him off with impatience, though. How odd. I watched Vanessa approach the bridal table and lean over to speak. Cissy squawked in protest.

"Why can't you just take an aspirin for your headache?"

"I need my meds now, or I won't be functional tomorrow," she said. "You know how bad it gets. My skull feels like it's gonna explode."

Nick walked over and added his opinion. "Let her go upstairs and rest, or she'll be a hot mess for days. Worse than Kim right now."

I glanced where he pointed along with everyone else. Kim limped over to the bar and sat, head in her hands. I wondered what kind of drink she'd had, or was it another side effect from the extra Botox injections?

"Hey, Sasha." Eric waved a hand to catch my attention. "Go ahead, Maddie. Ask her what you wanted."

"Sorry, what?" I asked my sister and shifted on the uncomfortable chair.

"I wondered if you snuck any of the cannoli yet," she said. "I can't wait for this to end, so you better get your fill before we head out early."

"Me too," Eric said. "Hey, did everyone like my wine at the party on Tuesday?"

"They had mimosas and Jell-O shots," I said, "so I doubt they ever opened it. Too bad, because I wanted to try it."

"And we didn't stay long enough to find out," Maddie said.

Eric looked disappointed, but perked up when she

squeezed his hand. For a lot longer than I expected, too. Maybe I had missed what was going on between my sister and Eric. Hmm. He ordered a lot of graphic design work for the Silver Claw, according to Aunt Eve.

"So what's this about poker at the bachelor party?" I asked him.

"Yeah. I lost three hundred bucks to Dylan. Look at him now, laughing over in the corner. I heard him bragging that he dosed a drink with ipecac syrup."

"So that's why Kim got so sick! How horrible." Maddie sounded furious.

"Debbie mentioned at the bachelorette party, how she played that prank on Dylan long ago," I said. "Maybe he took the chance to pay her back for it."

"Yeah. That can't be a coincidence, only Kim drank it by mistake."

"Maybe Debbie gave it to her, if she saw Dylan spike it," Maddie said. "So tell me what happened at the bachelor party, and playing poker. You lost money?"

"Frank lost the most, I think," Eric said. "He accused Dylan of cheating. That's what sent Nick out of control, and the restaurant was a real mess afterward."

We stopped talking when the waiters brought the pasta course. After I wolfed down my marinara-drenched noodles, I nudged Maddie. "Let's try the restroom before the entrée."

"Yeah, and I got a few spots of sauce on my skirt."

Maddie followed me past the Antonini family table, where Gisele and Bob Vaccaro sat with Frank Antonini, his wife Claudia, and Martina. Zia Noemi was at the next table, regaling Barbara and Richard Davison with tales of Gus's childhood.

Debbie Davison jumped up from the bridal table. "Can you believe my luck? Now I've got marinara sauce on my dress. Good thing it doesn't show."

"I have a few spots, too," Maddie said. "Easy to spill—"

"I know! And this dress is dry-clean only. Plus my shoes smell like beer from when Dylan splashed it around."

"No big deal," Gus said, although she huffed at that.

"It is to me! Dylan was half-drunk before dinner started. He's such a loser."

"Get over him, will you? The guy's got no family to speak of, only a brother who moved out to California," Gus said. "I'm tired of hearing you whine about him."

"Dylan's taunted me whenever he passed by," Debbie retorted, sitting again. "I won't stop until he starts acting like a decent human being. Which isn't possible anyway."

She kept going on and on about their broken engagement, how badly Dylan had treated her, repeating his sins over the past year.

"I don't know why you two can't ignore each other until after the wedding, for pity's sake." Gus downed the rest of his wine. "Sasha, watch out—"

Vanessa's husband had suddenly backed into me, spilling his icy drink and soaking my jumpsuit. Steve pushed up his glasses and mumbled a lame apology. I waved him off, figuring I'd towel off in the restroom. Steve headed back to the bar.

"Hope we don't miss the main course." Maddie nodded to Nick Rizzo, who'd stepped aside with a low bow before she passed him. I followed her with a smile.

"Ladies first," he said, and winked. "You two are more ladies than the others."

"Charmer," my sister tossed back with a laugh. "Are you feeling better, Kim?"

She looked as pale as the linen tablecloth but opened a small plastic bag of dried cherries. Kim popped a handful into her mouth. "My parents grow these up north near Traverse City. They're the best thing for healing."

"I'm not sorry I passed on the Botox," I said.

"Yeah. It's my own fault for being so greedy."

"So where is Dylan?" Nick fiddled with his gold cufflinks. "I hope he didn't go after Vanessa. She's in a lot of pain from that headache. And I don't like the way he's been tomcatting around. Look at Steve, too. Getting another drink."

"Not surprised, especially when he can get hammered for free," Kim said. "Five to one Dylan's outside getting a cigarette."

"Glad I quit. That was the toughest bad habit to kick—"

"Sasha, come and help me get this marinara stain out." Maddie pulled me toward the narrow, empty hallway that led to the ladies' restroom. "I can smell the prime rib from here, so they must be ready to serve it. I need some protein."

"Me too. Although we'll have to order more bread."

"I ate three rolls. They were great, yeasty and warm from the oven, plus I was starving. Poor Eric didn't get any, but I told him to ask for more."

Inside the narrow room, the tile floor looked slippery. "What the—whoa." I'd skidded on a damp spot near the sink, which I grabbed for support. Faint pink streaks lined the porcelain bowl. I ducked into the first stall. "Maybe there's a leak somewhere?"

Maddie's heels click-clacked toward the handicapped stall, and I heard her yank on the door. She gave a gasp of disbelief. "Oh. My. God. Sasha? Sasha!"

"I'm trying to hurry," I said, wrestling with the zipper of my jumpsuit. Maybe I should have helped my sister first. "What is it?"

She started hyperventilating. "I-I think I found him. Dylan."

Confused, I unlocked the stall door and peeked past Maddie's shoulder. "What do you mean, you found—oh."

I stared at the best man, sprawled sideways on the floor,

between the toilet and the wall. Dylan Campbell faced us, eyes open and unblinking. Twisted, half on his side, the way he was stretched out on the tile. His white shirt stuck to his chest, as if wet. A pool of dark blood streamed toward the floor drain. But the strangest thing was seeing what protruded from the side of his neck, above his red-stained shirt collar.

A wooden-handled ice pick.

Chapter 5

"What the—"

Hands shaking, I nearly dropped my cell phone on the wet floor. Maddie had somehow dialed 911, however, and sounded calmer than she looked. At the sound of giggles outside the door, I blocked Gisele and Cissy from entering the restroom.

"Big problem, sorry. We've called for help."

"But I need to—"

"Later. Sorry."

Ignoring their puzzled looks and protests, I shoved a small bench and the metal garbage can over to prevent the door from swinging open again. And then sat on the bench for good measure. How many women had visited here since the dinner began? And how could Dylan have gotten in without being seen? I knew one thing for sure. The murder must have occurred after Kim tossed her cookies. She'd have noticed a dead body, no matter how sick.

I felt sick right now, in fact, and fought it. Maddie looked pale and leaned against the closed stall door, one hand on her stomach. She breathed deep, eyes shut, and then rubbed her temples. I tried to forget what I'd seen, although that failed.

Who had lured Dylan Campbell inside? And it didn't look like he'd fought back, either. From what little I saw, since I'd only gotten one quick glance. It seemed so unreal. He couldn't have been stabbed somewhere else and then dragged here, given all the blood.

The door slammed into the bench beneath me so hard, I almost fell off. "Ow!"

"Police, open up!"

I scrambled to my feet, pushed the bench and can aside, and was relieved to see Officer Hillerman instead of Digger Sykes. I didn't need to face my sister's high school friend right now, even if he was a cop, since he constantly reminded me about other dead bodies I'd found.

Hillerman raised his eyebrows at us both. "What's going on?"

"I—I found the body," my sister said. "Gus's best man, Dylan Campbell. He's back in the second stall. We didn't touch anything."

"Good. Are you both okay?"

We nodded. Hillerman quickly checked the second stall and then spoke tersely into his ear microphone, asking for backup along with the county medical examiner's forensics team. He stepped out for less than a minute, leaving the door ajar, and barking an order to prevent any of the bridal party from leaving the banquet room. Too late, since Vanessa Leeson had gone to her hotel room. When I told him that, Hillerman spoke quickly into his microphone again.

"Chief, we got a problem—"

Digger Sykes suddenly poked his head inside the restroom and grinned. "Ha! I knew it. Sasha the body magnet—"

"Shut up," Maddie interrupted, still shaking. "I found the

body, Digger. If I hear one more word out of you, I'll punch you in the nose. I'm not joking, either."

She sounded close to tears, which surprised him. His face beet red, Digger backed out into the hall. Hillerman followed, and I heard him ordering Sykes to retrieve Vanessa from her room. I grabbed a stack of paper towels and blotted my damp jumpsuit in the narrow hallway. Maddie looked so pale, I hugged her.

"You're not going to be sick, are you?"

"It's just weird," Maddie said, "like when we found Will Taylor. How could this happen? I mean, with so many people around?"

"I dunno. But let the cops figure it out."

"Remember what Debbie said five minutes ago? How someone should take him out."

"Yeah," I said grimly. "I remember."

We returned to the banquet room. Zia Noemi looked confused and helpless when tall, silver-haired Chief Russell arrived to help the other officers. She kept repeating the same phrase in Italian—which nobody but Gus understood.

"Che è successo?"

"Don't worry, the police are here now," he said, trying to soothe her, but Zia Noemi didn't stop until he squeezed her shoulders. "When I find out what's happening, Zietta, you'll be the first to know."

"Oh, Gus—I finally heard what happened," Cissy cried out, rushing toward him, her face pale. "At our rehearsal dinner, too!"

In full meltdown mode, Cissy wept against his chest. Even Debbie looked shocked, arms crossed over her chest, and inched her way to stand beside Zia Noemi. Gisele and Bob Vaccaro joined them, along with Barbara and Richard Davison.

Oblivious of what happened, waiters carried out stainless-covered dishes and set one at each place setting. I peeked under the closest one and noted julienned vegetables, red-skinned potatoes, and a huge cut of mouth-watering prime rib sprinkled with peppercorns. My stomach grumbled, but my appetite had vanished. For one thing, I couldn't get the sight of Dylan's blood out of my head. Who had killed him in such a crude manner?

"Miss Davison? I'd like a word, if you please," Chief Russell said to Debbie.

Cissy and Gus quickly surrounded her, along with the Vaccaros, forming a protective circle. "What about?" Debbie asked.

"Surely you must know." Russell gestured toward a corner. "Better take our conversation to a less public place."

I watched him escort Debbie, waving Gus and Cissy back to keep them from interfering. Bob and Gisele joined Steve Leeson at the bar. Given how often Steve scratched his beard, I wondered if Mr. Clooney's fleas had jumped to him.

I nudged my sister and spoke in a low voice. "Vanessa left earlier, but I wonder if she really did have a migraine. Or was that a convenient excuse?"

"You mean she might have had something to do with stabbing Dylan?" Maddie shivered. "I thought you said to let the cops figure it out."

"Yeah, but. We found him. I can't help wondering what really happened."

My curiosity was in overdrive, and I couldn't stop thinking about possibilities. Maddie pulled me back to our table. Eric Dyer sat alone, nursing a glass of wine, his eyes downcast. He looked dazed when I pulled out a chair and sank onto it. Maddie shoved a covered dinner plate to the table's center and sat beside him. Zia Noemi trotted toward me, her face red with anger. She plopped on the chair next to mine.

"Someone killed my nephew's best friend! What will his family think of us? And how could this have happened, tonight of all nights?"

Eric let out a deep breath with a whoosh. "Incredible, isn't it? I mean, I talked to Dylan only half an hour ago."

"Yeah, it is a shock," I said, "but the police will figure it out. Soon, I'm certain."

The older woman shook a finger. "Before tomorrow, though?" Zia Noemi shook her head. "The wedding is ruined, just like Cissy said would happen. She must be psychic."

"Uh—"

"Cissy knew the minute she met my Gus that he was the one. Instant head-over-heels," the older woman said, "and my nephew felt the same about her. So who would kill someone, right under all our noses? Even if that man was big trouble."

"How could Dylan be alive one minute, dead the next?" Eric asked. "He was the life of every party, laughing and joking. Unbelievable."

"And bragging, remember," Maddie reminded him, "about dosing that drink."

"Yeah, but it was a harmless prank—"

"Unless it happened to you, maybe. Poor Kim drank it by accident, Eric. She was puking her guts out."

He shrugged. "Maybe you're right."

"What was this?" Zia Noemi asked. When I explained, she looked horrified. "Young people nowadays, how can they behave like that. *Che schifo!* Cissy was right. Gus should have chosen his cousin as best man. None of this would have happened if he'd listened. What did I tell you? She's psychic, for certain."

Frank Antonini strolled over to stand by our table, a drink in hand. "So Dylan's dead and gone," he said. "Good riddance."

"The man's not even cold yet," Eric said, "and you're already dissing him."

"No different than Debbie complaining about him, over and over."

"That was different."

Frank snorted at that. "Gus should have chosen me as his best man."

"Yes." Zia Noemi looked pleased when Gus and Cissy walked over to our table. Nick followed them as well. "Gustavo, you should have listened to your bride. She told you to name Frank as best man."

"Yes, I know." Gus sounded grumpy, and Cissy wiped a mascara smear from her cheek.

"He didn't know this would happen, though," she said. "It's terrible."

"No one knew," Nick said, although Zia Noemi glanced at him in annoyance.

"That may be true, but Gus should have done as Cissy asked. For one thing, it would have avoided this tragedy—"

"Enough, Zietta," Gus interrupted with a deep sigh. "What's done is done. And Frank, what you did to Claudia wasn't right, smacking your wife around."

Nick nodded his head. "Yeah, dude—"

"My family, my business," he snapped at them both. "Stay out of it, or else."

Hands in the air, Nick backed away and walked off. Frank ignored Gus's dark scowl and returned to sit with his wife and daughter a few tables away. He leaned back, nonchalant, and grinned when Claudia scolded little Martina for tossing Mr. Clooney another roll.

"And you, Frank—how can you eat at a time like this?"

He cut into his steak and took a huge bite of meat. Then

he waved his knife in the air. "I'm not letting this meal go to waste. You two go on up to bed."

"The cops said we couldn't leave," Claudia whined.

"Then shut up and eat."

She picked up her fork, clearly unhappy, and toyed with her food. I didn't understand how she could stay with someone who abused her, emotionally and physically. Even if she may have brought trouble on her own head. Curious, I turned to Eric.

"Could it be true that Dylan and Claudia met earlier today," I whispered. "They both came late to the rehearsal at church."

He shrugged. "I wouldn't doubt it. Frank's got a hair-trigger temper—"

"Hey, Sasha, Maddie! How are things going?" Dan Russell, a rookie cop, sauntered our way. "I hear you two found the body. That's pretty crazy. My dad was so surprised when the call came in, you know, about another murder. He's over there talking to the hotel manager now."

"I see." I glanced around and spied Chief Russell talking to a man in a suit, who looked upset. "How do you like working under your dad at the station?"

"Cool, but he avoids me most of the time. Digger claims it's nepotism."

"Ignore him. Hey, I heard Dylan Campbell has a brother out in California." Maddie leaned forward and beckoned him closer. "I guess you'll contact him, right?"

"Yup." Dan motioned to the door. "The team from the coroner's office is here."

We swiveled around to watch a group of men and women in navy jackets who swarmed into the banquet room and carried cameras and other equipment down the hallway. Chief Russell quickly joined them and beckoned to Dan. The young man stretched yellow crime scene tape to block the hallway. I was relieved when Detective Mason from the county sheriff's office arrived. He greeted the local policemen and conversed with Chief Russell and Officer Hillerman.

I trusted his judgment, since Mason had taken over the last case from an incompetent colleague last December. He peeled off his heavy coat, revealing a sweatshirt with PROPERTY OF DEXTER CO. spelled out on the front, and ratty blue jeans. Mason also wore thick-soled boots. Could be he'd been off duty and didn't have time to change. He was built like a teddy bear, his light brown hair in need of a trim, and wore wire-rimmed glasses.

Mason took out his black Moleskine notebook. I imagined he still printed tiny, almost unreadable letters. I'd glimpsed a few pages in previous investigations and would need a magnifying glass to make anything out. Chief Russell whistled sharply.

"Everyone, listen up! This is Detective Greg Mason, who will work closely with Officer Hillerman on the investigation. I trust you'll all cooperate. We want to get to the bottom of this matter quickly. But no one is to leave until they take your statement."

The detective approached Gus and Cissy first. The bride scrubbed her mascara-streaked cheeks with Zia Noemi's handkerchief and then blew her nose. She and Gus nodded or shook their heads in reply to Mason, whose eyes were fixed on his notebook. If only I were a fly on the wall nearby to overhear.

I wanted to ask Eric more about Frank Antonini, but he and Maddie were chatting about other weddings they'd attended.

"Nothing as crazy as this one, though," my sister said.

"Ha. One time the best man toasted the 'new parents' at

the reception," Eric said, "and they hadn't told anyone about being pregnant. The bride's mom was furious."

"That's awful! I remember a few years ago, when one of the groom's friends announced that the bride once worked at Hooters, and how he'd tried to 'bag' her first . . ."

I left the table to discover more interesting information about Dylan. Who might know him best? Clearly Debbie would, but she was busy talking to Chief Russell again.

"I swear, it's only marinara sauce! Why don't you believe me?"

Whoa. The chief flashed me a look of warning, so I turned around and passed by Frank and Claudia's table. Martina pounded her fist with a fresh demand.

"How come I don't have a flower bunch, Mama? I want one like Cissy—"

"You don't get a corsage. Now finish your pasta," Claudia said tersely.

"If I don't get one, I'll stomp all over that stupid flower basket!"

Her mother tuned out the tantrum that followed, gulping more wine. Martina flung herself to the carpet, kicking her legs and pounding her fists, until Frank crouched down beside his daughter to calm her down. She resumed her seat but pouted in silence.

I wandered over to the bar and ordered white wine. The bartender quickly retrieved a glass. "Pretty crazy, isn't it," I said, glancing back at the room.

"Yeah. Never worked a gig where a murder took place before." He slid my wine across the wooden bar. "I seen that guy joking around with the others. Dylan, right? Said he doctored a drink for his ex, only she left it untouched on a table. Then another chick took it."

"Ah, so that's how Kim ended up with it, when he meant for Debbie." I turned around to check on Cissy's sister, who looked shell-shocked. Her parents tried to intercede with Chief Russell, but he waved them away. "And Dylan bragged about it, right?"

The bartender nodded. "Sure did. Guess I'm not surprised he ended up dead."

Hmm. I pondered that while sipping my wine. Why would Dylan go into the women's restroom? Someone must have lured him in there. And he certainly wouldn't have expected a woman to attack him. Was that why he hadn't fought back? It had to be someone tall enough to reach Dylan's neck. Come to think of it, Vanessa was statuesque. She also claimed to have a migraine, vanishing before Maddie and I found Dylan in the ladies' restroom.

That seemed suspicious in my mind.

Cissy suddenly gasped so loud, everyone in the room heard. "Oh, my God! Where are the wedding rings, Gus? Did you take them out of the satin bag on Mr. Clooney's collar?"

"I gave the rings to Dylan."

Zia Noemi wrung her hands. "Maybe they're in Mr. Campbell's coat pocket."

"They must be," Cissy said. "Our rings are worth a fortune."

"Okay, I'll go ask the forensics team," Gus said and hurried off.

I waited along with the rest of the bridal party. When he returned empty-handed, Cissy wailed in dismay. Debbie rushed over to hug her sister and then stabbed a finger at Gus.

"Whoever killed Dylan must have stolen those diamond rings," she said. "Everyone knew they cost thousands of dollars."

"Maybe Dylan gave them to someone else." Gus turned to Nick, who shook his head.

"I don't even remember you giving them to Dylan," he said. "Are you sure?"

"Of course I'm sure." Gus sounded cross. "Maybe one of the hotel staff—"

"That's not possible," the manager interrupted, who'd been hovering nearby. "We're careful to hire only the best people. We've never had any thefts reported. Ever."

"There's always a first time," Frank Antonini piped up, and waved his fork and knife in the air. "Decent steak, but the potatoes are overdone."

"Stop complaining, Frank," Claudia admonished him, and then scolded Martina. "And quit feeding the dog, for heaven's sake! Go away, you stupid mutt."

"Mr. Clooney is not a mutt! He has a very delicate stomach." Cissy marched over to the table, incensed. She led her reluctant poodle away and rebuked the dog when he pulled hard against her. "Stop it, Mr. Clooney. You're not allowed table scraps. No, no."

"Officer Hillerman, will you take statements from the staff while I finish in here," Mason directed, and beckoned Hillerman closer to ask a question. Too low for me to overhear, though. He nodded at the policeman's answer. "Good. Thanks."

Once the detective walked over to speak with the bartender, Nick snapped his fingers. "How about we search for the rings?" he suggested, his voice low. "Maybe Dylan dropped them and they got thrown out by accident. It wouldn't hurt to look."

Gus heartily agreed. "Yeah, let's do it."

They enlisted Eric and crept to the kitchen. I followed but peeked through the half-closed door, wondering if Chief Russell might consider their efforts as tampering with a crime scene. The murder had taken place in the restroom, though. All three men donned nitrile gloves and pawed through trash bags and garbage containers; they made a royal mess on the tile floor. At last they finished, giving up hope, their moods sour afterward.

I followed Eric back to our table. Mason was questioning Steve Leeson, who scratched his beard and shifted on his barstool, clearly nervous. I changed direction to the bar near the ice sculpture, inching sideways until I could overhear their voices without straining my neck.

"—time did your wife leave the room? Before they started serving dinner?"

"I don't know."

"You didn't notice her leave?"

"Yeah. She told Cissy she had a migraine." Steve mumbled something else, his voice dropping. "Happens a lot. The doctors gave her meds for it."

Mason turned a page in his book. "Did you notice Dylan Campbell leaving the room?"

"Nope."

"See anyone he might have talked with tonight?"

"Uh, a lot of people. Like almost everyone here, except me and my wife." Steve finished his beer. "Listen, Officer, let me be honest with you."

"Detective. And sure, I like honesty."

"I didn't like the guy, it's true. But Vanessa and I had nothing to do with his death. We didn't talk to him at the church, either. And since we got here, I've been sitting in this spot the whole time. The bartender will confirm that."

"He said Dylan was talking to Vanessa."

Steve raised a shaggy eyebrow. "News to me. When she gets a migraine, she gets dizzy and nauseated. If she doesn't take her medication, she's sick for days."

Mason perked up at that. "So you let her drive home?"

"We live in Rochester Hills, over an hour one way. We booked a room here at the hotel for the weekend."

"So you didn't speak to Dylan Campbell, even when he visited the bar to get a drink?" Mason asked, checking a previous page, but Steve shook his head. "Several people mentioned him boasting about a prank he played."

"I ignored him." Steve scratched his thigh this time, one foot tapping on the chair's metal rung. "Dylan brags about a lot of things. Bragged, I mean."

"What's your room number?" Mason beckoned to Dan Russell, who brushed past me in his eagerness to obey. The younger man whispered something in the detective's ear. "Go back, and this time tell her it's not a request. If she refuses, tell Mrs. Leeson I'll have her taken down to the station instead for questioning."

"Yes, sir."

Dan hurried off. To my annoyance, Cissy blocked my view of Mason, who resumed questioning Steve. She wailed again to Gus about the missing wedding rings and drowned out everyone's conversation in the room.

"But where could they be? Someone must have seen them at some point!"

"They'll turn up," Gus said.

"What if we never find them? You had the engagement ring designed to show off your grandmother's diamond," she moaned. "My wedding band has a double row of more diamonds to match. Yours has a row of black diamonds and two-tone gold! From Cartier."

"Hope you have insurance, dude," Frank said, passing by on his way to the bar, "in case they're gone for good."

"That isn't helping." Claudia said, and hugged Cissy. "They're bound to turn up."

"I don't like turnips," Martina said, making a face. "I won't eat 'em, no way."

Gus turned to me, leaving Cissy and the others, and beckoned me to a corner beyond the bar. He lowered his voice. "You found Dylan in the bathroom, right?"

"Actually Maddie did, but I was with her."

Frank must have overheard and joined us. "Maybe they took the rings—"

"That's a lie," I shot back.

He shrugged. Gus said something in Italian, which angered Frank enough to stalk off with his wife and daughter. Martina stuck out her tongue at me. I ignored her rudeness.

"Cissy's a wreck." Gus glanced back at Mason, who'd left to question Nick Rizzo at a table, and leaned closer to me. I could barely hear Gus's low voice. "She's afraid Debbie might have done something stupid. She threatened him, you know, several times. Everyone heard."

I nodded. "Threatening isn't the same thing as committing murder. But yeah, it's not a good thing. Even if Dylan did treat her badly in the past."

"Don't spread this around, but Chief Russell wants to test her dress for bloodstains. She claims she spilled marinara sauce. I sat next to her, and I don't remember her eating any pasta. But maybe you can talk to Cissy and her mom, huh? Calm them both down."

"Uh, I'm not sure—"

Ignoring my half-hearted protest, Gus hurried off to talk to Nick, Eric, and Steve at the bar. With a heavy sigh, I walked toward Debbie's family, who huddled around her. Richard Davison looked grim. Barbara rushed over to grab my hands.

"Sasha, you've got to help us." She sounded desperate. "You helped the mayor's wife before Christmas. Now Chief Russell thinks my daughter killed Dylan. You can't even see any stains on her red dress! But he advised us to hire a lawyer."

"Innocent until proven guilty," Richard Davison said. "Remember that." He hurried off to speak to Detective Mason. Debbie suddenly burst into tears.

"I swear to God, it's not blood on my dress! But now I'll go to jail—"

"You will not," Cissy cut in, hugging her. "We'll make sure of it."

Debbie's anger had morphed into rancid fear. I hated to say anything. We'd all heard her threats to take revenge on Dylan, multiple times. But Barbara was right, I couldn't see any stains on the dress given its red hue. Well, maybe there were a few dark spots. Hmm.

"It's marinara sauce, Sasha. Honest." Debbie covered her face. "What if I do end up in prison? What will happen to my bees?"

"Hush, darling," Barbara said. "You won't go to jail, and nothing will happen to your bees. Sasha will prove you didn't kill anyone."

I hadn't actually promised anything. Cissy turned to me and gripped my hands so tight, I almost cried out in pain.

"You'll help Debbie, won't you?" she begged. "Please!"

"Well—"

"Oh, good!" Barbara Davison had interpreted my hesitation as acceptance, and now waved to someone entering the room. "I'm so relieved that the lawyer was having dinner here tonight. Mr. Hanson, over here! I'm so glad you could come to our aid."

I turned to face my ex-husband, kicking myself for not seeing this development. Flynn never turned down any opportunity to make money, no matter what the circumstances. I wasn't surprised he'd leave Cheryl and her parents—if that was who they were—if that situation was so awkward. Flynn grinned at me.

"Hey, Sasha. Guess I'm not surprised you're involved."

I glared at him. "What's that supposed to mean?"

He ignored me and turned to Barbara, Debbie, and Cissy. "Thanks for calling me, Mrs. Davison." Blond hair slicked back, hands folded in front of his bespoke suit and deep maroon tie, he quickly assumed a look of deep concern. "Whatever you need, I'm willing to help."

Chapter 6

I gazed down at him, wondering if Flynn had shrunk a few inches. Then again, I wore four-inch heels that were killing my feet. He also seemed far more lightweight compared to Frank Antonini's and even Eric Dyer's muscular builds. But Flynn made up for any physical lack with his suave and confident manner.

"It's a sticky situation," Mrs. Davison said. "The police suspect Debbie of being involved since the best man, Dylan Campbell, was found dead. Stabbed, quite horribly."

"Really." He quirked an eyebrow. "So Sasha found another murder victim, this time at a wedding rehearsal dinner?"

I bristled at his sly comment. "Maddie and I both found him, actually."

"Close enough. Everyone knows you're a jinx." Flynn turned to Richard Davison when he returned. "I'd prefer consulting in a private room. You can explain there why the police believe your daughter is a suspect."

"Sasha agreed to prove Debbie's innocence," Barbara said, "but only if you think it's necessary, of course."

"The police would be the ones to object, so I'll leave that decision to them. I don't know why, but murders have been following Sasha like stray dogs." Flynn flashed another grin at me and then led the Davison family to a side room just outside the doors.

Flustered and angry, I marched in the opposite direction. Bad enough that Digger Sykes called me a "body magnet." Now Flynn had labeled me a jinx. He seemed to insinuate that I'd brought about this latest murder, too. That was nuts.

"Hey, Sasha. Are you all right?" Kim patted the chair beside her, so I sat at her table and tried not to stare at the dark bruising beneath her eyes. "Guess what? Claudia asked that detective if she could leave, but he turned her down flat. She's furious now, because she thinks he considers Frank a murder suspect along with Debbie Davison."

"Really?" Maddie suddenly popped up behind me, along with Eric and Nick. They all drew out chairs at the table. "Is it because Frank didn't get along with Dylan?"

"More than that, I bet," Kim said. "They never talked if they could help it."

"Yeah. And Frank's got a history of violence," Nick said, and cracked his knuckles. "His wife's black eye is proof. Not the first time he's smacked her around, either."

I shrugged. "That's not enough for the cops to think he killed Dylan."

"Didn't you tell Frank that you saw Claudia meeting Dylan this afternoon?" Eric asked Nick. "Although she denied it."

He looked a little shamefaced. "Yeah. I didn't mean to cause trouble, though."

"Frank didn't believe her story about that shopping trip," Kim said. "None of us did. And remember that Claudia mentioned how Frank gets 'insanely jealous' Tuesday night."

I shrugged. "Takes a lot to commit cold-blooded murder, though."

"That may be true, but Frank was a real hotshot in the military," Nick said. "Not like me, or Eric here. We were just ordinary chumps."

"What kind of hotshot?" Maddie asked, her fingers tapping the table. "Some kind of specialist? And which branch of the military?"

"Army," Eric said. "We both were in basic training at Fort Bragg, but he qualified for Special Ops training. I bombed out because I couldn't carry all that heavy equipment and run around for hours on end. Nick, too. But Frank excelled at all that, plus he trained as a paratrooper for special missions in Afghanistan and Iraq."

"So you're saying Frank would know the best way to kill." Nick shook his head. "Sasha's right. Takes guts to do something like that."

"We all had a good reason." Eric shrugged. "Dylan cheated us at poker during the bachelor party. Gus said he has to pay his boss for all the damage we caused at Flambé. That fight got so out of hand."

Bob and Gisele Vaccaro walked over to our table. "Hey, everyone." Gisele slid onto the only empty chair beside me. "I overheard you talking about the bachelor party. Bob said Dylan cleaned you all out." She laughed. "Suckers."

"But Nick started the fight," Bob added, one hand on his wife's shoulder.

"I didn't like the way Dylan lorded it over us," Nick retorted. "I never threatened him."

"Not that night, maybe."

"Well, Vanessa told me Debbie wanted to poison him with arsenic. She said that at the bachelorette party, right?"

Gisele nodded. "I heard her, too—"

"Who's ready to make a statement?" Detective Mason interrupted, and then flashed his badge. "I'd like to hear more about the bachelor and bachelorette parties."

I waited to hear what everyone would say, but Kim and Gisele remained silent. So did Nick, Eric, and Bob, who all glanced at each other while Mason asked several pointed questions. It seemed as if they were signaling to keep quiet.

"Okay, then I'll interview you individually, in private. Stay put until I call your name." Mason ambled over to Debbie Davison, whose hands shook at his approach. "You're the bride's sister, is that correct? I have some questions for you."

"Like what?" Debbie's eyes grew to saucers. "Chief Russell already asked me all kinds of questions."

"I'm glad to hear that." The detective opened his small notebook. "So when was the last time you spoke to Dylan Campbell?"

"When he spilled beer on her shoes," Gisele said, passing by, and loud enough for Mason to hear. "Boy, was she mad about that."

Debbie burst into a fresh flood of tears. "I didn't kill him, I swear to God! Yes, I was mad at him, but that's all. And this really is marinara sauce on my dress—"

"Excuse me." Flynn Hanson popped up out of the blue. "Ms. Davison will not answer any further questions. I am representing her now."

Mason looked peeved and walked over to consult with Chief Russell. Flynn led Debbie away, one arm around her waist. She cried harder, both hands covering her face, wailing her innocence. Cissy rushed over to hug her.

"It's okay, Debbie. It's okay!"

"Now they'll think I'm guilty for certain—"

"No, they won't," Flynn said, "and remember that anything you do tell them can be used against you. If they do end up charging you, that is." His voice trailed off when he followed the sisters to rejoin Barbara and Richard Davison.

"Is that true?" Maddie looked at me. "Does that apply to us, too?"

I shrugged. "I suppose it would. Eric, why didn't you tell Mason your theory? That all the groomsmen may have had a reason to kill Dylan. He's bound to find out."

"Oh, man," Eric muttered. "I don't know about the rest of you guys, but I blame myself for losing so much money to Dylan at the bachelor party."

"I only lost a few hundred bucks," Bob Vaccaro said.

Gisele screeched at that. "You told me fifty!"

"Dylan laughed in our faces," Nick said. "He refused to admit he cheated, too, even when I saw him palming a few cards."

"You couldn't prove it, though. Unless you took a video," Eric replied.

"It's too late to argue about that," I said, "so tell me more about Frank's background in the military. What exactly can Special Ops do?"

"Anything they're called to do—counterterrorism, hostage situations, search and rescue," Nick said. "They're sharpshooters, and trained with knives or any kind of weapon."

"He was stabbed—"

"Sasha, can I talk to you for a minute?" Maddie dragged me from the table, her voice low while we walked away. "You're not supposed to tell people what we saw, remember? The police haven't finished questioning everyone. That might affect their answers."

"Oh. You're right." I felt sick and embarrassed. "Must be all the champagne I drank. We never did get more than salad and pasta to eat, too. I wonder why Flynn decided to represent Debbie. After all, he's moving his practice to Ann Arbor."

"I hear the Legal Eagle lawyers are furious that he's leaving them in the lurch. They turned down another friend who wanted to join their firm, back in September, to make room for Flynn. Now he's dumped them after less than six months."

"And all that publicity, although it did help boost their client list—"

"Hey, you two, quit being so secretive."

Kim Goddard waved us back to the table, so we returned to sit once more. She looked less pale, her long blond hair combed back from her face. Nick and Eric had gone off to refresh their drinks at the bar, where Steve quaffed another beer.

"So are you going to tell that detective what Debbie said at the bachelorette party?" she asked. "Vanessa's back. Doesn't look like she has much of a migraine."

Kim gestured to Vanessa, who was pacing the area behind her husband. She looked angry. Or was it only nerves? Dan Russell hovered near her, as if worried Vanessa would bolt again before Mason could question her. Officer Hillerman was talking to Richard and Barbara Davison, along with Zia Noemi, on the room's far side. Mason jotted notes in his black notebook while he questioned Gus and Cissy. He finally closed it with a snap.

Mason walked over to our table. "I need to know exactly where you all were sitting this evening," he announced, "and whether you left the room. What time, either before or after Mr. Campbell's body was discovered, too." He wrote down what Nick, Eric, and the Vaccaros told him, plus Maddie and I, before he turned to Kim. "And you, Ms. Goddard?"

"I was sick," Kim said. "Someone told me that Dylan doctored the drink, because he bragged about it. I didn't know he meant it for Debbie. I mistook it for the glass I'd left on the table, but it did taste funny. And then I rushed to the restroom."

"Did you notice Vanessa Leeson leaving the room?"

"No. I've been sitting here ever since, and didn't pay any attention to anyone else."

Mason asked a few other questions she couldn't answer and then headed over to speak to Vanessa. I watched her twist her wedding ring around her finger, eyes downcast, avoiding his gaze. Once Mason began to question her husband, Steve, she seemed to relax.

After untying the bows of my high-heeled shoes, I slipped them off. My toes looked red and pinched, and I didn't care if my feet got cold. I was too tired to think past when Chief Russell or Detective Mason finally agreed that we could go home. I also wondered about the wedding tomorrow, and if they'd delay it. After all, the murderer might be one of the bridal party. None of the hotel staff had any reason to kill Dylan.

Hopefully, the wedding would be postponed, so I could rest my poor feet.

Vanessa rushed past me to the exit. Mason blocked Steve Leeson from following her, however, and opened his notebook again. I sat back. Waiting around was no fun, so I checked my cell phone. Jay had texted me long ago with a *Home yet?*

I replied with *Sorry, big delay. Tell you more tomorrow.* I had no idea what else to say, since I couldn't explain that a murder had taken place via text messages. Plus Detective Mason would be livid if word got out beyond the hotel.

I'd been warned in the past about giving information to the gossip mill. Even Digger Sykes had been guilty of that. And tonight I'd nearly blabbed about the ice pick as the murder weapon. My world had shrunk to this banquet room. Everyone else was enjoying their Friday evening—the beginning of a whole weekend to celebrate the holiday of the year for romantics. And on Sunday, Valentine's Day itself, I'd be working at the Chocolate Bear Bar event.

Jay was supposed to come to the wedding tomorrow, but that might change given this incident. And we agreed not to celebrate the holiday until later. We both disliked the crazy commercialism. Did we really need Valentine's cards, flowers, or presents to show our love? I sighed. I bought a present for him, but now I wondered if Jay had bothered.

I quickly grew bored playing Candy Crush, so I switched to a different game app. I'd never gotten into Pokémon GO or the latest fads. Maddie was a whiz at Piano Tiles. I preferred Solitaire, ZigZag, and word games.

"Ms. Silverman?" Mason towered above me, eyebrows raised.

"Oh, uh. Yeah, I'm coming."

I nearly dropped my phone, I was so surprised to hear his gruff voice. He glanced at the others in the bridal party, fixing his gaze on Gus, who cradled Cissy on his lap. Holding my high heels by their ribbons, I followed Mason in my stocking feet to a table near the bar.

"Have a seat." He waited until I perched on a chair. "Maddie explained how she found Dylan Campbell. Must have been wrenching for you both."

"Yeah." I frowned. "But I'm not a jinx, or a body magnet."

"You just happened to be in the wrong place, at the wrong time. Again."

"Hey—"

"I'm kidding, really." Mason poked up his wire-rimmed glasses with a sly grin. "Things happen beyond our control, like my hunting trip up north being canceled at the last minute. I was already past Clarkston and had to head back on I-75. Now, let me confirm a few things with you. First off, what time did you visit the ladies' restroom?"

"Um, right after the pasta course. Maddie spilled a little marinara sauce on her skirt, so it's possible Debbie Davison did as well—the pasta was really messy. I didn't check my phone for the exact time, though." He looked skeptical at that, but I shrugged. "There's no clock in this room, either. We first went there after the salad course, but Kim was sick. So we waited."

"Okay." Mason flipped through his notebook pages. "Dylan spiked a drink, only he meant it for Ms. Davison. Maddie mentioned how 'Vanessa Leeson stood at the door and warned us not to go in.' Was that before she left to go to her hotel room?"

"Yes. After that I heard her telling Cissy she had a migraine."

"You didn't see her at any point afterward?"

I shook my head. "I don't think so."

"What about Debbie Davison?"

"What about her? I didn't notice her leave."

"Not going to the bathroom, then."

"Not that I remember—"

"But you heard the threats she made about Dylan Campbell, at the bachelorette party?"

"Uh, yeah."

"What about at the church?"

I nodded, uncomfortable confirming that, but he kept his eyes on his notebook. Mason waited me out. "I doubt if she meant anything by it, though. I saw Debbie sitting with Cissy and Gus when we passed by on the way to the ladies' room."

"Close enough to slip away, and then back, without being seen?" I didn't reply, so Mason turned a page. "Did you hear either of the Davison sisters say something about getting rid of Dylan and choosing another best man?"

"Oh." I wished my dad were here, as a lawyer, to advise

me what to answer. "They did complain about him a lot, and that Gus's cousin should have been the best man."

The detective flashed me a skeptical glance but dropped his gaze once more. "What did people say when Mr. Campbell showed up at the bachelorette party?"

I shrugged. "He was drunk, so that didn't go over well with anyone. Dylan apologized to Vanessa and said he was innocent. Several times, which I thought was kind of strange."

Mason scratched his jawline. "Innocent about what?"

"Nobody explained what it was about, so I don't know. Her mother wasn't happy, either, with Dylan showing up that night."

"So what happened?"

"Gus arrived, along with Nick and Steve, and they dragged Dylan out. Nick Rizzo did say something earlier about how Dylan didn't understand why people hadn't forgiven him. That's all I know about it," I added.

Mason scribbled furiously and then poked up his glasses. "Heard anything interesting about Frank Antonini, by any chance?"

"That he has a short temper," I said bitterly. "He gave his wife a black eye, or didn't you notice? Because Frank heard that Claudia met with Dylan this afternoon."

"Heard from who?"

I shrugged. "I think Nick. She claimed to be shopping, but didn't have any bags when she came to the rehearsal. And Dylan showed up right after."

Mason nodded. "Okay. I'll check on that."

"What about the missing wedding rings?"

"What about them?"

"They're supposed to be worth a fortune. A couple thousand bucks, each, I guess. Cissy can verify that." I nodded in her direction. "I think Gus used his grandmother's diamond in her engagement ring. His ring has diamonds, too."

Mason consulted his notebook. "I believe the dog had them in a bag on his collar?"

"Satin, tied with a red bow, yes. He wore it at the church rehearsal." I studied the ceiling tiles above, trying to remember. "Gus said he gave the rings to Dylan at some point, though. At least I think that's what he said."

"And now they're missing."

"Yeah." I watched him continue to read through his scribbled notes. "Why wouldn't they use imitation rings for the rehearsal, if they were that valuable?"

"Why let the dog carry them around on his collar in the first place?" Mason countered. "Happens all the time, people not taking precautions with their valuables."

"Is it possible one of the staff might have learned how expensive those rings are? The bartender sure overheard everything that was going on tonight."

"He saw and heard a lot, but didn't know anything about the rings. Neither did the staff. We asked. Several times."

"That doesn't mean they're telling the truth." I waited, but Mason was busy writing and didn't answer. "I'm curious. What did the bartender actually say?"

"Do you really want me to answer that?" The detective glanced my way, his gaze frank. "Remember how dangerous it is, crossing paths with a murderer. I didn't think I had to remind you of that after the last three times."

"Hey, you were pumping me for information."

"That's my job, Sasha."

I couldn't help sighing, which did little to ease my frustration. "So what about the wedding tomorrow? Is it still going on?"

"Postponed. Best man murdered, maid of honor a prime suspect along with the groom's cousin," he replied. "The wedding wouldn't be a happy one if they went through with it."

"So was Dylan actually killed in the ladies' restroom? That was a lot of blood."

"The body wasn't dumped there, if that's what you mean." Mason flipped to a fresh page. "Anything else you might have picked up from conversations today?"

I tapped my finger on the tabletop. "Frank Antonini trained as Army Special Ops."

"I'll check his military record then."

He added a few more lines to his notebook and then rose to his feet. Mason straightened his sweatshirt and then turned back to me as if he'd forgotten something. The overhead lights glinted on his lenses, hiding his eyes.

"Sasha, stick to selling teddy bears—"

"Yeah, thanks. I know."

"And if anything else comes up, call or text me."

Mason stalked off. Although I resented his offhanded dismissal, I grabbed my shoes and returned to the table. Zia Noemi had joined Maddie and Eric, while the detective approached Frank Antonini at the bar. That didn't go well, apparently, since Mason stepped back when Frank raised his voice. He also clenched his fists, as if ready to take a swing. Officer Hillerman quickly walked over to join the detective as backup.

"Perhaps we can continue this down at the station," Mason said.

Frank shook his head. "I told you everything I know."

"And I'd like to go back over some of the questions and your answers."

"No way—"

"Can't it wait, detective?" Gus jumped in to defend his cousin. "He suffers from PTSD after serving so long in the Army. That's why he acts a little squirrely."

Cissy marched over, her cheeks beet red, and her voice rose to a screech. "Who cares about how stupid Frank is acting? Chief Russell told me a few minutes ago that we have to postpone the wedding! What about the reception's food, going to waste? Shrimp and crab appetizers, filet mignon and salmon entrées—"

"I'm sorry," Mason interrupted, "but it will have to wait until Chief Russell gives you the go-ahead." He signaled to Hillerman, who gripped Frank's elbow and led him toward the exit.

"It wasn't some cheap chicken cutlet buffet," the bride-to-be wailed. "And what about the cake? My mother special ordered it! Rose-flavored buttercream, five tiers, with dozens of red roses surrounding the base and all the layers."

I had a feeling Cissy was more upset about the postponement than any gruesome murder. Especially Dylan Campbell's. Gus folded his arms over his chest, shaking his head, and sounded weary when he replied.

"Come on, babe. There's nothing we can do about it. And remember, my Zietta baked over five hundred cookies. She spent weeks in the kitchen, baking and icing all of them, but we're not whining about it."

"You can freeze the cake, and the cookies," Kim said, trying to be helpful.

Cissy muttered something about where to put those cookies. Gus grabbed her arm. "My best friend is dead," he said tersely, "so we'll have to let the police find out who killed him first. And then we'll get married."

She shook herself free. "I warned you that Dylan would ruin my wedding!"

Maddie glanced at me, her mouth in the shape of an O, leaned back in her chair, and then exhaled a long breath. I fought to suppress a smile, but Zia Noemi shook a finger in my direction. She didn't bother to whisper.

"Didn't I tell you, and I was right. Cissy is psychic."

Chapter 7

My alarm rang a scant five hours after I crawled into bed. I groped to shut it off, but only managed to knock the clock radio off the nightstand. Rosie and Sugar Bear grumbled when I pushed them aside and reached over the bed—and rolled onto my fluffy rug.

At least not on the hardwood floor. But still, ouch.

"Okay, clock, I'm up. So leave it."

I punched the button and set it back on the nightstand with a thump. Dragged myself into the shower, ran hot water over my head until my eyes opened wide enough to face the day. After last night's fiasco, I had only one positive thing in mind. Rest today, read, relax. Thank goodness I'd asked Renee Truman to cover for me at the shop. I was supposed to get my hair done at Luxe for the wedding, along with a manicure and pedicure. I hated to deprive Lynn of such a major appointment, given the busy holiday season.

Then again, she might be happy to cancel me off her tight schedule.

I shut off the water and toweled myself dry. Chose casual

jeans and a sweater, plus boots, and then combed out my wet hair. Ponytail? Braids? Bun? I chose the first, since I was too tired to make an effort. I returned to the bedroom, checked my phone's calendar, and called the salon.

"No problem, Sasha. Maddie canceled, too, but Cissy's here," Lynn whispered, "and she wants the works even though the wedding's been postponed. Her friends came with her, along with her future sister-in-law. We'll be busy enough."

"Great, now I don't feel bad. Thanks."

Downstairs, I spied a note on the kitchen counter near the coffee. Maddie's handwriting was usually illegible, so she'd printed. "Renee has the flu. Sorry." Dang. I returned upstairs to change into my usual work uniform of black pants, silver sweater, and teddy bear earrings. Then I spent another half hour blow-drying my hair and adding makeup. I scooped Sugar Bear and Rosie off the bed and carried them down to the kitchen. Already nine thirty, and that meant a rushed breakfast for us all. I opened the back door and shivered in the cold wind.

"Come on, you lazy pups. Out you go."

I had to laugh at Rosie's reluctance, the way she slunk down the steps to sniff a high snowbank. Sugar Bear shook herself and then raced along the sidewalk after my older dog. She quickly finished and returned before Rosie; once inside, Sugar Bear charged at Onyx, barking her little head off. Maddie's black cat had been sitting on the cushioned window seat but hissed at the tiny poodle, arching her back, her tail as thick as a brush.

"Stop it, both of you. Sugar, focus! Focus." When I pointed my finger at her, Sugar Bear squatted on her butt in hopes of a treat. I waited the correct amount of time and rewarded her for being quiet. "Good girl. Now leave Nyx alone, okay? Please."

I couldn't discipline Onyx, however, who continued to stare at Sugar Bear with venom. The cat-and-dog wars had decreased in number each day, but I knew a fresh skirmish could flare up at any moment. Onyx disliked all dogs, although she'd grown tolerant of Rosie over the years. She wasn't happy about having a second dog around the house. And given Sugar Bear's feisty attitude and boundless energy, Onyx might never adjust.

"Breakfast time, girls. Here you go."

They gobbled their kibble, racing to see who could finish first and sneak extra bites from the slower eater, but finished at the same time. Sugar Bear looked disappointed. Rosie burped. Laughing, I grabbed a protein bar for myself, filled a thermos of coffee, and then let the dogs out once again. Both rushed off the porch. But the moment I glimpsed a beige blur running toward them, I raced outside without a coat.

"No, Mr. Clooney," I yelled. "Shoo! Go on, go back home. Silly dog."

I did not want him to pass on fleas or terrorize Sugar Bear. My little poodle cowered in fear. The larger dog steered away from my waving hands and loud voice, thank heaven. Mr. Clooney rushed back toward the Davisons' house and jumped the fence. Sugar Bear had rolled onto the snow in submission and now her curly fur was caked. I cursed under my breath. I'd have to towel her dry and brush her, which would definitely make me late to open the shop.

"Brother," I muttered. "Of all the days for this to happen."

By the time I walked through the office to the shop's front, I found Aunt Eve waiting on a customer. She looked marvelous in a midcalf plaid skirt and white blouse, and her cherry red cardigan had a feathery collar. I always enjoyed seeing her unique fashion style. Her blond hairdo reminded me of Lauren Bacall's smooth bob with its slight wave.

"Your girlfriend will absolutely love this bear. Buy a box of chocolate to go with it, and your Valentine's Day date will be off to a great start."

"Thanks."

His face flushed, the teen hurried out the door. Aunt Eve couldn't help laughing. "Poor kid, he wants to impress a new girlfriend. We'll have lots of guys coming in at the last minute to buy something for their wives and sweethearts."

"That reminds me. Mary from the florist needs more teddy bears." I checked my phone for her text message. "White if we have any left, since they look better with her red roses and baby's breath arrangements. So now Renee came down with the flu? That's harsh."

"Yep. Fever, aches, flat-out tired. A few of our factory staff have recovered."

"I hope Renee feels better soon. And I'm glad the wedding was postponed, because my feet need a break. Those heeled shoes are murder—oops. I mean, uncomfortable."

"Maddie said someone was killed last night, so what's the whole story?"

"Hang on until I deliver those bears to the flower shop. Then I'll fill you in on the dirt. And boy, howdy, is there plenty to spread around."

Aunt Eve cocked her head. "A bushel, huh?"

I laughed. "Enough to fill a cornfield."

She shooed me off since another customer arrived with two kids in tow. I packed half a dozen white bears, along with a few beige and brown ones, drove over to the florist shop on Main Street, and delivered them. Mary and Norma were swamped with orders and didn't have a minute to spare, so I set the boxes on their back table and quickly wrote out a receipt. They could square up with Aunt Eve next week.

Then I stopped by Fresh Grounds for my favorite espresso, a Mint Mocha, and splurged on a decadent chocolate-drizzled raspberry scone. Garrett Thompson, my best friend's husband and part owner of the coffee shop and bakery along with his uncle, steamed my almond milk and poured it over my cup, then topped it with whipped cream and syrup. He set it before me with a flourish and pushed a lock of dark hair from his eyes.

"There you go, Sasha. Happy Saturday. And Valentine's Day, early. I heard Jay's up north for the weekend at some winter festival."

"Yeah. So how was Mary Kate's ultrasound?" I asked.

"Good, good." He straightened to his full height. "Everything looks okay."

"Do you know if it's a boy or girl, or are you waiting to be surprised?"

"Mary Kate prefers not knowing, although I have an idea."

Garrett looked pleased, so I guessed it might be a boy. "You never know for certain."

"I'm painting the baby's room a pale blue just in case. And if I'm wrong, I'll do it over in pink. Or add purple stripes to the blue."

"That would work."

He leaned over the counter and spoke in a low voice, so that other customers sitting at the tables wouldn't hear. "So, Sasha. I heard Cissy and Gus's wedding is on hold. Is it true Debbie Davison stuck the guy who dumped her with a steak knife?"

"Who told you that?" I sighed. "Gus's best man was killed, but the investigation is in the early stages. The gossip mill must be churning away like crazy, huh? I heard Chief Russell on the radio, saying they won't release any name until they notify next of kin. And we didn't have steak last night for dinner, it was prime rib. We didn't get a chance to eat it, either."

"Whatever. But he was stabbed, right?"

"I can't say. You'll have to wait until the police hold a press conference."

"Uncle Gil told me that you agreed to prove Debbie's innocence. And your uncle said that would be a piece of cake for you."

"Really," I muttered. "I suppose those two met for breakfast at the Sunshine Café, as usual. That means the chief's wife overheard them talking."

"It's possible." Garrett tapped the side of his nose. "You know and I know that Lenore Russell keeps whatever she hears to herself. That's a good thing. Too much gossip circulates around the village, and it usually ends up hurting people."

"Says the man who wanted to hear gossip," I teased him. He only grinned. "Tell Mary Kate these scones are the best yet."

"Hey, Sasha! I baked those," Wendy Clark sang out while she wiped down the nearest table. She'd been working at Fresh Grounds since last fall, and a good thing too, given the shop's popularity. "I used Mary Kate's basic scone recipe, with lemon oil and peel, plus raspberries. That's dark chocolate for the drizzled topping instead of streusel crumbs."

"Mmm," I said, my mouth full with the large bite. I sipped my coffee. "Great combo. I'll tell Maddie. She's wild about raspberries."

I waved to my cousin Matt behind the counter in the adjoining bookstore. He rang up a purchase for a young mother and her child. My other best friend, Elle, Matt's wife, rushed over to referee when their kids started arguing over a puzzle at a corner table.

"Girls, I'll send you to Grandma's if you can't behave—"

I headed back to work, happy that The Cat's Cradle looked busier than ever. Matt faced closing his business last year after being questioned as a murder suspect. The bookstore survived to reap an abundance of sales over the Christmas holidays. I would have hated for Silver Hollow to lose that unique shop. Elle and Matt enjoyed hosting events for customers and their children throughout the year, from book club meetings to author appearances.

By the time I returned to the Silver Bear Shop, Aunt Eve had finished bagging a panda bear for an older woman. "My granddaughter will be surprised. Her parents don't celebrate any holidays, can you believe it? I want to give Kyla some love on Valentine's Day."

"How sweet! And she'll adore this ballerina outfit for her bear."

"Yes, she's really into purple."

Once the woman left, my aunt pushed back a blond lock from her face and perched on the stool behind the counter. "Time to tell the story of what happened last night, Sasha. Must have been rough at the rehearsal dinner. Maddie's still upset about finding the best man's dead body and had a horrible nightmare."

I felt bad for my sister, knowing full well how sleepless nights had affected me after I'd discovered our sales rep's body last fall. And the second time was worse. My mother had found Mayor Bloom's body before Christmas, and that had been bad, too.

"—doubt if she'll get much done today at her studio," Aunt Eve was saying.

"I'm in the same boat." I yawned wide. "I can barely keep my eyes open, and this triple-shot espresso doesn't seem to be helping much." Leaning against the wall, I finished my drink. "Plus later today I've got to help set up for tomorrow's Chocolate Bear Bar."

"Okay, but hurry and explain before another customer comes in."

I tossed my cup in the trash and then related how we'd found Dylan Campbell, how Detective Mason had kept us at the restaurant long past closing time, and how he'd asked the same questions in a different way, no doubt hoping someone's story would change.

"We didn't get home until three in the morning. I haven't told Jay the whole story. I did text him that he doesn't have to come back today for the reception. He'll stay and hang with his friends at the Frostbite Festival," I added. "I have no idea when Cissy and Gus will reschedule their wedding, given the investigation."

"At least not until after the autopsy," Aunt Eve said, "or even when the case is officially closed. Mr. and Mrs. Davison must be worried since Debbie is a suspect."

"Especially the way she kept threatening Dylan. Did Mads tell you what she said at the bachelorette party?"

"No—"

We both broke off when the bells over the door jangled. An older man walked into the shop, clearly nervous, bundled up in a heavy coat, muffler, and wool hat. He took it off to wipe his sweaty forehead with a monogrammed silk handkerchief. I noted how his thinning hair had receded to the top of his skull. His gloves looked as expensive. He didn't smile, but managed a cautious nod.

"Can we help you, sir?" Aunt Eve chirped. "Are you looking for a teddy bear?"

"Yes. In fact, three dozen. They must be in a firm sitting position, however."

"Sitting?" Puzzled by that, I glanced back at our shelves. "Most of our bears can sit. Of course, when a child plays with them—"

"No, no. I'm looking for this type."

The man produced a slick magazine page from his coat

pocket and held it up for us to view. I recognized the toy as a Bears of the Heart teddy bear, produced by Teddy Hartman's company, before he sold it to another businessman.

"It must have a front seam, like this one."

"Our bears are made from a different pattern. Sorry."

"Perhaps you could do a special order? I want the best quality teddy bears. Several friends told me about your shop, and I also checked your online website."

"We produce our bears in the factory behind our shop," I said with a touch of pride, "but we only use our own patterns."

Aunt Eve moved closer to view the photo. "That's Benny Bear, from Bears of the Heart. We could create a special pattern for you, but we'd charge a setup fee to cover that. Are they not making those bears anymore?"

"No. That's why I'm willing to pay whatever is required." The man stuffed the photo away.

"Let me get my order book," she said cheerfully. "I'll be back in a jiffy."

While my aunt zipped to the office, an alarm bell clanged in my head. I didn't like the idea of copying a Bears of the Heart style of bear, for one thing. And why did he need a sitting bear? I reached behind me and grabbed a fifteen-inch firmer bear.

"There's no front seam, but this bear will sit without flopping to one side," I said. "We have plenty of these in stock. Are you donating the toys to charity?"

The gentleman looked down his nose at me and sniffed. "Do you always ask customers why they order products?"

"I thought you might have a specific charity in mind. On our tours, people can see each step in the production of our bears, from cutting fabric to sewing on the tags. And then watching the staff embroider the face."

"I'm not interested in that." He patted his sweating neck and face again. "I can pay cash, if you will make out the order. Three dozen bears. The fur color doesn't matter. They must be sitting and have a front seam," the man repeated sternly. "Perhaps I should have ordered online from a different company and saved myself the trip here."

"So you're from out of town?"

He glanced at me in surprise. "I am paying cash, like I said. I didn't think more than a name would be necessary for such a transaction."

I disliked his attitude, and the bad vibes this guy gave me. Maybe last night's events colored my instincts, though. I decided to dig in my heels and demand far more than a name and payment information on the order form. Luckily, Aunt Eve rushed back with several order sheets and signaled with a thumb—our code that she'd been called to the factory. No doubt Uncle Ross needed help. That left me to deal with this nervous customer.

When he mopped his forehead again, I poised my pen above the form. "Special orders do require more than a name," I said innocently. "Phone number, address, and credit card."

"All that isn't necessary—"

"I'm afraid it is, in case we have any questions about the pattern or if we encounter any delays in production."

The gentleman huffed in dismay and slapped his gloves against one palm, as if thinking. "Perhaps I'll just take those bears on the display shelf. Do you have more in stock?"

When he pulled out a huge wad of bills, I shook my head in amazement. I also positioned my cell phone and managed to capture a photo without him noticing. Something was off about this guy. I watched as he examined the toy's side seams and squeezed the stuffing.

"I'd have to check on that, of course." I retrieved eight more behind me. Two white teddy bears, three dark brown, and the rest tan in fur color. "So far, we have nine bears."

"How much are they?"

"Twenty-two dollars each."

He looked taken aback at my remark. "I paid twelve for Benny Bear, and that included tax with free shipping."

"You wanted the best quality, if I remember right," I said. "The price reflects that."

"I'll take only one now," the man said, clearly angry, "and see if it fits our requirements. If it does, then I will return and purchase more."

The bells over the front door jangled again. Uncle Ross entered the shop with a large box, cursing a blue streak about the changing weather, followed by Aunt Eve. Snowflakes scudded across the floor. My difficult customer snatched two bears, tossed a fifty-dollar bill onto the counter, and rushed outside. The door slammed behind him.

"I thought he wanted to order three dozen bears," Aunt Eve cried out in dismay.

"I bet Uncle Ross scared him off," I said with a laugh. "You do resemble a sailing captain with that hat and your beard. Plus your salty language."

"Hey. I 'yam what I yam,'" he said, quoting Popeye, and winked.

"Really, Ross, you should watch your language in front of customers," she scolded him, and eyed the empty order form. "So you didn't get his name or contact information."

I shook my head. "But you should have seen the big wad of cash in his pocket."

Uncle Ross grunted. "Like a mobster, huh? Eve told me some guy came in yesterday, right before closing, and paid cash for five bears. Younger, already balding, wore glasses."

"Renee called me to lock up last night, since you were at

the rehearsal," Aunt Eve said with a shrug. "She started feeling terrible, around five o'clock."

"Staff's dropping like flies in a summer heat wave. You better not get it," my uncle said to her. "I need you to take care of me if I come down with the flu."

"You will get sick if you don't take elderberry syrup like I do, and a zinc pill with your breakfast. I haven't had a case of flu in over twenty years." Aunt Eve turned to me, clearly disappointed. "Too bad you didn't get that special order, Sasha. We need a new project since we finally finished shipping out all the Beary Potter wizard bears."

"Maddie came up with wedding bears," I said. "How does that sound? June will be here before you know it. And we're standing up in Cissy and Gus's wedding."

Uncle Ross groaned. "A pair of bears? Twice the work."

"It sounds wonderful," my aunt said. "The bride bear can have a white lace veil at least, if not a gown. The groom bears could wear a bow tie and vest, maybe a little top hat—"

"No hats," he said firmly. "We had enough trouble with the wizard robe and scarf, plus the wand. The wedding veil would be simple to sew on, but the vest and tie are enough. There's only two months until May."

"I suppose you're right." I hid my disappointment, since the idea had really grown on me and Maddie's quick sketches looked adorable. "How about adding a little bouquet of silk flowers for the bride, though?"

"We'll see." Despite his grumpy tone, Uncle Ross seemed to accept the plan. "We'll make up a few samples. Maybe one of the grooms can wear a plaid vest and a kilt."

"And his bride bear will wear a red dress like mine," Aunt Eve said happily. "How sweet would that be to remember our special day."

I snapped my fingers. "Wow, that's a great concept! Special order 'anniversary bears,' and we can promote that along with the final design of the wedding bears. So what did you bring in the box, Uncle Ross?"

"White bears. We finished a dozen yesterday," he said. "Mary Monroe called and wanted at least this many, so you can deliver them during lunchtime."

"I already took over what we had on hand." I examined the seams of the bears that I'd brought down from the shelf. "I wonder if that customer wants a front seam to make it easier to hide drugs, like we found was happening last year."

My aunt's jaw dropped. "What? I never heard that story."

I explained the sordid details and checked the photo I'd taken of the man. He was so bundled up I couldn't make out his features. Too bad. If it turned out he was a criminal, that would have helped the police identify him. I didn't delete the photo, though. Just in case.

"Okay, you two," I said to my aunt and uncle. "Back to work."

"I've got to finish all the tax info. Not fun at all." Aunt Eve hugged me and then took Ross's arm. "See you later, gator."

As Saturday wore on into the afternoon, the shop was inundated with customers. I called Isabel French, former co-owner of the Silver Scoop, to help me out. She arrived, cheeks pink and breathless from the cold, shaking her dark hair out from her knit cap. Isabel tossed her parka over the stool behind the counter. She never regretted leaving her sewing machine for a chance to interact with customers, especially an adorable set of twins.

"How can I help you girls?" Isabel asked.

"We don't want the same color bear, though," one said. "I want a tan bear with a pink tutu, and fairy wings."

"And I want a white bear in purple," the other sang out. "With sparkles!"

"Let's see what we can find."

Isabel led the pair around the shop, showing them all the various costumes and accessories, while I helped a middle-aged man choose a small teddy bear to accompany a box of candy. He leaned closer and asked if any shop in the village sold women's lingerie.

"No, but here's a business card for someone who does." I tucked Devonna Walsh's hot pink postcard into the bag with the stuffed bear. "She'll be glad to help you out."

My feet ached, so I perched on the stool behind the counter. Thank goodness Cissy and Gus's wedding was on hold. Deon Walsh called at five o'clock; he and Tim Richardson had already moved all the sewing machines to one side in the factory's big room, set up the round tables, and swept the floor. What a relief. I was exhausted after so little sleep, and they saved me by prepping for the Chocolate Bear Bar event. I headed over there after closing time.

Joelynn Owens arrived shortly after six thirty. I was surprised to see Cheri Furness following her from the parking lot. She waddled through the factory's door, clutching her lower back and moaning with the effort, then quickly grabbed the nearest chair.

"I'm so ready to take a knife and do an emergency C-section in my kitchen," she said with a laugh. "This little dude's been kicking me for months, but he's quieted down at last. I'm hoping that means he's ready to arrive."

"No idea," I said, although Isabel nodded.

"My mom's a nurse. She told me that's one sign."

"Good." Cheri rubbed her back again. "How's your dad? Everything okay?"

"Slowly deteriorating," Isabel said sadly. "It's so tough . . ."

While they chatted, Joelynn drew me aside. "Before we set up, I have to ask you about Cissy Davison. What happened to postpone the wedding?"

"Yeah, she's been talking about her dream of a romantic

Valentine's wedding for years," I said. "So you didn't hear that the best man was murdered?"

"Whoa! You're not joking?"

Cheri and Isabel overheard me, so I explained what little I could. "Maddie and I sure didn't expect to find his body. Truthfully, after meeting him twice—well, let's just say the guy didn't impress me."

"So you think he deserved it?" Isabel asked, wide-eyed.

"No one deserves to be murdered," I said, "but someone resented him enough to kill him. But let's get started on setting up for tomorrow, or we'll be here all night."

I chose not to tell them that Gus and Cissy's wedding rings had gone missing, and that they were worth thousands of dollars. Greed was equal to revenge as a motive for murder.

The question was—had the killer stolen them after stabbing Dylan?

Chapter 8

Sunday dawned with another gray sky, but no fresh snow. I was grateful everything was ready for today's Chocolate Bear Bar. Last night Cheri had supervised from a chair. While she enjoyed it to the max, I noticed whenever she winced in pain.

On my way back from church, my cell phone rang. I quickly swiped it to take Joelynn's call. "Hey, girl. What's up?"

"Cheri had her little boy five minutes after two this morning," she reported. "Ten pounds, eleven ounces. Talk about a bouncing baby! I had a feeling Cheri had gone into labor, but she never said a word to me. I guess her water broke after Terry drove her home."

"Whoa, that was cutting it close. What did they name him?"

"Lukas."

"Aw, I'm so happy for her. So, are you ready for this afternoon? Kids, chocolate, and all kinds of fun. Let's hope they don't start throwing marshmallows."

"They might. I'll be over in about an hour, okay? I'm

really grateful Isabel French and your sister offered to help. That was sweet of them."

"They both love kids, and so do I. And I'm giving Isabel comp time for assisting at the event, because she could use it to help care for her dad. Her mom's exhausted."

"Yeah. Alzheimer's is a terrible disease," Joelynn said. "See you in a few."

I clicked off my phone and pulled into our parking lot beside the Silver Bear Shop. I'd thought hard about what to wear for the Chocolate Bear Bar and decided casual black was best. ChocoLair was such a darling name for Joelynn's business, and she had ordered a special canvas awning in striped brown and white to decorate the tiny shop's entry door. That helped set it off from the neighboring Mexican carryout restaurant.

I sent a text to Maddie and Isabel as well, and they agreed to wear black. I slid my feet into black ballet flats. No heels for a long while. My toes had yet to recover. I clapped my hands to gain my dogs' attention.

"Okay, sweeties, outside. You ready, Sugar?"

The tiny poodle waited by the door, her tufted tail wagging, so I whistled for Rosie. My older dog had no intention of leaving the window seat, however. Not with Onyx sitting nearby, washing her face, as if disinterested. That cushion was fair game whenever empty.

"Come on, Rosie, get down. I won't let Nyx steal your favorite spot."

I had to drag her off and ignore her grumbling. Both dogs rushed out into the cold, did their business, and then scurried back inside. Onyx had indeed curled up on the cushion, and meowed in protest when I shooed her off. Rosie reclaimed her place. I lifted Sugar Bear up so she could share it with her older sister, knowing she'd soon grow bored. Thankfully, the dogs had formed a bond and curled up together without fighting.

I boosted Onyx to her cat tower perch. "Sorry, kitty, but I promised. Dogs can't get up high like you."

Once I freshened the animals' water dishes and then rewarded all three with a few treats, I grabbed my coat. The biting wind chilled me to the bone during the short walk to the factory. Joelynn arrived a few minutes later, along with Isabel.

"Whoa. Don't trip and fall on that icy patch," I warned them. Especially since Joelynn carried two heavy satchels. "Let me take one of those."

"Thanks. I forgot to bring a few things last night."

"Hey, you're all late," Maddie called out from the factory's big room. "I've already covered the tables and set up chairs."

Joelynn smiled. "Great. I hope the weather holds so people won't skip coming. I also have a surprise for you three." She pulled out long brown aprons with CHOCOLAIR printed on them in white letters. "This way you won't mess up your clothes. Although if you do get some on a shirt or pants, chocolate will come out if you rub some dishwashing liquid on the fabric, and soak it in cold water for thirty minutes. Then you can wash as usual in the machine."

"Good to know." I cheerfully donned an apron. "I'm betting more chocolate will land in our stomachs than on our clothes."

"Ha! That's why I brought extras of everything," Joelynn said. "Dark, milk, plus lots of treats. Plenty to sample during the event."

She directed us to place each attendee's supplies at all six tables. I set out adorable teddy bear and heart molds, vinyl gloves, dipping tools, precut waxed paper squares, and paper towel rolls, along with plastic containers of wipes. Isabel distributed large water bottles for the adults and smaller ones for the kids, plus take-home cartons and boxes. Maddie arranged the packages of Oreo cookies, pretzel rods, and marshmallows in the tables' centers, plus individual bags of popcorn. Last of all, I added plastic shakers of colorful sprinkles.

Joelynn set up metal stands over unlit chafing fuel canisters at three stations on a separate table. She placed an enameled pot on top of each, and then measured chocolate wafers into them. "I'm going to sell any leftover chocolate afterward."

"Do you really think there'll be any left?" I joked. "We'll see."

"We need to make sure people don't crowd around and tip these over," she said. "Not that the chocolate will be that hot, but the pots are metal. Each parent will guide the child to use tongs and dip the cookies, and thread the marshmallows on the wooden skewers for them. The pretzel rods are easier for the kids, since only the bottom half is coated. They can spread the popcorn on waxed paper and drizzle chocolate over it."

"Sounds like such fun for the kids," Isabel said. "I can't wait."

Maddie shook her head. "Just wait till the sugar rush hits them."

By half past one, almost all the attendees were present. Elle walked in at the last minute, right before two o'clock, with her two adorable girls. Cara waved to her friends, quiet and reserved, but Celia squealed in delight and raced over to hug me.

"We're making chocolate teddy bears, Aunt Sasha!"

"Yes, we are." I smoothed her brown hair back from her face. "Our table is over here, but your mom is helping you today. I'm helping Cara."

"But I want you to help me!"

"Celia, Aunt Sasha has to help other people besides your sister," Elle said, "We'll make a great team." When Celia climbed onto a chair, kneeling like several other younger girls, her mother brought over a booster seat. "Sit down, please. If you fall, you'll get hurt."

Joelynn counted heads and then went around to light the fuel canisters. By the time she finished, the last parent and child arrived. "We're all here, that's wonderful! Happy Valentine's Day, and welcome to ChocoLair's first Chocolate Bear Bar. My business partner Cheri Furness had a baby boy this morning. Wasn't that great timing?"

Maddie and I joined in the applause.

"All right, shall we get started?" Joelynn first explained the rules. "No dipping fingers in the warm chocolate. No leaning over the pots, and please let the candy-coated treats cool down on waxed paper before you taste anything. Make sure everyone gets the same number of treats, and you can take home whatever you don't eat here."

I scurried around the first hour, helping parents and kids at my assigned tables, and Cara if she needed guidance with her treats. Maddie and Isabel covered the other four tables. Joelynn walked around the room and offered advice, plus she demonstrated special techniques to avoid messiness. But my attention swiveled to the entrance, noting an unexpected visitor. Burly Detective Mason stood at the door, watching the proceedings. What was he doing here?

"Ms. Silverman? Can I have a word?" Mason held up his notebook.

"Um—if you can wait until we're done, that would be better." I stirred the chocolate in the pot before Cara dipped her marshmallow. "I'm a little busy right now."

"Sorry, but I'm due to meet with Chief Russell at three thirty."

"Why not go ahead and see him, and then come back. I'll still be here cleaning up."

"This won't take a minute," he said, "if you don't mind."

Elle motioned me off. "Cara's done with her treats, so go ahead."

Swallowing my resentment, I followed Mason to a corner of the factory. "What do you need from me that's so important?"

"Let me ask the questions, Sasha."

"Okay, but I hope you interviewed the restaurant staff again. It's possible one of them killed Dylan and stole the wedding rings to pawn them."

"We're keeping an eye out for that," he said. "Have you talked to anyone outside of the Davison family about the murder?"

"Only my aunt and uncle. Oh, I told Joelynn and Isabel that Gus's best man was killed, but didn't say anything more. Why? I've been busy here at the shop and factory."

"I stopped into Fresh Grounds this morning for coffee and a muffin. Seems like everyone knows far more than I expected. Like how Dylan Campbell was murdered, and where, and that Debbie Davison was arrested. Which isn't true, by the way. She's home."

"It's a small village. Word gets around fast," I said. "Nothing can be kept secret for long, especially after the last few murders."

"Things are getting out of hand, though. Does anybody realize how hard it makes my job to catch the perpetrator?" Mason grumbled. "We wanted the murder weapon kept secret, at the very least, but now that's out of the bag. You and Maddie were the only ones who saw the scene of the crime. And I doubt we'll get any fingerprints off that ice pick."

"I have no idea who spread that around." I was grateful that my sister had shut me up before I let it slip to the rest of the wedding party. "I doubt if Cissy or Gus would have said anything, or the Davisons. They don't want any scandal for the family."

"Yeah. I got the third degree from Richard Davison."

His wry tone suggested more than frustration. "Why does he blame you?" I asked. "It has to be someone in the bridal party spreading information. They weren't happy sticking around so late on Friday, or staying in town until they're cleared to leave. Most of them don't live around here, except for Vanessa Leeson's mother. She hosted the bachelorette party last Tuesday night. Oh, wait. Eric Dyer is a local."

Mason consulted his notebook. "Yeah, I got his address. Gus's sister and brother-in-law, Gisele and Bob Vaccaro, live in Chicago."

I nodded. "So do Frank and Claudia Antonini."

Maddie joined us, keeping her voice low. "Sasha, you'd better get back. Elle can't handle Celia and Cara both."

"I'll make this quick," the detective said in a rush. "You mentioned that Claudia Antonini had a black eye. When I saw her that night, I didn't see the evidence."

"She hid it with concealer," my sister said promptly. "She must have slathered it on, like someone who had lots of practice."

I looked at her in surprise. "How could you tell?"

"Remember I helped in high school and college with theater makeup. There's a few tricks to hide bruises." Maddie pointed to her cheekbone. "But we saw her reddened skin and a bit of swelling. I bet she layered on foundation and powder over the concealer. Plus her brighter red lipstick drew attention away from her eyes."

"Okay, then. I'll take your word for it."

"I have a quick question, although it's unrelated." I held up my phone to show Mason the photo I'd taken yesterday. "This customer wanted to order special bears, with a front seam, like the kind Bears of the Heart used to produce before the owner sold his company. I thought he might want them to hide drugs. Does he look familiar?"

Mason eyed the photo. "If you see him again, call the cops. Try not to let him be aware of it, though, if you can help it."

"So he is a criminal?"

"I can't confirm that. Go on back to the chocolate festival."

"Chocolate Bear Bar," I corrected, and then rushed back to Elle's table.

Given the way Celia shrieked and squirmed, Elle looked relieved when I took over the job of washing smears of chocolate from the little girl's face, hair, and hands. My friend packed up extra treats with a sigh.

"She's on overdrive," Elle said. "I'd better take them both home."

"I don't wanna go home! I want more chocolate bears," Celia wailed.

I scooped her into my arms. "We'll make more bears some other day. But you know what today is, right? Valentine's Day, and you love your mom. So be good, because you don't want to miss the next Chocolate Bear Bar. Okay?"

She sagged in my arms. "But why can't we make more now?"

"Because Ms. Joelynn needs to make chocolate to sell at her shop. And I've got to clean up all the tables. If I find any extra chocolate bears, I'll save them for you."

"Okay!" Celia kissed my cheek and slid down to grab her mother's hand. "Come on, Cara, let's go home so Daddy can have the treats we made him."

Isabel broke up the ring of kids, Cara included, who used their plastic-wrapped pretzel rods as pretend swords. When they raced back to rejoin their parents and retrieve cartons and boxes, I sighed with relief once they filed out of the factory.

"You ought to be a teacher, Isabel. I don't have your patience."

She shrugged. "With Dad so sick, I can't go back to school right now. Not when Mom needs me."

"It's something to think about for the future." I noticed that Detective Mason, his cell phone against his ear, hadn't left yet. Or he'd returned after his meeting with Chief Russell. "Seems everything went pretty well, don't you think?"

"I'm so glad." Joelynn brushed her dark curls with the back of one gloved hand. "Whew. The kids enjoyed everything, and ate way more than I expected. Good thing I brought extra chocolate and marshmallows. Those were a big hit."

"Let's hope they visit ChocoLair for more treats in the coming few weeks. That's what you need—steady customers."

"Several moms wanted to order Easter bunnies and eggs. They also asked about teachers' thank-you gifts for early June. That should keep me busy for a while. Without Cheri, I might need to hire someone to help until she's ready to return to work."

Maddie held up a hand. "I know someone who might work out at ChocoLair. Do you know Mia Donovan? She and her mom both work at the Queen Bess Tea Room, but Mia wants a different job than serving tea and scones."

"If she can ring up customers and take phone orders, that would be great. Even Cheri hasn't had official classes in chocolate making, like I did."

"Where did you take classes?" I asked.

"At the Ecole Chocolat, in Vancouver," Joelynn said with a proud smile. "If Mia can help out, that would take the pressure off for the next six or eight weeks. And if our business takes off, I could hire her full time."

Detective Mason sidled over and introduced himself. "So what's this Chocolate Bar about? Like where you order chocolate drinks?"

"I wish." I winked at Joelynn. "Just think, hot chocolate, a little coffee flavor in there, maybe a nip of brandy."

"And whipped cream on top," Isabel added. "Mmm."

"I'll show you the kind of treats we made today." Joelynn opened a box and brought out a chocolate-coated cookie. "Here you go. Take a pretzel, too, and a bag of popcorn. The kids ate all the marshmallows, though. And the chocolate bears."

"The hearts, too, don't forget. They were all so high on sugar, they floated out of here," Maddie said with a laugh. "But they had a blast."

Mason munched on the cookie with interest and then pointed the pretzel rod at Joelynn. "How well do you know Cissy Davison or Gus Antonini?"

"Me? I'm new in Silver Hollow."

He turned to Isabel. "How about you?"

"I know Cissy," she said, clearly reluctant, "but not very well. Kristen Bloom is friends with her, though, but we don't work together anymore. She opened a yoga studio last month. You could ask her, because they've been close since high school."

"Kristen might know Gus, too," I said. "She and her ex-boyfriend, a cop, went out several times with Cissy and Gus."

Mason nodded. "I plan to talk to Phil Hunter." He turned back to Isabel. "What about Debbie Davison? You knew she was engaged at one time?"

"We all heard about Dylan and how badly he treated her. Multiple times." Isabel crossed her arms over her chest. "Most women would have given up, but he's Debbie's favorite subject. She always said she'd get back at Dylan, but I never took her serious."

"I always thought Debbie was all talk and no action." I turned to Mason. "So you didn't find anything suspicious about the hotel staff? Any one of them could have gotten the wedding rings out of that little bag on the dog's collar."

"So could one of the bridal party members." Mason closed his notebook. "The rings haven't turned up yet, but we're working every angle."

"What about the stains on Debbie's dress? Wouldn't the bloodstains have turned dark if she had stabbed Dylan?"

He sighed. "While I appreciate your help, leave investigating to the professionals."

Mason ambled toward the door and zipped his heavy jacket. I studied the factory's high ceiling and counted to ten, wishing he wouldn't remind me so often. Besides, if I didn't get involved, I'd never be able to prove Debbie Davison's innocence.

Joelynn and Isabel laughed, so I turned to face them. "What did I miss?"

"We could ask you the same thing," Isabel said. "Your head's in the clouds."

"What's this about stains on Debbie's dress?" Joelynn asked.

"Debbie claimed it was marinara sauce," Maddie said, "so they have to test the stains to see if she's telling the truth. How odd, though, the way Mason popped in here to complain about gossip in the village. And then warned you about staying out of the investigation."

I waved a hand. "Yeah, I know. I'm not gonna do much."

"Really? I saw that look on your face."

"What are you talking about?"

"That bloodhound look." My sister raised an eyebrow. "After what happened last time, are you going to track down the murderer?"

"No. Only prove that Debbie isn't responsible." They all burst out laughing, which annoyed me. "What? That wasn't my idea, remember. Barbara Davison roped me into it."

"No matter what you say," Maddie said, "you'll do a lot more than that."

Apparently none of them believed me, no matter how hard I protested.

Chapter 9

"So the best man was stabbed to death. Why would someone risk that with so many people around? Good thing I didn't leave my ice pick behind at the hotel." Jay scratched his stubbly jaw. "Where was he killed?"

"In the ladies' restroom—oops." I clapped a hand over my mouth. "If Detective Mason asks, you never heard that from me."

At a loud pop from the fireplace's log, I snuggled closer to him on the sofa. The clock struck half past ten. Jay had driven straight here once the Harrison Frostbite Festival ended. Despite being tired after helping all afternoon at the Chocolate Bear Bar, I was excited to see him. Jay also brought an oblong box with a dozen red roses, their scent heavenly, and dark chocolate truffles. I trimmed the flower stems and arranged the roses in a crystal vase while he built up the fire.

After that he opened his Valentine's Day present. I loved seeing Jay's ecstatic expression as he examined every inch of a special carving tool, from the wood handle to the finely honed blade. We shared truffles in between a make-out session, and then discussed the ice festival before I related the wedding rehearsal events, at the church and at the Regency Hotel.

"So the cops think Debbie is a suspect, along with Gus's cousin," Jay said.

"Yeah, and Mason said they've ruled out the hotel staff," I replied. "So I'm wondering if someone else in the bridal party had a motive to kill Dylan. Vanessa mentioned her niece was injured in a car accident. What if he was somehow involved?"

"I remember Kip O'Sullivan telling me something about an accident," Jay said slowly. "He owned that art gallery in Traverse City, remember, when Gus worked at a restaurant up there. They hung with the same group of friends."

"That must be it." I snapped my fingers. "Kim Goddard's parents have a farm up there, too. And Debbie Davison took beekeeping classes near Traverse City. They all knew each other. Kip, Nick and Dylan, Kim, Debbie, plus Gus and Cissy. So when was this accident?"

"The weekend I drove up north for some party. Kip had to work, so I turned around and went home—I didn't know the others, and wasn't in the mood to stay. But he told me Gus's friends had gone barhopping. That's all I remember about it."

"I wonder if Maddie heard anything, since she dated Kip for a few months." I reached for my phone and dialed her number. "Hey, did I wake you? I thought you'd still be up reading. It can wait till morning—"

Maddie had already hung up, though, and soon descended the stairs wrapped in a fluffy robe and slippers. She yawned wide. "What? I was hoping to hear from Eric, not you."

"So you are dating!" When Maddie nodded, I smiled in satisfaction. "Guess you didn't mind pairing up with him after all for Cissy's wedding."

"I didn't like him at first when he hired me to do some graphics," she said with a shrug, "especially since Eric didn't know what he wanted for his business. It's not easy to come up with ideas for clients without some input. But we found out we have a lot in common." Maddie turned to Jay. "So how was the Frostbite Festival up in Harrison?"

"Good, for the most part."

"He's too humble to say he got an honorable mention for his teapot carving," I said. "But was it worth the time and gas money driving up north?"

Jay laughed. "They named the festival right, because a brutal wind whipped through the park and straight across Budd Lake. People up there must be used to it, I guess. But you missed seeing the outhouse race and golfing on the ice."

"I take it you didn't do the Polar Dip?"

"No way. One of the guys dared me, even swore he'd give me fifty bucks, but I didn't bite." Jay rubbed his hands together. "My fingers are so stiff, I'd like to crawl into the fireplace. But maybe I could warm up a different way."

I shrieked when he slid his cold bare fingers up the back of my sweatshirt. "Gaah!"

"Hey," Maddie said flatly. "I didn't come down to witness you two fool around."

"Sorry." I shivered and wrapped an afghan around us both. "I wanted to know whether Kip O'Sullivan ever told you about a car accident up north. Involving some of Gus's friends, and if Kip knew them that well."

Her eyes widened. "Yeah, he did mention an accident. I'd forgotten all about that. Kip told me that one of Gus's best friends was driving. It could have been Dylan."

"It's definitely something to go on." Yawning wide, I turned to Jay. "I've got to get some sleep, and it's almost twelve. Are you staying the night?"

"Sorry, I've got an early breakfast meeting with a brewery in Ann Arbor. They want a big carving of a wolverine to mount above their sign." He kissed me and stood. "I wonder how much they're willing to pay. That's gonna be a tough job, if they want it full size, baring its teeth, and bigger than real life."

"You love a good challenge," I said, and hugged him. "See you later, then."

Jay headed outside, followed by the dogs. Maddie had already gone back upstairs. I shut and locked the back door once Rosie and Sugar Bear returned from the yard. I couldn't help wondering what happened at that accident up in Traverse City. If Dylan was driving, was he drunk? Why else would Vanessa associate it with Gus's parents' tragic deaths? Maybe a Google search would turn up information.

I dragged myself to the bedroom, following Rosie and Sugar Bear, and yawned. Maybe tomorrow. I crawled under the covers, smiling when my dogs curled up together, warming my feet, but kept waking every few hours. Dang.

My mind spinning, I slid my laptop from its case. I waited with impatience while it booted up, and then searched on Michigan's government website. Then I typed in Dylan Campbell's name, hoping to hit pay dirt. Any criminal conviction would be part of the public record, although a misdemeanor offense might not specify details of any sentence, whether time was served or a fine and community service assessed.

I had trouble accessing court records, which meant I'd probably have to pay a visit to a clerk in person. Unless I could find out using a sneakier way. I closed my laptop and composed a text message on my phone.

Flynn owed me after that nasty comment Friday night. I wasn't a jinx.

On Monday morning I checked my texts for a reply. I knew my ex-husband wouldn't bother looking up the information himself. He'd assign the task to one of the law clerks or office staff at his new firm in Ann Arbor. If Flynn had opened for business, that is.

I also wondered if my ex sought bigger fame to match his fiancée, Cheryl Cummings, a television weather reporter. She was extremely popular in the region. Flynn had ramped up his television commercials, too. Oh well. He wouldn't pop up in the village often. No doubt he'd send over a junior lawyer if Debbie Davison needed further help with the police.

I was in the middle of checking sales receipts when my cell's ringtone announced a call. The "Ex On the Phone" message played, "You labeled this person your ex for a reason." That made me smile. I swiped my phone to answer.

"Hey, Flynn. I figured you'd be too busy and would delegate this to an assistant."

"We're all busy. I don't have much time, Sasha—"

"So what else is new?"

He huffed at my interruption. "I'll do this favor for you once. After today, I'm bowing out of all these Silver Hollow dramas. Cheryl doesn't want me getting involved in any other murder investigations. It's bad publicity."

"But you agreed to represent Debbie Davison."

"Like I said, this once and never again. So Dylan Campbell, Grand Traverse County, three years ago. Misdemeanor, first offense. Possibly an OWI—"

"What's an OWI?"

"Operating while intoxicated."

"Did the cops do a Breathalyzer test?"

"They must have, but my information doesn't show the result. His driver's license was suspended for thirty days, and Campbell paid a thousand-dollar fine. Also performed forty-five days of community service. The passenger who was injured—"

"In his car?"

"The other car, young girl, not wearing a seat belt," Flynn replied. "She didn't show any symptoms right away. If the judge knew how serious her closed head injury was, Campbell would have served up to five years in prison."

"Wow." That surprised me. "So when did she develop symptoms? I don't suppose the report listed her name, and any contact information?"

"Nope. Gotta run."

"Okay, thanks," I said, but he'd already disconnected the call.

The injured girl had to be Vanessa's niece. It all made sense now, the way she was so upset talking about the accident before the rehearsal, and why Dylan showed up to apologize at the bachelorette party. Maybe the family felt guilty about that lack of a seat belt, too. Who could I ask for more information? Vanessa's mother would know, but I couldn't show up out of the blue to ask. I'd have to figure out another way.

Thank goodness Monday morning at the shop was always slow, and no customers interrupted me. I spent a few hours going over the supply spreadsheet. The numbers didn't register, though. My head spun between the information Flynn provided about Dylan's misdemeanor offense and his gruesome murder at the Regency Hotel Friday night.

At last I turned the OPEN sign to CLOSED FOR LUNCH and fetched my dogs. Rosie was stretched out on the window seat, while Sugar Bear played with her ball—letting it roll away, then running to grab it, over and over. Onyx was nowhere in sight.

"Probably up in Maddie's room, taking her daytime nap.

And you, Rosie, are getting too lazy in your old age. You're only six." I hooked the leash's coupler to her collar first, and then to Sugar Bear, who wriggled with excitement. "No, Sugar. Down."

All January, I'd worked hard on training the five-pound toy poodle to walk without any pulling or tugging against the leash. This month I started walking them with a two-way coupler, which worked for the most part. Next to Sugar Bear, Rosie ignored the squirrels. Almost as if she wanted to set a good example, and I certainly didn't mind. The weather was chilly, not quite forty degrees, but springlike for the middle of February, and without any sharp wind.

Despite their sherpa-lined coats, I knew Sugar Bear wouldn't make it all the way to the Village Green and back. Instead we walked down Theodore Lane, past Silver Moon. I waved to Maddie behind the huge picture window glass. She and Zoe Fisher worked together on a layout design, probably for a business flyer. I didn't want to bother them, so I headed toward the Queen Bess Tea Room. Usually the business was open on Monday, but I knew they hosted a special Valentine's Day tea yesterday. A 'CLOSED' shingle hung beneath the sign out front.

"Hallo!" Trina Wentworth waved to me when she let her dogs out the door. They raced to the gate, barking a welcome. Rosie and Sugar Bear wagged their tails and whined a greeting. They loved Prince and Queenie, both black-and-white Cardigan Welsh corgis. "How are you, Sasha? Sold all those Harry Potter wizard bears?"

"Beary Potter. And yes, we did," I called out over the dogs' noisy barks. "Now we're starting a new project. Wedding bears."

"Wonderful. Care for a cuppa? If you can spare a moment, love, bring the lovely little dogs in, too. Precious lambkins," she cooed. "Prince, get back. Queenie, you know better than to jump. Off! Bloody buggers. None of that, now."

Once all the dogs had their fill of butt sniffing, Trina ushered them inside. I followed, glad to see the changes to the former bed-and-breakfast. The Wentworths had brought in some wonderful furnishings from England; a huge black walnut sideboard dominated the front parlor, displaying a variety of teacups and saucers. Pink, green, and gold rose-patterned chintz chairs added brightness, along with gold-framed paintings of English castles and landscapes. The whole place seemed cheerful despite winter's gray skies.

Maddie and I had helped at the first annual Cran-beary Tea Party, which opened Silver Hollow's Oktobear Fest last fall. We had a ball serving scones and tea to parents and children. Trina and Arthur Wentworth had hosted a Christmas tea, also, with a huge turnout. And despite being held the same day as the Chocolate Bear Bar, their adults-only Valentine's Day tea had been well attended. They'd done a great job advertising the fairly new business.

Trina still wore a necklace of red and white hearts over a thick red sweater, plus jeans and sturdy boots. She updated me on her event's success. After she poured out two cups of Lady Grey, Trina pushed a plate of fresh lemon-and-blueberry scones my way. I couldn't resist.

"So what's the story about that juicy murder of the best man? It's all so Agatha Christie," she said. "Done in by the maid of honor, from what I heard."

My heart sank. "Uh, the police are still investigating—"

"Come on, Sasha. It's brilliant. Three murders since we hopped the pond! I told Artie we should've come over sooner." Her blue eyes sparkled, and she tucked a strand of her blond bob behind an ear. "A wedding murder, though. That's a new one."

"Where is your husband?"

"I sent him round to fetch some teacups and saucers, either at the antique shop in the village, or over in Chelsea. Anywhere he can find some. So what happened?"

I fed a bit of scone to Rosie and then scooped up Sugar Bear, who gobbled a piece as well. "I don't think Debbie Davison killed the best man."

"Was he poisoned? Stabbed? Strangled?"

"I really can't say until the police release more information."

Trina bit her lower lip, clearly disappointed. "Ah, well. Seems to me she would've used the knife she had on Friday afternoon."

"What?" I choked on my tea, sputtering until I could speak again. "Wait a minute. You saw Debbie Davison with a knife?"

"Nah, just something I heard around the village." Trina sighed. "All right, ducky. But I'll tell you what else I learned, about a certain house on Theodore Lane."

I gulped. "You mean the Davisons' house."

"Up for sale already, quiet like, without a sign out front. Our good friends, the MacRaes, are set to come over from Edinburgh. They've already put in a bid."

"That's great."

"We're chuffed for them." Trina beamed. "Soon there'll be an English tearoom and a Scottish boutique, only two steps away."

"That would be amazing," I said. "When will they move in?"

"Only one problem. Someone else is in the running to buy the house."

"Oh? Do you know who?"

"Someone from New England. Teddy Hartman."

I choked again, this time on a bite of scone, and coughed with such violence that Trina pounded me on the back. Sugar Bear jumped down, whimpering. Queenie, Prince, and Rosie all crowded my legs, but I didn't have breath to speak. Wheezing, I gulped my cooled tea. I petted all four dogs to let them know I was all right and finally managed to croak out a few words.

"No. Way."

"Sorry?"

"I mean, that's crazy."

"Unfortunately, it's true. If you're feeling better, tell me who this bloke is."

I nodded, sipping more tea, and then explained part of the story. "My dad and Teddy Hartman have been rivals for years. He used to own a company called Bears of the Heart in New England, which made teddy bears as well, before we opened the Silver Bear Shop and Factory here in Michigan. Dad always saw Hartman at all the trade shows. They argued about production quality, choice of fabrics, and advertising."

Trina nodded. "Luckily the tearooms here aren't big rivals. More than enough business to go around, but why would Hartman care if he was over in New England?"

"Hartman chose the cheapest route to make his bears and resented poor reviews. He blamed Dad for posting them. A man who rarely uses a cell phone or email."

"Sounds like Hartman's a nutter. Doesn't make sense why he'd want to buy a house here, so close to your shop." Trina jumped up again and hurried to the door. "Artie's back, maybe he can explain. Hartman popped in one day for a chat while I was out."

Arthur Wentworth walked in, his thick glasses frosting up from the room's warmth. He snatched them off and polished them while the corgis circled his legs. Trina grabbed his hat and then unwrapped his muffler, both wool, while he peeled off his gloves. I marveled at how easy they acted together. Arthur removed his coat, shook it out, and hung it on the coatrack by the door. He stooped to give all the dogs a rub, fluffing their fur, and then straightened.

"Hallo, Sasha. Are you okay?"

"Uh, yeah. I'm fine."

Trina laughed. "That means 'what's new?' not 'are you sick?' or anything. Tell her what that Teddy Hartman fellow said to you, Artie. What is he up to, something dodgy? Wanting to buy the place across the lane."

"Oh. First a cuppa, if you don't mind." He claimed a chair at the table and leaned down to scratch Rosie behind her ears. The corgis stretched near him. Sugar Bear jumped onto his lap, so Arthur warmed his hands around her furry middle and smoothed her curly fur. "Hartman said he'd open a bed-and-breakfast and push selling his teddy bears."

"Oh, brother." I didn't bother to hide my disgust. "I can't tell you how often he's passed out flyers for his Bears of the Heart at local events. We never invaded his territory back in New England, though. He sold his company to another toy factory, so it doesn't make sense why he'd do that here. Especially a bed-and-breakfast. That's a lot of work."

"I'm sure he'd hire all that to be done," Trina said. "I suppose Hartman wants to get back at your dad in some way. And right next to your shop. Both buildings are so alike, too."

"I never thought of that," I said. "He was so jealous after we won the Magic of Christmas contest last year with our limited-edition wizard bear."

Arthur shrugged. "Then it makes sense he'd undermine your company."

"I better ask Dad what he thinks."

Chewing my thumb, I worried that Teddy Hartman was

once more attempting to steal customers from the Silver Bear Shop & Factory. He resented our hard-won success, and the boost we received in sales and national exposure last December. And I didn't want to recall the other nasty tricks he'd pulled in the past. What if the Davisons ignored their years of friendship with my parents and sold their house to him?

In my opinion, that would be unforgivable.

Chapter 10

Tuesday and Wednesday at the shop flew by, given the three staff meetings we held to finalize the design for the wedding bears and begin production. I hadn't seen Maddie, either, since she was swamped with extra work at Silver Moon.

After work, too lazy to warm up any leftovers, I popped a frozen mac-and-cheese dinner in the microwave. Mom wouldn't approve, but I was in no mood to bother with prep or cleanup. And too bummed about Teddy Hartman's devious plans. The idea of him running a bed-and-breakfast, showcasing Bears of the Heart to compete with ours, sent me into a tailspin.

Maddie breezed into the kitchen. "Hey, we brought pizza."

Rosie and Sugar Bear both barked at Eric Dyer, who followed my sister. Even Onyx hissed a warning from her cat-tower perch. After a few treats and several sniffs of his hiking boots, jeans, and hands, my dogs accepted his presence.

"Sorry we've been missing each other—uh-oh. What's wrong, Sasha?"

My sister had a knack for identifying bad moods, and zeroed in on my despondency. But I waved a hand. "It's nothing. At least not yet."

"Oh, come on. Spill."

She set down the pizza boxes on the kitchen table, which drew me like a hummingbird to nectar. Mmm, the scent of ham, pineapple, and extra cheese, my favorite, made my mouth water. I fetched plates, grabbed a fistful of napkins, and some beers from the refrigerator. I popped their caps, set the bottles at three places, and pulled out a tall stool at the island. Maddie dug in to the cheese and pepperoni. Eric opened the third box, the extra-meat and veggie pizza.

"I talked to Trina Wentworth Monday at lunchtime." I took a huge bite of thick, crispy crust and felt sauce dribble down my chin. How embarrassing. Eric had wolfed down an entire triangle before I scrabbled for a napkin. "She had plenty of news."

"So do we." Maddie looked sly when she bit into her pizza. "Hey, what do I smell?"

"Oops." I quickly retrieved the mac-and-cheese tray from the microwave, stirred it, and set it on the table. "I'll have to let it cool before I store it in the fridge."

Eric grinned. "I wonder how that would taste as an extra topping."

"Ugh!"

Ignoring my sister's protest, he slopped some orange goop on his second slice. I had to admit adding it to a meat and veggie pizza looked gross, but hey, cheese is cheese. Eric took a bite and then shrugged.

"Not bad. Macaroni could be a little more al dente. Crunchy instead of soft," he joked, but Maddie groaned. "What? It's all going—"

"To the same place," my sister and I finished for him, and then laughed. "Dad says that all the time," I told Eric. "Okay, enough about food. What news do you have?"

"Oh no, we're not stealing your thunder. You first."

Once I explained about Teddy Hartman, Maddie stomped around the kitchen in a rage. "You are kidding me. You're not kidding? That is evil, pure evil! After what he did to you long ago? How dare he—"

"I'd rather not remember that, Mads. And when I saw him last fall, during the Labor Day parade, he didn't recognize me at all. Or look guilty about what happened, either."

"What a sleazebag. Wait till Mom and Dad hear about him wanting to open a bed-and-breakfast. In the Davisons' house, of all places. They're gonna be livid."

"Barbara hasn't sold to him yet. But if she does, I'm sure Mom will pitch a fit. I hope she never speaks to her again."

"Since the Davisons are moving to Florida, that won't matter," Maddie said.

"Who's Teddy Hartman?" Eric looked puzzled.

My sister enlightened him on our shop's rivalry with Bears of the Heart. I chimed in with some of the tricks Hartman had pulled—taking out ads in the *Silver Hollow Herald*, passing out flyers to showcase his bears, recruiting his staff to make crank calls, and placing online orders that would be canceled right before shipment. Teddy Hartman had also sold a number of cheap black bears to the Bloom Funeral Home for display.

"His version of a 'Magical Christmas' bear had a red robe, white gloves, and a blue hat covered with gold stars," I said. "A Disney lawyer got on that immediately, sending a 'cease and desist' letter, since the costume looked too similar to the Mickey Mouse sorcerer's apprentice. That burned him to no end."

Maddie nodded. "And then he changed the costume to a

red felt cape, without the gloves and hat, and glued a holly branch to the bear's paw."

"And so cheaply made, the holly fell off and the robe frayed. The few customers who bought it demanded refunds." I finished off my pizza slice. "He must have lost so much money, it could be why he sold his company."

"Competition is tough in any field," Eric said.

"Okay, enough of all that. Time to tell Sasha about the bachelor party." Maddie selected another wedge of pepperoni pizza. "Just wait till you hear this."

"Something else than Dylan cheating at poker?" I asked.

Eric tossed the rest of the macaroni-slathered slice in the trash and reached for two fresh pieces. He ate one at a snail's pace while we held our breath, and then laughed when my sister poked him hard in the shoulder.

"Okay, okay. We started with dinner at Flambé. Most of the guys wished we'd gone to Quinn's Pub for a burger and beer when the appetizer came out—prawns with garlic, which is basically a big shrimp. For dinner we had chicken cordon bleu, clams and linguini, and bacon-wrapped pork loin with pesto—"

"That sounds delicious!"

"I'd have rather had pulled pork with extra barbecue sauce. Christophe Benoit strutted around like he cooked everything, and kept asking if every course was up to standards."

"Whose standards?" I asked, but Eric held up a hand.

"The food didn't matter, since Dylan hired a belly dancer as entertainment. That girl had talent. She could bend like a snake—" He glanced at Maddie, his face and neck flushing scarlet in contrast to his pale blond hair, and cleared his throat. "Anyway."

"Yeah, anyway," she encouraged him, suppressing a smile.

"Then Dylan actually invited the belly dancer to the wedding. Gus was sure shocked at that. She was ecstatic to get a related gig, and said she'd charge half price."

"To entertain at the reception?" Maddie laughed. "How ridiculous."

"No kidding. And then when Dylan started the poker game, he let some of us win a hand or two before he started cleaning up." Eric blew out a breath. "I didn't mind so much, but a few really lost big-time."

"Who was playing that night?"

"Everyone, even Bob Vaccaro. But he was smart enough to know he'd lose and stopped. Nick Rizzo was so steamed over Dylan's cheating that he started the fight."

I nodded. "And that's how the restaurant was trashed?"

"Patience, young Padawan. I'm coming to it."

"Well, hurry up. Jay should be here any minute."

"Want me to wait?"

"No!"

We'd both shouted that at Eric, who winced. The doorbell rang at that moment, the dogs started barking like mad, and I almost tripped over Sugar Bear when I rushed to answer. Jay stalked past me, looking furious. Uh-oh. I waited while he shrugged out of his jacket and gloves, shook Eric's hand, and thanked Maddie for the beer she handed to him. I filled a plate with half of my Hawaiian pizza. In return he gave me a quick kiss.

"You gotta do something about Mr. Clooney, Sasha. Frozen poop, remember?"

"But Mom talked to Mrs. Davison—"

"Wait, wait," Maddie cut in. "I asked her about it, but Mom said she's been too busy with the election campaign. I walked out of Silver Moon's back door this morning, carrying a big box to take to the post office, and stepped right in a big pile. I wasn't happy, either."

"You're sure it was from Mr. Clooney?"

"I saw him running off."

I sighed in frustration. "I doubt if Mrs. Davison will listen to me, so that's why I asked Mom. All it takes is a simple phone call. She can't be that swamped."

"Why isn't the mayoral election on the second Tuesday of the month?" Eric asked.

"No idea, but the village council scheduled it for this week," Maddie said. "Mom's been making calls all day long, and visiting the village shop owners."

"Okay, I'll have to visit Mrs. Davison," I said. "Then I can ask whether she's had any showings, and if she plans to sell the house to Teddy Hartman."

"I wouldn't ask," Eric said, "because she might do it to spite you guys."

"Since when is the Davisons' house for sale?" Jay asked.

He reached for a second slice of pizza and listened while Maddie and I took turns to explain the two bids—Hartman's bed-and-breakfast versus the Scottish-themed boutique. Jay perked up at that news.

"Cool. My grandparents were born in Scotland."

"Isn't Kirby an Irish name?" Eric asked.

"Yeah, but my mom's grandparents were born north of Edinburgh. I took part in the Highland Games over in Livonia, at Greenmead. Couple years in a row, doing the caber toss," Jay added. "I've even got a kilt, with a sporran and dagger."

"Do you wear anything underneath that kilt, or go stark naked?" I snickered. "You never mentioned any of this before. Which clan tartan do you have?"

"Gordon, although Sinclair is also in our ancestry at some point. It's complicated, the way they figure out the clan families now." He winked. "Guess you'll find out if I wear shorts or nothing under my kilt later on this summer."

Maddie waved her hands. "Okay, okay. Let's get back to what Eric saw at the bachelor party. You should have told Detective Mason—"

"Only because I forgot until yesterday," Eric cut in. "I didn't think it was that big of a deal. I guess you're right, though, given how expensive those wedding rings were."

"What about the rings?" I asked, curious now.

"Nick started the fight and claimed Dylan was cheating. I was trying to settle them down, except I got a punch or two for my efforts. Bob Vaccaro did, too. Steve Leeson was drunk and not much help at all."

"That's not surprising. So what about the rings?"

Eric grinned. "I'm finally getting to that. You know how Frank acts macho all the time, and he'd thrown a few punches. Suddenly he backed off. That surprised me until I saw him pocket some of Dylan's winnings."

"Okay, but I still don't get it."

"Dylan got back at Frank by arranging to meet Claudia."

Maddie folded her arms. "That didn't work out so great for her."

"Yeah, but mostly because Nick claimed he saw her with Dylan. If he'd kept his mouth shut, Frank might have let it go."

"I doubt that," my sister argued.

"But what does it have to do with the rings?" I asked.

"Gimme a minute. The fight at the bachelor party soured the whole atmosphere. Gus was mad when the belly dancer grabbed money from the poker pot, too. She rushed out before he could shake her down. By the time Dylan counted his winnings, he missed six hundred bucks. He accused Frank, who blew him off. So maybe he stole the wedding rings Friday, too."

"But why? Gus is his cousin—"

The dogs' loud barking drowned me out. Rosie stopped

on command, but I couldn't control Sugar Bear's shrill yapping. I figured my parents had stopped by, although my sister's surprised cry at the side door startled me.

"Aunt Marge! Come in, it's wonderful to see you."

My diminutive aunt entered the kitchen, her beaming smile half-hidden by a thick scarf and fur-trimmed coat. I rushed over to hug her. Outside Uncle Hank lifted two leather suitcases from the car's trunk. The dogs had darted over and circled him, barking like mad. I exchanged my slippers for boots and hurried out to help.

"How much more luggage do you have?" I asked him.

"Girls, hush! I'm so sorry they're making so much noise."

"Doesn't bother me. I'm used to dogs." He kissed my cheek. "Marge has a smaller case in the front seat, plus a few boxes. I hear we're staying with you."

"Yeah, Mom and Dad's condo renovations aren't finished. She feels so bad."

"Not a problem. From what Alex tells me, she ends up here most of the time to cook for you girls." Uncle Hank laughed. "Can't get her out of your hair, is that it?"

I wasn't about to answer that. "I bet you're hungry."

"All we need is a bed. We stopped for dinner a few hours ago."

Uncle Hank strode toward the porch, his cowboy boot heels clacking on the sidewalk. He wore a Stetson on his balding head. He and Aunt Marge had moved out to Tucson after he retired from government service. When I was a child, I suspected he worked as a spy; he was always so secretive, although his job entailed computer systems and security rather than overseas missions. Uncle Hank often had friends send me postcards from London, Paris, Hong Kong, and once from Saint Petersburg, with his name scrawled in different handwritings.

I hadn't caught on to that trick for a while.

Shivering hard, I retrieved the boxes and Aunt Marge's case from the car, locked it, and then trudged back to the house. Maddie crouched to rub caked snow from between Sugar Bear's tiny paws, and Jay finished drying Rosie's thicker coat. The dogs raced off to gain Uncle Hank's attention. While I hung up my aunt's coat and scarf, she claimed the family room recliner and covered her legs with a heavy afghan. Once Uncle Hank sank into the oversize armchair, both dogs jumped into his lap.

"Hello, hello! Friendly dogs, that's for sure."

"Rosie and Sugar Bear," I said. "And this is Jay Kirby, and Eric Dyer."

Eric touched Maddie's shoulder and mumbled something about having to work early tomorrow before he departed. Jay threw another log on the crackling fire and then headed toward the door as well. I trailed after him.

"Sorry," I whispered, although he grinned. "Call me tomorrow."

"Promise me you'll talk to Barbara Davison about Mr. Clooney."

"Okay."

Jay kissed me and then slipped outside. I wasn't surprised he left, since he'd been so busy with the carving festival, plus networking with other artists. Jay and I both believed that family came first, too. After I brewed some herbal tea, I carried the cups to the family room and handed them out. Maddie was curled on the sofa, so I chose a chair opposite my aunt and uncle.

"I told Judith and Alex we'd get in around nine-ish, so we're only a little bit late," Uncle Hank said. "A minor accident on the freeway slowed us down."

"I'm betting Dad's on the way, but I'll call him." Maddie dug out her phone. "If he has his cell phone, and the battery's not dead."

"He doesn't have voice mail set up, either." My uncle shook his head. "Judith's the opposite. Sends me texts, those little emoji things, and photos all the time."

"Since Mom's running for village mayor," I said, "she may be pulling an all-nighter at her campaign headquarters. In her gallery, Vintage Nouveau. She sells local Michigan artists' work as well as gift and vintage items. I'll call and tell her you're here."

"Nah, we'll see her in the morning."

Despite his protest, I speed-dialed Mom, but the call went to voice mail. After I texted her and explained that Uncle Hank and Aunt Marge had arrived, she texted back. "So Mom just said that Dad's on his way, but she may come later tonight. She's still making calls. There's a campaign breakfast at eight tomorrow morning, and she says you're invited."

Aunt Marge held her teacup between her hands, warming them. "We'll see how cold it is that early. I'm not used to Michigan winters anymore. It was seventy-eight degrees when we left Arizona, and now it's thirty-seven! My bones are aching."

"Today felt like spring," I said, "but that is a big change for you." The dogs barked before Dad walked in the door. Rosie raced around my father's ankles, nearly tripping him, along with Sugar Bear. "You goofballs, get over here. Rosie, come."

At least she listened and sat near my feet. Sugar Bear jumped back onto Uncle Hank's lap. Once Dad shed his coat, hat, and gloves, he claimed my chair. Rosie followed when I joined Maddie on the sofa.

"We have news to share," Uncle Hank began, "and I'd rather tell you before Judith hears. It might be a shock to her, like it was for us. But we have to accept things that come . . ."

When his voice trailed off, I glanced at Maddie. She looked as puzzled as I felt. "Bad news?" Dad asked. "I hope not."

"I'm afraid so." Aunt Marge sipped her tea. "Hank wants to protect Judith. She never wanted to hear anything negative. At least that's what we always thought in the past."

"Marge is right," my uncle said. "Judith never could accept bad news. When our parents filed for divorce, she resented them for years afterward. I bet you girls may not know much about that side of your family history."

"Oh, we do." Maddie snorted. "How Grandpa Allen drank too much, and Grandma threw him out of the house and changed all the locks. Years before she finally divorced him. Too bad she didn't take that step right away."

"Things were different back then," Aunt Marge said, her tone light. "Women didn't file for divorce without being able to prove their husband committed adultery. Alcoholism was a given, and not considered a problem. You drank too much, Hank, when we first married."

He rubbed his jaw. "I wised up, though."

Dad shifted in his chair. "Judith married me, thinking my family was more stable, but my parents weren't saints. Everyone has secrets from their past. But tell us what this bad news is you have to share, Marge."

She set down her tea on a coaster, clasped her hands, and met my gaze before glancing at Maddie. "My granddaughter has a brain tumor. Katya's only five. My daughter Angela has had a terrible time dealing with everything, plus two other kids."

"She's divorced, isn't she?" I asked.

Aunt Marge nodded. "Her ex was denied custody, with limited visitation. She can't count on him at all. It's been difficult, to say the least."

I swallowed hard, trying to come up with comforting

words, but failed. A child with brain cancer—what could possibly be said? Aunt Marie had died after a lung tumor spread to the rest of her body. We'd been devastated. My cousin Matt, her only son, spent years in denial and anger. Once he met Elle, she helped him get through the pain. And we all remembered the local University of Michigan coach's grandson who died of an inoperable tumor several years ago. That had been a heartbreaking situation. Hot tears blurred my vision.

Now another five-year-old child was suffering.

Dad cleared his throat. "If there's anything we can do, Hank and Marge, just ask. We're so glad you came to visit. I'm sorry the renovations haven't been completed, though."

"Don't feel bad, Alex." Aunt Marge sighed in contentment, watching the dying fire in the hearth. "I'm looking forward to staying with the girls. I'd also love to tour the teddy bear factory, and meet customers who want to buy your products."

"I have a tour scheduled for Friday afternoon," I said, "with a group of elementary school kids. You used to teach third grade, right?"

"I did, and I'll do my best to keep up with them. If they don't mind a crotchety old lady hanging around."

Maddie and I both laughed. "You're not old or crotchety, Aunt Marge."

"I wish the mayoral election wasn't taking up so much of Judith's time," Dad said, but Uncle Hank waved a hand in dismissal.

"Judith loves being the center of attention. We wanted to visit with you before we meet Angela and Katya at St. Jude's Hospital in Memphis, probably next week. Angela will let us know when they're leaving North Carolina."

"If you or Angela need any money for airfare, gas, meals, motel costs, whatever, we'll support your family," Dad said. "Let's hope and pray the treatment works."

I tried to hide my worry. Maddie nodded, unable to speak, clearly upset by the bad news. We'd only met Angela twice as kids, and didn't have much in common, but family was family. Any parent going through a health scare with a young child was difficult. It was hard enough providing kids with a loving home, nutrition, warm clothing, and a good education. My sister and I had yet to experience all that.

Poor little Katya. Life wasn't fair sometimes.

Chapter 11

Although Maddie's bedroom door was shut, I knocked softly and then entered. Curled up on her bed, my sister cuddled with Onyx. I perched on a chair, sensing her unease, and struggled to find words. We both had trouble dealing with bad news, like Mom.

I knew she'd be hysterical. Uncle Hank, Aunt Marge, Angela, and her kids were all the family Mom had left. Grandpa Allen died when she was eleven, and Grandma Allen only five years later, so we'd never known them. Uncle Hank had been big brother and substitute parents for her until she'd graduated from college, met my dad, and then married. I sensed Mom had never gotten close to Grandma Helen Silverman out of resentment for losing her mother. She refused to accept anyone else encroaching on that sacred ground.

I didn't blame her for that.

Nor did I blame Mom for putting heart and soul into the mayoral campaign. I'd been the one encouraging her to run. Gil Thompson had grumbled to Garrett and Mary Kate that he fully expected to lose the special election. I wasn't so sure, though. People might hesitate to vote for a woman. But if Mom did win, they'd know she could get things accomplished. She proved that after taking over the Christmas parade and tree lighting ceremony in early December. She was a go-getter, and my sister and I found that inspiring.

Now I wondered what we could do to help Aunt Marge's granddaughter. Katya's future looked so bleak. Poor Angela, facing such a crisis without help from her ex-husband. At least her parents were fully behind her. And our family would help, too.

Maddie shook her head in sorrow. "We can't just mope around about this, Sasha. We've got to do something."

"That's exactly what I thought," I said.

"I don't want to set up a GoFundMe page, though."

"Maybe we could host a charity fundraiser at the park. A 5K run and walk, maybe, all around the village. That was popular before Christmas."

"It's too cold, though. And if we wait till spring, people will be signed up for early May's Relay For Life at the park," Maddie added, "so that won't work."

"We gotta think bigger." I paced her bedroom and nearly tripped on the pink shag rug. After kicking off my slippers, I snatched them up and clapped the soles together to help me think. "How about asking people to bring teddy bears and set a world's record for the largest gathering in one place? Like at the school gymnasium. We could charge admission."

"How much?"

"Um—maybe a buck a bear?" Throwing myself into Maddie's rocking chair by the window, I warmed up to the idea. "People who sign up could get businesses around here to match donations up to a certain amount. Like if they bring in ten teddy bears."

"How would we keep track of people's stuffed animals? They'd want them back."

Maddie was the practical one, which amazed me. "You're right." I thought harder. "We could tie tags on them. Or they could seal their bears in plastic bags with their names on them. Then we could have the event outside, in case it's raining or snowing, and provide bags, masking tape, and magic markers in case some people forget."

"We could still ask for monetary donations," Maddie said, "for brain cancer research. That's always a good idea."

"Sure. I wonder what the Guinness World Record is, anyway?"

While Maddie brushed her teeth and changed into flannel pajamas, I did a quick Google search on my phone. The largest bear, over sixty feet, was in Mexico. A woman in South Dakota apparently had the largest collection with eight thousand teddy bears. I also read that one group gathered over five thousand stuffed animals, including teddy bears, in a Massachusetts school gym. We faced a lot of work to beat any of those records.

"I wonder what color represents brain cancer." At the sound of soft scratching, Maddie opened the bedroom door to let Rosie inside. Onyx hissed and fled under the bed. "Purple is for pancreatic, and pink for breast cancer. Whatever the color is, we could design special shirts."

"It's gray. For brain matter, according to the website." I looked up from my phone. "We could tie that into the bears somehow. Koalas are technically marsupials like kangaroos, not bears, but there is a subspecies of the American black bear. The glacier bear is silver blue or gray. We could use that."

"There's only eight types of real bears, right?" She flopped down on her bed. "Remind me again what they are. Cinnamon is one, I know."

"A subspecies," I said. "The eight main types are giant panda, polar, brown bear, Asian black bear, sloth bear, sun bear, spectacled bear, and then American black. Under that are the cinnamon and the glacier. Cinnamon has more of a red brown fur. Glacier bears are only found in Alaska, the southern part of the state."

"Thank you for that science and geography lesson." Maddie pillowed her head on her arms and yawned. "But Katya lives in North Carolina, a long way from Alaska."

"Okay, but you're the one who came up with a T-shirt idea. How about gray shirts with a silver blue bear on them? And maybe Jay could build a fenced corral of wood or plastic, in the shape of a teddy bear. That way everyone could toss all the bears in one spot, after paying their fee to attend the event."

"Do they have to be teddy bears?"

"They should be if we're going for a world record."

"Hmm. It sounds ambitious."

"The largest gathering of teddy bears in the shape of a bear would draw the most people, don't you think? And it's unique enough for the Guinness people to come and check it out, too," I added. "We could produce our smallest-size bears in silver blue and gray. People who don't have a teddy bear can buy one and toss them into the corral."

"Maybe, but then we ought to donate part of the proceeds." She still didn't sound totally convinced. "It would be a royal nightmare getting all the bears back to whoever they belong to, even with tags on them."

"Then they can donate the teddy bears. Like the teddy bear toss at ice rinks, here in Michigan and in Pennsylvania. We'll send them to children's hospitals after the event."

"I like that idea. And I bet Eric would help Jay build the bear corral," Maddie said. "I'm glad they get along. He's trying to make friends in the village."

"Good, and helping us might boost his business. Vintage Nouveau and the Silver Bear Shop could cover the cost of the flyers, and if Eric donates, that would give him exposure."

"Sounds great. People need to learn about his brewery and winery. I designed a new logo of silver claw marks for his wine bottles. Did you know his dad wants him to stick to making IPA beers? Eric prefers wine, though."

"I thought his dad supported him."

"He does, for the most part." Maddie sighed. "Eric's really sweet, but he feels a little unsettled after moving here from Traverse City. He had a lot of friends up there, so I'm trying to introduce him to everyone I know."

"I like him, he's a lot of fun." I'd found paper and jotted a few notes. "I wonder if Isabel French and Abby Pozniak would volunteer to help build the corral. They've worked on houses for Habitat for Humanity. Mom will help in some way, too."

"You mean if she isn't too busy after winning the election."

"Win or lose, I bet she'd get behind it." I turned around when the bedroom door opened. "Speaking of the next mayor of Silver Hollow."

Mom stood in the doorway, her eyes glistening. "That's a bit soon, don't you think? We don't know how the election will go tomorrow."

"I'm confident you'll win." I waved my notepaper. "So, have you already talked to Uncle Hank and Aunt Marge?"

She nodded. "I was shocked to hear about her grand-daughter's diagnosis."

"We're brainstorming a fundraising event."

"That's one way to put a positive spin on the situation." Mom held out her arms for a three-way bear hug. "I'm so grateful for you two."

"It's getting late, you know." Maddie sounded cranky, but we hugged and then pulled apart. "Time for bed."

Dad poked his head into the bedroom. "Hey, Judith. Remember we're distributing flyers tomorrow in the village.

Can you girls bunk in together? That way Mom and I can get some sleep and we can hit the ground running in the morning."

"Sure." I glanced at my sister, who shrugged. "I'll change the linens in my room."

"The girls have come up with a charity fundraiser," Mom said. "Sasha will explain."

I updated Dad on my idea, which he loved, but I put off planning further details. A lot depended on Gus and Cissy's new wedding date. I hadn't heard the latest developments in the investigation, since Mason had warned me to keep out of police business. That meant I'd have to get it from the horse's mouth. I decided to call Cissy Davison, a confirmed night owl. Maybe she'd know something.

After I changed the bed linens for Mom and Dad, I speed-dialed her number. Cissy had ordered the bridesmaids to program it into our phones, to update us on every wedding detail. That came in handy now. I was dying to know if Debbie had been arrested.

"Oh, Sasha! I'm so glad to hear from you," Cissy gushed. "The police have questioned Debbie several times, along with Frank, at home and at the police station. Did you hear Chief Russell at that press conference on the radio? They're still following leads, I guess. Claudia is furious, she wants to go home."

"I'm sure things will work out."

"That's what Gus keeps telling me, but I'm not so sure. As for the wedding, we're going to reschedule it for the end of February."

"Okay, but—"

"Tell Maddie, and then have her call me. I'll need new invitations printed, a rush job. I'll need to mail them to all the guests by this weekend, or they'll never get them."

"Couldn't you just text people, or email them?"

Cissy sniffed, apparently disliking my idea. "No, no. You must have some small white bears we can use for decorations, right? I'd love to hang them on the pews, right beneath those frilly net bows that Zia Noemi made—"

She chattered on so fast, I couldn't get a word in edgewise. Our smallest-size bears only came in assorted colors, but I wasn't about to set off another bridal tantrum by telling her that bad news. I doubted Maddie could produce new invitations in a few days, either. It had taken weeks to do the original invitations with embossed red hearts and swirls. Plus her assistant had addressed the inner and outer envelopes with calligraphy for an extra charge, and added confetti with tiny hearts.

"Cissy," I interrupted, cutting into her long-winded explanation of how she was ditching the Valentine's theme. "If the wedding is still in February, you can keep the heart theme. We're wearing red dresses, remember."

"But I'd rather change everything. Wait a minute, let me ask Gus."

"Okay—ow!"

I held the phone away from my throbbing ear, since Cissy had shrieked his name. I didn't appreciate the front-row seat to their argument over a new wedding theme. I knew, given what had happened already, that the bride was not going to give up her idea without a fight. I hoped Gus talked sense into her, however. The bridesmaids might have trouble finding new dresses, at the very least, to fit properly, as well as shoes. But another problem arose, apparently.

"Every weekend is booked? How can that be?" she screeched to Gus.

Forgetting I was also listening, besides believing that everyone in the world had to adjust their schedules to fit her plans. I decided not to offer an opinion, and wondered how long this would play out.

Cissy's voice rose higher in panic. "No way am I going to

get married on a Monday! What will people think? Don't you 'darling' me, Gustavo Antonini. I will not relax."

"Which Monday?" I asked, my curiosity growing, but she didn't hear me.

"You'll just have to call them back, because that is unacceptable—"

I hung up. Cissy had forgotten I was on the line, and no doubt had plenty more to say to Gus. I yawned, plugged my cell into the charger on my dresser, and laughed when Rosie jumped onto the plush coverlet. My parents would have to sleep with both dogs. Onyx would never stand for them being in Maddie's room. The cat barely tolerated my sister being in the bed. I had a feeling Onyx would not appreciate me tonight, either.

"Great, Sasha. Thanks." Dad carried Sugar Bear in his arms and placed her next to Rosie on the coverlet. "I let them both out already. Your mother's telling Hank and Marge about the fundraiser, but I'm bushed. I think my ear went numb today, calling so many people to ask for their votes. Let's hope she wins tomorrow."

"I know she will," I said, and collected fresh clothes for the morning.

"I saw that article in Dave Fox's *Herald*, about the murder," he said. "From what little I've heard, the police haven't tracked down Dylan Campbell's brother yet. That's a shame. Nothing takes the place of family."

I kissed his cheek. "Don't I know it. I'm grateful every day for mine."

"I've always wondered if people gamble or drink because they miss out on what we've always taken for granted." Dad shook his head. "Winning money or partying can't ever take the place of close friends and family. Am I wrong?"

"No way." I smiled. "Can you hang around until Uncle Hank and Aunt Marge are ready to leave for Tennessee? Since

Maddie and I work all day, that would help. I'd hate to have them sitting around being bored, so you could keep them entertained."

"Good plan. I'm sure your mother wouldn't mind. She feels a bit isolated out at the condo with only Ross and Eve for neighbors. And they're here every day."

I added pajamas and my toothbrush to the clothing pile before I headed to my sister's room. Maddie was already asleep. That didn't surprise me. Her usual bedtime was nine thirty or ten at the latest. The digital clock glowed eleven forty-eight.

Onyx blinked at me from her spot on the pillow, but I shooed her off. Tough luck. I slid under the covers and opened my Kindle. The latest mystery I'd downloaded, a cozy about a young woman helping run her aunt's floral boutique shop in Oregon, held my attention for a bit until I dozed. And dreamed that hundreds of bears rained down on me while I stood in a deep hole, fighting to breathe. Stuffed animals kept bonking me on the head. I fought my way up between the furry piles that mounted higher. One bear slapped me in the face.

That woke me fully. "Nyx. Get off me, you silly cat."

I sat up, hoping my dream wasn't a bad sign about an unsuccessful fundraising event. Maybe Aunt Eve could help, since she had more savvy about planning details. Maddie grumbled in her sleep and turned over, hitting me with her elbow.

I slid closer to the mattress's edge and gave her more room. The house creaked and groaned over the next half hour while I counted backward from two hundred. That didn't put me to sleep, so I started at five hundred and made it all the way to three hundred and two before giving up. Onyx crept in between me and my sister, purring aloud. If only I'd brought my laptop with me to check email and social media.

I didn't want to wake my parents and fetch it from my bedroom. Instead I grabbed my robe and headed downstairs. I tiptoed to the kitchen, where I poured myself a glass of milk. Maybe I'd add a little nip of brandy. But a scratching noise caught my ear.

"Nyxie? Did you follow me?"

Cats usually nosed around at night, although Onyx wasn't a normal feline. She was also fairly old at fourteen and slept a lot. Had the noise come from the hallway? The cat often opened doors. I rattled the knobs of the double doors between our living quarters and the shop. Locked, as they should be. I heard the noise again, but this time outside the window. My heart leaped into my throat. I hadn't brought my cell phone downstairs.

Using my long sleep shirt, I wiped frost from a pane of glass. A shadow fled out of sight. My heart in my throat, I raced back to the kitchen and grabbed the landline phone. Dialed 911. And then quickly hung up. No way was I going to wake the whole house with the police coming to check the yard and neighborhood. I hadn't noticed a flashlight beam, after all. Was it an actual prowler? Perhaps some animal, or Mr. Clooney, had been nosing around the shrubbery. At least I'd scared whatever it was away.

And we did have a working alarm. If anyone tried to force a window or door, the police would be here in minutes. I waited, pacing the kitchen, living room, library, and down the hall, checking the doors to the office and shop once more, and back to the kitchen, until my heart stopped thumping. I took several deep breaths, and then returned to Maddie's bedroom.

Peering out the window, I noted my parents' SUV, my uncle's luxury rental, Maddie's car, and mine, all untouched in the lot. As far as I could tell, anyway. Maybe my imagination was on overdrive after that lucid dream of drowning in toys.

I could still feel the furry fabric rubbing against my hands, face, and arms. Ugh.

"Get a grip," I said to myself, and settled under the covers. "And if you swat me again, Nyxie, I'm gonna bring the dogs in here. Fair warning."

The cat only blinked.

I curled on my side, my thoughts wandering to the Hotel Regency's banquet room. Who was sitting where? I hadn't noticed anyone leaving at any point, and kicked myself for not paying more attention. Wait. Debbie Davison must have left at some point.

Cissy had been looking for her, since she sent Vanessa to track her down. The men had been back and forth from the bar, and in and out of the room to smoke outside. Where had Dylan chosen to sit? With Gus and Cissy? I counted on my fingers, trying to place everyone in the bridal party, but kept getting confused pairing up names with all the tables. I yawned wide. Tomorrow I could draw a seating chart. That might help.

Maybe Dylan had never gotten a chance to sit anywhere before his untimely death.

Chapter 12

After a late start Thursday morning, I checked on Renee Truman. She'd recovered fully, although she still had a minor cough, but assured me she could handle customers and any orders. I headed outside. Today was the mayoral election, and I had to show up at Vintage Nouveau. Dad and Uncle Hank had gone to the Sunshine Café before Mom left for the gallery. Aunt Marge decided to skip breakfast, so I was on my own.

Somehow I found a parking spot in Ham Heaven's lot and walked to Main Street. The village clock pointed to half past ten, so I'd have to settle for leftovers. Unless the campaign staff had eaten everything, but there had to be plenty of coffee. If that was depleted, I could always fall back on Fresh Grounds. I squinted into the sunshine toward the coffee shop and bakery, noting the long line snaking out the door. Dang.

"Hey, Sasha!"

I spotted Debbie Davison with her mother, waving to me near the hair salon. Barbara wore her Burberry coat, plaid scarf, and fur-lined gloves. Her daughter was bundled up in a puffy down jacket, jeans, and heavy boots, with a black-and-gold knit hat. I'd worn a lighter coat, given the warmer temperature predicted today. Fifty-five, although now I shivered in the stiff breeze. Maybe I'd been too optimistic.

A petite blond woman stood waiting across the street, in front of Vintage Nouveau, and listening to music via earbuds. She kept checking her cell phone, too. Was she a campaign worker? I tamped down my curiosity. This might be my only chance to ask Barbara Davison about Mr. Clooney. Jay's frustration had reached its peak. Maddie's, too. I joined Debbie and Barbara with a hesitant smile.

"Morning. Did you realize Cissy's dog is wandering all over the neighborhood, jumping fences? His droppings leave such a mess."

Barbara flushed in embarrassment. "That crazy dog! I'll have to get a special harness, since he keeps slipping out of every collar I've tried so far when I walk him."

"He scares my little toy poodle, too," I said ruefully.

"Oh, my, I'm so sorry. I'd better see Judith before the crowd gets too big."

Barbara rushed across the street and through the gallery's doors. Debbie eyed me with concern. "Mom's upset about having to take care of Mr. Clooney for Cissy. He's such a pain. So how is it coming along? Proving I'm innocent, I mean," she added. "The police analyzed the stains on my dress and said some of it is blood. I forgot to tell them I cut my finger."

I wondered if that was true. How could she have forgotten something that important? "So they'll have to test to see if it's yours or Dylan's, then. By a DNA sample."

"Yeah, but the lab's taking forever."

"Maybe they're swamped."

"You don't think I killed Dylan, do you?"

"Uh, no. But you should have told them about cutting your finger."

I felt awkward chiding her, even though I wasn't totally confident of her innocence. Debbie seemed relieved, however. "Everyone thinks I'm guilty. One of my friends gave me such a dirty look the other day, and wouldn't talk to me! She's known me my whole life, so how can she think I'd kill someone?"

"Let's hope the lab results will prove it's only your blood." I couldn't help feeling sorry for her, since Uncle Ross had once been a prime suspect. "Try to be patient."

Debbie quickly changed the subject to Cissy and Gus's wedding plans. "So a Monday wedding, that's weird. I guess the reception hall didn't have any other option, and Mom won't get a refund on the deposit if they don't accept that date. At least this time Frank will be the best man, like he should have been from the beginning. I dunno why Gus chose Dylan in the first place. He treated all women like dirt. Not just me."

"So you found that out before or after breaking up with him?"

"Before, because I found out Dylan cheated with a few married women." Debbie stepped closer to me. "Did you know that Nick saw him with Claudia, the day of the rehearsal?"

"Yeah, I did."

"Bet you don't know where, though. Nick said he saw them making out, around two o'clock. Guess she had a little afternoon delight instead of retail therapy."

"Why did Nick tell Frank, knowing he gets so jealous?"

"Who cares," Debbie said. "Maybe he was a little jealous of Dylan. Nick's a terrific salesman, but he never gets the same attention from women. He pestered me about going to a club with him, after the rehearsal dinner, but I refused."

"I thought Nick was married."

"His wife threatened divorce, but she hasn't filed yet. Besides, what does that matter? Guys love to get some on the side, Sasha, if they can get away with it. Everyone knows that."

Although I'd learned the hard way that Flynn cheated, I didn't believe every guy had that attitude. I changed the subject. "What do you know about an accident up north, that Dylan was involved in? He was driving drunk."

"I don't know if he passed a Breathalyzer test," Debbie said, "although Dylan admitted he'd had a few beers. Vanessa's sister lives up north, and she was driving the other car. Her kid wasn't wearing a seat belt. She acted okay at first, but ended up with terrible seizures. Hasn't gotten any better, either. The weather that night was bad, heavy rain with fog."

"Is that why Dylan claimed he was innocent at the bachelorette party?"

"I guess so. The guys were out celebrating that night. Dylan, Gus, Nick, and a few other friends. They barhopped, but Gus had just been hired at the Capitol City Grille in Lansing. He had to report early for work, so he left the group—"

I lost the thread of conversation, watching the blonde across the street who held a cell phone up to her face. Had she taken a photo? The sun emerged from a cloud and almost blinded me, however. I shifted my focus back to Debbie, who continued talking about the accident.

"—her niece. Vanessa begged Nick to tell the cops that Dylan was drunk and at fault. Nick felt so bad, like he was betraying a friend."

I held up a hand to stop her. "Wait. Why is that woman taking photos of us?"

"What woman?"

Debbie turned around, but the strange blonde had already

pocketed her cell. She tossed her thick tweed scarf over one shoulder and hurried down Main Street. Hmm.

"Do you know that woman?" Debbie looked puzzled, so I pointed. "Walking toward the courthouse, see? I'm pretty sure she was watching us."

"Why would she?"

I didn't answer, because I recognized the man who emerged from Mary's Flower Shop. The same guy who'd asked about ordering sitting teddy bears, and he carried a rectangular box with vases of red roses. Several bears accompanied them. The guy set the box into the open rear hatch of a black SUV on the street corner, parked illegally. Once he'd cut the plastic ties that held the bears in place, using a small penknife, he dumped the flowers and vases in the trash.

Then he drove off. With half a dozen teddy bears.

But not before I'd snapped several photos with my phone. Given Mason's warning about him, I hoped the police could verify the guy and maybe track him down. I hoped Mary Monroe had gotten his name and credit card for six arrangements post-Valentine's Day.

"—didn't serve time in jail, but Dylan's license was suspended." Debbie waved a hand before my face. "Hey. Are you paying attention, Sasha?"

"Oh, sorry. Give me a minute, will you? I'll be right back."

I dashed down the street, but another car blocked my line of sight. Unfortunately, the guy turned the corner. I hoped his license plate number was visible in the photos I'd taken. I walked back to Debbie, who looked a bit miffed. At least she verified what Flynn had told me.

"You said Dylan never served time in jail?" I asked.

"Nope, he paid a big fine and only got community service." Debbie rubbed her mittened hands together. "Vanessa is still mad about that."

"How old was her niece at the time of the accident?"

"Ten or eleven, I think. Poor kid seemed dazed at first. Then she started getting seizures, and couldn't remember things at school. She got worse despite physical therapy and meds."

"Did she ever improve?"

"Nope. She can barely function. Her family takes care of her full-time."

Wow. No wonder Vanessa was so upset. "I better get back to my mom's gallery," I said. "The special election is today, and I haven't voted yet."

"I'm so grateful for your help." Debbie looked worried, however. "Remember, I sat with Cissy and Gus the whole time on Friday night."

"Except when Vanessa brought you back from the restroom."

"But Dylan wasn't in there! I avoided him because he was being such a jerk."

"Except when you threatened him," I reminded her again. "You also said that someone needed to stop him at the bachelorette party."

She quailed at that. "I didn't mean he should be killed! I was mad, yeah. Dylan called me all kinds of nasty names under his breath, whenever he passed by. Like gold digger, and witch, and said that I was crazy. But he was crazier than anyone I know. You've got to believe me, Sasha. The cops are still calling me, asking questions over and over again."

I took her hands and squeezed them hard. "I'll do what I can, but don't talk to anyone about the murder. There's enough gossip going around."

With that, I walked across the street to the Vintage Nouveau gallery. It used to be Cissy Davison's Time Turner boutique before her cousin turned it into the Magpie's Nest selling vintage items. My mother bought it, lock, stock, and barrel, when Maggie Davison left Silver Hollow; Mom kept the best items and donated the rest to charity. An adjacent shop, The Birdcage, sold varieties of birdseed, feeders, and squirrel baffles, plus specialty feed, cages, toys, and more supplies for pet birds.

In the gallery window, Mom had artfully arranged vintage items set among paintings, sculptures, and several of Jay's carvings. One included a set of tiny polished teak animals surrounding a Noah's ark, priced at $200. My favorite was a sweet rabbit holding a basket of flowers. And the seated lion with an elaborate curly mane, fashioned from a stairway's newel post, had a SOLD sign on the tag.

Thrilled, I called Jay in case he hadn't heard the news. "Yeah, your mom told me yesterday." His voice was tinged with pride. "She got five thousand bucks for it."

"Whoa! How much of a commission will she take?" I asked.

"She deserves forty percent, which is what we agreed on in the contract. I'm happy someone wants it. Kind of unique, and I figured nobody would buy it. I did that piece on a commission three years ago, and the client gave me the wood."

"From their house, I take it."

"Yeah, he was building a new one. But then he backed out because the builder had so many problems with subcontractors. The builder never installed it, and then the client ended up taking a job out of state. Never paid me the balance, so I'm glad someone wants it."

"Hey, have you voted yet?"

"Nope. How about we meet at the courthouse, two o'clock?" Jay suggested.

"Sounds great." I heard laughter and applause inside Vintage Nouveau. What was going on? "I gotta run, so I'll see you then."

I slipped the phone into my purse and reached for the

gallery door's curved brass handle. Vintage Nouveau had fresh-painted gray walls, metal and glass shelving units with a variety of art, plus paintings grouped in eclectic ways instead of media similarity. Muted watercolors mingled with pen and ink, oil, and vibrant acrylic paintings. Mom kept florals apart, however, from modern splashes or geometric and color-block designs. Landscapes hung beyond them, in an alcove formed by a jutting brick wall.

Loud applause emanated from the long, narrow back room. I waved to my mother's part-time assistant at the desk near the front window. Ryan Martinez studied an open textbook before him, no doubt art history or anthropology. He was dying to go on a dig overseas, but his parents hoped he earned an MBA and would one day take over their Mexican restaurant. Ryan covered any phone inquiries and handled paperwork for the gallery sales.

"Hey, Sasha. I managed to grab coffee and a bagel before the crowd arrived." With a grin, he set his book aside. "Everyone's in a great mood."

"I hope Mom wins, or she'll be so disappointed," I said in a low voice.

"Nah. Mrs. S told me she'll roll with the punches."

I knew my mother better, however. Judith Silverman was too much like my ex-husband, Flynn Hanson. They both craved the three *A*'s: attention, adulation, and admiration— the latter from a mirror, if not from other people. Flynn was far more extreme as a narcissist, though.

"Great." I'd pushed aside the beaded curtain that hid the back room, something Maggie Davison had left behind. "No more food."

The long table held half a dozen empty plates with bagel and muffin crumbs. I held a cup under the coffee urns and pumped, but realized they'd been drained as well. I should have stopped by Fresh Grounds after all. When she saw me,

Mom's face brightened. I didn't dare sneak out again and remained at the back of the crowd jamming the hot, narrow
room. At least the door and window to the alley were open
for fresh air.

"—thank everyone for coming today, and for your votes,"
my mother was saying. "I've ordered more coffee and bagels
from the Sunshine Café. I didn't feel right ordering from my
opponent, Gil Thompson, at Fresh Grounds across the street."

Many people snickered at that. Mom raised her voice
when some of the older retirees signaled they couldn't hear.
Her auburn hair glinted in the bright lights overhead. She
wore a gold sweater and earrings, plus black pants and boots.
Her infinity scarf had swirls of silver and gold, adding to her
snazzy appearance. Bracelets jangling, she waved to Uncle
Hank.

"I want to introduce my older brother, Henry Allen. He's
supported me over the years, and always gives great advice
whenever I call. Take a bow, Hank."

When he tipped his Stetson, the crowd applauded. Dad
whispered something in her ear and then stepped back, beaming. Mom held up her hands once more for silence.

"Alex said the poll numbers look great, although how he
learned that is a mystery. No shenanigans, Mr. Silverman! We
don't want anyone to question the election results."

"So when are you gonna announce your win, Judith?"
someone called out, to more chuckles from the crowd. Mom
shook her head.

"Not until voting is over tonight and we've received official word. Or Gil Thompson concedes, but the residents will
decide the next mayor of Silver Hollow."

"And village council president! Gil's been sitting on his
hands long enough, so it's time to get things done," one man
shouted. Everyone applauded again.

Dad beamed at that. "May the best woman win!"

The crowd cheered. My parents joined Uncle Hank and Barbara Davison on one side of the room, near the muslin sheets covering stacks of boxes. A white pod sat in the alley outside, so I figured Mom had stored all the extra merchandise there. Resourceful.

Rusty Monroe, the owner of the local cinema, sidled up to me. "Your mom will win, hands down. Judith will get the council to vote on stuff they've been putting off, like tearing down the empty building next to mine. I've been waiting years to pave that for a parking lot. Theodore Lane should be opened to traffic at Main Street, too."

"That would be so helpful," I said, "for the tearoom and our shop."

"I hope she gets the county to blacktop the gravel road, too," he said. "Cal Bloom always promised to convince the road commission, but failed in the long run."

Rusty turned to another business owner and continued discussing village improvements, so I slipped through the doorway. I doubted if Mom and Dad noticed my departure. I also wanted a chance to ask Mary Monroe, Rusty's sister, about the customer who bought the white bears.

My curiosity was in overdrive.

Chapter 13

Despite my yearning for coffee and something to eat, I crossed the street and headed to Mary's Flower Shop beyond the Luxe Salon. A brass ironwork archway flanked the florist's entrance. Large buckets and baskets of fresh, mixed bouquets in the bay window made a lovely display, and more filled the interior aisles. I walked in to tinkling bells, and waved to Norma Drake at the back. Mary Monroe stood near the cash register.

"Sasha, what brings you in? I told Maddie the flowers wouldn't be ready to pick up until later." At my confusion, she added, "The congrats bouquet for your mom."

"Oh! Mads didn't mention anything to me," I said lamely, "but what a great idea. I'm here to order a small basket for my aunt."

Flowers might cheer up Aunt Marge about her granddaughter, and cover the real reason for my visit. Mary Monroe resembled her brother Rusty, with thinning blond hair, gray eyes, and fair skin; they could be twins, with the same thin frames and mannerisms. But Mary's smile was infectious, and she had a green thumb to envy. She loved making unique arrangements, and her floral teddy bears designed for new mothers were in high demand.

"I have a quick question," I said and surveyed the shop for our teddy bears.

"How about if you choose the flowers first." Mary led me to the back counter and opened her receipt book. "Is this a special occasion, or just a cheery pick-me-up?"

"Yes, a cheerful bouquet. I like that," I said, pointing to a white basket filled with African violets. "But with fresh cut flowers that won't last too long. My aunt won't be able to take it with her when she travels again."

"I bet she could, packed in a box, if they're still blooming. How about gerbera daisies? They're lovely with baby's breath."

"Add in some purple flowers, too."

"There's a finished arrangement back here," Norma called out. She opened one side of the double-door floral cooling unit and brought over a woven basket with huge, bright yellow daisies, white carnations, and tiny purple flowers. "I made this today, so it's fresh."

"It's perfect." I rummaged through my Dooney & Bourke satchel for my wallet. "Can you deliver it for me? I've got a few errands yet, and I'd like her to be surprised."

"Sure, no problem." Mary handed me back my change. "Three o'clock is our next run."

"That's fine. Who was that guy, your last customer? The one who bought half a dozen white teddy bear bouquets."

"Yeah, that cost him almost three hundred dollars," Norma said, her eyes wide.

Mary straightened the till's drawer. "You should have heard him complain about your shop. How unhelpful you were, and how he wasn't able to buy the bears he wanted. I wouldn't sell them without the flower arrangements, though."

"So he asked for the bears by themselves," I said slowly.

"Yeah, but I wasn't about to take them apart. Plus he wanted a discount," she added with a laugh. "Said he'd take them off my hands, since the holiday was over. I usually give a ten percent discount to regular customers, but I'd never seen him before."

"We figured he'd leave," Norma said, smiling, "and then complain about how unhelpful we were. Instead he pulled out this fat wad of cash. I was so surprised."

Mary shrugged. "Then he rushed out of here like his tail was on fire."

"So you didn't get his name or address? Phone number?"

"He wouldn't give one, since it was a cash sale."

I nodded. "Let me tell you what he did after leaving your shop. He cut the bears free and then dumped the flowers and vases in the trash."

Norma and Mary exchanged shocked glances. "You're kidding."

"Come and see the proof."

We trooped outside to the street corner. Mary shivered, since the sun had dipped behind a bank of gray clouds that looked menacing. Norma let out a cry and plucked an intact vase from the metal trash can. I peered inside and noticed the jumble of ribbons, broken glass, and red roses among the discarded cups and other items in the bottom.

"The guy's a lunatic," Mary said. "Totally crazy."

"Detective Mason wouldn't explain, but this guy may be up to some kind of criminal activity," I said. "Notify the cops if you see him again."

"Will do. And congrats to your mom. I'm sure she'll be the next mayor."

"I voted for her," Norma added, and then dashed back to the shop.

Mary followed, shivering hard, and waved before the door closed behind her. I eyed the gray clouds and felt misty drops on my cheek. Rain, for now. It would turn to snow once the temperature dropped below freezing after sunset. Winter in Michigan was no fun.

In the courthouse lobby, I warmed up near a heat register. Jay wouldn't arrive for another half hour, so I called my sister. I wondered if Cissy asked Maddie about the new invitations, but her phone went to voice mail. I didn't leave a message. Instead I sat on a bench and played a few games on my cell until the clock struck the quarter hour. Then I headed back outside. The cold hit me hard, and I wished I'd worn a thicker coat.

Jay waved from across the street and rushed to meet me. "Is there a line?"

"Nope. Maybe most people have already voted."

We returned inside and headed down the hallway to the clerk's office, showed our IDs, and received our ballots for the special election. A few people arrived after us, so we handed in our folded papers and walked to the exit.

"How about taking in a three o'clock matinee?" Jay suggested. "I could use a break after last weekend's ice festival. And the brewery owners who want the wolverine postponed this morning's meeting."

"That's too bad," I said, "but sure. Let's go."

Hand in hand, we strolled down Main Street past Vintage Nouveau and The Birdcage, stopped at Ham Heaven for a sandwich, and then passed by Quinn's Pub with its scrumptious scent of burgers. Across the street, the Silver Maple Theater's brick building, dating from the early 1900s, looked its age. The interior's mustiness and threadbare carpet was another sign of decay. Rusty Monroe filled a huge bucket of popcorn for us.

"And one cherry slushy, coming up."

I glanced back outside through the wide windows onto the street. "Was there a car parked in front of here last Friday? With slashed tires."

"Yup. I saw that car."

"Don't suppose you happened to see someone near the car, by any chance?"

Rusty leaned over the glass counter with a huge grin. "You mean, did I see little Debbie Davison sneaking away from that car? Sure did. With a knife in her hand."

I almost dropped my slushy. "A knife?"

"Yep." Rusty hooked a thumb toward the door. "I went out for a smoke, and saw her take off like she'd just done it. Digger Sykes told me the owner never reported the vandalism, though, since the dude was killed at the hotel. Bummer for him. Cops hauled his car away yesterday. I've got a surveillance camera, so they can check out the tapes anytime."

Jay and I headed inside the theater. I remembered that Dylan asked Nick for a ride Friday night. Had he seen Debbie slashing his tires? Or figured she had, since she'd threatened revenge. And then doctored that drink with ipecac syrup as payback. Only Kim Goddard intercepted it.

I bumped into Jay. "Oops. Just daydreaming a little."

"No problem. Where do you wanna sit?"

Rusty had hired a crew to tear out the old theater's wide stage, pipe organ, and the tiered box seats that lined each side of the second floor. They'd built a wall down the center to house two movie screens, although each separate viewing area had only eight original plush seats in each of a dozen rows. The cushions sagged when we sat down, and the velvet looked crushed and ragged. Many villagers drove to Ann Arbor to attend the chain cinemas instead.

Except for diehard locals, like us.

Jay glanced at a group of older teens who filled the back row. They jostled each other, threw popcorn, and laughed uproariously. Ignoring them, I explained to Jay what we needed for the charity fundraiser. He readily agreed to make the teddy bear–shaped corral.

"I'll ask my brother if he'll donate wood."

I kissed him soundly. "Thanks! I wish I could think up a name for the event. I'm drawing a total blank."

"What was the name of your childhood teddy bear?" he asked me.

"I had a Care Bear, besides Grandpa T. R.'s bear—wait!" I snapped my fingers. "Cure Bears, I wonder if anyone ever thought of that. Or Bears for the Cure."

"Either one would work."

The previews ended, so we quieted down. Jay and I crunched popcorn, shared sips from the slushy, and relaxed. The movie had a good twist, and I didn't regret taking time away from my normal routine. Plus I didn't think once about Dylan Campbell's murder.

Afterward, we waited for the kids to leave first. I tossed the empty bucket and slushy cup in the trash on the way out of the theater. A cold wind drove tiny snowflakes into my eyes. Dusk had fallen, and I wished again for a warmer coat or extra sweater. Despite my reluctance, Jay led the way toward Fresh Grounds. The coffee shop usually closed at six, and Garrett Thompson was busy wiping tables and collecting garbage. He grinned at me.

"I hope you didn't come to gloat. Uncle Gil already conceded to your mom."

"He did?" I couldn't help feeling pleased.

"He never wanted the temporary mayoral job in the first

place," Garrett said, "but was roped into it after Mayor Bloom was killed. Nobody else would take it on."

"Yeah, I understand all about that. I got roped into proving that Debbie Davison is innocent of murdering her ex-fiancé."

"So I've heard."

"Well, she is a friend. I don't think Debbie did it," I added, sinking into a chair, "so I'm willing to try. Someone else must have had a good reason to kill the guy."

"But you told me she threatened him," Jay said. "Sounds like a good motive."

"I know, I know. Don't remind me."

Garrett smiled at my obvious frustration. "Either of you want coffee or tea?"

"Nah, we're good. How's Mary Kate?" I asked. "When's her actual due date?"

"The doc said right around tax time. She's got a few months to go, but bed rest is driving her crazy." He locked the door, since it was a few minutes before six, pulled a chair around, and sat on it backward. Garrett rested his forearms on the top edge. "So I heard Gus and Cissy's wedding was rescheduled?"

"They're lucky they could do it at all," Jay said. "Every hall in the area is booked solid from now till October. Gus didn't want to wait that long, so he talked Cissy and her parents into Monday, March first. The reception is at an exclusive golf club near Ann Arbor."

"Richard Davison is a member. He took Dad golfing there a few times," I said.

Garrett nodded. "My uncle knows the owner, too. He said the Davisons didn't want to lose their deposit, almost twenty grand."

"Cissy may have another beef with Gus." I waved my phone. "Got a text from her, and she's upset because he wants to skip the ceremony at church. Gus figures both the wedding and reception can take place at the golf club. Most of the guests will be coming straight from work. He has a point, really."

Jay nodded. "Especially given traffic around Ann Arbor. A nightmare at rush hour."

"There may not be a wedding," I said, "given all these exclamation points in Cissy's text. She is steamed. And Gus might get burned."

"Speak of the devil," Garrett said, and pointed to the window.

I turned to see the prospective groom peering through the glass. Gus Antonini walked to the door and rapped hard. Garrett had already risen from his seat and ambled over, not in any hurry, and waved toward the door's sign.

"We're closed. Sorry!"

Gus gestured wildly, mouthing something, so Garrett let him in and relocked the door. Melting snowflakes slid down Gus's leather jacket. He pulled out a chair to join me at the table and ran a hand through his dark, damp hair, slicking it down.

"I've looked high and low for you, Sasha, all over the village. Your mom had no idea where you'd gone. The staff at the Silver Bear Shop said you took the day off."

I nodded. "Is your cousin Frank still a suspect in Dylan's murder?"

Gus frowned. "They took him to the station for questioning, let him go on Sunday, and then brought him back down to the station Tuesday. Then they let him go this morning, since they couldn't charge him without evidence. Detective Mason told him not to leave Silver Hollow, though. That's why I hired a team of private investigators—"

"You hired a PI team?" I sputtered.

"I know, it's too expensive," he said, waving a hand, "but

I'm not taking any chances. Go ahead and prove Debbie is innocent, but I need a professional to clear Frank. Dylan flirted with his wife, after all. Claudia refuses to tell me why she met him Friday afternoon, too. And Frank won't talk to me, either. That's why I figured a PI might get better results."

"Why would Frank tell them anything?" Jay asked.

Gus shrugged. "They could follow him around, see what he does. Ask who Frank's been talking to since he came here. And maybe pressure Claudia to explain why she's caused so much trouble. She didn't have to meet Dylan, after all."

"I know Nick claimed he saw them, but how do you know he's telling the truth?"

Gus stared at me, as if I'd told him the moon was green. "Why would he lie?"

"I don't know, but it sounds like you blame Claudia instead of Frank," I said in disgust. "They're both at fault, in my opinion."

"Hey. I need to clear this whole thing up soon, so me and Cissy can get on with the wedding." Gus rested one bent leg on his knee. "The PI's said they're gonna do background checks on the entire bridal party."

Jay grinned. "Including the dog?"

Gus didn't seem to appreciate his joke. "I don't trust the cops to figure things out. Look how Sasha helped them solve the murders here last year. They're so lame."

I didn't appreciate his implication, that a mere woman could beat the police at their own game. Jay scowled as well, but I knew saying anything was futile. Given his attitude, Gus would ignore any criticism. But I was glad he'd hired professionals. Maybe they could work on the case with Mason. That woman I'd seen on the street, with her cell phone and earbuds, must be on the PI team. I had no doubt now that she'd listened to our conversation.

Her partner might be doing the same with Frank Antonini. I'd love to corner Claudia, in fact. She was bound to spill a few secrets about Dylan Campbell. Maybe Frank had bragged to his wife about killing Dylan.

"So where are your cousin and his family staying?" I asked Gus.

"Zia Noemi insisted they stay with her until the wedding. She's got a huge house, a pole barn, lots of dogs and cats. That should keep little Martina busy."

"So it's not a problem for his job, then, if Frank stays on? What does he do that he can take more time away from work?"

"He consults for a private security firm, mostly online," Gus said. "If they need him, he's one click away. Or so Frank told me."

"A security firm," Jay mused. "Bet they were impressed by his military experience."

"Oh, big-time. Frank was an expert sharpshooter during his service." His voice was tinged with pride. "The most accurate of his team, in fact. His knife skills were excellent, too, so his CO recommended him for special training. But all his missions were top secret."

"Knife skills," Jay said, glancing at me, "which means he knows exactly where to stab someone for a clean kill. Quiet, too."

Gus glared at him. "You don't know that for sure."

"I'm only speculating. You're the one who said Frank's an expert."

"He's a security expert."

"With excellent knife skills." Jay spread his hands. "I'd say Frank has the best motive so far, given how Dylan messed around with Claudia."

"And he's bad-tempered, given the black eye he gave his wife," I added.

"Nick should have kept his mouth shut," Gus said. "Pics or it didn't happen, but now everyone believes the story."

Gus rose and walked toward the door. "In case you didn't know, Nick served in the National Guard. Maybe he's skilled in handling a weapon. Eric Dyer, too. He was in basic training with Frank."

"Only they weren't Special Ops," I said, "or sent on top secret missions."

"Listen, Sasha. What really matters is getting this wedding off the ground." Gus leaned against the door's jamb. "Cissy's not answering my phone calls or replying to my texts. I love that woman, but she can be a real pain in the—"

"I don't blame her," I interrupted. "Why a Monday, instead of Thursday? Or Sunday."

He sighed. "Yeah, well, the golf club was the real problem. I said skip the reception, but she had a fit about that. Did Cissy order new invitations?"

"I don't know for sure."

"Great. Maybe you can talk to her, get her to call me. Or text. Whatever. She'll listen to you, Sasha, because she's not being reasonable with me." He opened the door with a whoosh. "Thanks. I owe you."

Garrett relocked the coffee shop after him. I let out a deep sigh, unhappy with all this pressure from Cissy's family and now Gus. How did I get myself into these situations? If only someone else besides Maddie had stumbled on Dylan's body in that restroom.

"Now I'm supposed to act as a marriage counselor as well as prove Debbie's innocence. Which will be almost impossible, since Rusty Monroe saw her slash Dylan's tires," I said. "With a knife, no less."

"Wow," Garrett said. "And Dylan was killed with a knife?"

"No." I hesitated. "An ice pick. Anyone could have gone up to that cupid ice sculpture on the bar and taken it without being noticed. The bartender was busy filling drink orders."

"But still risky," Jay said. "Someone could have seen him, or her."

"Hmm." Garrett perched on a chair and tipped it back. "Any guy going into a ladies' restroom would have been noticed, don't you think? So maybe a woman killed Dylan. Where was the wound? In the back?"

"In the neck," I said, giving up on trying to keep details secret. "But Debbie is so short, she probably couldn't have reached that high. Vanessa is tall. Dylan kept telling her he was innocent in the accident that hurt her niece. That could be a motive for revenge."

"Maybe," Jay said. "But Frank, Nick, and Eric all had military training, while Debbie or Vanessa would have to rely on luck. With a knife, you can slash a throat and let them bleed out, but an ice pick? It's not the same. And if Dylan knew what the killer intended to do, he'd have fought back and not let them get close enough."

Garrett nodded. "That's why I think it had to be a guy. Frank could have done it, quick and dirty. Dylan never saw it coming, if his back was turned."

"And all of the guys lost a bundle of money at poker," I said, pondering that. "But why would Dylan have gone into the ladies' room in the first place, unless a woman lured him there. So maybe Debbie, Vanessa, or Kim were involved."

"Maybe, but it sounds crazy," Garrett said. "And no one's talking, I bet."

"Nope." Jay held up a finger. "But you didn't hear any of this from Sasha."

"I'm not like my uncle. I won't even tell Mary Kate."

"She doesn't need to worry about murder." I changed the subject. "Did you hear anything about the Davisons selling their house, Garrett?"

"Only that they've gotten multiple offers. I guess your dad's rival, Teddy Hartman, hopes to buy it. Uncle Gil told me about a knock-down fight at some toy show. Was it New Jersey, or somewhere else?"

I breathed deep, wishing I could avoid answering that. Dad and I never told Mom how that fight began years ago, and how close Dad had been to being charged with assault. He and Hartman agreed to avoid scandal and put that issue to rest, given the fallout.

"New Jersey," I finally said. "Hartman resented Dad for opening a business in Michigan. It didn't make sense to me, because Bears of the Heart was far enough away in New England to keep competition at bay. At least that's what Uncle Ross always said."

Jay folded his arms over his chest. "Competition is tough in the toy market, or any market for specialty items. I bet even the big coffee chains cut into Fresh Grounds' business."

Garrett nodded. "We get enough locals to keep us going, though. Everyone loves to hear my uncle's stories, even if he gets the information wrong. Today Uncle Gil told someone that Dylan Campbell was found with his head in the toilet."

"Wow, that is so wrong!" I couldn't help laughing. "I can't believe some of the gossip people pass around."

"Your Uncle Ross is just as bad. He said one of Cissy's bridesmaids looked like a lady wrestler, her eyes all puffy and bruised. Is that true?"

"He must mean Kim Goddard. She had a bad reaction to Botox injections from Tuesday night's bachelorette party."

"Kim Goddard?" Jay cocked his head to one side. "Blond? Tall, a bit pudgy."

"Hey, I could be called pudgy," I protested.

"Nah, you're curvy. She's almost six feet of solidness. Like a barrel."

Garrett doubled over, laughing. "Man, you better stop now before Sasha rolls you like a barrel out the door. How do you know one of Cissy Davison's bridesmaids?"

Jay eyed me with an apologetic air. "Okay, okay, she's not pudgy. Or a barrel. Just built like a—never mind. Anyway, my brother Paul dated Kim Goddard for a few years. He even met her parents, who own a small orchard up in Traverse City."

"Kim mentioned that," I said. "She had a small bag of dried cherries on Friday night, and said they're good for healing bruises."

"Paul said she's really into hunting. Guns of all kinds, actually. Not just rifles."

"Did he break up with her?" Garrett asked.

"She dumped him. My brother's not the most inventive guy," Jay admitted. "She set up everything they did together, and I guess Kim got tired of him being so passive. She's licensed to carry a concealed handgun. Paul said Kim shot a blank at him one night."

Shocked, I gulped hard. "Why?"

"He forgot their one-year anniversary. No candy, or flowers, or a card."

"That's some overreaction."

"Firing blanks can be dangerous," Garrett said. "An actor killed himself playing around with a gun loaded with blanks."

"I heard about that." Jay rubbed his stubbly jaw. "A television star, young guy? I don't remember his name, but heard he was joking about the production delays. Held the gun to his head, pow. The explosion's force drove a piece of his skull into his brain."

"Wow. So Kim could have killed your brother, firing a blank at him like that," I said.

"Paul sure didn't mess with her after that. He was relieved when she dumped him. Saved him from having to break up with her."

I still had Frank Antonini on the top of my list. He knew how to kill. And he had the best reason to exact revenge on

Dylan—cheating with his wife. Nick Rizzo being jealous of Dylan's ability to hit on women seemed a weak motive. Vanessa Leeson blamed Dylan for her niece's injuries, plus she'd left the banquet room with a migraine. A perfect excuse to lure Dylan into the restroom, murder him, and then flee to her hotel room.

Then again, Kim Goddard might have been angry about Dylan's ipecac syrup prank. But was she angry enough to stab him? Kim was smart enough not to use her handgun. That would have pointed suspicion right at her, and using the ice pick may have been a sudden inspiration. She could have swiped it and hidden the weapon in a skirt fold. I doubted if Dylan would have suspected her of anything more than harmless flirting in the restroom.

Reluctantly, I added her name to my suspect list.

Chapter 14

On the following Saturday morning, Maddie pointed her spoon at me. "Debbie is still a suspect, I think," she said, "given what you told me about Rusty Monroe seeing her with a knife. And she actually slit Dylan's tires."

"Yeah, it sounds so juvenile. We should ask Digger Sykes if he's had a chance to watch any surveillance camera video."

"Remember that Debbie threatened Dylan, too."

"I'm supposed to prove her innocence, not her guilt." I wished again that I'd turned down that request. "She doesn't come across as a killer to me."

"We've said that before about people we've known. Last December—"

"Okay, okay. You don't have to remind me that I've been fooled before."

Maddie nodded. "Let's not think about it. We've got to finalize the plans for Katya's fundraiser, for one thing. I wanted to ask Mom her opinion, but I bet she won't be up for a while. She's been working nonstop since her election win."

"I'm glad Aunt Marge went to breakfast this morning with Uncle Hank and Dad," I said. "You should have seen her yesterday during the tour with the third-grade kids at the factory. She asked more questions than the students did."

"Mm, hmm." Maddie's mouth was full, and she swiped her phone to check Facebook.

I cut up a banana into my steaming oatmeal. Aunt Marge had loved watching our staff finish several bears. Uncle Hank had also joined the tour yesterday, and was impressed by how Uncle Ross handled production, oversaw packing and shipping orders, plus either repaired or called in experts for any machinery problems.

After work, we headed home where Mom had cooked her famous lasagna to celebrate her election win. Maddie and I made an antipasto salad and garlic bread, while Dad had picked up a scrumptious cassata cake from the Pretty in Pink bakery.

Now I yawned wide and sipped more coffee. "Maybe I ate too much last night."

"Or you're too worried. You kept kicking me."

"Did not."

"Did, too. I was glad when you rolled out of bed," Maddie said. "What were you doing on the computer?"

"Checking the social media profiles of Cissy and Gus, going back several months. Plus a few more in the bridal party."

I explained about trawling through photos of the "trio of blondes"—Cissy, Kim, and Vanessa—drinking in every bar around Ann Arbor and Ypsilanti. Too bad Vanessa hadn't posted anything recent about her niece, though. I did find a link to a GoFundMe page, along with a few photos of a therapy session.

After adding brown sugar plus a handful of blueberries, I

waited for my cereal to cool before eating. "Let me ask you this. Why would Debbie vandalize Dylan's car that Friday night? She could have gotten caught and arrested, and ruined Cissy's wedding plans."

"True, but she must not have thought of it. And then Dylan's murder overshadowed that." Maddie held up her cell phone. "Did I show you the photo that Cissy wanted me to put on the new invitations? It shows them on a bench with Mr. Clooney sitting between them."

I studied the photo. "Cute enough, but not as fancy as the first invitation. I texted Cissy about his fleas, by the way. She had a fit, of course, and rushed Mr. Clooney to the vet."

"I bet she expected them to get rid of the fleas for her."

"Not a chance," I said. "She got flea shampoo and powder for the carpet."

Maddie laughed. "Wanna bet Cissy stuck Debbie or her mom with giving the dog a bath and vacuuming the house?"

"Maybe Barbara will hire someone to do it." I watched Sugar Bear do a little circular dance on her hind legs for a treat, and then rewarded her. "Rosie, sit. Shake."

When my older dog yawned, Maddie and I both laughed. After a bit more encouragement, Rosie sat and held out a paw. When Sugar Bear tried to steal the treat, I scolded her. The smaller dog slunk away and picked up her ball for comfort.

"Good girl, Rosie. It's okay, Sugar, you're both sweet girls." I tossed another treat for the younger dog, who gobbled it. Her ball rolled toward me, so I threw it across the room. Sugar Bear happily chased it, but didn't bring it back. I turned to my sister. "I take it you got Cissy's new wedding invites done on time, then. I know she wanted to mail them out."

"I'm dropping them off today," Maddie said. "She could

have texted or called everyone instead, and saved a lot of money."

"No kidding. Didn't Cissy want the envelopes addressed with calligraphy again?"

"Zoe's hand cramped up so bad the last time, she refused."

"I don't blame her." I set aside my empty oatmeal bowl and crunched a piece of butter-and-honey-drizzled toast. "Guess what I found out about Kim Goddard. She has a permit for a concealed weapon, and dated Jay's brother. She's on my suspect list now, but I also found out something new about Gus."

Maddie raised an eyebrow. "He knows where Jimmy Hoffa's body is buried?"

"Very funny. Remember how Vanessa told us his parents died in a car accident. That led me to research newspaper accounts and death notices, although I had to dig back a ways. Gus's Uncle Lorenzo, Zia Noemi's husband, was driving the car." I noted her shock and nodded. "He had multiple drunk driving incidents on his record. That was before the laws changed and Michigan cracked down on DUIs. I bet Zia Noemi feels guilty about what happened."

"That could be why she treats him like a son."

I pulled up Facebook on my phone and scrolled to the Antonini family photo I'd seen in my search. "A few years ago one of Gus's cousins posted about the accident, and that Uncle Lorenzo died a few days later from his injuries in the car crash."

"Wow," Maddie said with admiration. "You're turning into a real sleuth."

"Ha. So what do you think about Kim Goddard as a suspect?"

"Dylan wasn't killed by a gunshot," she said, "but you're right that Kim wouldn't use her own weapon. She lives with the guy who owns the shooting range she works at, doing all the paperwork and giving lessons. It's located in Stockbridge."

"Talk about turning into a sleuth!"

My sister shrugged. "I found all that out from Abby Pozniak, whose older sister Alyssa graduated with Kim. Superior Defense is the name of the shooting range, and Kim's worked there at least five years. She also doesn't like kids."

"How do you know that?" I demanded.

"Didn't you see her deal with Martina Antonini at the rehearsal? Remember the brat kept untying our shoe bows."

My curiosity rose. "Okay, but what did Kim do?"

"She crouched down and whispered something. Martina ran off to her mom, wailing."

"I feel sorry for that kid. You can tell she doesn't get much positive attention from her parents, so no wonder she acts out."

Maddie swallowed her last bite of toast. "Martina's spoiled rotten. An only child who wants everything that Cissy has—a fancy dress, flower bouquet, you name it. Frank finally told her if she didn't behave, they'd get a girl dog to walk down the aisle with Mr. Clooney."

"That must have worked like a charm," I said with a grin.

"It did. Remember you told me Gus hired a PI team? I saw a man and woman at Fresh Grounds, sharing photos on their cell phones. They sat in the corner, and I overheard something about Debbie Davison. They left in a hurry when I sat down at the next table."

"Blond woman, petite? She wore a thick scarf. Tweed, I think."

"Yep. That sounds like her."

"Wish I knew if they found anything out about Frank Antonini," I said. "Anyway, I'm not so sure Kim Goddard would have killed Dylan just because he spiked that drink."

Maddie nodded. "Yeah, that does sound lame. What about

Gus's sister Gisele? She flirted with Dylan. Maybe her husband was jealous, like Frank."

"Bob Vaccaro? He comes across as a pushover, and oblivious to Gisele."

"I guess. Hey, maybe what we need to do is get all the bridesmaids together again, like at the bachelorette party." Maddie's eyes brightened. "What if we host a paint party, with plenty of wine? That would draw them like flies to honey. They'll spill their guts about Dylan. Maybe we'll learn more of what happened during his engagement to Debbie Davison, too. I bet she'll brag about slashing his tires."

"First I'd better ask Cissy if the wedding's still on. Remember she wasn't happy about his plans. And he wants me to smooth things over, since she isn't talking to him. Isn't that crazy? Like Cissy has ever listened to me."

I grabbed a notepad from the kitchen counter and started composing a text message to the bride and bridesmaids. Once Cissy replied, with a gushing text about loving the idea, Maddie checked her work schedule, texted Zoe about a project deadline, and then turned to me.

"Next Wednesday is good, less than a week from the wedding itself. I'll ask Eric if we could host it at his brewery. He has IPA beer, wine, even hard cider. The Silver Claw has a tasting room, and we could cover the tables with plastic to avoid paint spills."

"Sounds great, if he has that date open," I said. "Frank Antonini can't leave town because he's still one of the prime suspects. He and Claudia are staying with Zia Noemi. She's a sweet lady, but from what Gisele said, she drives people batty."

"That means Claudia would love getting a break from her company."

"You know Zia Noemi will invite herself along," I said.

"I bet Barbara Davison will want to come as well, and maybe Vanessa's mom."

"Whatever." Maddie wiggled her phone. "Eric says Wednesday is good for him. I'm glad we don't have to use my studio, because Jay started work on that wolverine carving. It's huge and taking up all the extra space we have."

"Okay, next Wednesday it is. But what time? Seven or eight o'clock?"

Maddie grabbed her coat, hat, and purse. "Make it six thirty, and that means we'll get started around seven. I'll order the canvas and paints, plus come up with a few designs. Better find out if everyone can make it that Wednesday. Eric said Thursday is open, but not Friday. He has a Harry Potter trivia party scheduled that night with a ginger beer tasting."

"That sounds like fun." I glanced at the clock. "Okay, now you're running late."

A few minutes after Maddie left for work, my mother strolled into the kitchen. Her auburn hair looked brushed, but she still wore a thick velour robe and slippers. Mom yawned and poured herself a cup of coffee, then topped it with cream.

"That little basket of flowers really surprised your Aunt Marge. That was very sweet of you girls to send." She kissed my cheek. "And I love the bouquet you two sent me."

"How does it feel being mayor? Busier than you expected?"

I checked the water level in the crystal vase filled with pink roses, purple and white ball-shaped hydrangeas, daisies, baby's breath, greenery, and a variety of snapdragons. Maddie had nailed Mom's taste in flowers. The bouquet looked gorgeous as a table centerpiece.

"Not more than I expected. You were right, Sasha. I do love being mayor, even if I'll have way more on my plate to deal with this year."

I smiled. Mom and I had often been at odds before my

parents returned from "retirement" in Florida. We'd had a rocky relationship since childhood, actually, but forged a truce of late. I was thrilled at her victory, since I'd suggested she run against Gil Thompson. Now Mom could focus her energy on serving the village; she'd been bored while Dad puttered around Silver Hollow, meeting friends for breakfast or golf, visiting the gym, and consulting on the factory's production— whenever Uncle Ross asked his opinion, of course.

Since my parents were staying here to help entertain Uncle Hank and Aunt Marge, my sister and I didn't feel guilty. As much as we wanted to spend more time with my aunt and uncle, we both had obligations at work.

"Before I head to the shop, what's the latest news about opening Theodore Lane?"

"That's first on the agenda for our next council meeting." Mom looked pleased. "We'll also discuss Rusty Monroe's request to pave the lot beside his movie theater. The Davisons have never been able to rent that building next door. They found a contractor to renovate it, but it's too far gone. It's going to be demolished."

"Wow, and you've only been mayor a few days," I said. "Have you heard whether the Davisons sold their house yet?"

"Don't get me started on that." She breathed deep. "If they do sell to Teddy Hartman, Barbara will be dead to me. That man has tried hard to undermine the Silver Bear Shop, for years." Mom perched on a tall chair at the kitchen island. "Hartman printed up a brochure, with illustrations, so they could visualize his bed-and-breakfast plans."

"Illustrations? You've got to be kidding."

"Each bedroom showcases one of his Bears of the Heart, in a holiday theme. Like the Valentine's Love Shack Bear, the St. Paddy Whack Bear, the Spring-Fling Bear, the Spook-Nik Bear, and the Christmas Cash Bear. With order forms in every room."

I choked on my coffee and coughed hard. "That will definitely cut into our business."

"Your father wants to talk to a lawyer, but I told him to hold off. I'm hoping the Davisons won't sell to him, and that Barbara takes our friendship over the years into consideration." Mom crossed her fingers. "Teddy Hartman is notoriously cheap, too. He may bargain with her about the price. If he does, she may accept the other offer."

"I hope so." I related what I'd learned about Trina and Arthur Wentworth's friends from Scotland. "I'm sure they have plans to live above the ground floor boutique, like we do here. This street is zoned a mix of residential and commercial, right?"

"Yes. The Walshes rent that little cottage across the lane, but Barbara may sell that property as well. I should ask her. I'm dropping in on the county road commission's meeting next week to ask about paving the road out to Richardson's Farm. That's a long overdue project. I hope the commission will approve it for spring."

"What about fencing the Village Green? I never heard what the council decided."

"They're still 'on the fence' about it. Gil Thompson accepted a motion to adjourn at the last meeting before that came up for discussion," Mom said. "I'll try to bring it up under old business, but our agenda is already five pages long. We'll see what happens."

"Everyone loves the open feeling around the courthouse. It's ridiculous that a few people complained about pet owners who don't clean up after their dogs."

"Aren't you supposed to be working?" Mom laughed when I glanced at the clock and gasped. "Fifteen minutes late, and on a busy Saturday."

"Whoa." I rushed my bowl over to the sink, filled it with

water, and headed toward the double doors leading to the shop. "What are your plans with Aunt Marge today?"

"Afternoon tea, and shopping. I need a relaxing break after this week."

I rushed down the hall, although Aunt Eve stopped me near her desk in the office. "Hey, Sasha, hang on. Your mother and I think the charity fundraiser is a wonderful idea."

"Great! Can we talk about it tomorrow, because I'm late. Oh, and can you ask Mom to let the dogs outside again for me? Thanks."

"But I have a question. Actually two—"

"I'd better check to make sure no customers are waiting."

When Aunt Eve's phone trilled, she waved me off. "I'll come after I take this call."

I raced off to unlock the shop's front door and found an impatient customer on the porch. Although I greeted him, he walked past without a word. I changed the sign from CLOSED to OPEN. The man had a curled mustache streaked with gray, a red felt cap, and leather gloves. He pulled them off while glancing around the shop at all the shelves of teddy bears.

"Sorry for the wait," I said. "Can I help you with anything?"

"Yes, I hear you have quality toys. Not made in China, correct?"

"We produce them in the factory behind our shop, and they are finished by hand."

He took the silver bear I handed him and ran his fingers over the fur and seams. "Very nice. What kind of Poly-fil do you use? I'd like to take some filling out." The man looked closer at the side stitching. "My grandchildren like to squeeze softer stuffed animals."

"That might damage them, though. And the faux fur we use for our bears is the softest on the market in the US." I pointed to the framed magazine cover near the register that highlighted our prize-winning Beary Potter wizard bear. "We fulfilled all the special orders for the Magic of Christmas bears last month."

"Yes, I saw the article and tracked down this shop. Do you have pink teddy bears?" he asked, smiling. "My granddaughters prefer that color."

"Only the smallest size, in that bin with other color bears."

He looked disappointed at that. "Perhaps I could special order a large ten- or twelve-inch bear, in a sitting position, in pink." The man reached into his overcoat, a mix of wool and cashmere in a herringbone pattern, and brought out a roll of hundred-dollar bills. "How much will it be? I'll even pay extra for a rush order."

Alarm bells rang in my head. "A sitting position? Our pattern that we use is like this silver bear, which can sit propped against a shelf or—"

"How much would it cost to design one like this?" He took out a folded magazine photo, which I recognized as Benny Bear from Bears of the Heart. The toy was permanently sitting, with a front seam as well. "I'll pay extra if you can design a pattern."

I swallowed, glad to hear Aunt Eve's high heels clicking on the hallway's wood floor. The man glanced at the door in alarm when she entered the shop; he backed away, clearly wary. He pocketed his money when she smiled.

"Okay, Sasha, I'm here with my questions about the fundraiser. I didn't mean to interrupt anything, though. Shall I come back later?"

"No, no, I'll return another time."

Aunt Eve raised her eyebrows when he rushed out the door. "Another guy with a roll of cash? That must have been six or seven hundred bucks!"

"He wanted pink bears. Sitting bears, like that other creepy guy." I explained how I'd seen him at the florist and about the bouquets he'd trashed. "This is getting crazy. Two men who offered to pay extra for a special design, to make a sitting bear like the one from Bears of the Heart. And he asked about taking some Poly-fil stuffing out, too."

"I don't get it. Why come here?"

"Let me check something." I was already searching Google on my phone for any Bears of the Heart toys still available for sale. "Benny Bear is no longer being produced. Hmm. I wonder what's going on, and why these guys want that specific type. Maybe they want to put something else in the bears, like illegal drugs. He checked the seams and stitching."

My aunt smoothed her billowy red plaid skirt. "Apparently I scared him off, but do I look that bad for an old broad? Don't answer that."

"Stop it." I hugged her and then patted her cardigan sweater with a smile. "You always look so fashionable."

"Nice of you to say," she said. "Looks like he forgot his gloves, though."

I stopped Aunt Eve from touching them. "Good, because maybe Detective Mason can get a fingerprint off the leather, and see if he has a criminal record."

It was definitely worth a try.

Chapter 15

Aunt Eve nodded. "I hope so. But I still don't get why people would use a child's toy for hiding drugs."

"You don't think like a criminal, that's why." I composed and sent a text to Detective Mason. "So, what questions did you have for me?"

"Oh, that's right." Aunt Eve took a notepad out of her skirt pocket. "Judith thought the Village Green might be the best place to hold the event—"

"The only problem is parking."

"Let me finish. She thought of that and then suggested the high school football stadium. Judith said she needs to call the office and find out when track and field is going to start. That might be the only fly in the ointment."

I sighed. "We could always ask the Quick Mix factory if we could use their parking lot. But then we'd run into the same problem with where people would put their cars. Not at the elementary school, because they barely can fit buses in that lot with all the cars."

"That's because so many parents drive their kids to school

now," Aunt Eve said. "In my day, we walked—rain, snow, sleet, you name it. Now they won't let kids out for recess if the temperature dips down to freezing."

I suppressed a smile. Uncle Ross always told us stories of walking to school five miles, and uphill both ways. "The windchill factor plays a role in that, I suppose."

"Windchill, hmph. We survived that and plenty worse. No seat belts in cars, no bicycle helmets, no cell phones or computers. And we drank from the hose in summer. Young people have it so easy now." She consulted her notebook. "Anyway, I found a vendor for silver blue faux fur, except it looks more gray than blue. How much should we order?"

"Did you ask Uncle Ross what he thinks?"

"I've already told him what I think, so that settles it. He's been so grumpy the last few weeks. Although I wasn't much better about how we survived growing up, was I?"

We both laughed. "You're nowhere near as bad as him," I said.

"I thought taking a weekend honeymoon would be enough of a break, but Ross is back to his old bearish self. Maybe he's tired of working so long and hard."

Alarmed, I voiced my fears. "He isn't thinking of retiring?"

"No, not at all. But maybe we need a longer vacation this year." Aunt Eve checked her notepad again. "I love this job, so Ross will remain supervisor as long as I'm here."

"Whew. You had me worried." I perched on the tall chair behind the counter. "I don't think we could keep production running smoothly without him. If you do take a vacation, Flora Zimmerman will have to sub for him again."

"Don't tell your uncle that, or he'll never leave. That woman bugs him to death about every little thing, and being in charge makes Flora feel like she owns the place. Not a good thing, according to the staff. At least that's what they told Ross at the last meeting." Aunt Eve waved a hand. "Flora didn't attend for some reason, or the others would never have admitted that. I think you'd have a mutiny on your hands if she supervises again."

"No one else has as much seniority, though, or knowledge of how things are run."

"Doesn't matter. Flora Zimmerman is very pushy."

"Yeah, that's true." I propped my elbows on the counter. "Guess I'll have to take over for Uncle Ross if you two decide on a real vacation. How about a cruise?"

Aunt Eve waved her pen and pad. "Too late for spring or summer, and Ross won't spend the money on another trip. I've never heard him complain as much, though."

"Let's make an executive decision right now. We'll produce a hundred small bears using the silver blue fur, as a special run, and sell them for eight dollars. And for every sale we make, three dollars can go straight to the charity fund. We can always make more bears if they sell out. Or do you think we should produce two hundred?"

"Yes, at least! Kids love those small bears."

"Maddie can start promoting the event once we nail down the name and date. I came up with Cure Bears, sort of a take on Care Bears. Or we could always go with Bears for the Cure, if you like that better," I added.

Aunt Eve tapped a finger against her chin. "I prefer Bears for the Cure. Care Bears is trademarked, and Cure Bears is too similar to that name. Remember you told me that Teddy Hartman had trouble when he nearly copied that Mickey Mouse costume for his magical bear. We don't want to end up with a trademark infringement."

"Okay. I'll call Maddie."

My aunt scurried off, high heels clacking. "I hope Bears for the Cure isn't too long of a name for your promotion plans," I said when my sister answered the phone.

"I love it, and no—it's perfect." Maddie sounded excited. "I'll start planning designs, so let me know when the date and time are set."

After helping several customers, I closed the shop for lunch and headed to the kitchen. Rosie slumbered on the window seat, while Sugar Bear played with her ball. Mom walked in while I fetched their leashes. Her eyes matched the sky blue sweater she wore over blue jeans and low-heeled boots, and she'd added a silver necklace and matching earrings. Her auburn hair was gathered into a messy bun, which looked chic.

"Eve called me," Mom said. "I love Bears for the Cure as the event's name! The best place to host is the high school football field. They have a huge parking lot, so it's ideal. Which weekend did you have in mind?"

"Not until March, don't you think?"

"I was hoping you'd say that. The school superintendent told me the baseball and track teams start practicing outside in early April, depending on the weather. We'll have to chance rain or snow on whatever Saturday in March that we choose."

I checked my phone calendar. "Snow would fit with the glacier bears. How about the twelfth? Unless you think people will be celebrating St. Patrick's Day early."

"Hmm." Mom gazed at the ceiling. "Make it the first Saturday, March fifth, so we'll have time to fly Angela and Katya here to participate in the event. You can start collecting teddy bear donations right away and sealing them in plastic. I'll call the Quick Mix factory. I bet they'd let us borrow a semitrailer to store them all, and get some free publicity that way."

Her excitement spurred my own eagerness. "That sounds great," I said. "Once we know we've got enough donations to beat the Guinness World Record, we can gather volunteers to toss the teddies into the bear corral at the football stadium. I bet Dave Fox will be glad to photograph the event, too.

Someone around here must have a drone to get some aerial views. I'll ask around, see who's tech savvy. Will you act as master of ceremonies?"

"Of course!" Mom looked ecstatic. "The mayor is supposed to act as the community's spokesman. Calvin Bloom was a whiz at it."

"You'll be good at that, too."

"Thanks, honey. A mayor has to be diplomatic, in every situation, or so Cal always told me." She cocked her head to one side. "Now that I think of it, he told me a lot about how the mayor should act in all situations. Cal said he learned everything 'on the job' during his terms. How to handle people during conflicts, getting the council members to compromise, that kind of thing. No wonder he was successful for so many years."

"Maybe he was mentoring you without realizing it."

"I doubt that. Cal would have stayed on as mayor for life," Mom said, her eyes twinkling. "Or at least until his wife put him in the Silver Birches nursing home. I heard the gossip about her dating Eric Dyer's dad so soon, but Alison seems happier now. I'm sure she would have divorced Cal, if he hadn't been killed."

I changed the subject. "So will you write up a speech for the event?"

"Of course. People need to know how more research and funds are needed. Brain cancer is one of the leading causes of death in children besides accidental injuries," she added. "Marge and Hank told me how much a cancer diagnosis affects families. Not just parents. It's so heartbreaking, really, to see the emotional toll it takes."

"I'm sure Aunt Marge and Uncle Hank will participate in the event, too," I said. "Oh, and Jay told me that every football field's dimensions are the same. One hundred twenty yards long by fifty-three and a third wide. His brother Paul is donating the lumber."

"Wonderful." Mom blew me a kiss and headed to the door. "I'm off to meet Marge at the antique shop. She's been browsing around the village since breakfast."

Once I devoured a yogurt for lunch while waiting for the dogs to return inside, I made several phone calls. The bridesmaids were ecstatic about next Wednesday's paint party. They all agreed to attend. I had to leave a message for Cissy, however, but she soon called back after I'd returned to the shop. She loved the idea, and kept chatting despite my broad hints that several customers had arrived. Cissy moaned with true diva drama.

"It's all been so terrible! Debbie's been dragged into the police station a few more times, and Gus's cousin Frank has been giving Zia Noemi fits, acting like a big gorilla. Claudia's eye is still puffy and bruised. Everyone thinks getting married on a Monday is odd—"

"As long as you do get married."

She sailed on as if she didn't hear my comment. "—and Kim and Vanessa are being so uncooperative. They hated my idea of green and white for new wedding colors."

My heart sank. "You're changing things at the last minute?"

"I can't. They refuse to buy new bridesmaid dresses." Cissy wailed and ranted on and on, so I let her talk until she finally ran out of steam.

"Red and white, along with hearts, still fit as a wedding theme," I pointed out. "Plus we'd never be able to find green and white dresses in time for March first."

"I suppose you're right. Oh, I have another call coming in."

I chuckled when she hung up on me. Cissy didn't mean to

be rude, since I was far down on her list of important people. Plus, I noticed a customer waiting to gain my attention. I slid my cell phone into hiding under the counter.

"I'm so sorry. I didn't realize you needed my help."

"No problem, although it sounds like your friend needs some," the woman said.

"Nervous bride," I said with a smile. "I'm in the bridal party."

"My daughter was a wreck, so I understand. Do you carry teddy bear stickers?"

"Yes, we do." I showed her our selection along with notebooks, folders, and other school supplies, so she chose several to buy. "We'll be hosting a Bears for the Cure charity event in early March to raise money for childhood cancer. I'm sorry we don't have any flyers ready yet."

By the time I finished explaining, the woman pressed a ten-dollar bill into my hand for a small glacier bear. "I don't live in the area, but what a wonderful project. My best friend's child died of leukemia, long ago. Thank you for doing this."

"Thank you for donating. Would you like a receipt?" I also made a note for Aunt Eve to compose a tax-deductible letter to print out and have on hand. "I can send you an email with it, plus updates on the project if you join our mailing list."

"Yes, I'd like that."

The bells over the front door jangled. Surprised to see Detective Mason, I handed the woman her bag with the stickers and then perched on my tall chair. He waited until the customer departed and then ambled toward the counter. Mason wore an overcoat, slacks, and a tweed sport coat, minus tie, instead of jeans and a sweatshirt. He waved his cell phone.

"Got a text about picking up some evidence?"

"Yes, that's right," I said and explained about the pair of gloves.

"So another guy wanted teddy bears, huh? Seems your shop isn't the only one getting these visits."

"Really." I brought the bagged evidence from under the counter. "This was a different man, but he also checked the seams and asked if stuffing could be taken out. He also wanted to know if we could design a sitting bear, like the one Bears of the Heart used to produce."

"Hmm. Sounds like this guy's a friend of your other customer."

"Is it possible they're working together?"

Mason nodded. "Yeah, a group of child predators. Two or three of them get a dozen or so of these bears, and a tech guy sets up the video camera inside them. Then they stream the kids playing, getting dressed, or worse. After that, they trade the recordings online."

"That's disgusting," I said. "Aren't the parents aware?"

"Not always. Some of these guys are family members, and handling these cases can get tricky. Especially if there's been ongoing abuse."

"Is it happening more often, or is technology making it easier?"

"Both," Mason said, "but technology also makes it easier to prove a case. If we get the evidence before the perps destroy it, that is. Thanks for being so diligent, Sasha. Here's hoping we can get fingerprints off these gloves."

He pocketed the bag, checked his cell phone, and started toward the door. I blocked his path, however. "Have you made any progress on Dylan Campbell's murder investigation? Maybe you could update me."

"Sure, I could. But I won't."

Grinning, he tried to dodge me but failed. "Come on, Detective." I stretched my arm farther in case he managed to get past. "I helped you out on this predator case, so tell me what's going on with Debbie Davison. Is she the prime suspect, or is Frank Antonini? Have Cissy and Gus's wedding rings turned up yet?"

"Nope." Mason rubbed his jaw. "We have contacts at the local pawn shops and jewelry stores around the area. All the way to Ypsilanti and as far as Jackson."

"In case you didn't hear, Frank Antonini stole some of Dylan's poker winnings at the bachelor party held at Flambé. Several groomsmen accused Dylan of cheating. When the fight started, Frank took advantage of the chaos and helped himself."

"Okay, but that's hearsay coming from you. None of them would admit to anything that happened that night during questioning. They all said they had a great time."

"That's bunk."

"Welcome to police work, Sasha. People usually lie."

"But remember, Frank has a motive for the murder," I argued. "When Dylan found out about Frank stealing his poker winnings, he arranged to meet Claudia Antonini in revenge. Frank found out, and boy was he angry and jealous."

Mason shrugged. "It's a big jump to murder."

"Oh, come on. It makes sense." I folded my arms over my chest in frustration. "I also found out that Debbie slit Dylan's tires the night of the rehearsal, near the church. Rusty Monroe witnessed her using a knife. And there's a surveillance camera if you want evidence."

"Is that so." Mason jotted down a note in his black book and then sighed. "Aren't the Davisons expecting you to prove Debbie's innocence?"

"Aren't you supposed to keep an open mind when investigating?" I shot back.

"Yeah, but I'm swamped as usual with more than one case." This time Mason slipped past me before I could react. "I heard Gus Antonini hired a PI team, too, but remember what I've said before, many times. Stick to selling teddy bears."

"You never said whether Debbie or Frank is your prime suspect."

The door slammed shut behind him. I banged a fist on the counter, wishing he'd come clean with more information. My curiosity had built to such a high point, I couldn't give up. I'd thought Debbie was innocent, but now I wasn't so sure.

If only she hadn't slit Dylan's tires.

Chapter 16

After a relaxing Sunday, I spent all Monday morning checking inventory on the shop's shelves. I enjoyed the slow pace, since I'd always been stressed at the week's beginning in my previous job for a nonprofit. That hadn't lasted long. Less than my marriage, in fact. Now I filled the accessory racks with our spring fashions. We sold dresses sized for our medium and large bears, some with shamrocks or flowers, but most in pastel colors, along with tiny T-shirts and denims, shoes, hats, and backpacks.

Kids loved to dress up their teddy bears.

Surprised to hear the village clock chiming twelve, I glanced up at the clock above the shop's counter. "How time flies when you're having fun."

"Talking to yourself? Is that a good sign?" Aunt Eve smiled in the doorway. "Run along and take the dogs for their walk. Remember you have a tour later on at four."

"Oh yeah, I forgot. Thanks for the reminder."

My sweet fur babies seemed eager to head outside, despite

the chilly wind. "Come on, Sugar, walk nice." I stopped for the third time and untangled the coupler on their leash. "You're supposed to be watching Rosie and walking nice like her."

What I hoped to be a quick stroll down Theodore Lane to Main Street soon evolved into keeping my little poodle on task. Sugar Bear hadn't been this distracted for weeks. I didn't have the heart to keep tugging her along, but my patience nearly ran dry. At least the sun shone and the temperature had climbed to almost fifty degrees. Plenty of other people also were outside to enjoy a noon stroll along Main Street.

When a squirrel dashed across the pavement, Rosie whined and pulled me sideways. The leash wrapped around my legs, and I had to rescue Sugar Bear from being choked. I made them both sit and focus for a long minute before giving them a treat.

"You girls! Honestly."

I took the shortcut to the blocked-off portion of Theodore Lane, bypassing the small grove of trees. A small car pulled into the parking lot of the Queen Bess Tea Room, right in front of me. The driver, Claudia Antonini, wore sunglasses. Zia Noemi climbed out of the passenger seat before Gisele Vaccaro parked her sporty red Corvette behind them. This was my chance to interview Claudia, on neutral ground, although the other women might discourage her.

Especially about volunteering information her husband may have told her regarding the wedding rehearsal. Or maybe something Dylan Campbell confided to her during their time alone that Friday afternoon. That would be ideal.

"Hi, Sasha! What cute dogs," Gisele called out. "Look, Zia. How sweet."

"What a little darling!" Gus's aunt laughed when Sugar Bear danced around on her hind legs in excitement. "Can I pet her?"

"Of course," I said. "You're lucky, because Mondays and Tuesdays are the best days to visit the tearoom. They're booked solid on Saturday."

"Yes, so we heard," Zia Noemi said. "So what's your dog's name?"

"Sugar Bear, she's a toy poodle. She loves attention. And this is Rosie, a Lhasa Apso and Bichon Frise mix," I said. Claudia kept her distance, however. I thought fast, wondering how to engage her, and smiled her way. "Guess you're not an animal lover, huh?"

"Nope."

"Claudia had a bird at one time, though. Didn't you?" Gisele asked.

"Yeah. Big mistake on my part. Frank left the window open one day, on purpose."

We all gasped in shock. "That's a shame," I said. Claudia only shrugged. "What kind of bird? A parakeet or a parrot?"

"I'd rather not talk about it." She settled her sunglasses on top of her head.

"I think dogs are easier to take care of," Zia Noemi said, "although cats are really the least trouble. You can leave them for a few days and they'll be fine."

"You have to clean their litter." Gisele shuddered. "No thanks."

"That's nothing compared to picking up after a dog every time they go out—"

While she and Gisele argued about that topic, I sidled closer to Claudia, who pushed a strand of red hair away from her pursed lips. "So Cissy's getting married a week from today." She nodded, still silent, eyes downcast. At least her black eye had faded. "I guess that means Frank is Gus's best man, right?"

"He hasn't decided yet." Her anger rang clear. "I'm sick of this whole thing. Some PI came to talk to us, can you believe it? I told him to jump in the lake, and so did Frank. If Gus had chosen my husband as best man from the start, we wouldn't be in this mess."

"Like Debbie's been saying all along," I added.

"You got that right," Claudia said. "I'm beginning to wonder if Frank and Debbie worked together to get rid of Dylan. They were thick as thieves at the rehearsal."

"Why would you think that?" I asked, curious. "It's true Debbie slashed Dylan's tires, but I doubt if Frank told her to do that."

Claudia barked a laugh. "But he might have let her borrow his knife. Frank always carries one with him. And he believes in karma, big-time."

"But would they have plotted together to kill Dylan?"

"It's possible. Frank expected to be Gus's best man, given all they've been through since they were kids. They grew up together in the old neighborhood. Frank even wrote a toast to the bride and groom, and memorized it."

"That's true," Gisele said, joining our chat. "He recited it for me the other day."

Zia Noemi shook her head. "Enough of this. What's done is done—"

"But it isn't," Claudia said. "I wonder if Frank stabbed Dylan."

"Did he tell you he did it?" I asked, deciding to be blunt.

She turned to me, her blue eyes troubled, and her freckles stood out against her pale complexion. "No. But Frank's been acting so strange."

"That's nothing new." Gisele waved a hand. "I've got stories from family get-togethers long ago. Frank never wanted anything to do with any other kid except Gus. The two of them went off to the creek, bringing back spiders, snakes, toads, you name it. Then he'd scare us other cousins and freak out the adults."

"I remember that." Zia Noemi shuddered. "No matter how much my Gustavo tried to discourage him, Frank did whatever he pleased."

"He scares Martina with creepy stories, too," Claudia said, "and she has nightmares. What kind of father would do that? He won't stop, even when I beg him."

I didn't want to voice my opinion out loud—like father, like daughter. Martina had taken pleasure in terrorizing Mr. Clooney, untying the bridesmaids' shoe bows, and disobeying adults. But Zia Noemi had no qualms about speaking the truth.

"Your husband is a bad example for your little girl," she warned. "Little Tina is learning all the wrong things. And you are not strong enough to handle either of them."

"I don't need advice from you," Claudia snapped back. "You're not one to talk, the way Uncle Lorenzo acted. Getting drunk all the time—"

"Hey, hey. Airing dirty laundry in public doesn't help." Gisele glanced at me and drew them both away. "Come on, we're almost late for our afternoon tea."

They walked arm in arm toward the Queen Bess Tea Room. Dang. If only I'd gotten more answers from Claudia about Frank. Sugar Bear shivered from the cold, despite her sherpa-lined coat. I scooped her up, unzipped my coat, and stuffed her inside.

She licked my face. "Poor thing, I'm sorry that took so long," I told Sugar Bear. "Come on, Rosie, you look cold, too. Let's head home."

My older dog didn't mind jogging beside me back to the Silver Bear Shop. We headed around to the back porch and into the kitchen. Once I dried their paws and underbellies, I gave both dogs their Kong toys filled with peanut butter. I set treats for Onyx on the cat tower, since she was hogging the sunny window seat. Maybe that would get her to share. Eventually, when she was good and ready to move.

"Be back later, and no fighting." I hurried through the hallway, made certain the double doors locked behind me, and rushed past the office. "I'm sorry, I didn't realize how long it would take," I called out to Aunt Eve, who held one hand over the phone's receiver.

"No problem. Maddie stopped by, so she's covering for you."

I slowed, hearing my sister's voice and another customer in the next room. What a relief. The dogs needed exercise every day, and I didn't relish taking them out in the cold after sunset. Plus the village streets didn't have enough lamp lights.

Maddie suddenly laughed. "We nearly ran out of white bears due to how well they paired up with the red rose bouquets at the florist. They do get dirty easy, though."

"If that's the case, I'll take a darker color. Even if it ends up sitting on a shelf."

Sitting on a shelf? I groaned, hoping this wasn't another guy who wanted a sitting teddy bear. I peeked around the doorway and spied a man, probably in his late twenties or early thirties, with thick dark hair, dark glasses, and a heavy overcoat.

"Did you need any accessories today?" Maddie asked.

He shook his head. "Nah, just the bear. Do you have more like it?"

I fumbled in a pocket for my cell phone. What was it with these guys, targeting young kids? I'd better take a photo in case he was involved in the predator ring that Detective Mason had mentioned. Before I hit the camera's button, I heard the customer speak again.

"—niece wants to give the second bear to her friend in kindergarten. The family's apartment caught fire from a space heater. They lost everything."

"I heard that story on the radio. Didn't they live across from the elementary school?" Maddie asked. "A lot of the kids in every grade are donating toys."

"Yeah," the guy said. "I heard Dave Fox is doing an article in the next issue of the *Silver Hollow Herald*. I saw him taking photos of all the damage."

"We'll give you a twenty-five percent discount for buying two bears, with two coupons for a free accessory. That way the kids can come and choose what they want, along with a parent. Thanks for coming in today."

Maddie passed me, followed by the man, and processed the sale at the counter. She tucked the two teddies into silver tissue paper and nestled them inside one of our logo bags. My cheeks burned. Thankfully I hadn't taken a photo and sent it off to Mason. Talk about making an embarrassing mistake. Once the guy departed, I faced my sister.

"Late again. Good thing I needed to bring the mock-ups for the fundraiser," she said, one hand on her hip. Maddie laughed when I stuck out my tongue. "Poor Aunt Eve was frantic, because she had more than one customer."

"You both have my undying thanks."

"Remember Aunt Eve covered for you Saturday morning when you were late. What gives? Wait, don't tell me. The murder investigation, right?"

"I ran into Claudia Antonini, along with Gisele and Zia Noemi, on my walk with the dogs." I smiled at her look of surprise. "Uh-huh. See, you're interested to know what I found out. Don't try to fool me that you don't care."

"It's not that I don't care, but—"

"But what? I should stick to selling teddy bears? That's what Detective Mason keeps saying. I know I've been distracted from work, but the more I find out, the more curious I am about what really happened to Dylan Campbell."

Maddie sighed and ruffled her spiked pixie haircut. "I get that, but I don't want you to get in danger again. I can't help worrying."

"I'm not gonna take any risks again," I promised her. "The last time was a fluke, trust me. And it turned out okay."

"Barely."

"Do you want to know what I found out, or not?"

"Yeah, but first look at this." She drew an envelope from beneath the counter, opened it, and extracted a few sheets of thick paper. "What do you think?"

"This one might be too close to the Care Bears trademark." I pointed out the gorgeous rainbow behind a group of sketched teddy bears. "If we get in trouble, we might have to cancel the event. And it's only a few weeks away, remember."

Maddie pushed her orange sweater's sleeves farther up her arms. "Hmm, I forgot that the rainbow was associated with those bears. We're not pushing people into buying the glacier bears, right? They can bring new teddies to donate."

"Yes. But whoever doesn't bring a bear can buy a small one."

Aunt Eve breezed in, carrying a light blue ten-inch bear. "Look what I found in a storage room upstairs, isn't it adorable? It can be a prototype for that glacier bear."

I examined the bear's tag, the faux fur, and soft body. "What did Uncle Ross say?"

"I asked him, but he doesn't remember this at all."

"That's not like him," Maddie said, "since he decided that fur color was too pale."

"That's right," I said, "and Will Taylor pushed us to use that vendor. We chose another vendor to provide a mottled blue fur. He was steamed over that."

"Never mind, then. These flyers are wonderful, Maddie," Aunt Eve said. "Except for this one with the rainbow design."

"Yeah, we already decided—"

I glanced at the door when tinkling bells announced customers, a mother with two small children in tow, followed by an older couple. Planning for the fundraiser would have to wait until later on. Aunt Eve leaned in to whisper in my ear.

"By the way, Judith said that she asked Flynn Hanson to help out with Bears for the Cure. He'll call you later."

Oh, joy. I felt abandoned when she left along with Maddie, who swept up her sample flyers and followed my aunt to the office. The last thing I needed was a chat with my ex. Flynn no doubt expected a chance to plug his new Ann Arbor law practice in exchange for appearing at the event. He always thought of himself first.

"Excuse me, I have a question," the older woman asked and pointed to the pale blue bear on the counter. "Isn't that produced overseas?"

"This one is, yes, but it's a prototype. Several years ago we committed to producing bears in the factory behind our shop," I replied. "All of our teddy bears come in realistic shades of fur except for our smallest-size bears. If you'd like, you can sign up for a guided tour. I'm hosting one today at four o'clock."

The older woman smiled. "Good, we'll be back then."

"We'd love to see how teddy bears are made." The young mother drew gift certificates from her pocket and handed one to each child. "Grandma and Grandpa bought these before Christmas. Can you help us choose which bears to buy?"

"Of course."

I explained the various types, from grizzly and sloth to polar and glacier bears. The kids were sweet, choosing a black bear and a panda, plus accessories. After bagging their purchases, the group headed off for a late lunch. I turned to see Maddie leaning against the doorway.

"I forgot how much you deal with people face-to-face," she said. "I was on the phone most of the time when I worked in the office. At Silver Moon, I only talk to people when clients ask for an actual meeting."

"Lucky you. I don't mind customers visiting," I said. "It can be fun."

"Mom said we ought to contact radio and television stations for interviews."

"Ugh. Now that I wouldn't like." I frowned when she laughed at my obvious discomfort. "I get too nervous in that kind of situation."

"I came back so you can update me on what you learned from Claudia." Maddie's eyes widened once I'd related my chat. "Really? She thinks Frank gave Debbie his knife to slit the tires on Dylan's car, and maybe plotted together to kill him?"

"Remember it takes proof. Seeing them talking together doesn't mean squat, and no one else mentioned overhearing that conversation."

"Or seeing him give her the knife to use," she said.

"Frank will never admit that he gave a knife to anyone. And Claudia has a good reason to get her husband in trouble with the cops. He's an abuser."

"Didn't you say Rusty Monroe witnessed Debbie slitting the tires?"

"He said he saw her walking away, holding a knife. And that's hearsay, according to Detective Mason. I'm hoping he'll watch the surveillance tape at some point, though." I shooed her to the door. "Unless you want to cover for me during the tour at four o'clock, you better get busy printing those flyers so we can pass them out to all the village shops. Even if Claudia thinks Frank might be guilty, it's only her opinion. Too bad he didn't confess."

"Bazinga."

I suppressed a smile when Maddie bundled up in her coat, scarf, and gloves. For all her teasing, I was glad she showed interest in the case. Any help was welcome, from her, from Jay, and my other friends. After all, I promised to prove Debbie Davison's innocence.

That wasn't proving to be an easy task.

Chapter 17

Wednesday evening, I studied my closet's interior to get dressed for tonight's painting party with Cissy's bridesmaids. Everyone had RSVP'd, with excitement, along with Zia Noemi, Barbara Davison, and Vanessa's mother. Things had been fairly calm since the night of Dylan's murder. I'd learned nothing more to either clear Debbie Davison, or prove she stabbed her ex-fiancé with Frank Antonini's help. I also hadn't seen the PI team lately in the village.

Maybe they hadn't gotten far, either.

"Why did I choose this outfit?" I tore off my blazer and sweater, then donned an old sweatshirt instead. "If I get paint on this, who cares."

My sister honked from the parking lot. I rushed to the window and waved, and then realized she couldn't see me. Maddie's car headlights beamed toward the fenced yard. The sun had gone down more than an hour ago. I blinked. Unlocked the window, slid it upward, and leaned out. Was it my imagination, or had I seen a shadow slinking against the house?

"Oh, no!" I watched as a large poodle's lean body cleared the fence and loped off. "Mr. Clooney's running wild again. And I'm sure he pooped all over the yard."

I'd discovered several piles the day after that late-night visit, when I'd nearly called 911. Now I knew that dog was the true culprit. Sighing, I snatched up my coat, purse, and gloves. Lucky for me, I'd already taken care of feeding Rosie and Sugar Bear after a brief walk. They were both stretched side by side on the braided rug before the gas fireplace's warmth.

"I just saw Mr. Clooney jump our fence," I told Maddie while fastening my seat belt. She muttered a curse under her breath. "I'll clean up the yard, don't worry. Mom said she asked Barbara to take him on a leash whenever he goes outside."

"I doubt she would bother. Plus he's an escape artist whenever they open the door." Her tires squealed on the slick pavement. "Oops, sorry."

"We're not late, are we?" I asked.

"We will be if I don't hurry. And if traffic's bad."

We rode in silence to Eric Dyer's brewery and winery out on Baker Road. Maddie parked next to his van in the rutted lot and then led the way to the low gray-painted building. Heaps of dirty snow blocked a few windows. I skirted some nasty ice patches, grateful that I'd changed from work shoes to thick wool socks and hiking boots.

"I think Eric ought to install some lighting in the lot here."

"Yeah, he said he'll get to that in the spring." Maddie pointed to the rough painted sign above the entrance. "Eric wants to commission Jay to carve a full-size bear and install it on the roof, but that would cost a fortune. I told him a bear's head with one paw and silver claws is enough to get the idea across. Come on. We've got to set up everything."

I tugged and pulled at the heavy oak door and finally managed to open it. "Wow. This thing weighs a ton." Maddie only laughed.

"You need some biceps workouts at the gym."

"Me? I hope you're joking."

"You can't just walk the dog or bike ride, Sasha, and expect to stay in shape."

I sighed. My sister had a Pilates machine in her bedroom, used it faithfully, and visited the local gym at least twice a week. I was lucky to walk the dogs a few days a week in winter, given the cold weather. Forget bike rides. I'd researched treadmills, but I didn't have a spot for it, and spring was coming. Once warmer weather arrived, daily walks would be the norm again. I'd never denied being lazy about exercise.

Not too lazy to thaw leftover Christmas cookies from the freezer, though.

Eric met us inside the dim interior, kissed my sister, and smiled at me. "Great to see you two. Come on back. One of my staff will direct your guests to the tasting room."

"Good, because it's kind of a rabbit's warren in here," Maddie said. "Is your dad on-site? I wondered if he'd help set up the tables tonight."

"Nope. Out with Mrs. Bloom for dinner."

I nodded, not daring to ask how he felt about the gossip in Silver Hollow. Many people felt Alison Bloom shouldn't be dating so soon after her husband's death. Then again, love spurred people to take action without considering the consequences. So did hate, given the way Debbie slit Dylan's tires. Passion could send people in either direction and change the outcome of their future, and not always for the better.

"Quit dawdling, for heaven's sake," Maddie said.

"I was just looking at all this wine," I fibbed.

She dragged me past the floor-to-ceiling racks to the tasting room. Two huge oak trestle tables dominated the large space. A pair of rustic chandeliers glowed above each table, and hefty wood chairs lined the walls. I perused several framed newspaper articles about Silver Claw's business around the room. One described a hops farm in Goodrich, and another featured Eric's dad when he retired after thirty-five years as an engineer. Wow.

"Dad loved his job, but the grind really got to him."

"He seems to keep himself busy," I said.

"Busier than when he worked a nine-to-five job, for sure. Dad wasn't thrilled about this paint party tonight. I bet he thinks you'll leave a big mess to clean, but Maddie said she'd keep things under control."

"Of course," my sister said cheerfully. "First we'll cover the floor with plastic."

Once Eric and I moved both tables, Maddie rolled out long lengths of white plastic on the floor. We all moved the tables back, then covered them with plastic as well and taped the corners underneath to keep it in place. Maddie set out acrylic paint, canvases, a variety of brushes, plus jars of clean water at each chair. We also placed easels at each end of the tables with simple designs on each canvas.

"They can choose to paint white daisies against a wooden barn wall," my sister said, "or the lake scene with a silver moon."

"Nice going, Mads. I figured you'd have us paint hearts and red roses."

"Cissy wanted something like that, but daisies are easier." Maddie shrugged. "I've got a photo of red roses instead of daisies, if anyone wants to try it, but good luck with that. Come on, Eric. Let's choose the wines for tonight."

They headed off, leaving me to wait for the bridesmaids. Kim Goddard was the first to arrive, and her eyes looked normal without bruises. Gisele Vaccaro and Claudia Antonini walked in a few minutes later with Zia Noemi, who was clearly skeptical of the chandeliers.

"Will there be enough light to paint? It seems so dark in here."

"I'll try to find a lamp, if you need one."

I excused myself, and hoped to scrounge up a canvas apron like Eric's wait staff wore. The other women wore casual jeans and sweatshirts, but Zia Noemi had a long-sleeved blue silk floral dress. She would not be happy splashing water or paint on it.

"Thank you, dear," she gushed when I tied an apron around her waist.

"Better safe than sorry," I said and then plugged in the small lamp on one table. "Acrylic paint doesn't wash out, so please be careful. We're so glad you could come tonight."

"We left little Martina with her father, thank heavens for that. Frank begged us to bring her but Claudia put her foot down. I was so surprised!"

"And if Tina throws a tantrum, Frank can deal with that, too," Claudia said with a scowl. "I hope you're happy with how I handled it, Zietta."

The older woman nodded. "Yes, indeed. Oh, Sasha—I brought some dessert." Zia Noemi gestured to several boxes on a side table. "I put them all over there."

"Wonderful, thank you. Welcome to the Silver Claw, please come in," I called out. Ginger, Vanessa Leeson's mother, strolled into the room.

"Isn't my daughter here yet? I'd better text her."

She pulled out her cell phone and then squinted at the screen. "I have trouble seeing at night, especially when I'm driving home. My eyes are getting bad."

"You'd better paint with me at this table," Zia Noemi said. "We have a lamp."

"Maddie should be back any minute," I said, "so we'll wait for everyone to arrive before we get started."

Eric brought platters into the room with assorted cheeses, meats, olives, and a variety of breads and crusty rolls. I arranged the fruit tarts, biscotti, anginetti, Florentines, and profiteroles that Zia Noemi had brought without sampling more than a few. That was a hardship. Several of Eric's wait staff brought bottles of wine and glasses. The women's chatter grew louder after they chose chairs around the two trestle tables, far enough apart to give everyone enough room for food and drink as well as their painting supplies and canvas squares.

Cissy finally arrived with Debbie and Barbara Davison, and waved to everyone. "I'm so glad we can all get together before the wedding next Monday! I'm excited."

"We all are." Debbie clapped her hands. "This will be such fun."

"I didn't expect it to look so nice in here," Cissy said, looking around, "but I'll warn you now, Maddie. I can't draw a straight line."

"You don't need to, as long as you follow directions." My sister signaled me. "I think we're gonna need a few more aprons."

I dashed off. Cissy had dressed for the occasion in a rabbit-fur vest, a cashmere sweater, black leather pants, and high-heeled red boots. She needed a floor-length poncho, but the apron covered most of her outfit. Debbie had worn sweatpants and a tattered shirt under her puffy winter coat, but Barbara Davison wore a silk blouse and wool slacks. The other ladies continued to chat, sipping from full glasses of wine, while I helped Cissy's mother tie her apron.

"Where's Vanessa?" Kim asked Cissy. "I thought she was coming early."

"Me too. Didn't you see her today, Eric?"

"Nope. I've been here all day," Eric said, "although I've

been cooped up in the office." He turned to the server who brought out a tray of IPA bottles. "Did anyone come by earlier, five or six o'clock? Or maybe three or four?"

She shook her head. "Nobody except customers picking up orders."

"Vanessa will show before long," Debbie said, "so let's get painting."

Maddie agreed and tapped her wristwatch. "Okay, everyone, you have two minutes to choose either the floral design or the moon-over-the-lake landscape. I can help you prep your palette with the specific paints you'll need. Everyone has a plastic tray, right? Plus a container of wipes handy for emergencies. Let's begin."

I watched Cissy, Debbie, and Kim giggle over the wine and argue about which design would be easier to paint. They squealed when Cissy poured too much paint onto her tray. My sister had far more patience than I did. I'd take a tour of fifty elementary school kids over adults, any day. Gritting my teeth, I focused on helping the older women, Zia Noemi, Ginger, and Barbara Davison, choose their paint colors.

I hoped Barbara could explain what happened between Debbie and Dylan that soured their relationship. Unfortunately, she seemed dead set on avoiding any chitchat and turned away whenever I sidled closer to her spot.

"Mom, look at mine! Hey, yours is coming along great, too," Debbie called out. "Sasha, can you get me fresh water? Thanks."

Frustrated, I took her jar and emptied it at the huge sink in the next room. After refilling it, I plunked it down near Debbie's hand. Maddie gave her pointers on adding a few dabs of brown to her daisy centers.

"There, see? Just a touch adds a little depth, and makes it seem more real."

"You're right, that's so cool."

I turned to watch Cissy, who apparently had mended things with Gus without my input. She gushed about his latest phone calls and the huge bouquet of flowers he'd sent; Cissy also complimented Zia Noemi whenever the older woman dabbled tiny bits of paint on her canvas. Given her cautious method, Gus's aunt might end up with a pointillism master-piece in a month or two. Both of them spent more time chatting than actually painting.

Zia Noemi smacked a hand over her heart with dramatic flair. "You should have seen my little Gus when he was in third grade! So handsome, even then. That dark hair, those eyes like melted chocolate," she raved. "And he was an angel in school, with wonderful grades. So polite to all his teachers—"

"Practically perfect in every way," Maddie muttered low, so only I could hear.

I suppressed a laugh, which came out like a pig snort, and coughed hard to cover my embarrassment. Both Kim and Debbie raised their eyebrows in my direction. Luckily Zia Noemi had not heard me. She peppered Cissy with questions about their Tahitian honeymoon.

"Like Gus said, it will be a unique experience. The travel agency changed our flight and tour tickets," Cissy said. "Good thing he bought insurance."

"My Gus, always the smart one! You will never be sorry in your marriage, Cissy," Zia Noemi said. "All that matters is your happiness."

Cissy hugged her and nearly upset a water jar. "Thank you, Zietta. Keep telling stories about Gus when he was small. I love hearing them."

I moved on around the tables, more interested to hear Debbie's complaints about Dylan, and how he was to blame for the car accident that hurt Vanessa's niece. Ginger didn't look happy about that. When she brought up how Gus's parents died, Zia Noemi moaned about her late husband and all his faults.

"Lorenzo, that man! He never listened to me, *un uomo stupido.* He insisted on driving them home, when he had more wine and whiskey than both of them together! I couldn't tame him. And I blame myself, for that and many other things."

"Now, now," Cissy said. "Gus doesn't blame you."

"That man of yours, my sweet Gustavo, is a saint! A saint, I tell you. Did he explain how we broke the news to him about that night?"

Despite the bride's quick nod, Zia Noemi launched into the story and droned on about how brave Gus was, how heroic during his parents' double funeral, and how he'd supported her throughout Uncle Lorenzo's visitation and service. Cissy finally changed the subject to list all the wedding gifts they'd opened. Weary, I switched to hear Gisele's and Claudia's complaints about their husbands.

"Bob is so dull, it's like being married to a lumpy sofa," Gisele said and refilled her wineglass. She plucked up the bottle and studied the label. "This tastes great, what is it? Chardonnay, with overtones of pear, peach, and apple, citrus and vanilla, plus cream. You wouldn't think a wine would have so many flavors in it, would you?"

"It is lovely." Claudia sighed. "My Frank drives me nuts. Moody, that's his middle name! And for the past few months it's been famine in the bedroom, if you get my drift. It's either too much, or a desert. Can you blame me for meeting Dylan?"

She'd missed covering a slight tinge of purple near her eye with makeup. Claudia leaned closer and lowered her voice, so I inched closer to overhear their exchange.

"—happened?" Gisele asked.

"Dylan sure could kiss," Claudia whispered. "I felt it right down to my toes!"

"I told you so, didn't I?"

"He flirted with me right off the bat, when we first arrived from Chicago. Dylan met us at the hotel, you know," Claudia admitted, her voice rising in excitement. "Frank was jealous then, but I kept telling him it didn't mean anything."

"Dylan meant it, girlfriend," Kim said, who was passing behind the two women. She stopped and waved a hand. "He was such a player, it made me sick. He targeted me a few weeks ago at a bar, and I caved. It was only the thrill of the chase, you know. Once he got what he wanted, good-bye. It's a good thing you didn't go farther."

Gisele smirked. "Yeah, good thing your husband took action."

Claudia protested at that. "Hey. Frank didn't kill Dylan!"

I was surprised by her comment—clearly she'd changed her mind about his possible guilt since I saw her near the tearoom. But Cissy rolled her eyes with a deep sigh.

"Oh, please. Everyone suspects him. That's why the cops told him he couldn't go back to Chicago. They're looking for more evidence."

"Must we talk about such unpleasantness?" Zia Noemi pleaded, but the women all ignored her.

"Gus had motive, too. You told me he nearly lost his job," Claudia said, "because his boss blamed him for letting Dylan trash that Flame restaurant."

"Flambé, actually," Kim said, finishing her IPA bottle. She flipped a hank of blond hair over one shoulder. "This stuff is too bitter for my taste. Fruity, but not enough."

"I prefer the wine," Cissy said, topping her glass. "This one tastes like strawberries. And Gus didn't lose his job. Everyone else was fighting, not him."

"I still think Frank is guilty," Debbie said, slurring her words, and finished her beer. No one paid her any attention, so she lurched back to pick up her paint brush.

I filed away Kim's confession about having a fling with Dylan. What if she was lying, and they'd had a full-blown affair? What if Dylan wanted to end it, preferring to play the field instead? Would Kim have been as bitter as Debbie?

Maybe she craved Dylan's attention, and was devastated when he suddenly ended things. Debbie had slashed Dylan's tires, after all, over a year after his rejection. That wasn't like her nature at all. And Kim had been furious with Jay's brother Paul.

Either one of them could have taken outrage to the point of murder.

Chapter 18

Gisele leaned closer to Claudia. "Tell me more about Dylan."

"Take back what you said about Frank first," she said, frowning.

"Okay, okay. I'm sorry, but how far did you get with Dylan?"

"Not far enough, because I saw Nick drive past in his Jeep." Claudia frowned. "That squashed my mood flat. Dylan only laughed. He said Nick spied on him a few times."

"Really? That's weird."

"Yeah, but Nick said he only wanted to keep Dylan from making a mistake. He has a big heart. Cares too much for his friends."

"To me, it sounds like he won't mind his own business," Gisele said with a laugh. "Nick tried to talk me into a monthly spa visit to lose weight. Talk about insensitive."

"But you always complain about wanting to shed twenty pounds," Cissy said. "Nick can be pushy, though. He tried to sell us a honeymoon cruise package to the Bahamas after Gus had already finalized our trip to Tahiti."

"I turned Nick down on the spa package," Gisele said, "despite the huge discount. He couldn't guarantee I'd lose anything except my money. I pamper myself enough, according to Bob, getting manis and pedis. And hair color, and facials. I deserve it all."

"I wish Frank wasn't so cheap," Claudia said. "I have to ask him for gas money—"

"Sasha, can you do me a favor?" Barbara Davison called from the next table.

Drat. I trotted over to help, since she'd gotten paint in her hair and couldn't see where or how to get it out. I managed to strip the dried bits off. Maddie rushed over to help.

"Acrylic paint dries so quickly. Your painting looks great," my sister added. "The barn door background is so realistic with all those thin lines, just like wood."

Barbara beamed with pleasure. "I took a few painting lessons long ago. I'm going to sign up for more down in Florida, too. I hope it comes back to me."

"Like riding a bike, yep. Keep going."

By the time I circled back around to eavesdrop on Gisele and Claudia, they were arguing over handbags—whether Kate Spade, Coach, or Dooney & Bourke were the best buys. I sidled over toward Kim, who was chatting with Zia Noemi and Debbie. Kim's moon painting was nearly finished, except the sky colors resembled stripes instead of being blended together.

"You ought to come to Superior Defense for lessons," Kim said.

"I don't know," Debbie said. "I'm not sure if I could pull a trigger."

"You get used to it. It's so rewarding after a month or two of target practice, when you see improvements, and how accurate your shots get. I love it."

I raised an eyebrow over that. If Kim took pride in her marksmanship, would that transfer to wielding a different weapon? Like an ice pick.

Barbara waved a hand from the other table. "You make it sound easy, but my husband tried to teach me to shoot a rifle once. Richard loves to hunt, but I didn't like it."

"I bet you didn't like the kickback, is that it?" Kim nodded. "But a handgun isn't the same, and you can wear headphones to cut down on the noise."

"Noise, that's my nemesis. Cissy's dog is driving me crazy with his barking. I can't control Mr. Clooney. We should have trained him, I suppose, because he barks at every car that drives past, and every delivery. At our house or anywhere on Theodore Lane."

"And he's been wandering into our yard," I muttered under my breath.

Apparently Barbara heard me. "That dog slips his collar like Houdini. I tried using a harness, and somehow he managed to get out of that."

"Because you didn't put it on him the correct way," Debbie said. "You should have bought an easier one, Cissy."

"How do I know what kind to buy?" her sister complained.

Zia Noemi waved her brush. "He must be a good watchdog, though."

"Ha. If anyone offered Mr. Clooney a treat, he'd invite them inside," Cissy said. "Probably show them my jewelry case, and where we keep the wall safe."

Debbie laughed, but Barbara shook her head. "It's gotten

dangerous in Silver Hollow with all these murders. That's why we're moving to Florida."

"It's no safer there than in Michigan," I said.

Barbara glared at me. "We bought in a gated community."

"Anyone can guess the access code, like too easy passwords," Kim scoffed.

"That's true." I hated to burst anyone's bubble, but it was easy. "A lot of people use one-two-three, or a string of zeros, or their birthdate. And pet's names for their online passwords. Then they wonder why their computer accounts get hacked."

"I can't remember all the passwords to everything," Cissy wailed. "And when I write them down, I can't find where I put the notebook."

"All this computer talk," Zia Noemi said. "I have no interest in such things."

"It keeps your mind sharp," Kim said, but Gus's aunt hooted at that.

"Italian wine, that keeps my mind sharp enough."

"You could think of a phrase, something meaningful, and then use the first letters of every word as a password code," I offered. "As long as you remember to add in a number and a capital letter somewhere."

"That doesn't sound simple at all." Barbara tossed back her wine and refilled the glass. "Oh well. I suppose you heard that Teddy Hartman wants to buy my house, Sasha. I'm waiting for a counteroffer from the MacRaes. If they withdraw, I'll consider Hartman's proposal. Silver Hollow needs a new bed-and-breakfast. The Regency Hotel is too pricey."

"You're right," Kim said, "and that's why I'm driving back and forth from home."

"But Teddy Hartman is a ruthless businessman," I argued. "He's trying to undermine our sales, and he'll probably hurt other shops in the long run."

"That's your opinion," Barbara said. "It's none of my business what Hartman plans to do. No one should dictate how a business owner decorates or renovates. I don't care if he hangs teddy bears from every ceiling fan, or serves mush for breakfast."

"Or teddy bear pancakes," Debbie said, giggling.

"How about those sticky bear claws." Kim grabbed a bottle of red wine. "Ooh, Merlot. I'm gonna try that next."

Barbara ignored her. "He might turn around and sell the house, for all I know. Especially the way he's trying to get it for such a cheap price."

Maddie quickly changed the subject. "Did you want to try doing the other design, Mrs. Davison?" she asked. "We have extra canvases."

"I'd like to do the daisy one. This moon painting's pretty hopeless." Kim glanced around. "So Vanessa had to work late?"

"She said she had a meeting." Ginger dabbed a few highlights on her daisies. "My son-in-law gave me a ride here, although he's getting ready for some business trip. Probably going to Vegas so he can gamble. He and Dylan used to do that together."

"They played poker out in Vegas?" I asked.

"Oh, yes. Out there, online, plus betting on sports, horses, you name it. Vanessa once told me Dylan owed thousands of dollars. That was back when they were dating."

Surprised, I didn't reply to that. Nobody had mentioned Vanessa's former relationship with the best man before, or his gambling debts. They sounded serious, too. No wonder Dylan had been upset to learn that Frank Antonini swiped money from his winnings. He needed every penny to pay off creditors. And how long had he dated Vanessa? They must have been involved long before Dylan and Debbie's engagement.

"Why hasn't my daughter replied to my texts," Ginger said, clearly worried. "It's not like her to ignore me."

"Why don't you call her?" Zia Noemi suggested.

"I hate to bother her, though, if she's still in that meeting."

Kim gulped her wine. "Maddie, I can't get the barn to look like the sample."

"You're waiting too long, that's why," my sister said. "You've got to get into acrylic layers right away, or it dries up and you can't blend them. Paint over what you have."

"I'd rather you show me. I want this to look good enough for my wall."

Maddie demonstrated, stroking over Kim's canvas with dark brown, then adding tiny lines of gray to give it depth. "Now for the daisies. Take the brush, dip it into titanium white, and push and lift to make the petals. They don't have to be perfect."

"Wow, that is so neat. Thanks for the tip."

I hung back, watching the women working on their canvases. Cissy suddenly shrieked. "Oh my God, I have paint on my hand! Roll up my sleeves farther, Debbie, hurry. My sweater is brand-new. It cost me over a hundred dollars—"

"I can't get it off!"

"Rub her skin with a wet wipe," Maddie instructed me.

Both sisters calmed down once I cleaned off the paint. "My leaves look like blotches compared to yours, Maddie," Cissy said. "I can't get them to look real."

"Chill, for heaven's sake." Debbie swigged the rest of her wine. "This is supposed to be fun, remember. We're not gonna sell these trashy paintings."

"How can I relax?" her sister snapped back. "Vanessa hasn't shown up or called tonight, and Frank is bugging us to be the best man. He's driving Gus crazy. I'm worried about having to choose another maid of honor if the police arrest you for Dylan's murder."

Debbie shrugged. "They won't. Flynn Hanson said so, he's a top-notch lawyer."

"What if they do, like the day before the wedding? I'd be stuck with another delay. And someone in this room is supposed to prove your innocence."

They both shot me a dirty look. Cissy turned back to painting, but Debbie simpered in satisfaction when Kim, Zia Noemi, and Barbara Davison also glared at me. I decided to answer that with a raised eyebrow.

"How can I possibly prove anything when Rusty Monroe saw you with a knife? The night of the rehearsal, right before Dylan found his tires slashed."

Except for the Davisons, everyone in the room gasped in shock. I bit my lip, wondering if I'd made a mistake announcing that. Even Zia Noemi's complexion turned pale beneath her pancake makeup and bright pink blush. Debbie threw down her paint brush.

"He dumped me, without warning, so Dylan deserved a little inconvenience. And I cut my finger doing it. That's how I got blood on my dress."

"Did Frank let you borrow his knife?" I asked.

Gus's aunt gasped again, although the others remained silent to hear Debbie's answer. She hesitated, glancing at the door as if she wanted to escape. Maybe I shouldn't have put her on the spot like this, but it wasn't fair for her to expect so much from me.

A cell phone's faint ringing caught everyone's attention.

"Whose phone is that?" Barbara Davison asked. "It must be outside this room."

"Vanessa's." Ginger held up her own cell. "I dialed it a second ago."

"Call her number again," Kim suggested, "so we can track it down."

"It doesn't make sense that she'd be here and not answer her phone," Cissy said. "She must be somewhere in the building."

Maddie and I exchanged worried glances. I didn't like this development at all. We both followed the group out of the tasting room and threaded our way through the back storage area, listening for that catchy electronic pattern of Vanessa's ringtone. I circled a stainless keg with metal taps screwed into its side. More lined the cement floor. The ringing was less faint but soon faded. Ginger dialed again and then cocked her head.

"There it is again. Do you hear it?"

I nodded. "Yeah, but—oh. Here's Eric."

He stood in the doorway, clearly startled, and held up a small leather purse. The ringing was audible from its interior. "Is this someone's bag?"

"That is definitely Vanessa's," Ginger said. "Where did you find it?"

"One of my staffers found it outside in the lot, around four o'clock. We figured whoever dropped it by accident would return. That's why I kept it in my office."

Maddie grabbed the wine-colored leather strap before Ginger, and then searched inside. She brought out a wallet, opened it, and held it out. "This is Vanessa's license. Are you sure you didn't see her at some point today, Eric?"

"No. She never came inside the brewery," he said. "Only our regular customers came in to pick up their online orders."

"So where is she?" Ginger asked, her tone tinged with

panic. "How could Vanessa drop her purse in your parking lot? I called Steve, but he didn't answer. His plane isn't supposed to leave until tomorrow morning."

Zia Noemi tsked aloud. I'd already sent a text to Detective Mason, in case we didn't find Vanessa. If it was a false alarm, no harm done. Why would she abandon her purse, an expensive Gucci? Something strange must have happened to her. And now her husband was MIA, according to Ginger. That didn't bode well.

"Let's form a search party." Barbara Davison looked at Eric for approval. He seemed as confused as the rest of the group. "Vanessa might be in trouble—"

"Oh, Mom, why would she be?" Debbie shook her head. "Maybe she got here early, and her purse fell out of her car. What if she didn't see it, and thought she left it at home. She may have gone back to get it. Your parking lot is so dark, Eric."

"I hired a contractor to install lights," he retorted, "but he's booked till spring."

"We should call the police," Maddie said quietly. "Even if she did return home, she should have been back by now."

"It's nearly half past eight," Ginger said, wringing her hands. "Vanessa and Steve have been quarreling a lot worse, ever since Dylan's murder—"

"That's crazy," Kim interrupted, clearly bored. "Hey, I bet that's Vanessa now."

We all turned at the sound of footsteps, but one of Eric's staff entered the room. Steve Leeson ambled after her, and stopped short when Ginger stabbed a finger at him.

"Where's Vanessa?"

"Isn't she here?" He tore off his knitted cap and scratched his untidy red hair. "She told me she had some meeting and then this paint party. I called Vanessa a few times earlier, but she never answered."

Maddie held up the cell phone. "It's locked, so I can't tell who's called."

"But where could she be?" Cissy asked.

Steve took the phone from Maddie and swiped a pattern on it. "Her voice mailbox is full. But see, I did call. So did Ginger. I haven't seen Vanessa since breakfast."

Cissy tossed her blond hair from her eyes. "She's never late for anything."

"That's weird."

Steve avoided our gazes, however, and I smelled alcohol on his breath. Was he telling the truth? He'd also been drinking a lot the night of the rehearsal dinner, too. And his business trip seemed a little convenient, to my thinking.

"What kind of meeting did she have?" I asked him.

Steve shrugged. "No idea. She never tells me much about her work."

"You never ask her!" Ginger sounded exasperated. "I doubt if you ever cared when she stayed out late before. It's true Vanessa is a bit secretive, but a husband should know where his wife's going in case she runs into trouble."

"Hey, she always takes her phone with her—"

"Not today," Zia Noemi said, her tone firm.

"How would I know where she is?" Steve glanced around, as if we'd snap our fingers and produce his wife. His defensive tone also didn't gain much sympathy from anyone. "I called her a bunch of times. You must have seen her, Dyer."

"No, she didn't come inside," Eric said stubbornly. "None of the windows face the parking lot, so we never know who's out there. Punks have been racing around, in fact, but only the neighbors witnessed that. I'm going to install a few cameras along with lights, but not until the contractor can get out here."

Eric's dad suddenly hurried into the back room. He wore a heavy overcoat and gloves, and looked startled to see us all gathered together. As tall as Eric and muscular, but with silver hair and blue eyes, Keith Dyer cleared his throat.

"Can I talk to you, son? It's important."

"What?"

"An emergency, Eric. We'd better speak in private."

I didn't like the sound of that.

Chapter 19

Eric blinked. "What emergency—"

"Wait." Maddie faced his dad. "We need to call the police, Mr. Dyer. Vanessa Leeson, one of the bridesmaids, is missing. She never showed up for the paint party, and someone found her purse in the parking lot outside. We believe she must have been here at some point, though. So if there's been trouble, we ought to call 9-1-1."

Keith Dyer let out a deep sigh. "I called Chief Russell. He's sending a squad car."

"Is it Vanessa?" Ginger shrieked. "What happened?"

Gisele and Claudia grabbed each other's hands, and Zia Noemi moaned in dismay. Even Kim looked sick. "Where is she?" Cissy demanded.

"Ladies, please," he said, and held up his hands. "Give us some time to talk for a minute or two. Go on back to your painting."

"But something must be wrong if you called the cops," Debbie said. "Tell us."

Keith didn't look pleased. "I understand you're all upset, but I can't explain anything until the police arrive."

"You found Vanessa, didn't you? Is she hurt?"

Ginger sagged in a near faint, but Barbara Davison snaked an arm around her waist and kept her from falling. Cissy clutched her rabbit fur vest, whimpering. Keith gave a brief nod to Eric, who gazed at Maddie with helplessness. She walked over and clasped his hand.

"Where's Vanessa?" Debbie demanded. "What happened to her?"

"She's at the hospital," Ginger said, her tone hopeful. "I bet she was in a car accident! Our family's cursed—"

I could tell something far worse had happened to Vanessa, given Keith's refusal to reply. That didn't help the older women, either, who drew Ginger away to sit on a nearby bench before she collapsed. Cissy and Debbie murmured together. Kim looked pale and cradled her stomach, as if in pain. I inched closer to Maddie and whispered in her ear.

"I'm going outside. You coming?"

I heard the police siren's wail while we grabbed our coats. Eric led the way through the maze of barrels to the back door. His dad switched on a huge flashlight before we headed into the night. My boots crunched on the rutted snow. When I skidded on a patch of ice, I gripped Maddie's arm. We couldn't see much except what showed in the circle of light ahead of us, since we were so far behind the man. I bumped into a large wooden barrel.

"I thought Eric used metal kegs for his beer." I rubbed my sore elbow.

"He uses these for wine making. It's more traditional, using oak."

"Gotcha. They're a lot bigger than the ones inside, that's why I asked."

"He bought these wholesale," Maddie said. "Remember

he wants to do more ice wine, and other types if the grapes grow in the orchard he bought."

"He must be doing okay, if he's expanding into wine."

"I don't ask about his business, since he's risking a lot. He knows I'm in the same boat. Starting a new venture takes guts and a ton of money."

"You know Mom and Dad would loan you anything you need."

"Yeah, but I'd rather not." Maddie sounded wistful. "If Silver Moon tanks, I'd feel bad not being able to pay them back. Work's coming in, don't get me wrong. But things can change in a heartbeat. Look what happened to Kip O'Sullivan and his Traverse City art gallery."

"He brought trouble on himself," I said, "but let's not talk about all that."

"I know. It's too painful—"

She stopped when a Silver Hollow police car careened and bounced over the parking lot, and then slid sideways. Snow and ice spewed in a wide circle. The car stopped a few inches from a sleek black Lexus. Whoa. That was close.

"You almost hit my car," Keith called out in anger.

Officer Sykes scrambled from behind the wheel. He didn't apologize, however, and swaggered over to join us near the brewery's farthest end. I couldn't tell what Keith had found, or where, given the row of wooden barrels that marched off into the darkness.

"The medical examiner's team should arrive any minute."

I hadn't noticed that Ginger and Zia Noemi had followed us, until the older women both moaned aloud. "She's dead," Ginger cried. "Oh, my poor baby—"

"Take her inside," Keith ordered, so Gus's aunt obeyed. He turned to Digger Sykes, his flashlight beam pointing upward to the sky. "Do you want me to show you the barrel?"

He shook his head. "Better not mess up any footprints near the scene."

"Or tire tracks," Maddie whispered to me. "Digger already ruined that."

Cissy had trudged out to join us also, but now waved a bare hand and turned back toward the brewery's door. She pushed Debbie along despite her sister's protests. "I can't handle this," Cissy said. "I'm calling Gus."

Shivering, she marched Debbie to meet Barbara Davison in the doorway. Gisele and Claudia turned and ran inside the building like frightened rabbits. I wished I had a flashlight, but I noticed how Steve Leeson hung back, unwilling to stand near the other men.

Kim Goddard's breath steamed in the air when she walked up to me. "Think I'm gonna pass on this, too, Sasha. You can tell me what happens later."

"Sure."

I watched her trudge to the back door. Maddie nudged me, so I turned to see Digger wave at an approaching van. It bumped over the snowy parking lot and halted near him. The forensics team piled out, conferred with Digger for several minutes, and then pulled out their equipment from the van's back; they quickly set up tall lights, prepared cameras and evidence bags, and then roped off the area with crime scene tape. They worked faster than I'd expected.

Following Eric, Keith, and Digger, Maddie and I carefully picked our way over the icy ground. The team surrounded a row of oak barrels at the farthest end. A few had been knocked on their sides. I stumbled over a broken wooden pallet in the darkness.

My sister grabbed me before I fell. "Whoa, Sash. Those boards are dangerous with all the nails sticking out of them. Eric should clean this lot up in daylight."

When Keith pointed out a particular barrel, the forensics

team began their investigation. In the light's strong beams, I noted plenty of boot and shoe prints marking the snow. Many crisscrossed each other. Eric's distress was plain.

"Someone should identify the body," he said, his voice low.

Digger overheard him. "You're the husband, right?" he said to Steve Leeson. "Guess you're the one to do it."

The forensics team showed him exactly where to step in order to walk close to the barrel. Steve chewed on his bottom lip and then slowly peeked over the metal rim. He staggered backward with a pitiful whimper.

"Yes. It is—Vanessa."

I turned away, sick at heart. Steve Leeson sank to his knees, head in his hands, and rocked back and forth. A pair of evidence techs lifted the crumpled figure from the interior and laid Vanessa on a large plastic sheet. Her long blond hair fanned out behind her head, which lolled to one side. Horrified, I noted her bluish skin, bloodshot eyes, and protruding swollen tongue. My heart leaped into my throat when I saw deep bruises around her neck. The killer had choked her and then stuffed Vanessa into the barrel like a discarded rug.

Steve Leeson struggled to rise, lurching a bit. "Who did this to my wife?"

"The investigation is beginning, sir. Calm down."

"I'll kill him—"

Keith and Eric dragged Steve, who continued to curse and rant, back to the brewery. Maddie and I lingered. Digger didn't speak, leaning down to peer closer at Vanessa's face and neck. The medical examiner pointed out several things, his voice low, before Digger backed away. Then he rushed off into the darkness. We heard retching sounds.

"I bet he'll stop joking about you being a dead-body magnet after this," Maddie said. "How can homicide detectives and forensics professionals remain so calm? I'm feeling sick to my stomach. Come on, let's go."

I followed her back toward the building, wondering the same thing about Detective Mason. Then again, he usually arrived at a homicide scene after the investigating team had bagged the body and processed evidence. Maybe Mason had grown numb after visiting crime scenes during his career. I knew I'd never get to that point, where the senses were dulled to the aftermath of evil.

My hands shook, and I had a sour taste in my mouth. Something odd struck me. Vanessa had been wearing a pink blouse with a bow, and a bedraggled black skirt. But no coat.

"I wonder if whoever killed her brought the body here."

"Why would you think that?" Maddie asked.

"Where's her winter coat?" I tapped my phone and opened Google. "It's pretty cold today. She would have worn one, if she was meeting someone here."

"That's true."

"The cold temperature may have kept rigor mortis from setting in, too. This website claims it takes effect within four hours, unless the body is frozen. Vanessa could have been killed early this morning, put in a car's trunk, and then brought here."

"And no one on staff would have seen them," Maddie said, a little breathless, "because there's no windows facing this lot. Unless a neighbor noticed something."

"Maybe." I checked the weather app on my phone. "It's twenty-five degrees now, and it didn't get up past the freezing point today, despite that sunshine we had around noon. I walked the dogs for ten minutes. They didn't want to stay out long."

Digger Sykes walked slowly back to join us at the brewery's door. He looked shamefaced until Maddie touched his arm. "It's okay. We understand," she said softly. "Vanessa Leeson was one of the bridesmaids in Cissy and Gus's wedding."

"Gotcha. Pretty sad, all around."

A low-slung sports car, probably a Mazda and fairly new from what I could tell in the dim light, pulled into the lot. I groaned when Detective Phil Hunter climbed from behind the wheel, locked his car, and then loped over to join us.

"What's going on?"

"Didn't expect to see you," Digger said. "Where's Mason?"

"Busy, I guess." He hooked a thumb in my direction. "How come the Silverman chicks are always around when someone gets murdered?"

Maddie caught my arm before I could speak. To my surprise, Digger clenched his fists. "Why don't you go crawl back under your rock?"

"Watch it, or I'll report you for mouthing off to a superior."

"Superior, my foot! Go soak your fat head—"

An SUV bumped its way over the parking lot. Detective Greg Mason jumped out, pulled on a heavy parka, and then ambled our way. He was a far cry from lean and mean Hunter in his pricey cashmere coat and leather gloves, and whose wary, ice blue eyes studied everything. I still preferred Mason's easygoing manner. The stocky detective crammed bare hands into his pockets and eyed us with interest.

"Heard a woman was found strangled."

Mason ignored Hunter's glare while my sister and I explained the whole story. "What if the killer is trying to frame Eric by leaving Vanessa's body here?" Maddie asked.

He looked skeptical, however. "It's too early for theories."

"But it's possible she was killed somewhere else," I said, "since she isn't wearing a coat. This has got to be tied to Dylan Campbell's murder. They're both in the wedding party."

Phil Hunter chuckled. "That wedding's got a bad vibe going for it."

"Another inappropriate comment," Mason said to him, "like last week. Guess you forgot what the captain said at the meeting."

He left abruptly and walked to the brewery. Phil Hunter's open contempt annoyed me, but Maddie turned to Digger.

"Do you think these murders are connected?"

"Yeah. Some people will do anything for love or money."

"Like you have a lot of experience in crime solving," Hunter said.

He followed Mason toward the brewery. Digger gave him the finger in reply, although the detective's back was turned. I shivered in the cold wind.

"What a piece of work," Maddie said. "Why does he bother helping with Mason's cases here, if Silver Hollow is so unworthy of his attention?"

"He's gotta stroke his ego," Digger said. "Forget him."

"Come on, Sash. Let's get warm inside."

My sister led the way back over the dark parking lot, slipping and sliding on ice. Maddie followed me when I made a beeline for the restroom. Even after splashing warm water on my face, I stood before the row of sinks. Numb, breathing deep and avoiding my reflection in the mirror, I waited another five minutes until I felt calm enough to think straight. But I couldn't banish the sight of Vanessa's body from my memory.

Had she realized some important information about Dylan's murder, and planned to meet the killer? And then realized too late what he might do? I hoped she'd fought against a sudden attack when he grabbed her throat, and clawed him deep enough to leave marks. It had to be a man. Nobody else could have gripped her throat and hung on, fighting against her

struggles. She'd broken off at least one of her acrylic fingernails, after all.

"Are you okay?" Maddie asked. "I feel like someone
punched me in the gut."

"Me too." I took another deep breath. "Who would have
done such a coldhearted thing? Strangling her and then dumping her in a barrel like that. I think you're right. Someone is
trying to frame Eric."

Maddie nodded. "Why leave the body here, otherwise?
They could have left Vanessa anywhere around Silver Hollow. Even Phil Hunter's right. Cissy's wedding is turning out
to be a real fiasco. First Dylan was murdered, and now
Vanessa."

"I don't care what Mason thinks, they're connected. And
wouldn't you say the killer is a guy, given those deep bruises
on her neck? I think they were finger marks, anyway."

"Some women might be strong enough to do that."

"Hmm. Maybe, but whoever killed Dylan must have
wanted to eliminate Vanessa."

"But why?" Maddie asked.

"Either she found out something, or said something at one
point to make the killer think she knew what he did."

"So you think Vanessa saw something at the Regency
Hotel? Like whoever lured him into the women's restroom!
She stood near the hallway, remember."

"Or she could have seen the killer leave, with blood on
their clothes."

"We could be wrong about this whole thing. Remember
what Ginger said, that Steve and Vanessa weren't getting
along lately. What if he killed her?" My sister bit her lip. "The
spouse is usually the first suspect in any murder, you know."

"Yeah, that's true. And it could be Steve wants to throw
off suspicion by letting people think her death is tied to
Dylan's murder."

"We need to find out a lot more about Steve and Vanessa's relationship," Maddie said. "Even if it means questioning Ginger."

"There's something else I noticed. Vanessa only had one shoe, did you see that? Where's the other one? That might point to where she was killed."

"So we need to figure out how bad their marriage was, if they were close to divorce."

I nodded. "And where Vanessa left her coat. Either at home, or at work."

Plus find her missing shoe.

Chapter 20

I stopped halfway through the maze of barrels, hearing angry voices. Maddie bumped into my back. "Oof. Sorry," she whispered. "What's going on?"

"Mason is questioning Steve Leeson."

We peeked around the closest barrel. Mason stood, notebook in hand, while Steve Leeson perched on a chair. Eric and Keith Dyer blocked the way to the tasting room. Cissy and the other women were chatting in high-pitched voices, muffled by the closed door.

To my eye, Vanessa's husband seemed far more agitated than grief-stricken. "I told you, I only saw her at breakfast," Steve said.

"What time?"

"I don't know! Eight, or maybe seven thirty."

He refused to meet the detective's gaze. That was another mark to put in the suspicious column. Over the past six months, since our sales rep's murder in our factory, I'd read about how police questioned suspects and what to watch for in their reactions. Especially if they were lying. Mason turned to Eric next.

"When did you say that Mr. Leeson arrived today?"

One of his staff answered. "Around noon."

"To pick up my order," Steve added in irritation.

I nudged Maddie. "He came here earlier today? Whoa."

Mason didn't look up from his notebook. "What did you pick up, a keg of beer?"

"A couple of growlers. Is it against the law to buy beer?"

"I never said that, Mr. Leeson."

Mason waited, as if expecting him to reply, but Steve kept silent. The detective jotted more notes and flipped a page. I suspected that was a deliberate ploy to make a subject rethink their answers. It also made Steve more nervous. His already flushed face turned darker. He kept wiping his face, shifting on the chair, scratching his beard, and tapping his knees with his fingers. After several minutes of silence, he finally spoke.

"When I got here today, I didn't see Vanessa or her car. I didn't expect to see her. She was at work in Ann Arbor, at the real estate company."

"What time was her meeting?" Mason asked.

He shrugged. "She didn't tell me."

"Where were you at noon, Mr. Dyer?" The detective had turned to face Eric, who looked startled. "You were on the premises, correct? Did you see Mr. Leeson?"

"No. I was on the phone talking to a distributor around that time. Patti can verify that. She takes over in front for me when I'm too busy to handle customers."

"That's right," the woman offered, hands in her apron pockets. "Mr. Leeson came in around five minutes after twelve."

Phil Hunter spoke up. "What type of beer did Leeson order?"

"Our specialty IPA, called the Crow's Nest," Patti said.

"It has six different flavors: nuts, pineapple, grapefruit, orange, passion fruit, and mango. Our most popular."

"So, given this guy's red hair and beard, you recognized him."

She nodded, her blue eyes bright behind wire-rimmed glasses. "Mr. Leeson's ordered it many times before today, and always picked it up here."

"Because I can't find it in any stores." Steve sounded sullen.

"That's why I was talking to a distributor," Eric said. "Nick Rizzo recommended them, but I'm not sure if we're ready for that. Bottling is an expensive process."

"How busy was it here during the day?" Mason asked next, eyeing both Patti and Eric. "Did you have other customers, up until the ladies arrived for their paint party?"

"Half a dozen, I'd say," Eric said. Patti nodded as well. "It's quieter during the week, although we get a lot of people in on Friday and Saturday."

Hunter addressed Steve. "So your wife didn't tell you who she was meeting, or where? Not even with a text message?"

"No. I said that already." He gazed at the ceiling and then beyond Hunter, as if Steve could see the women in the tasting room. "No matter what my mother-in-law says, I did ask Vanessa. She kept secrets from me, all the time."

"You're scheduled for an out-of-town trip," Mason said, checking his notes.

"My boss is sending me to Chicago." Steve sounded defensive again and clasped his hands together. A bead of sweat trickled down his face. "A training session that starts tomorrow. I work in computer software analysis, and network security."

"Seems awfully convenient," Hunter said. "You never denied killing her—"

"What?"

"It's pretty obvious you met your wife this afternoon in the parking lot, strangled her, and left her in that barrel outside."

Steve Leeson stared at him openmouthed. "I didn't kill Vanessa. I swear to God, you've got to believe me."

"Funny thing, that's what a lot of guilty people say." The detective hooked a thumb at Digger, adding, "How about if Bozo and I take Leeson to the station, Mason? We'll fingerprint him, make sure he doesn't have any record of domestic disputes. I'd say it's possible he showed up tonight to make sure the body was found."

"Are you crazy?" Steve's already red face turned purple, and he banged a fist on the nearest table. "If I had killed Vanessa, I'd have left town already!"

"Uh-huh." Hunter snorted. "Sure, dude. Easy for you to say now."

"What is this, bad cop, good cop? Am I under arrest?"

"No." Mason looked annoyed. "I'm sorry for Detective Hunter's statements, sir, and want you to know I appreciate your cooperation."

"I love my wife. I'd never hurt her."

"I understand that. Did you go back to work, Mr. Leeson, after you left earlier?"

But Hunter had muttered something under his breath about a lawyer—if I'd heard right. Steve overheard it as well and ignored Mason's question. He pulled out his phone.

"Good idea. I'm calling a lawyer right now."

"Tell him to meet you at the Ann Arbor station," Hunter said. "Not the dinky one in Silver Hollow that looks like a roach motel."

"Hey!"

Digger looked indignant. Maddie and I had been hanging

back, but we stalked forward as one to glare at Hunter. Even though I suspected he'd said that to bait us all. He'd succeeded, too, given Mason's piercing gaze.

"Enough, Phil."

"What? It's rectangular, with black windows."

"I said enough. Maybe you could—"

"Take a hike?" Hunter grinned. "I'd rather take this guy to the station."

Steve had finished his phone call. "My lawyer told me I don't have to answer any further questions without him being present."

Mason held up a hand. "We'll be in touch, Mr. Leeson, if we have anything else to ask you. But please inform your employer that you cannot leave town for the near future."

"But I need that training in Chicago."

"Have your boss call me if he has any questions." Mason handed him a card. "And our sincere condolences on the loss of your wife."

Steve blinked, owlishly, as if remembering Vanessa was dead. Without another word, he ambled in a daze toward the brewery's entrance. Hunter watched him for a minute and then let out a blue streak of curses.

"What the hell are you doing, letting him go like that?"

"He lawyered up, Phil, thanks to you," Mason shot back.

"How much you wanna bet that guy killed his wife when he was here at noon? Two birds with one stone, that's my take. Probably took out a whopping life insurance policy on her, too. What more do you need to figure this out?"

"Evidence. But we'll check out the life insurance angle, just in case, and wait for the ME report. We don't have a time of death yet, Phil, for God's sake. So calm down—"

"We still need his fingerprints—"

"We'll get them, if they don't show up in the database."

Hunter slapped the table, still fuming. "What's the lab result from that ice pick, Perry Mason? Any fingerprints? What about a search warrant for Frank Antonini?"

"All in good time." Mason moved closer, a few inches from the other detective's face, and his tone held a warning. "The name's Greg. Not Perry Mason or any other insult you toss out. You got that? I'll get a search warrant for Leeson's computer and residence. Remember how you were supposed to call Chicago PD and find out any information on Frank Antonini. Have you done that yet? Yeah, I didn't think so."

The tension between them was so thick, I could smell it. Maddie whispered "Wow" in my ear. The two detectives faced each other, fists curled, their bodies stiff. Hunter towered over Mason, a good three or four inches taller. I shouldn't have been surprised to witness this match, given their past history of antagonism. Hunter looked furious, eyes flashing to me and my sister, but he didn't get a chance to reply before Mason spoke again.

"Go write up your report and email it. I'll check the lab report for the time of death and text you. When I get a chance."

"Sure. You do that."

Hunter vanished into the maze that led to the parking lot. The back door slammed, echoing in the building, and the sound rose to the beamed rafters before it faded. Maddie's worry increased while Mason questioned Eric about his business hours and staff.

"You don't have any available surveillance videos?" the detective asked.

"I didn't think we needed security cameras." Eric wiped his hands on his jeans. "We've only been in operation a few months. It's quiet out here, just farms and little traffic."

"Not many people in the area know that Silver Claw is here, in fact," Maddie offered. "That's why Eric's been hosting taste-testing parties and trivia nights. Every visitor gets to sample his specialty wines, too."

Mason turned to Keith Dyer. "How did you find the body?" he asked.

"Saw a wild animal nosing around the barrels in back," Keith said. "So I checked it out."

I knew without a doubt that the notoriety of a dead body found in a wine barrel behind Silver Claw would soon draw a huge crowd. During every factory tour with the exception of elementary school groups, I had to field questions about Will Taylor's gruesome murder. That was unsettling at first, and then annoying—especially since people wanted to see where it took place. No doubt the same thing would happen to Eric's microbrewery.

While Mason continued his questions, my thoughts strayed. Was there a connection between Dylan's and Vanessa's murders? I wondered if Vanessa saw Frank Antonini enter the ladies' restroom the night of the rehearsal dinner. Would she dare ask to meet him, knowing he had a dangerous temper? Was Claudia right about Debbie Davison being his partner in the crime? After all, she'd used his knife to slash Dylan's tires.

Maybe Debbie had lured Dylan into the bathroom, where Frank waited. But I doubted if Dylan would fall for that ploy. He didn't trust Debbie. I also doubted that she had enough strength to strangle Vanessa, dump her body in the wine barrel out back, and calmly show up to the paint party. She was thoughtless, given her act of vandalism, but a second murder might cancel her sister's wedding altogether. Debbie wouldn't risk that.

"So you knew Mr. Campbell and met him before the bachelor party?" Mason asked.

Eric nodded. "I saw him in Traverse City a few times, but only when Gus invited a bunch of his friends. I didn't really know Dylan."

"How much did you lose at poker at that party?"

"Three hundred bucks. Same as Frank."

Mason jotted that down. "How well did you know Mrs. Leeson?"

"Not very well. Beyond saying hi to Vanessa and Steve, that was it," Eric added. "But they're close friends with Cissy and Gus."

I watched as Zia Noemi led Ginger out of the tasting room. They both wore coats, and shook their heads when Mason hurried over to intercept them. He flipped to a fresh page of his notebook, but Ginger swayed on her feet.

"Give the poor woman some time to recover," Gus's aunt scolded. "Call on her later if you must ask questions."

Mason let them go, frowning as he watched, along with Gisele, Claudia, and Barbara Davison. Cissy and Debbie huddled together inside the tasting room, whispering together. Kim Goddard walked out holding a full wineglass, her coat and purse slung over her arm. She seemed to radiate a steely resolve. I wondered why she didn't follow the others, but Kim hung back. As if curious to overhear Mason when he resumed questioning Eric.

That intrigued me. I hadn't eliminated her from my suspect list, after all. And using an ice pick instead of her handgun would have diverted attention. What if Kim had lured Dylan into the restroom, to his death? Maybe Vanessa had witnessed her involvement, either acting alone or in league with Frank Antonini. Was it possible? I tapped a finger against my chin, wondering if those two had worked together.

"—started the fight?" Mason had resumed questioning Eric. "The night of the bachelor party, at Flambé."

"Pretty sure Nick Rizzo threw the first punch. Frank got in a good one, too, and so did I," he said, sounding weary. Maddie folded her arms over her chest.

"Is there any surveillance video of what happened?" she asked.

"I'm still waiting for the owner to get back to me," the detective said.

I considered the rest of Dylan's friends as possible suspects while listening to Mason's interrogation. What if Vanessa had shown up early this afternoon, surprising Eric, and accused him of murder? Would he have strangled her? And then put her body out back, not having much time to hide it—but he'd looked as shocked as everyone when Keith Dyer arrived to tell him the news. I doubted if Eric could maintain a feigned innocence for long.

Maddie's theory of the killer framing him made far more sense.

I didn't think Bob Vaccaro knew Dylan at all, and he hadn't played much poker. But Nick Rizzo did, and he'd been angry over Dylan's cheating. He'd also spied on Dylan and Claudia— then told Frank. That led right back to Gus's cousin. Frank checked all the boxes with a double motive. Dylan cheated him at poker, and then tried to cheat with Frank's wife as payback for stealing his winnings. Frank also knew how to kill with any weapon close at hand.

I stopped, a sudden thought taking form in my mind. What if Frank had asked Vanessa to lure Dylan into the restroom? Eliminating her tied up that loose end. Would he have asked her to do that, though? I wasn't sure she knew him that well. Hmm.

"Too bad Vanessa didn't tell someone about who she was meeting," Kim said, her voice low. She drained her wine and raised an eyebrow at me, as if expecting an answer.

"Who's her closest friend, I wonder. Cissy?"

"Or me, if she couldn't get Cissy. We usually called each other every day or so, but then Vanessa hasn't been acting like herself since Dylan's murder. I asked her a few days ago what was wrong, but she wouldn't talk about it."

"Do you think Steve killed her?" I asked bluntly.

Kim shrugged. "I dunno. But Vanessa's mom is right, because their marriage was on the rocks. They were seeing a counselor for a while."

"Is it true that Vanessa dated Dylan a few years ago?"

"Oh, yeah. Long before he met Debbie. Steve was jealous, even though Vanessa ended things with Dylan before she started dating him. I think Steve worried that she'd divorce him, maybe go back to her old flame. Although that seemed unlikely, given what Dylan did." Kim leaned against the tasting room's doorway. "I mean, she never forgave him for that accident. Why else would he show up at the bachelorette party, claiming he was innocent?"

"But he wasn't, if he ended up with a conviction," I said. "Right?"

"I guess so. Wonder if Steve snapped. Maybe got rid of Dylan, and then Vanessa when she suspected him—"

"Hey, Sasha." Maddie's interruption startled me. My sister beckoned from inside the tasting room. "I promised Eric we'd clean up after the party."

Kim handed me her empty glass. "Guess you might want this, then."

I followed Maddie with a backward glance at Mason and Eric, who continued to answer questions. Inside the tasting room, painted canvases had been abandoned on the tables along with crumpled paper towels, open paint tubes, and ruined brushes. What a shame the party had been ruined by more tragedy. My sister and I sorted and collected supplies, storing everything in boxes, and then stuffed the plastic table coverings in the trash. Cissy and Debbie huddled in one corner, clearly uninterested in helping.

Maddie frowned after counting the bottles of unopened

wine. "Wanna bet Gisele and Claudia hid some under their coats? Three are missing, and that's gonna cost me. Oh well." She plucked up a canvas and walked over to Cissy. "Here's your painting. It's dry."

"No way do I want that." Her voice was tinged with hysteria. "That would remind me of what happened tonight. Poor Vanessa! And if the police expect me and Gus to postpone our wedding again, we'll just elope."

"You will not, because I'll never get a chance to be maid of honor again." Debbie waved a hand toward the door. "Let's go."

Digger Sykes blocked them, however. "Sorry, ladies. You can't leave until Detective Mason takes a statement from you."

"We didn't have anything to do with Vanessa's death," Debbie said, her cheeks pinker. "I'm sure Steve did it. I heard what that other detective said. The guy that Kristen Bloom dated, only she broke it off on New Year's Day."

"He dumped her," Digger said. "That's what I heard."

"Nah, she got tired of his antics—"

"Officer Sykes!"

He bolted from the room to answer Mason's bellowed summons. Cissy and Debbie both giggled. Everyone knew Digger couldn't resist gossip. Maddie sighed, glancing at the ceiling, and tried to wash out a few paint-caked brushes.

Kim walked into the tasting room, clearly amused. "I saw Detective Hunter at the casino downtown in Detroit. I didn't realize he was a cop at the time, though."

"Oh? When was this?" I asked her.

She helped me move a table so that Maddie could collect the floor plastic. "Early in January. Phil Hunter, right? He was with a tall, leggy redhead, but I didn't catch her name. Both of them were dressed to the nines. He wore a tux, she had a slinky gown, sequins, and high heels. The works in terms of hair, nails, and makeup, too."

Maddie shrugged. "Maybe he was working undercover."

"No idea," Kim said. "I met Dylan that night, for some fun. But he had a streak of bad luck. Lost a few grand, so no wonder he cheated during the bachelor party's poker game. Probably needed to make up that big loss."

"That's why he got mad when Frank swiped some winnings," I said.

"Gus's cousin is a real wild card," Kim said. "Gisele told me he always takes advantage whenever he sees an opportunity."

"That's true," Debbie said. "Frank's money hungry, too. Claudia told Gisele that they're so much in debt, he won't let her spend an extra penny."

"Then why did she use shopping as an excuse when she met Dylan that Friday afternoon, before the rehearsal?" I asked. "No wonder Frank didn't believe her."

"I don't care anymore," Cissy said, and turned to Debbie. "We're leaving. And if that detective tries to keep us here, call Flynn Hanson. He told you to call anytime they bother you. See you all at the wedding Monday, but don't expect a rehearsal."

Debbie led the way past Digger Sykes, who stepped aside when both women glared at him. He looked over at Mason, who was still busy with Eric's staff. Kim shrugged and retrieved her two canvas paintings.

"Thanks for hosting the party tonight," she said, "and it's too bad Cissy hasn't shown any gratitude. All she thinks about is herself, but she's always been like that. I want my work, even if they're not that great. Do you think the cops will postpone Cissy's wedding again?"

"I don't know," Maddie said.

"I shouldn't be surprised that Debbie slashed Dylan's tires," Kim said. "She can be so vindictive. Dylan told me they loved pulling pranks on each other, only Debbie never bragged about that like he did. Once he put a tarantula in her bedroom. She freaked out! I saw the video he took, so she sprayed sugar water on his clothes and then asked him to help her one day with her bees. That's why they went after him."

"Is he allergic?" Maddie asked.

"He got stung enough to require treatment in the ER." Kim slipped into her coat. "Oh, you might not know this, but Dylan and Frank hated each other from the time they first met. I'm not surprised one of them ended up dead."

I listened to her echoing footsteps until the heavy front door slammed shut. I wondered if Kim was trying to deflect suspicion from herself, though, given all the details she'd mentioned about Debbie. The pranks she and Dylan pulled clearly pointed to immaturity. A tarantula was mostly harmless, as well as spiking a drink with ipecac, but slashing car tires? And getting stung by enough bees to require an emergency room visit sounded serious, too.

Kim also confirmed bitter animosity between Frank and Dylan, but I'd have to verify that with Eric or Gus before I believed it. While I still thought Frank Antonini was the most likely suspect, I wasn't about to rule out anyone else yet.

Without evidence, though, solving either murder seemed impossible.

Chapter 21

On Sunday after church, I pulled into the Silver Bear Shop's parking lot. "That silly dog, running around again," I muttered. Mr. Clooney raced down Theodore Lane to Silver Moon before I hopped out of the car. "Better catch him. If that's possible."

The sun peeked out of the gray clouds while I hurried after the poodle, but a stiff wind blew. Luckily, I had warm gloves, a scarf, and my wool peacoat. March might come in like a lamb or turn hellish with a lionlike roar. Michigan weather was so unpredictable.

"Here, Mr. Clooney! I've got a treat for you—" A bold-faced lie, since I only had an old tissue in my pocket. I needed a leash to hook on his collar. If he wore one at all.

Mr. Clooney ignored me and raced around the brick-and-glass building. Formerly the Flambé restaurant, it now housed Maddie's graphics design company in the front half and Jay's carving studio in back. Zoe Fisher hunched over a table near one window, immersed in a project, and returned my wave. I continued the chase, but the dog ignored my pleading calls.

Suddenly I slid on muddy ground and ended up flat on my back. Right beside a steaming pile of fresh dog poop. Gross.

"That's it! Get over here, you mangy cur." Sidestepping the ominous pile, I made a wild grab, but he zipped right past me. "Dang. You are one stubborn mutt."

Good thing Cissy hadn't heard me call her prize-winning poodle a mutt. A ray of sunlight touched on something that gleamed, half-hidden, in a thawed clump of dog poop. I needed a few bags. Jay thought the Davisons ought to clean it all up, but I was tired of the mess.

"What is that?" I used my boot's toe to nudge the wink of light within the goop, and then squatted down in amazement. "A ring! I wonder if—"

I raced to Silver Moon's back door, but it didn't budge. Locked. Instead I raced around the building and banged on the front window. Zoe hurried to the door, unlocked it, and stepped aside when I rushed inside.

"Does Maddie have any plastic bags? Anything I can use," I added, panting hard. "Sorry, I'll explain after I get back."

"Uh, let me look."

I helped to search cabinets and drawers. Zoe found a pair of long dishwashing gloves, and I unearthed a box of plastic sandwich bags and several wrinkled grocery sacks. I snatched them all and thanked her in my excitement.

"Bless my sister for not tossing things in the trash."

"She's a fiend about keeping everything organized," Zoe called out when I was half out the door. "Maddie uses those gloves for screen printing, so she might want them back—"

"I'll buy her a new pair!"

Certain I'd struck a gold mine, or was it platinum and diamond, I raced around the corner and returned to the pile. After poking around with a gloved finger, I unearthed a circle studded with dirty gems. A few more twinkled in the sunshine. I slid the ring into a sandwich bag, sealed it, and then resumed my search. So Gus had given the rings to Dylan that night, out of the little silk bag attached to Mr. Clooney's collar, and the best man must have pocketed them.

"But there's only one so far," I mused aloud. "I remember how Dylan threw his coat onto the chair, and it slid off. You shook it like a toy. I bet the rings fell out and then you ate them."

Gus and his friends searched the banquet room that night, including the kitchen trash bags, but came up empty. I was surprised the dog had not gotten sick after gobbling them down, or required a vet visit for an X-ray of his abdomen. Even surgery.

"Gus's ring has got to be here, too. Somewhere."

For the next fifteen minutes, I dug through every sodden pile left by Cissy's dog beside or behind Silver Moon. Then I moved on to the yard behind the Davisons' house. Nada. The grass was brown and muddy, but everything seemed pristine for winter. Even the garden beds. Perhaps Barbara had hired a service to collect the dog's waste. If the second ring had come to light, the crew no doubt pocketed it for themselves.

I moved on toward the Silver Bear Shop's picket-fenced yard and studied a few patches of unmelted snow. Larger paw prints left by Cissy's dog mingled with Rosie's and Sugar Bear's prints. I saw several large poop piles, too. Ugh. Using a discarded branch, I poked through them. In the fifth mushy pile near a large arborvitae shrub, I was rewarded to spy the large diamond-encrusted ring. Hopefully, going through Mr. Clooney's digestive tract hadn't done either ring permanent damage. I bagged it and then stood still, thinking hard.

"I wonder if Frank expected to find the rings in Dylan's pockets after he stabbed him. If that's true, maybe I could use these as bait to get a confession."

Then again, given Vanessa's murder, that plan might backfire.

I trudged toward the house, stripped off the rubber gloves, and headed inside. Rosie and Sugar Bear both dashed over to greet me before I removed my boots. I felt a wave of guilt, since Aunt Marge stood at the kitchen sink and washed long romaine leaves. That was supposed to be my job. Mom stood at the counter and chopped celery, onions, and grapes, then mixed up the chicken salad. She arranged scoops on the clean leaves for our family's Sunday lunch.

Mom glanced at me when I crept past. "What have you got there?"

I scurried to the bathroom. "Gotta wash up!"

It took me a good ten minutes to clean the rings—first scrubbing them with hot, soapy water, and then soaking them in a small plastic jar filled with rubbing alcohol. After washing my hands twice, I screwed on the jar's top and stuck it in a drawer.

"Sorry, Mom," I said once I returned to the kitchen. "I was cleaning the yard."

"Good. Set the table for me so I can change, all right? I have a funeral visitation this afternoon. That's part of the mayor's job, supporting the bereaved in the community."

"Anyone I know?" I asked. Isabel's father was on his deathbed, and I knew she'd taken time off to sit with him in Silver Birches' nursing wing.

"A council member's mother. Mrs. Schwartz, she lived in Chelsea."

I nodded and quickly set the table. Dad and Uncle Hank wandered in, still talking about the upcoming baseball season, and continued while we ate lunch. Conversation flowed around me, baseball statistics, the mayoral election results, and the Bears for the Cure fundraiser, but my thoughts centered on the investigation. I barely noticed when my parents left. I composed a long, explanatory text to Detective Mason, studied it, and then sent it off.

Aunt Marge nudged my arm. "Sasha? I'll wash the dishes if you dry."

"We have a dishwasher—"

"I'm old-fashioned, I suppose. It won't take long," she said.

I didn't have the heart to object. Leaving my chicken salad half-eaten, I gathered the plates, cups, and flatware and set them in the sink. Uncle Hank snored in my dad's favorite recliner—how had I missed hearing that loud noise? Talk about being in a daze. But I couldn't help worrying about how Mason would react to my text. Would he show up out of the blue to claim Cissy's and Gus's rings?

My aunt nudged me. "Thinking about the wedding tomorrow?"

"I haven't heard if it's still on, actually," I said.

Aunt Marge seemed surprised. "Odd how murder has disrupted the couple's plans twice. Your mother told me that her friend Barbara is a bundle of nerves."

"Yes, given what's happened."

I collected a fresh towel, dried each piece, and stored them in the cabinets. We worked in companionable silence. I remembered my mother's worries before my wedding to Flynn Hanson. My parents spent far too much money and effort to help in the preparations. At the time, given my own stress, I hadn't appreciated it. Deep guilt hit me hard after the divorce. That guilt played a big part in my accepting the job as manager of the Silver Bear Shop after Dad retired.

Reluctantly at first, but I never regretted it.

Aunt Marge handed me the last serving spoon. "So, Sasha. How are you?"

I blinked. "Fine."

"You don't look fine." She smiled at my confusion. "I've been worried about you and your sister. Maddie's so busy, but she thrives on it. Judith has kept me hopping since we arrived, but you seem distracted, and numb. If you want to chat, I have time now."

"That's so sweet of you, but I'm okay."

On impulse, I hugged her. No way was I going to burden Aunt Marge with how to prove Debbie's innocence, plus my worries about the upcoming wedding and the Bears for the Cure fundraiser. She had worries of her own. But I felt loved, and that lifted my spirits.

Aunt Marge ended our hug and pushed a strand of blond hair out of my eyes. "No matter what happens, Sasha, things always work out—"

"In the end," I finished. "That was Grandpa T. R.'s favorite saying."

"Sometimes he also told me that 'after everything is said and done, family is the most important.'" She smiled again. "I'm so glad you and Maddie are close as sisters. I hardly talk to my brother, even though he moved to LA and is not that far from us. But I'm thankful for Judith and Alex. We always enjoy a nice chat on the phone. Did you know they're thinking of coming out to Arizona for a week? If your mom can ever take a vacation."

"She'll find a way." I squeezed her hands. "Even if she has to work online, or take phone calls to keep on top of things."

"Too many young people have drifted apart from their loved ones in the world. They rely on social media, television, or playing video games." Aunt Marge's voice shook with sadness. "My Angela does, but she says it helps her handle stress."

"Everyone has to make choices."

Aunt Marge nodded. "I may be judgmental, but I wish she'd find more productive ways to deal with stress instead of falling back on nonreality."

I didn't know how to reply to that. "Everything will be great after the wedding. Then we can devote our time to the fundraiser."

"Another thing your grandfather said is 'All we can do is prepare the best we can, in the time we have, and worry less.'"

"I don't think he ever told me that—"

"Hey, you two." Uncle Hank stood in the doorway, bleary-eyed. "What's this about having time to worry?"

My aunt and I both chuckled. "Not quite," she said. "By the way, Angela called and she's bringing Katya next Friday, in time for the fundraiser. Alex and Judith bought their airfare. Isn't that wonderful?"

"I'll pay for half the cost." Uncle Hank frowned. "They've been squiring us around town, feeding us every day, and the girls have been putting us up for over a whole week."

"We should say putting up with us," Aunt Marge said.

"But we love having you here," I said. "Maddie's making a special welcome banner for the fundraiser on Saturday to hang over the football stadium's entrance."

"Hank is so blessed to have a generous family. We can't thank you enough."

"Everything she said and then some, kiddo." Uncle Hank hugged me tight. "I can't wait to see all those donated bears. I'll help build the corral, too."

"I want to call Angela back right now," my aunt said, "and tell her that I picked out a special outfit for Katya. Judith helped me shop for it this week."

Their infectious excitement lifted the dark, ominous cloud hanging over my head since the paint party. My cell chirped with an incoming text. I didn't recognize the number, but chose to open it out of curiosity. I was glad I did and grabbed my coat.

"Need to meet someone," I said. "Be right back."

Outside, my heart pounded in excitement while I race-walked across Theodore Lane and down the street. The text from Trina Wentworth sparked my interest. I prayed it wasn't bad news and waved to Tyler and Mary Walsh, who were busy taking down Christmas lights. Ahead, I saw Trina bundled up in a thick coat standing with a tall, lean man with gray hair. They chatted in front of the Davisons' house, right beside the SOLD sign.

"Guess who bought this house, Sasha," Trina called out. "Come meet my friend!"

I smiled at the stranger. "I take it you're from Scotland, and not Teddy Hartman."

"Never heard of the bloke. I'm Gavin MacRae," he said, and pumped my hand in a firm grip. "We accepted Mrs. Davison's counteroffer, because we didn't want to lose out buying this place. It's a risk, but we're good with it."

The man's Scottish accent delighted me. "So good to meet you, Mr. MacRae."

"We're in America, call me Gavin. Bonnie's still packing back home."

"I hope you'll love the village."

Trina squeezed my arm. "They will. And Sasha's mom is the mayor, Gavin, so that's a plus. She's already gotten the council to approve opening the lane onto Main Street, for two-way traffic and easier access. It's been rough every weekend, customers coming and going, with only one outlet to Kermit Street."

"And winter's nowhere near as busy as summer," I said. "Once they get bids from contractors, the work will begin."

"So I hear you've pulled off solving a few murders around the village," Gavin said with a mischievous grin. "Trina told me the other day. A real American Nancy Drew, eh? You wouldn't want to be called Jessica Fletcher, a young girl like you."

Tickled by his way of saying "pool" for "pull" and "gurr-el," I didn't correct him about being far beyond a girl in age. I didn't like being called Nancy Drew, Miss Marple, or Jessica Fletcher, but I refrained from admitting that.

"Really, I've only helped the local police."

"There's another case in the works." Trina rubbed her hands together with glee. "Who killed the groom's best man, and why? The wedding's tomorrow—"

"Sasha! I have news, can I talk to you for a minute?"

Debbie Davison waved from the front porch, so I excused myself and walked through the picket fence's open gate. I was halfway up the steps when Mr. Clooney bounded out the open door and almost knocked me off my feet. Luckily, I'd grabbed the railing and kept my balance. Since I'd found the wedding rings, I didn't have the heart to push him away. Debbie scolded him, though, but the dog ignored her.

Debbie slid her arms into her puffy coat's sleeves with a shiver. "Sorry about that. Mr. Clooney wriggles out of his collar every chance he gets. Cissy bought him a different harness, but it's more complicated than the other one."

She whistled when Mr. Clooney followed Trina and Gavin to the tearoom. I was shocked when the dog raced back to watch Debbie, as if expecting a treat. "Cissy is so mad, because the cops told her to postpone the wedding again," she said. "Can you believe it?"

"Given what happened to Vanessa, I'm not surprised," I said.

"Gus called the golf club, and they agreed to reschedule the wedding for next Sunday. Detective Mason said he needs more time to solve the case. If it's ever solved." Debbie let out a long breath. "I'm sure he suspects Steve or Frank. If one of them is guilty, that would leave you or Kim without a groomsman."

I didn't want to reply, since I thought pairing up the bridal party was a lesser problem than finding a killer. Debbie retrieved a piece of cheese from her pocket, held it out, and then while he chowed down, slipped the harness over Mr. Clooney's body and buckled it.

"People around here aren't happy about the first murder, and now there's been a second one." She sighed again and clipped a leash to the dog's harness. "The private investigators that Gus hired have talked to everyone in the bridal party—"

"Not me or Maddie," I interrupted.

Debbie blinked. "Oh. I dunno—maybe they figured since you two found the body, they could skip you. Or maybe the cops told them that."

"I hope it wasn't a wasted expense."

"Gus complained about the price, but it was his idea. They gave him a report, so they're done. He wouldn't tell me what they wrote, though."

I had no experience with how private investigators worked, or how they came to their conclusions, so I couldn't comment. "How much did they charge?"

"Seventy bucks an hour—unbelievable. At least with the two of them, it didn't take as long. Anyway, Gus told me the report was like twenty or thirty pages."

"Wow."

"I know. Cissy agreed to postpone the wedding one more time, but that's it. No matter what, even if the police don't have enough evidence to arrest anyone, they're getting married next Sunday at the golf club. Gus's aunt says that the third time's the charm. Nothing else should interfere with the wedding."

"I hope so." I meant it, too. "I better head home, but thanks for the update."

"By the way." Debbie's cheeks turned scarlet, and she clenched her fists. "You ought to know that Kim Goddard is a big, fat liar!"

"What do you mean?"

"She told you she dated Dylan, right? They had a casual fling, a one-night stand. That's all it was, and he never told Kim much at all."

I stepped back from her fury. "Uh—"

"She doesn't know squat about Vanessa and Dylan's relationship, either," Debbie rambled on. "He wanted to marry her, you know, but his gambling was a big roadblock. And then that car accident happened. Vanessa never forgave him for her niece's injuries."

"How long were they together?"

"Less than me and Dylan." Debbie sounded smug, as if she'd somehow bested Vanessa. When Mr. Clooney whined, she dragged him up the steps and shoved him inside the house. "And that was crazy when Dylan showed up at the bachelorette party, trying to convince her that he was innocent. My foot! Nick told me all about it."

"He was with Dylan, in Traverse City."

She nodded. "As a passenger, and he said Dylan couldn't see due to the fog and rain. Plus Dylan had a beer or two. That affected his reaction time." Debbie pulled on gloves over her reddened hands. "Nick admitted he'd had a few drinks, and felt terrible about giving testimony against Dylan in court. They've been friends since high school."

"If both of them were involved in the car accident," I said, "why didn't Vanessa blame Nick as well?"

"Because he helped her family pay for doctor's bills, and physical therapy. Dylan never gave them a dime, even when Gus and Nick suggested it. He'd racked up more gambling debts. Never learned to stop while he was ahead at the casino."

I glanced back at the Silver Bear Shop. Aunt Marge and Uncle Hank headed to their car. This conversation had been interesting, but I needed to walk my dogs. I suddenly remembered something else Kim had said, however.

"What's this about you and Dylan playing pranks on each other?"

"No big deal." Debbie's face flushed again, though, clearly in embarrassment. "Silly stuff, from the first time we met."

"He put a tarantula in your bedroom, and you sprayed him with sugar water—"

"Not that much," she cut in. "Dylan was such a baby. I asked him to help me move the hives, but he refused to put on protective gear. Then he smashed a few bees under his shoe, even when I warned him not to do that. So they swarmed him."

"The sugar water didn't help, though."

"I used the smoker to calm them down. It's not like Dylan needed an EpiPen. Just some antihistamine."

"But he did go to the ER, right? And you slashed his tires," I pointed out. "With a knife that Frank Antonini let you borrow. You said that's how you cut your hand."

"I didn't kill Dylan! I still loved him." Debbie's eyes filled with tears. "Sort of a love-hate thing, I guess. I know he hoped Vanessa would divorce Steve, and that could be why he got so jealous whenever Dylan talked to her. Maybe he's the killer."

I shrugged. "The police need evidence to prove anything."

"Yeah, I know." She brushed a tear from her cheek and then brightened. "Did I tell you they figured out my blood was on the dress? So I'm off the hook and so are you. I'm innocent, like I said all along."

"That's great," I said, wondering if Mason would confirm that.

"See you at the wedding next weekend."

Debbie quickly disappeared inside the house. I didn't cross her off my suspect list yet, but it did make things easier for my plan to work. Frank Antonini was dangerous, but Jay would be with me at the wedding. Along with Gus, Nick Rizzo, and

Eric Dyer. With that many men they could all handle him or Steve Leeson, however things turned out.

But I'd put money down on Frank for motive alone.

My phone rang while I walked back home. Mason wanted to know exactly how I'd found the wedding rings. "Given my caseload, though, I may not be able to pick them up until next week, at the wedding. Keep them safe."

"What did the coroner determine about Vanessa's killer?"

"I'm waiting for the fingerprint patterns on the victim's neck," he said. "If they don't match her husband, then we're back to square one. But don't get any crazy ideas, Sasha. We'll solve both murders, eventually, but you can't help us this time."

I disagreed, only Mason didn't have to know that.

Chapter 22

Monday morning, I received a phone call from a podcaster. Maddie had set up the interview to promote Saturday's event. Although I was nervous, and said "you know" and "uh" too often, Elizabeth was gracious and reassured me that she always edited the audio and deleted those. She was also surprised to learn the facts I'd researched about children's brain cancer.

"I had no idea how many kids are suffering with this," Elizabeth said. "I hope scientists can find a cure."

I nodded, despite knowing she couldn't see me. "Yes. That's the main reason we decided to call our event Bears for the Cure."

"I think that's a wonderful name. Everyone who's listening, use the link I'll post to send in donations. Either money or a new teddy bear, big or small, this Saturday." Elizabeth repeated the address and directions to Silver Hollow's high school. "There's also a Facebook page where people can donate money. Right, Sasha?"

"Yes," I said, and twice repeated the link Maddie had

written down. "Thanks so much for inviting me to be on your podcast today."

"You're so welcome! I'd love to hear whether you make it in the Guinness World Record book. Please let me know, and I'll update my listeners during the next episode."

"I'll do that. Right now we have over a thousand teddy bears, but we're hoping to get three times that number. The local Quick Mix factory loaned out a semi to store them, and we're so grateful. Once the event is over, volunteers will take them to several children's hospitals."

"What a great service to the community," Elizabeth said. "Thanks again."

I ended the phone call, pleased with the interview. When my cell buzzed again, however, I expected to hear the podcaster with a question she'd forgotten. Instead, Flynn Hanson's voice boomed in my ear and made me wince.

"Cheryl arranged for an interview on her station for Friday, with you and Maddie," he said. "On the morning show. You good with that?"

"I better ask—"

"Yes or no, because Cheryl needs to confirm."

"I guess, and thanks."

"Bring a few of those glacier bears to the studio. Judith told me something about T-shirts, too, so wear those."

Annoyed by his directives, I mumbled my thanks again. Despite the short notice, and the fact that we both had jobs, Maddie and I did need to promote the event—and that morning show was certainly popular. I was also grateful that Cissy's wedding wouldn't take place until after Bears for the Cure. We'd be able to devote all our time to adding more plastic-sealed teddy bears that half-filled the semi parked in our lot.

A sudden snow squall on Tuesday blanketed Silver Hollow with five inches of snow. The month of March had arrived like a lion, indeed, with high winds that created huge drifts. Snowplows had a difficult time clearing the roads. Even though our contractor pushed snow far away from the semi, the donations of teddy bears ground to a halt. A few customers braved the weather to buy glacier bears, but plenty more ordered them online to be picked up on Saturday during Bears for the Cure. That saved us the hassle of shipping, at least.

Wednesday and Thursday crawled along, and I read a book at the shop's counter waiting for customers. Only a few brought in bears, which discouraged me. Would anyone show up this weekend for the event?

By Thursday afternoon, the fifty degree weather melted most of the snow but left the ground muddy and soft. Cissy called me that night after dinner.

"The February Valentine's Day theme is all wrong for my wedding," she wailed. "Everything is red or has hearts, from the confetti on the tables to the chandelier hangings. March is all about green for St. Patrick's Day."

"But a lot of people use hearts, whether it's in February, March or October."

"What about the red tablecloths and bridesmaid dresses? I told you we should have switched the color scheme."

"Why not call Mary Monroe at the flower shop? It may not be too late to substitute white for red flowers, and add more greenery, like shamrocks and ivy."

"That might work."

"And then ask the clubhouse staff to use white linens on the tables at the reception. That way the red will be toned down—"

I held the phone away at her squeal of delight in my ear. Once again Cissy hung up on me. I wondered why she hadn't asked Debbie or her mom for ideas, though. I didn't need to deal with a frantic bride. I had my own worries regarding the

Bears for the Cure event, and I'd also been pondering theories about the double murder. But I shifted my focus to tomorrow's on-air interview with Cheryl Cummings.

Maddie and I showed up at six o'clock Friday morning to record the television segment. After undergoing makeup and hair checks, and being wired with microphones, we sat in the green room until called to the studio. I perched on a black chair, less comfortable in my skirt than my sister in her leggings, and kept my knees angled to one side like Duchess Kate. Instead of Cheryl Cummings, however, another on-air celebrity greeted us. Eyes bright, her dark hair perfectly in place, Anna took her seat and pointed to the camera.

"Don't be intimidated. When the little red light goes on, then you can get nervous."

I forced a smile, but Maddie laughed. "We thought Cheryl, the weather forecaster, would be interviewing us."

"If I'm on vacation, she'll do a few segments. Right now she's preparing her weather forecast," Anna said. "Are you both good friends with Cheryl?"

Tongue-tied, I let Maddie answer. I preferred not bringing up my ex-husband and his fiancée; friendship wasn't exactly how I'd term my relationship with Flynn. He annoyed me to no end whenever he turned up at unexpected times. I appreciated Cheryl's sweet nature, similar to her television personality, but I wished them both well in their future without being a part of it.

Maddie ended up fielding most of the interview questions. While my sister chatted with Anna about Bears for the Cure, and how we'd recruited men and women to build the bear corral, I channeled Vanna White in displaying our silver blue and gray glacier bears. That got a laugh from the cameraman. Then Maddie explained about Angela's daughter and her brain cancer diagnosis, and how we'd chosen teddy bears to help raise money for research. Plus our hope to set a Guinness world record.

"It sounds exciting," Anna said. "We also received a generous donation from Hanson's Law Firm—I have the check right here." When she brought out a printed cardboard rectangle, the cameraman zoomed the machine for a close-up. "A thousand dollars, which will truly help support children undergoing treatment."

"Thank you so much," Maddie said, her smile frozen.

"I hope you make your goal to gather the most teddy bears in one place." Anna faced the camera. "Please help this worthy cause. Those glacier bears are adorable, and I believe you still have a few left available for purchase."

"We'll produce more until all orders are filled," I piped up.

Anna asked several more questions after the red light blinked off. I was surprised when Cheryl raced over to congratulate us, her long black hair swinging behind her. She gushed over the interview and reassured us that we both did well.

"It's a shame Anna's booked for another event on Saturday, or she'd bring a camera for a live segment. Flynn and I plan to drop by around noon."

"Great." I smiled weakly. "See you then."

Maddie laughed hard once we left the studio building. "I should have known that Flynn would manage to promote himself on the air. But that was nice of Cheryl anyway, setting up the segment for today. Anna showcases a lot of causes all over the metro area."

"Anna's Angels, I know." I felt a little silly being so timid during the interview. "You were great, Mads, but I'm glad that's over."

"You did fine, but we've got a lot to accomplish today. Let's go."

My sister drove straight to the I-94 expressway and then to the sprawling Metro Airport. Once Maddie parked, I texted Angela to meet downstairs in the huge baggage claim area. Her flight had landed a few minutes early. I barely recognized my cousin, since we hadn't seen her in years. She recognized us, however, when we wove our way through the crowd of people.

"Hello, thanks so much for coming," Angela said, breathless. And stressed to the max, given her weary expression, wrinkled clothes, and limp brown hair. "We had to leave so early to catch our flight. This is Katya, by the way."

Maddie knelt beside the little girl's wheelchair. Katya's huge eyes stared at us, her arms hugging a ragged bunny, and she wore a thin scarf over her bald head. "We're so glad you came to visit Grandma and Grandpa in Michigan," my sister said. "Can you give us a minute while we fetch your suitcases?"

She nodded, so I rushed over to help Angela snag the two worn cases and a backpack from the slow-moving carousel. Katya shivered in a thin jacket. I handed her the fluffy silver blue glacier bear I pulled from my coat pocket.

"This teddy's been waiting to meet you, too."

Katya smiled shyly. "Will he be friends with Bun?"

"Of course! But your bear needs a name."

"Blue." She hugged the small bear close. "Bun says she loves him already."

Angela smiled. "Thanks. I usually don't mind early flights, but this turned out to be way more than I could handle. The airline staff helped, of course, and the pilot pinned wings on her coat. I'm lucky the ticket agent found a child-size wheelchair."

"Let's get you to Silver Hollow, so you can relax," Maddie said.

Katya shivered again, clearly exhausted. We tucked my sister's coat around her and headed to the car. Once she and Angela were settled in the back seat, Maddie pointed out various landmarks on the way to Silver Hollow. They both nodded off before we made it home. Uncle Hank, Aunt Marge, and my parents welcomed us all with hugs; we enjoyed a filling brunch of French toast, scrambled eggs, cinnamon rolls, fruit, and lots of coffee around the kitchen table. Hot chocolate for Katya, though, with whipped cream.

"We need to fatten you up," Aunt Marge said, caressing the little girl's cheek. "Explain what you've been dealing with, Angie. It's been rough, I know."

Angela explained her latest ordeals with doctor appointments, treatments, headaches with homeschooling, and the possibility of exposing her daughter to common viruses or unvaccinated kids—at home and while traveling.

"I'm lucky friends agreed to watch my other kids while I'm here. Thanks for sending the airline tickets, too, Uncle Alex. It's been such a hassle fighting my ex to get any child support payments. On time or late, as long I get them."

"Didn't you say the court threatened to garnish his wages?" Aunt Marge said. "I hope they follow through, because I am so tired of hearing his excuses."

"You and me both." Angela hugged her daughter. "Come on, sweetie, you need to eat. You love French toast."

"I want to sleep, Mommy."

"You can take a nap after you eat. We'll curl up on the sofa together, okay?"

"With the dogs?" Katya glanced at me. "Please?"

"They would love it," I told her solemnly. "Sugar Bear will sleep on your lap, but Rosie prefers the floor pillow. Right at your feet."

Katya smiled at that. After brunch, Maddie and I ran several errands. We ordered coffee and pastries to be delivered in the morning from Fresh Grounds, then stopped at the market to buy bottled water and juice, plus more plastic bags. We also drove to the football stadium and checked the wooden bear corral's progress. A few patches of mud dotted the field's edges, but Uncle Hank was busy spreading hay over them.

"Volunteers will be able to steer clear of the mud," I said, "so thanks. Ow!"

The whine of a power saw hurt my ears. I watched Jay cutting boards, while Eric lugged them over to Isabel French and Abby Pozniak. The women nailed them into place with Uncle Hank's help to align them. The team worked well together.

I turned to Maddie. "I'm gonna climb up to the top of the grandstand."

"I'm game. I hope they'll be done before dark. Eric told me Jay's brother couldn't deliver the lumber until noon, so they're a little behind."

"Wow. They've worked fast to get almost halfway." I checked my cell for the time. "It's almost three, so they should make it."

Once we reached the uppermost row of seats below the announcer's booth, I could take in the corral's rough outline. It resembled a teddy bear's lower body from this high vantage point. The crew started adding the rounded arms next.

"Will we have a drone taking a few aerial shots?" I asked Maddie.

"Zoe said a friend of hers will bring one, if he can get it to work. Guess it crashed the last time he took it up, though, but he's hoping it's fixed." She waved a hand. "But Zoe's going to take photos from the booth to prove our claim for the Guinness record book."

"Great. I'm heading back down," I said and raced her to the lowest level.

Maddie jumped into Eric's arms from the grandstand's last few steps. Jay whirled me around in a bear hug, too. "It's working out great," he said. "Even with all the mud. How about you two help carry the boards and give Eric a break?"

"Sure. I'd give you a break, too, if you teach me to run the power saw."

Jay agreed, watching Maddie and I work until the noise gave me a headache. I switched to carrying the boards to be nailed, and within a few hours, the bear corral was finished. We all applauded, tired but satisfied, and headed back to the stadium's parking lot.

"The ground's so soft, I almost lost one of my boots," Abby said. "See you all in the morning. My sister's covering the shop for me tomorrow."

"I'm helping my mom at Silver Birches," Isabel said, "but I can come early for an hour or so, collecting donations. Deon Walsh said he'd help seal up any teddy bears that come in without a plastic bag."

"Yes, that's the plan." I hugged her. "Thanks."

"I'm bushed." Uncle Hank stuck out a bruised thumb. "Popped it but good."

"Need some ice?" Maddie scooped up a tiny clump of dirty snow.

"Ha, no thanks. I'm ready for dinner. Burgers, on me. Is everyone in?"

The seven of us gladly trooped to Quinn's Pub for juicy burgers and beer. I pointed out Maddie's flyers tacked up by the front door. We also found them inside every menu. A plastic jar near the cash register had a flyer taped on it and was filled with coins and bills. Jay and Eric reported that businesses in the village were collecting money, too.

"Fresh Grounds has over a hundred bears that people do-nated," Jay said. "And the Cat's Cradle took at least that many to the semi already. Matt Cooper told me his kids baked cookies and sold them at school to raise money. His girls are bringing more to sell tomorrow, too."

"That is so sweet," I said, although my cousin had already texted me.

"Sounds like a wildly successful project." Uncle Hank raised his beer bottle. "A toast, to my nieces. May you always find joy in whatever you do."

"To Isabel and Abby. Plus our honey bears, Jay and Eric," I added. "You too, Uncle Hank. And let's not forget Jay's brother who donated the wood so we didn't have to buy it. Remind me to have Mom thank him in her speech tomor-row."

I noticed Detective Mason enter the pub. He unzipped his parka and headed straight to the bar. Brian Quinn filled a glass of beer with a head of foam. Mason tossed a few bills on the counter and then walked to our corner table.

"Evening, folks. Mind if I join you?" He took the empty chair across from me and sipped his beer. "Thought I'd update you, Sasha, about those gloves you gave me."

"What did you find out?" I was surprised and excited, since he usually didn't share his findings without being pressed for information.

"What's this about gloves?" Uncle Hank asked.

I spent the next few minutes introducing him to Mason, and then explained, without going into too much detail, about the odd requests for teddy bears. Once I finished, the detective traced a finger over his beer glass's condensation.

"Why did this guy leave his gloves behind?" Eric asked.

"Aunt Eve may have spooked him, for some reason," I said.

Uncle Hank laughed. "Not many women have her unique clothing style."

"So tell us who these guys are, and what they're doing," Jay said. "Or is it still under investigation, and you can't share."

"They're a ring of child predators," Mason replied. "We traced the prints to a guy who's on record for indecent exposure, plus other crimes."

"Why did these guys ask if we could make a bear similar to Bears of the Heart's Benny bear?" I asked. "It's not like ours, in a permanent sitting position. What's the deal with that?"

"Easier to take out the stuffing and put in a hidden camera. This group used the internet to contact victims and then sent the kids those teddy bears. Child porn is big, and predators can profit big time off live streams or from selling still photos."

"How sick, using innocent teddy bears," I said.

"Thanks to Sasha, at least this group's out of business." Mason shrugged. "We're also investigating Teddy Hartman, to see if he had any tie to these criminals. He sold his company, so it's not easy tracking evidence that would stick."

I winced, my fingernails digging into my palms, and then reached for Jay's hand. I was so thankful I'd found someone who valued family and children as much as I did. He squeezed my fingers in return. Maybe one day I'd share more about Teddy Hartman's sleazy nature.

"Good luck tomorrow with the fundraiser." Mason finished his beer and then rose to leave. "I can't guarantee we'll finish the murder investigation by Sunday's wedding. I'll try to be there or send someone. But remember, not all cases are solved."

"True enough." Jay sounded grim.

Eric ordered another round of beer. "Thanks for being so

cheerful. If it was my wedding, I'd have gone to Vegas. A quick ceremony in a chapel, with an Elvis impersonator."

"That's not an option in Cissy's world," Maddie said. "I doubt Zia Noemi would want Gus to elope for any reason. Even a third murder."

"Bite your tongue," Uncle Hank said. "Two is too many, am I right?"

I agreed, but Maddie was also right. No matter what happened, no matter how many people dropped out, Cissy and Gus yearned for their special day in the spotlight. Most couples wanted affirmation from family and friends. Was that a bad thing? I couldn't blame Cissy or Gus, even though they'd lost two friends to tragedy. Even though I knew firsthand how murder affected a normal routine, I couldn't judge their decision.

Back home, long after eight o'clock, we met Aunt Marge in the kitchen. "Katya's asleep," she said. "Poor little thing! She didn't eat much dinner, either."

Angela hugged me and then Maddie. "Thank you for everything."

"We can't imagine what you're going through," I said, "but we're glad you're here to share in Bears for the Cure tomorrow."

I slept that night, better than expected. I even dreamed that the bear corral overflowed with bags, rushing toward the grandstand like a tidal wave, filling the metal rows and seats, and spilling over the top booth into the parking lot. And woke up, jarred by Maddie's hard shaking, her voice tinged with panic. I rubbed my eyes and checked the clock. Half past six.

"Come on, Sash. We've got to pick up all the pastries, the coffee, and make sure the semi is in the parking lot before everyone arrives. Get dressed!"

"Okay, okay," I mumbled.

Yawning, I rushed to get a shower, don jeans, a long-sleeved polo shirt, plus the glacier bear T-shirt over it, heavy socks, and boots. The wind whistled outside and chilled me to the bone. Lucky for me Mom and Dad would deal with my lazy dogs this morning.

By the time Maddie and I fetched everything from Fresh Grounds, the sun shone dim in the east. We passed the elementary school on Quentin Street and noticed the apartment row where one unit had been boarded up from the fire. What a shame. I'd seen Dave Fox's photos of the kindergarten children hugging their classmate, with all the toys and bears surrounding them, in the latest *Silver Hollow Herald* edition.

Past the brick high school, I pulled into the parking lot. My heart soared when I saw all the volunteers, over a dozen, huddled near the semi. The truck blocked the wind which whistled through the football stadium's entrance. Jay greeted me, wearing only a puffy vest over his plaid shirt, and the same mud-streaked twill pants from last night. His work boots were caked, too, and I saw bits of dried mud in his brown hair.

After he kissed me, I rubbed my cheek with a wry grin. He laughed. "I overslept, and didn't take time to shave. Got enough coffee?"

"There's plenty. Help yourselves, everyone," I called out. "The Thompsons of Fresh Grounds donated the muffins, scones, and cinnamon buns."

They all cheered. We spent the next hour visiting before several volunteers gathered up the empty boxes and carried them to the trash. Others began unloading the Quick Mix semi, forming a human chain, and handing the sealed bags of bears in a line that snaked all the way to the football field. Three Silver Bear staff members counted the bags before the volunteers tossed them in the wooden corral. Unfortunately, plenty of bare spots showed.

"A little under two thousand," Isabel French said with a

sigh. "Our goal was at least three thousand bears. But we've raised over twenty-five hundred dollars in cash, so far."

"More bears are coming in, look." Deon Walsh gestured toward the crowd of visitors streaming past the stadium gates. "Right on time, too. It's almost ten o'clock."

"Did we set a time?" I blinked in the brighter sunlight. "I don't remember that."

"Then you didn't read the flyer." Maddie handed me another cup of coffee. "The event is scheduled for ten until noon, when Mom is bringing Angela and Katya. But we'll stay longer until we reach our goal. Zoe will take the official photos when we do."

"Dave Fox is coming, too, plus a camera crew from Anna's Angels," Jay reported. "Got a text from Flynn Hanson this morning telling me that. How come he didn't text you?"

I knew the answer. My ex probably expected a personal phone call to acknowledge that huge check. Flynn was no doubt steamed, but so was I. He'd arranged that on-air interview so he could promote his law firm and get a hefty tax credit. It bothered me that I had been so blind long ago to his motives and self-serving schemes. I hoped and prayed the monetary donations gathered by village businesses would eventually overtake his offering.

"Such an egomaniac," I muttered.

"What's that, Sasha?" My cousin Matt Cooper unloaded his van, filled with more plastic-sealed bears. I shrugged.

"Nothing. Want some help?"

"The girls need to set up their cookie sale table."

I smiled when his daughters climbed from the van's interior. Together we unfolded the card table and drew out dozens of boxes. Volunteers and visitors crowded around. Within half an hour, Cara and Celia had sold out. They gleefully added the money to the high school bake sale profits.

Celia jumped up and down in excitement, a glacier bear in each hand.

"How much did we make, Aunt Sasha?"

"I don't know, but it must be a lot." I shook the jar to hear the coins jangle. "Wow."

"We'll bake more," Cara said solemnly.

Matt drew a finger across his throat. "Help your mom clean the kitchen instead."

Since both girls wrinkled their noses at that suggestion, we all laughed. "I'll help," Matt said reluctantly, "but only if you two go to bed on time tonight." Celia hugged him.

"Okay, Daddy, but you gotta read us three stories!"

"Bribery," I said, and winked at my cousin. "Works every time."

By eleven o'clock, bagged teddy bears covered every bit of ground within the corral. We were still short of our goal, however. Volunteers cheered and waved whenever more people trickled in with their donations. Disappointment overwhelmed me.

"There's less than an hour left," Maddie said, her voice low. "Some spots in the corral are only a single layer. The photo won't look all that great unless we get a lot more."

"What if a bunch of people stand inside the corral? Each holding up two or three bags," Eric suggested. "The wooden sides are waist high. It might look better from the stands when Zoe Fisher takes the photos."

"I love that idea," I said. "We should have thought of it sooner. Let's do it."

We all rushed off to spread the word. Jay pulled apart one "foot" of the bear corral to allow easier access. Everyone took care to retrieve the sealed bags and not trample them, filing in slowly, until we had enough volunteers in every section. By the time my parents arrived, along with Uncle Hank, Aunt

Marge, Angela, and Katya, I had taken my place inside the corral with Jay. More people arrived and tossed bagged bears to fill in between us all.

Mom clapped her hands in delight. "It's marvelous! The television crew is pulling in, too, just in time. Where's my microphone?"

Isabel handed it to her, waved to the camera crew, and signaled to begin. "Thank you for coming to Bears for the Cure," my mother announced, her voice steady, until the loud screech of feedback made us all cringe. She waited until it died away. "Can I continue?"

"Go ahead, try it now," someone called out.

"This is a fundraiser for children's brain cancer research. As mayor of Silver Hollow, I'm proud to introduce my brother's granddaughter Katya. She'll be undergoing treatment in a Memphis hospital, so please keep her in your prayers—"

Everyone raised their bagged bears in the corral and cheered, drowning her out. Then Mom listed contributors to thank from the village and surrounding area, which took at least five minutes. Once she finished, the crowd applauded long and hard.

Dave Fox and Zoe Fisher climbed the grandstand to its highest point and snapped photos from all angles. While the television crew filmed, Flynn and Cheryl wormed their way into the throng inside the corral and waved fluffy bears high in the air. Not bagged in plastic.

"Bet they'll use that bit for the next 'Flynn Wins' commercial," I said to Jay. "I'm just grateful it didn't snow or rain today, and everything worked out."

Jay slid his arm around my waist. "All worth it, too."

"—for the Cure has officially raised over three thousand bears, and nearly four thousand dollars according to the latest count," Mom announced over the microphone.

"You're amazing, Sasha Silverman," Jay said and kissed me.

"No more than you." I snuggled up to him. "It takes a village, right?"

"True enough." He suddenly laughed. "Wouldn't you know, Flynn and his fiancée are announcing their engagement on camera."

"No kidding?" I whirled to see Cheryl flashing her diamond ring. "Oh, brother."

Angela walked over with little Katya, who hugged both her glacier bear and bunny. "We're leaving soon for Memphis, Sasha. Uncle Hank decided he wants to leave a few days early, taking breaks on the way, so Katya can rest before her treatment."

"I'm sorry we didn't get more time to talk," I said.

"I know. But we're so thankful for everything your family's done for us."

"Keep us updated about how things go. It's bound to be warmer in Tennessee. Let us know when you make it home, too." I crouched down to caress Katya's cold cheek. "You and your mom and grandparents can come visit anytime."

"Can I take your dogs with me?" she asked. Angela chuckled at that.

"No way, sweetie. They belong here in Michigan."

I leaned close to Katya. "Get better, and maybe your mom will give you a kitten one day. Maddie and I will try and convince her."

Jay stayed behind when I trailed after my cousin and her daughter to join my family in saying good-bye. I wiped a few tears away, too. Katya was so young to be suffering through this. What a comfort to see the entire community come together for a good cause.

"Hey, Sasha!" Mark Branson, a lawyer with the Legal Eagles, and my best friend's older brother, squeezed his way toward me. "Got a minute?"

"Sure," I said. "How's your sister doing? I need to call her."

"Mary Kate's bored out of her mind, being on bed rest for so long."

"We sure miss seeing her at Fresh Grounds."

"Yeah, I know," Mark said. "I sure won't miss Flynn Hanson, though, now he's moved on to greener pastures. It may be quieter around the office, but we can concentrate and get more done. We got so tired of being an audience for Hanson's drama."

"Don't I know all about that."

He pulled a slip out of his pocket. "Here's a check from our practice. Mike and I saw Flynn pull that stunt yesterday, during your television interview, so we decided to top him. But you don't need to announce it to the world."

I stared in surprise at the twenty-five-hundred-dollar amount, and hugged Mark. "We're taking out an ad in the *Silver Hollow Herald* to thank everyone. You can bet the Legal Eagles will be at the top of the list. That will bug Flynn to no end."

We both laughed before he strolled off. I rushed over to deliver the check to Maddie, who squealed in delight. She tucked it away. "I'll tell Mom once Flynn and Cheryl are gone. They're still sucking up to the television camera."

"Whatever," I said, and slipped my hand into Jay's when he joined us. "Tomorrow we have the wedding to get through, and I'm gonna take all day Monday to recover."

Jay snapped his fingers. "That reminds me. I forgot to mention that Kip O'Sullivan told me about Dylan, that he tried to blackmail Kip."

"Really? What was that all about?"

"Remember when Kip sold his gallery? He never repaid clients for commissions he didn't finish," Jay said. "Kip blew off Dylan, though, and said he could tell whoever he wanted about it. He wasn't gonna pay to keep that quiet."

"That makes sense, since Dylan had big gambling debts. Poor guy."

"Do you always believe people are good at heart? I figured these murders in Silver Hollow would have made you a little cynical by now."

I hesitated, wondering if that was true. "Maybe I am a little more suspicious of people's motives. But that could be due to my divorce, not the murders."

"Good. Keep looking ahead, Sasha, because you can't change the past."

Wise words. I clung to him, grateful for his warmth and love. For my family, and good friends who'd pitched in to make today a huge success. A niggle of worry rose in the back of my mind, however, over tomorrow's wedding. Despite Mason's warning, I needed a plan to identify the killer.

I didn't want to face the possibility of failure, either.

Chapter 23

Sunday proved to be a beautiful day for a wedding. In a cramped dressing room at the Ann Arbor golf clubhouse, I hitched up the red satin bridesmaid gown and its lining, adjusted my pantyhose, and then peeked in the mirror. I wore way too much makeup for my taste. Debbie had encouraged us to use eyeliner, heavy rouge, and lipstick. My false lashes resembled butterfly wings, and they tickled my cheeks with every blink. Curled and pinned, my blond updo sprouted ribbons and tiny white flowers. Maddie had insisted on all that decoration at the hair salon. In my opinion, I resembled a prom queen court attendant.

My sister tucked a stray hair behind my ear. "Some days I regret my pixie cut," she said wistfully. Her beribboned clip studded with flowers would be easier to remove later, though. "Need help tying your shoe ribbons?"

I stuck out one foot, still encased in a black ballet slipper. "No way am I putting on those four-inch heels until the last minute."

"Did you remember the garter?" Maddie raised her skirt

to show off the band of red satin just above the knee. "Like Cissy said, for luck. I bet you forgot."

"She's lucky I painted my toenails," I grumbled.

"These bows," Gisele groaned. "I've tied mine half a dozen times."

"You could knot them before tying the bows," Maddie suggested.

Kim Goddard checked her backside in the mirror. "This dress makes me look fat."

"Stop saying that, you look fine." Gisele Vaccaro patted her abdomen. "If anyone looks fat in this stupid dress, it's me. I even lost ten pounds. I'm still wearing Spanx to smooth down all my flab. God, I hate getting old."

"Zia Noemi said I shouldn't need any spanks." Martina tossed a handful of red rose petals like confetti into the air. "Whee!"

Gisele scolded her. "Pick those up, right now."

"But Mama said I should practice."

"I'll call your father in here if you don't stop."

The flower girl stuck out her tongue but then stooped to obey, much to my surprise. Her red silk and tulle skirt swept the ground each time Martina grabbed a rose petal. Halfway through the task, she scratched her rump and whimpered.

"I'm itchy, I'm itchy! I don't like this dress. Why can't I wear the other one that's all white with lace? I wanna look like Cissy—"

"Because you're not the bride," Kim interrupted. "What's itchy?"

"Let me see," Gisele said, and investigated beneath the little girl's dress. "You're not getting a rash, so what's the problem?"

"I hate how scratchy it feels."

I fetched my shoes from their box and slid them into my tote bag, wondering if I could get away with wearing flats. My dress was long enough to hide my feet. Nobody would pay attention to me, since the bridal party would all be waiting for the bride's procession. All eyes would be focused on Cissy, admiring her hair, her slinky white gown dripping with lace, her beaming smile. And little Martina, whose dark curly hair framed her angelic face. Her skirt looked flatter now, since Gisele had cut out one layer of tulle with scissors.

"It's still too itchy!"

Gisele snipped most of the second layer from under her dress. "Don't tell anyone about this, Tina, do you hear me? Zia Noemi will be mad."

"Okay, I won't," Martina said, giggling. "It's so much betterer. I saw Debbie's dress. How come it's different than yours? And why isn't she here with us?"

"She's helping the bride, that's what the maid of honor is supposed to do."

"I am not happy standing up with Steve Leeson," Kim said, smoothing her skirt. "He should have bowed out of the bridal party."

"Wait. Didn't Gus choose Frank to be best man?" I asked, puzzled.

"He chose Nick," Gisele admitted, "because Frank insulted Gus last night. At least that's what my husband told me. Frank said the wedding was screwed."

"And I heard Frank called Gus 'basic,' which is like the ultimate insult. You know how Gus is, so smooth and Fresh Prince," Kim said. "I can't even."

That must have really ticked Gus off, but I groused in silence. I'd be stuck with Frank Antonini after all, when I hoped to escape having to stand, sit, and dance with him. Plus he was at the top of my list for Dylan's murder, if not Vanessa's. Ugh. I shivered.

Maddie let out a deep breath and tried to re-glue a loose false eyelash. "I'm glad Cissy decided on these fur-trimmed shrugs. Otherwise we'd freeze all night." She turned to me. "What time is Jay coming?"

"Remember that wolverine commission? The pub owners wanted to meet him tonight and sign a contract, of all days," I added. "They called out of the blue, and insisted on five thirty. So I'm hoping he gets here in time." Especially given my plan to produce the missing wedding rings, although I hadn't told Maddie yet.

My sister adjusted her hair clip. "Are you ready, Sash?"

"No, but let's get this over with so we can eat," I said. "I'm starved."

"I wonder if we'll make it to dinner before someone else is offed," Kim joked.

Gisele gasped aloud. "That's the last thing Cissy and Gus need."

"Don't worry." Kim opened her clutch purse, drew out a small silver handgun to show us, and then shoved it back into hiding. "I got that covered in case of any more trouble. I'll check on Debbie and Cissy, who's probably having another meltdown."

Kim marched out of the golf club's dressing room. Gisele and Martina followed, heels skittering on the tile floor. I glanced at my sister.

"I wonder if Kim lured Dylan into the restroom?"

Maddie shoved her lipstick into her tiny handbag, along with her cell. "No idea. And the last thing I want to talk about is murder. Remember what Mason said, that he needs evidence to prove anything."

"I found the wedding rings." I dug into my tote bag, searching for the small purse to make sure. "That's one way to find out who killed Dylan."

"What?" Maddie blew out a long breath. "Sasha, don't tell me you've got something up your sleeve for tonight."

"I'm supposed to turn them over to Mason when he arrives," I said. "I'm hoping Frank will confess, especially if he wanted to steal them from Dylan. That and get revenge for cheating with Claudia. Oh, great. Where are they?"

"The rings?"

"I left them in the car," I said in frustration. "I'll be right back."

"You can't go outside! It's colder than blazes out there." Maddie handed me the shrug. "Put this on, and your coat over it. I'd better come with you, too. We've got a few hours to kill before the ceremony anyway."

Our long wool coats shrouded our gowns. I led my sister through one of the back doors of the elaborate, multiple-story clubhouse and out to the sloping parking lot. Her heels clattered on the cement. My feet froze. These ballet slippers didn't give much protection. Thankfully my car was close, considering how early we'd arrived to change. I unlocked the car, grabbed the small sealed envelope from inside the console, and slipped it into my purse.

Nuh-uh. Instead, I thrust it into my cleavage. The safest place, for now.

"Okay, I'm good." I slid my car key into my coat pocket. "Let's go—"

"Look who's on duty with Mr. Clooney. Didn't Gisele say Nick's the best man now?" Maddie gestured toward a white four-door Jeep Wrangler. "I wonder why Gus didn't ask Frank to keep an eye on the dog instead."

We both waved at Nick Rizzo. Mr. Clooney danced around several cars in the parking lot, ignoring any coaxing. Nick swung open his Jeep's back end and grabbed the dog's collar, harness, and leash. He crouched down, holding out his hand with a treat. The poodle inched closer, sniffed, and gobbled the morsel while Nick slipped the collar on. But then Mr. Clooney raced away to freedom.

He grinned, shaking his head in defeat. "Gus was mad

when Frank threatened to drown this dog in the golf course pond, so I volunteered to catch him. He's been running around like crazy for the past half hour."

"Good luck," I called out. Maddie headed toward him. Not a good idea, since the poodle had the bad habit of jumping on people. "Watch out, he might wreck your dress!"

"I'll be careful—"

Mr. Clooney jumped into the Jeep's back and grabbed a gym shoe between his jaws. "Gimme that, you devil dog." Nick wrestled the ripped sneaker away from Mr. Clooney but cursed when the dog rushed off to circle the cars in the lot. "Hey! Come back here."

Nick took off to chase him, waving his arms and yelling. Maddie wandered over to the open Jeep, shivering, so I followed.

"I wonder if he has more treats in here," my sister said, peering in the back.

"If that dog jumps the fence and escapes into the golf course, Nick will never catch him." I checked my coat pockets. Keys in one, but I found a rustling package in the other. One of Rosie's treat bags, a miracle. I stuck my fingers in my mouth, whistled, and then waved the plastic-wrapped packet. "Yo, Mr. Clooney! Come get a cookie, come on."

Nick laughed in amazement when the dog looped around the last car and headed straight for me. I prayed he wouldn't knock me over in this satin dress. But Mr. Clooney stopped short and gazed at the package I held high in the air.

"Okay, stay. Sit, be nice. Stay."

I waited until Nick slipped the harness around Mr. Clooney's body. While he fastened the buckles, I dropped broken pieces on the ground. The dog crunched them one by one, wriggling a little. Nick snapped on the leash and then wound it around his hand for greater control. Mr. Clooney strained against the leather strap but failed to escape again.

"Whew." Nick pumped a fist in victory. "Thanks, Sasha. You saved the wedding."

"You're welcome." Smiling, I led the way toward the clubhouse.

"Hey, wait for me," Maddie called out. She gripped her bulky coat together and scurried, heels clacking, until she joined us halfway across the lot. "I locked your Jeep for you, Nick."

"Thanks. Silly dog." He rubbed the dog's ears with affection. "Don't ask me why Cissy and Gus want him as ring bearer, since they never found those diamond rings. They're gone for good." Nick followed us inside, the dog trotting close beside him. "Gus could use what I found out here, as a joke, although I bet Cissy won't appreciate it."

"Use what instead?" I asked, curious.

Chuckling, he held out an aluminum beer can's ring-tab. "Do you know they first started making these pull-top things fifty years ago? They're officially historic."

"Wow." I opened the clubhouse's back door. "Watch him around food, remember."

Inside, Nick dragged Mr. Clooney away from the kitchen staff who carried items in and out of an open doorway. The wafting aroma of prime rib roast beef tickled my nose. We walked down a narrow hallway to the huge reception room. An elaborate tiered cake with red hearts and white buttercream roses stood on a tall table, surrounded by platters of iced cookies. Apparently, Zia Noemi had frozen and thawed them after all. Yum. I was so tempted to snitch one.

"Gorgeous cake," I said, "and I hope the cookies are still tasty."

Maddie sighed. "You're hopeless."

Back in the dressing room, I shed my coat once more. "Ugh. Why do I have to wear miserable, four-inch heels? With stupid bows."

My sister turned her back and fiddled with her skirt. "Suck it up, and quit whining." She smoothed the satin into place again.

"What are you doing? Or is the lining scratching you, too?"

"No, I'm good."

I scratched my thigh. My skirt dragged on the floor until I finished tying on my heeled shoes. The satin hid the elaborate bows, of course, and swirled a little behind me. All of the bridesmaids would need to avoid stepping on each other's trains.

Maddie and I headed back to the reception room. This time I avoided drooling over the cake and cookies and noted the glittering chandeliers, the tiny white lights that climbed the rough wooden pillars around the room, and the twisting topiaries that flanked them. More lights snaked over the long wooden tables lined with gold satin runners. Ivy, white gerbera daisies, and red roses were tucked between the china and crystal. A framed photo of Cissy and Gus sat at every place setting, along with tiny bags of sugared almonds.

Overall, the eclectic aura lent a simple beauty to the scene.

"Here are your bridesmaid bouquets, girls!"

Zia Noemi met us halfway to the door of the makeshift chapel. The thick stems of white lilies were wrapped in red satin ribbon. I sneezed, shaking pollen from my bouquet, and sneezed a second time. Uh oh.

Gus's aunt handed me a tissue. "Bless you."

She sparkled under the lights, her red sequined jacket shimmering over a floor-length gown with a floral design. Her updo rivaled mine for its curls and adornments—pearls, ribbons, and flowers. Zia Noemi shooed us, clucking like a mother hen, toward the adjoining chapel.

"Remember there's no procession like we practiced at

church," she said, and stepped aside. "Mrs. Davison will explain the rest of the changes."

Barbara nodded, looking regal in a dove gray gown. Lace covered her shoulders and arms almost to her wrists, and her dangling diamond earrings sparkled. "In the interests of saving time, the bridesmaids will stand on one side of the podium, with the groomsmen on the other. Then we'll wait for the minister—"

"But when do I throw my rose petals?" Martina wailed.

"You're going to wait with me at the back until the bride is ready," she said. "We'll send you ahead of Cissy to drop your rose petals."

"What about Mr. Clooney?" The little girl's voice trembled. "He's supposed to carry the wedding rings. In the little bag on his collar."

Zia Noemi stepped forward. "No, dear—" Martina burst into tears this time, but Gus's aunt hushed her. "We're not sure about the dog. Maybe he's not feeling well."

"He can't be sick," she wailed. "Not Mr. Clooney!"

"Where are the groomsmen?" Gisele asked. "I see Bob, but none of the others."

"They're behind that side door, probably keeping Gus from getting cold feet at the last minute," Kim said with a laugh. "Sometimes that happens."

"He won't," Gisele said, "or Cissy would kill—er, never mind."

I was glad she stopped. We didn't need any mention of murder.

Eric Dyer emerged from a side door, followed by Steve Leeson. I almost didn't recognize Vanessa's husband at first, since he'd shaved off his beard and mustache. He still wore glasses, and glanced furtively around the chapel as if checking for any police presence. Or maybe a way to escape if necessary. Frank Antonini, his black tuxedo straining at his wide shoulders, brought out Mr. Clooney on his leash and harness.

Martina ran to the dog and threw her arms around him. Her basket of rose petals spilled over the tile floor. The poodle whined, struggling to break free of the little girl's hold, and Frank cursed aloud. He yanked Mr. Clooney before he gobbled a few petals.

"Pick them up, Tina," he ordered. "Now!"

All the bridesmaids rushed to help. "Whatever it takes to get this over with," Maddie said under her breath. "I thought Detective Mason said he was coming, Sash."

"I thought so, too," I said, checking the chapel's pews, "but maybe not."

I stuffed the last handful of petals into Martina's white wicker basket. We all lined up with the groomsmen—minus the bride, groom, best man, and maid of honor, of course. The official photographer snapped several photos before Dave Fox arrived. I almost laughed at his rumpled suit and tie, scruffy loafers, and trademark ponytail.

Martina tossed a few rose petals in the aisle. "No, no, *non farlo*," Zia Noemi scolded. "The girls helped you, they won't do it again. Now behave yourself."

Poor Mr. Clooney whined, nervous from Frank's rough handling, and then had to endure another enthusiastic hug from Martina. "I love you. You're such a good boy."

Gisele grabbed Martina's hand and led her to the chapel's back. Debbie Davison opened a door. Her dark hair had been swept into a French twist, but she wore a deep burgundy dress, sleek, without ruffles. I figured she'd bought a new dress at the last minute. Lucky her.

Barbara Davison led Martina inside and shut the door again. Before Gisele returned to her place in line, Gus and Nick emerged from another side room. Gus's dark hair was slicked back, and he looked smart in his black tuxedo with a red satin bow tie. Nick slipped past Bob Vaccaro, while Frank flexed his muscular shoulders, keeping Mr. Clooney in a tight hold.

Pastor Lovett carried his leather Bible. "Ready to practice?"

"I thought we didn't need to practice," Kim piped up.

"Oh, right," he said, and waved us to move in closer. "Okay then, let's get started. At last Gus and his lovely bride will be married."

"Thanks, Pastor," Gus said. "About time, too."

Zia Noemi nodded. "We're so glad nothing else has undermined the wedding. The last few weeks have been a major headache, to say the least."

"I'm sure it has been a strain." Pastor Lovett glanced at Steve. "We have a little extra time, if anyone would like to share their feelings of those tragic events. Grief counseling can be such a comfort and help."

"I don't need counseling," Steve shot back. "I'm only here because I have to wait for the cops. They won't let me arrange Vanessa's funeral yet. It's ridiculous."

Startled by his hostility, the minister backed away several steps. Zia Noemi clucked in disapproval. "He's a man of God, Mr. Leeson. Show some respect."

Steve muttered a curse under his breath. I held my tongue, since an awkward silence descended. Kim looked bored, though, along with Bob and Gisele Vaccaro. Eric and Maddie exchanged knowing looks, as if they'd predicted that things wouldn't go smoothly. Poor Mr. Clooney coughed hard, whined, and panted as if thirsty. Frank tugged him back into place beside him, without any gentleness. The jerk.

"Gus, couldn't Eric handle Mr. Clooney?" I asked. "He's in distress."

"He's fine," Frank retorted. "I've trained military dogs."

"But Mr. Clooney's not—"

The poodle suddenly opened his mouth wide, as if choking, and then threw up. Some of the goo spattered on Frank's lower leg and shoe. He grimaced. "Oh, for the love of—"

"That's enough, Frank," Gus said sternly. "Give him to Eric."

Eric grabbed the dog's leash. "Go clean up," he told Frank.

Gus's cousin wiped his shoe with a handkerchief and tossed the cloth on top of the mess before he departed. Zia Noemi rushed to the restroom for paper towels, while Eric and Maddie led Mr. Clooney to a pew and soothed the poodle. Maddie petted the dog's curly fur and talked low to him until Mr. Clooney settled down, head on his paws. Zia Noemi, clucking to herself, returned to scrub away the mess on the tile floor.

I glanced around the chapel again. Where was Detective Mason? I didn't want to spring my news about the wedding rings until he arrived. But time was running out. I couldn't accuse the killer in front of the wedding guests, at least a hundred, when they arrived. And there'd be close to three or four hundred at the reception.

Maddie seemed nervous, too, now that Eric had to control the dog. Once Frank sauntered up the aisle, glaring at Mr. Clooney, I reached for the small envelope in my cleavage. Ugh, it had slipped a little low for comfort. Taking a deep breath, my stomach clenched tight, I fought to retrieve it. When Maddie burst out laughing, everyone turned to stare at me.

"Sorry—give me a minute." Finally I stepped forward, the sealed envelope in one hand. "I found something important the other day, when I was cleaning my backyard."

Gus and Nick looked startled, and Frank smirked. "What is this, show and tell?"

Kim spoke up. "Ignore him, Sasha. What did you find?"

"The missing wedding rings."

I tore open the envelope and held the glittering diamond bands high. Gus crowed in delight and rushed forward. Frank cocked his head, clearly shocked, and Nick's jaw dropped open as well. Steve didn't react at all, frozen in place.

"Whoever murdered Dylan may have wanted these rings. They're worth thousands of dollars." I turned to Frank. "Someone who wanted to recover his losses at that bachelor party, and also stole some of Dylan Campbell's poker winnings. Don't try to deny it."

"What a crock." Gus's cousin barked a laugh. "Who told you that lame story?"

"I did," Eric said. "I saw you take money while everyone else was fighting."

Pastor Lovett started to speak, but Frank waved him back. "So I stole a few hundred bucks. Dylan cheated us. And Nick lost the most money. Right, bro?"

Sweat beaded on his forehead, and Nick's cheeks flushed scarlet. "How did those rings get in your backyard?"

"Mr. Clooney ate them," I replied. "Remember he cleaned up whatever dropped on the floor during the rehearsal dinner at the hotel. I figured when Dylan took off his coat, they must have fallen out of his pocket."

"Ugh! Are you saying the dog pooped them out?" Kim asked.

"So what? They've been found, that's all that matters." Gus hugged me. "Thank you, Sasha! Cissy will be so relieved."

"But it doesn't answer the real question of who killed Dylan." I turned back to Frank. "You had the best motive. He suspected you of stealing his poker winnings. That's why

Dylan talked Claudia into meeting him that Friday. So you murdered him in revenge."

Frank looked furious. "I didn't kill that bast—"

"Who else would?" Gus interrupted, and stabbed a finger almost in his face. "Sasha's right. I've always wondered how far you'd go. I'm not excusing Dylan's rotten behavior, but for God's sake. Why kill him the day before my wedding?"

"I didn't kill him." Frank glanced around at the entire bridal party, clearly surprised we would think that. "Sure, Dylan deserved what he got. I wish I had stuck him. A fitting end, you know, given the way he stuck so many women."

Zia Noemi gasped at his crudeness. Gisele folded her arms over her ample chest, glaring at her cousin. "That's uncalled for, even if it was true!"

"Did you murder Dylan?" Gus demanded.

"I'm not gonna stand for this, man. The cops ran me ragged with their stupid questions, but I didn't kill the guy," Frank said. "I didn't even know he had those rings in his pocket. And no way would I steal those rings from you, Gus. We're family!"

He chewed his lip and turned to me. "Can you prove that he's the murderer?"

"No, she can't," Maddie said, "but I can prove who is."

Chapter 24

Shocked, I stared at my sister. All the women gasped when Maddie reached under her skirt and retrieved something secured in her garter. She held it up in triumph—a heeled black leather pump.

"This is Vanessa Leeson's shoe." Maddie slowly turned, shoe raised high, so everyone in the bridal party could see it. "Steve, is this a match to the one Vanessa had on the day she was killed? Remember the police only found one of her shoes at Eric's microbrewery."

Steve walked over and examined the heel and sole. He also checked the leather's inner lining. "Yeah. That's her shoe size, at least, and the cops will be able to match it with the other one as evidence. So who strangled Vanessa?"

Everyone in the bridal party inhaled a sharp breath, including me. I glanced at the doors, hoping that Detective Mason would arrive. Or even Digger Sykes, of all people. Anyone with authority to arrest the real killer. Gus ran a nervous hand through his hair.

"So what gives, Maddie? How did you find that shoe?"

My sister took a deep breath. "I'm hoping the man who murdered both Dylan and Vanessa would come forward on his own," she said. "It's time for the truth."

Maddie's gaze was fixed on Steve Leeson, whose face turned purple. "I didn't kill my wife. I barely knew Dylan—"

"And it wasn't Eric," she said, her tone angry. "The killer tried to frame him."

"You knew them both." I faced Nick Rizzo, who visibly flinched. "My sister found that shoe in your Jeep today. Isn't that right, Maddie?"

"Yes, when we went outside to fetch the wedding rings." My sister gestured to the dog. "We saw Nick chasing Mr. Clooney when he ran off with a gym shoe. That's when I saw this shoe in the Jeep's back. So Vanessa arranged to meet you on that Wednesday afternoon, but she didn't expect you to kill her. You put her body in your car and drove to the microbrewery."

Nick hung his head. "Gus, I—I never meant to hurt anyone."

"That's a lie," I said. "You planned to kill Dylan. Like Frank said, you lost the most money at poker. A lot more than anyone else. He cheated you then, but I bet he blackmailed you to pay off his gambling debts. You wanted to stop him."

Nick stammered something we couldn't make out. Gus and Frank looked ready to tackle him if he made any move for the door, and I clenched my fists just in case. Like Mason warned me, murderers were unpredictable.

"Or maybe Vanessa asked to meet you," I said, "because she either saw you going into the ladies' restroom, or coming out."

Shoulders sagging, Nick wiped his hands on his trousers. "No one saw me. Vanessa made sure of it. She lured Dylan inside, and he didn't realize I was waiting for him. I tried to reason with him, but he wouldn't listen. I never intended to kill Dylan—"

"Then why take the ice pick with you?"

Nick blinked in silence. "And then you killed Vanessa, to shut her up?" Kim pointed her small handgun at him. "You planned to kill her, didn't you? Quit shaking your head, you liar!"

"That was an accident—"

"No, it wasn't," she snapped. "Vanessa told me she didn't trust you, but she never told me why. She agreed to help you, but she had no idea you intended to kill Dylan." Kim's hand remained steady, but her voice shook. "When Sasha and Maddie found his body, Vanessa flipped out. That's why she ended up with a migraine!"

He slumped in defeat. "I wanted to get my money back from Dylan. He laughed at me, and said I'd better keep paying him. Or else."

Steve choked up. "So why did you kill Vanessa?"

"She figured out the truth about the car accident," Nick said. "Vanessa got suspicious when Dylan slipped up at the bachelorette party, insisting he was innocent. She'd already agreed to lure him into the restroom the night of the rehearsal dinner. Then Vanessa kept hounding me about the accident. So I told her, that I'd been driving—"

"Oh, man," Gus said in disgust. "All these years, you kept that secret?"

"I couldn't risk ruining my career, or my reputation."

"Why didn't Vanessa tell Detective Mason that you killed Dylan?" I asked Nick.

"Because I told her they'd arrest her as my accomplice." He loosened his tie, his hands shaking. "I'm sorry I had to keep her from going to the cops. But I'm not sorry about Dylan. He deserved what he got."

"So what really happened in Traverse City, the night of the accident?" Gus grabbed Nick by the arm and dragged him to sit in the front pew. "Time to explain everything, bro."

I slid an arm around Maddie, who inched forward with Eric and Mr. Clooney. The rest of the bridal party held back, however, except for Kim. She nodded at me, handgun ready for any trouble. Bob Vaccaro had already sent Pastor Lovett off to call 911 and fetch the golf clubhouse manager as well, while he blocked the doors to prevent any guests from entering.

Nick slumped further on the pew. "Okay, okay. I was driving that night. I had too many beers, plus the rain and fog didn't help."

Zia Noemi clutched Gisele. "*Dio mio—*"

"I remember you saying how bad the weather was that night," Eric said.

"Yeah, Dylan said I ran a red light." Nick shook his head. "I don't remember much, and the other car came out of nowhere. Dylan yelled, but I couldn't stop in time. I couldn't think straight after the crash. But then he offered to take the rap for me. For money, of course."

"You thought fast enough to switch places behind the wheel," I said flatly.

"I had a previous DUI. He knew I was in big trouble."

"So instead of manning up, and taking the consequences, you let Dylan blackmail you?" Gus demanded. "That's just crazy, man."

"Yeah, I know." Nick bent over his knees and clasped his hands together. "Dylan was a friend, and I trusted him. It was a first offense for him. He swore nobody would ever find out, and at the time we thought nobody was seriously hurt. We didn't find out about Vanessa's niece until a few months later."

"And because of the fog, and rain, no one could tell who

was driving—you or Dylan," Maddie said. "How much did he want as payment?"

"Couple thousand." He shook his head. "And then he kept asking for more later on, to keep quiet. Dylan kept gambling, the idiot, and he wouldn't stop. I helped pay for the kid's medical bills and therapy. Doesn't that count for anything?"

"Money, that's always been the answer for you," Gus said. "Your family has loads of it, and you wanted to protect your sales career. It's all about you!"

"What about Dylan? He's not innocent—"

"I don't care if he cheated at poker, or gambled too much. And you're to blame for letting him blackmail you. Sure, that was wrong, but murder? How could you, to a friend? And then strangling Vanessa. She only wanted you to admit the truth."

"You would've done the same," Nick retorted.

Gus waved a hand. "No way, man. I'm done with you forever."

When Detective Mason entered the chapel, along with Officer Hillerman, I sighed in relief. Frank and Steve flanked Nick once he stood, head down in shame. Kim's handgun had disappeared, so I figured she probably hid it beneath her skirt. I doubted if she carried her permit in her cleavage.

"Here's your murderer," Gus said. "Get him out of here."

Mason looked puzzled and then glanced at me. "What did you do?"

"She found the wedding rings," Kim said, "but Maddie found Vanessa's shoe. They got Nick to confess, and we're all witnesses. Perfect timing, because the wedding's supposed to begin in like ten minutes."

Eric held out his phone. "I recorded Nick, so he can't deny anything."

"Good." Mason pocketed the cell and hooked a thumb

toward the back. "There's like a crowd of people waiting to get in here. But I'd like to ask a few questions first."

The detective listened to our answers, took Vanessa's shoe and bagged it, and then he and Officer Hillerman escorted Nick out the side door. Steve Leeson looked relieved. His mother-in-law would feel the same, no doubt. Poor Vanessa could rest in peace.

I wasn't so sure about Dylan Campbell, but at least the case was solved.

"Ready?" Pastor Lovett hurried up the center aisle. "Places, everyone!"

Within minutes, the doors opened. People streamed into the chapel and hurried to fill the seats. The noisy scramble drowned out the opening strains of Mendelssohn's "Wedding March," which played through the speakers in the ceiling overhead. Until several shrieks echoed through the chapel and stopped the music. Gus had popped his head through the door in back and now rocked backward on his heels.

"Don't you know it's bad luck to see the bride before the wedding?" Debbie wailed.

"I just wanted Cissy to know what happ—"

"We know," Barbara said, and slammed the door in his face.

When the other bridesmaids snickered, I pulled Maddie aside. "You realize that the bridal party's not an even number anymore, so I'll step out. Especially since Frank will take Nick's place as Gus's best man."

"Oh, no you don't. You're the official dog walker." Maddie wound the leash around my hand, wrist, and arm. "Gus is not gonna risk losing those rings again by putting them anywhere near Mr. Clooney. You can follow Martina, and Debbie can follow you. Then Cissy will walk up the aisle with her father. Go!"

Maddie retreated to stand with the other bridesmaids. The music started again, so I hurried around one side of the filled seats. And almost tripped on my dress's train. Drat. Mr. Clooney had recovered his energy and dragged me to the chapel's back, as if hoping to escape again. I stopped short, however, when Jay appeared. He wore a dark suit, red silk shirt, and a matching tie. Clean-shaven, too, with his light brown hair slicked back. He smelled great.

"Not too late, I hope," Jay said with a grin. "Starts at six, right?"

"I'm supposed to go first," Martina said with a scowl.

She gripped her wicker basket of silk rose petals tight, eyes wide, since everyone in the crowded chapel turned to watch us. I hoped the flower girl hadn't suddenly frozen in fear, but Claudia Antonini leaned out from a pew, halfway up the aisle. She beckoned.

"Throw your petals, Tina," I whispered. "Go on, you can do it."

Martina walked slowly, one deliberate step at a time, and dropped a single petal to the floor. Jay took my arm, although I hadn't expect that, but why not? Together we trailed behind the little girl. People burst out laughing, however, which confused me until I glanced down. Mr. Clooney was eating a silk petal. He refused to release it and kept chewing.

"Leave it!" I stared at Mr. Clooney, who gave me such a sad face that I couldn't help joining the laughter. "Silly dog."

Giving up, I steered him away from any others Martina dropped. A futile measure, since he stretched his neck and scarfed a few more. If he survived swallowing diamond rings, maybe a few rose petals wouldn't hurt.

Jay escorted me to stand beside Martina and then slipped away to sit in a side pew. Gus straightened his shoulders, smiling at his cousin Frank, before they both focused on the maid of honor coming up the aisle. Debbie sported a silver-and-gold honeybee pin against her lace shoulder and clutched the stems of her lily-and-rose bouquet.

The music swelled louder when Cissy finally started up the aisle between her parents. Everyone stood, oohing and aahing over her strapless bead- and lace-encrusted sheath. Ruffled chiffon flared out below her knees in mermaid-style. A sheer veil sprouted behind her elaborate coiffure, fastened in place by a pearl-studded tiara. Cissy kissed her parents and then took her proud groom's arm.

After a brief prayer of welcome, Pastor Lovett addressed everyone. "We all know the difficulties Gus and Cissy have faced over the past month. They stand here now, after celebrating good times and enduring bad the past few weeks."

I noticed Cissy brush a tear from one eye, and Gus clasped her hand in his.

"They ask every guest here to encourage them, to believe in them, and also to support this community of Silver Hollow," the minister continued. "Do you accept this union and believe these two should be married today? Please respond with 'We do.'"

Everyone murmured approval.

"Every marriage will be tested by change, conflict, and strife. Will you remind them that love conquers all, that after such difficult and stressful times, if these two cling to each other, they will gain strength and courage? Please respond with 'We will.'"

Once again the crowd agreed. Pastor Lovett turned to Frank. He handed over the diamond wedding bands. "These rings serve as a promise, and reminder, of their love . . ."

Once the wedding ceremony ended, the bride and groom headed down the center aisle as man and wife—at last—to everyone's applause. Frank and Debbie followed, arm in arm. Martina raced after her father, her empty basket bobbing on one arm.

The rest of the bridesmaids and groomsmen paired up to trail after them—Bob and Gisele Vaccaro, Eric and Maddie, Steve and Kim. I brought up the rear with Mr. Clooney, who seemed reluctant halfway down the aisle. Jay tapped me on the shoulder.

"Uh, you might want to do something about that," he said and winked. "I hate to say it, but I told you so."

"Don't even—" I glanced backward and sighed.

The dog had dropped something after all, but not a rose petal.

Read on for a sneak preview of the next Teddy Bear
Mystery from Meg Macy . . .

BEAR A WEE GRUDGE

Coming soon from Kensington Publishing Corp.

Chapter 1

"Mama, Mama! My teddy bear—"

I quickly stepped out of the crowd of walkers and snatched up the furry toy before one of the focused joggers in the middle of Roosevelt Street could kick it away. Brushing a smear of dirt from the bear's nose, I dodged runners in shorts and sweaty shirts. My sister Maddie kept power-walking toward the park, arms pumping hard, oblivious to my rescue effort. I struggled to avoid bumping into others before I caught up to the woman, who'd halted her child's stroller.

She smiled in relief and gratitude. "Thank you so much!"

"No problem," I said. "Sorry, but it's a little dirty."

"I want my bear," the little girl wailed, wriggling in the stroller's seat. She looked adorable with light brown curls and huge chocolate brown eyes.

"That's the third time you dropped it this morning, Gracie," the mother scolded her child. "I think you're doing it on purpose."

"Gimme my bear!"

"Not until we get home. Which will be sooner if it rains

like last night." The mother stuffed the toy into the backpack hanging from the stroller's handle. "If you behave, I'll let you have your teddy bear in the car."

"I want it now!"

"No, stop whining." She turned to me once more with a deep sigh. "Thanks again. I'm sorry if we messed up your timing this morning."

"Oh, not at all. I wasn't timing, just walking." I wiggled my foot. "Got a blister, so I'm slowing down more and more with each step."

The woman nodded and pushed the stroller off, her child still wailing in misery. Had my sister noticed that I'd stopped? I shielded my eyes from the bright spring sunshine, trying to spy Maddie up ahead. Giving up, I limped to the nearest boulder bordering a lawn. I should have worn sneakers instead of my comfortable sandals. I'd never had a problem walking a few miles before in them. But now a blister had formed on my right heel from the leather strap.

I kicked myself for taking a break. I should have kept walking, because getting motivated to start again would be tough.

"Are you okay, Sasha?" Maddie had suddenly appeared before me and shook her head when I explained. "This will help cushion it, until we get home."

She handed me a strip of gauze, waited while I wrapped it around the sandal's strap, and then pulled me to stand. Maddie led me toward the street once more, but I hesitated. The sun shone between the bank of clouds overhead, but at least the balmy temperature of seventy degrees helped. Especially in late April, when Michigan could suffer from overnight frost. The park was only a few blocks. Good thing, because I was dying to sit on a bench.

I took a long drink from my water bottle. My silver bear tee shirt felt damp between my shoulders, too. Ugh. I needed a shower. I pushed a stray blond hair out of my eyes. Took another drink, sipping slower, until I drained it.

"Hey, Mads. Got a ribbon by any chance?"

"I found this scrunchie on the ground, and it's not that dirty."

"Beggars can't be choosers." I gathered my long hair into a ponytail. One more thing I'd forgotten to do this morning. "Okay, let's go."

"You can make it, right?" Maddie asked.

"I'll manage." I gritted my teeth and limped forward to the street once more. "I feel like such a baby. The Teddy Bear Trot is only what, three miles?"

"Four, I think," Maddie said absently. "At least the shorter route is. The joggers' route is six, and I did half of it earlier when I waited for you to show up this morning."

"You're a glutton for punishment."

Ignoring the pain of my blister, I focused on the trees overhead. They had already filled out with tiny leaves after a rain-soaked March. Clusters of yellow daffodils and the earliest tulips had bloomed and left their green stems behind. Late-blooming tulips of every color would soon brighten the village flower tubs and line the front of houses and sidewalks. Dogwoods and azalea bushes sprouted tiny flowers, along with forsythia with their bright yellow blooms.

I loved spring in Michigan, except the heady scent of hyacinths and Easter lilies. Every time I'd walked past the spiky flowers, inside or out, I sneezed hard. Luckily I didn't suffer as much as Jay Kirby, whose spring allergies to tree pollen drove him crazy.

But flowers and loamy earth didn't mean winter was forgotten. Snow or deadlier ice storms had come to Michigan up to mid- or late-May. Right now, I drank in the sunshine's warmth, the distant barking of dogs around the village, and the scent of fresh mown grass.

I hoped rain would hold off. The newly formed Silver Hollow Entrepreneurs and Business Association, commonly shortened to the acronym SHEBA, had plans to host a Scottish-themed Highland Fling on the third weekend of May. Local bakeries would sell scones, oatcakes, and other treats, and vendors would display all types of goods from kilts to swords and armor. Dancing and music, herding dog trials, plus athletic games filled the tentative schedule.

My mother, recently elected the village mayor, had joined forces with the village coordinator to assist SHEBA. A huge crowed was expected.

"We both missed the first committee meeting for the Highland Fling." I winced when a stray pebble hit my sore toe. "Not that much happened, or so I read from the minutes Mom had on hand. Remind me why we volunteered to help."

"Because we're dorks and let Mom twist our arms."

I laughed. "Fair enough. I wonder why they haven't come up with a better name."

"Yeah, because 'Highland Fling' is boring." Maddie steered me around a group of seniors who rolled their walkers, many with teddy bears strapped onto the fronts. "I suppose the 'fling' refers to the dancing, but the games and food are bigger draws."

"I'm just glad we don't have to put 'teddy bear' somewhere in the name," I joked. "Bears in kilts are adorable, though. And they'll be a big hit."

"I'll put one in the promotional flyers."

"Scotland holds all kinds of festivals on the Isle of Skye, and Inverness, all around the country. But the Ceres Games in Fife is the oldest. That's where the oldest golf course is, too. Old St. Andrews."

"How do you know that?"

"Gavin MacRae told me, and I googled it out of curiosity.

Robert the Bruce gave the village of Ceres a charter in the fourteenth century. Now that's old."

Maddie laughed. "I'll try to remember that for trivia night at the Silver Claw. Maybe Eric could get some Irn-Bru for people to taste, and some haggis."

"He can't import it," I said. "The USDA doesn't allow any products made with sheep lung, so he'd have to find a different recipe. Gavin and Molly might know one."

My sister slowed her pace again. "I guess SHEBA is sticking with plain old 'the Silver Hollow Highland Fling' for a name. I bet you could talk Uncle Ross into making teddy bears using plaid fabric instead of fur, as well as the ones wearing a kilt."

"Good idea. I'll bring it up at the next staff meeting."

Maddie circled me a few times, dancing around to expend extra energy, while I limped forward to the park's entrance. "I thought you prepared for this Teddy Bear Trot, Sasha. You did Pilates using my machine, right? And you promised you'd walk at least thirty minutes, minimum each day, from January until today."

"Um, sort of. I did what I could—"

"Sasha!"

"Hey, it's been crazy busy lately."

I didn't have to explain further. Maddie knew that while our Silver Bear factory was working overtime producing teddies for spring and summer, as well as the kilts for the Highland Fling, the shop itself was closed. We'd hired painters for the interior and exterior, a long overdue project. That meant I had to deliver inventory at the local shops, especially Mom's gallery, plus around the region, and help process online orders. All the office paraphernalia had been relocated to a small corner in the factory. That created another problem, of course.

Aunt Eve and Uncle Ross had recently remarried after

years of being divorced. While they loved each other, close proximity day and night was taking a heavy toll on my aunt's sanity. Production staff usually tolerated Uncle Ross's growls, barked orders, and bristly manner, but his wife craved peace and a happier working atmosphere. Any attempt to change her husband's attitude led to flare-ups between them. I acted as a liaison more than a dozen times.

The last thing I'd thought about was finding time to exercise.

"A lame excuse." Maddie sighed. "I paid for a yearly gym membership as a Christmas present for you, and you've used it what? Twice?"

"How do you know?" I asked, more curious than annoyed.

"You're on my plan, remember, so I can see when you check in," she said airily. "But I've got another idea. Remember that Kristen Bloom runs Blissful Yoga in the house she bought from the Davisons. I'm surprised Mom doesn't miss Barbara now she's gone to Florida."

"Mom's too busy being mayor."

"No kidding. Anyway, Kristen offers regular yoga classes, but also does goat yoga out at Richardson Farms. The baby goats are adorable! You might want to try it, since you're clearly unmotivated to go to the gym. You need a regular schedule."

"Yeah, I know." Two visits in three and a half months was pitiful, I had to admit. My flabby thighs told me so, too. "What happens in goat yoga? They jump all over you while you're doing all the poses?"

"Pretty much. But it's a lot of fun."

"Sugar Bear and Rosie already jump on me whenever I do Pilates."

"They're a distraction, wanting to be petted. The goats

don't care. Ignoring them is such a challenge and helps you focus on what you have to do."

I almost laughed, although my sister sounded serious. But I had challenge enough finding time—no, making time—to exercise. I wasn't a morning person, and I hadn't been walking the dogs often enough at lunchtime, either. That meant after work. Ugh.

Maddie jogged up the sloping wooden bridge spanning the narrow Huron River, which meandered through several tiny lakes farther north, and entered our own Silver Lake a hundred yards behind the Davisons' house, which was now transformed into the Kilted Scot Boutique. The river skirted the village's eastern edge and wandered past the park. Then it widened and flowed southeast toward Ann Arbor. Unfortunately, the banks tended to overflow in spring.

Our village park was a misnomer, given the open sward bordered by evergreens and forest. Less than an acre, with a few picnic tables at one end, a volleyball net near the parking lot, it also had an old metal slide and a newer jungle gym playscape.

But not enough space for the Highland Fling event.

"I think the committee expects the event to draw up to a thousand people," I said. "It's too crowded here for our annual Teddy Bear Picnic over Labor Day weekend."

"True enough. They'll have to find another place to hold it. Let's ask Mom."

She headed toward our parents, who'd just arrived at the Teddy Bear Trot registration table. I was glad I'd asked friends to take on that task early this morning, since I worked late last night putting all the name tags in lanyards, alphabetizing them in boxes, and tucking fee payment receipts into envelopes. I'd stapled them to a flyer which listed upcoming village events and information about donating to a volunteer group making

fleece blankets for sick kids. With a sigh I limped over to join
Maddie at the registration table.

"Hey, Dad. Mom," I added. "Did you enjoy the trot?"

"Of course," my mother said, although she didn't look
happy. "It's such a good cause."

"Your mother slipped when we cut across a field, instead
of sticking to the route," Dad said, and showed off the dried
mud on his khaki pants and sneakers. "She pulled me down
when I reached out to help her up, too."

"Oh, Alex! You didn't have to tell them that." Mom
brushed off the back of her denim capris with a frown. "I
admit, that was a mistake."

"Then I won't say I told you it was a bad idea."

"It's not too bad, really," I said, surveying her clothes.
"I'm in worse shape. Got a blister on my heel from these sandals."

"What in the world is he doing here?" Dad glowered past
my shoulder.

I whirled to see Teddy Hartman ambling over the bridge.
I tamped down the familiar sick feeling at the sight of him. He
had little resemblance now to the actor Billy Crystal, since his
hairline had receded farther, and his face had more lines and
wrinkles. Last fall he'd passed out flyers for his company at the
Labor Day parade, not caring about competing with our local
business. Hartman wore red canvas sneakers, faded jeans, and a
white cotton T-shirt.

Not that he couldn't register and participate in the Teddy
Bear Trot, but he'd failed to buy Richard and Barbara Davison's house to open a bed-and-breakfast. I figured Hartman
would leave the area for good. Clearly I was wrong.

"I sense trouble," Maddie muttered under her breath.

The woman beside Hartman wore a blue velour jogging
suit that matched the teddy bear she carried, and the headband

around her shoulder-length curly dark hair. She also held a blue leather leash attached to a small shaggy dog.

A few walkers crossed the bridge behind them. "What an adorable Yorkie."

"He's a Morkie." Annoyed, the woman quickly scooped up the pooch into her arms and turned to Hartman. "How much longer is this gonna take?"

"Not long, Lucy. We just have to collect our badges and paperwork."

Pouting, Lucy muttered complaints under her breath. She reminded me of Lucy Van Pelt from the Peanuts cartoon strip with her crabby attitude. "Isn't that the corrupt mayor you were telling me about?"

Hartman snickered. "Yeah—"

"Still full of yourself, Hartman?" Dad interrupted, his voice low but firm. I'd only witnessed that simmering anger once before, at the New Jersey trade show. "Putting others down so you can brag about yourself, and spread lies."

"I'm only telling it like it is," he said, "after talking to residents here. Plus one of the village council members. Your wife likes to throw her weight around."

Mom bristled at that. "Oh? What exactly are you referring to, Mr. Hartman? Because if there's a problem, I'm right here and you can discuss the issue directly to me. Along with this unnamed village council member."

Hartman eyed my mother and then me, his thin brows furrowed. "It's not my job to tell you where you're falling short. Talk to anyone around here—"

"I'm talking to you," she said, "since you and your friend here mentioned corruption. If you make a claim like that, you ought to back it up with facts."

Lucy stepped forward, and shushed the dog when it growled. "The SHEBA group of business owners talked about how you're ramming stuff down people's throats, so why don't you ask them?"

My mother cocked her head, her auburn hair glinting in the sun, and placed a hand on Dad's arm before he could speak or react. "I will, thank you for that comment. SHEBA is a new group, and I believe Mr. Hartman organized it. Isn't that right?" she asked him, her tone saccharine sweet.

He shrugged. "So? We're opening a business here, where the ice cream shop used to be. A pet boutique. That means we'll be keeping an eye on you and Alex, plus your network of cronies." Hartman suddenly snapped his fingers at me. "Oh, yeah. I remember you from a while back. Running around that trade show in New Jersey. What were you, thirteen or fourteen? A little spy, taking notes for your dad."

Both my parents stiffened at his words, but I waved my hands in the air to keep them from losing their tempers. "That was research," I said, "to help gather ideas for the Silver Bear Shop my family wanted to start."

"Stealing ideas, that's what you really did."

He grinned when Dad curled his fists, clearly angry and trying hard not to lash out. I shook my head. "I didn't steal anything, Mr. Hartman, but you might want to watch what you say. Remember what happened back then."

"What? Nothing happened. I wouldn't touch such a fat, ugly girl—"

Maddie darted toward him before Dad could and landed a hard punch right on Teddy Hartman's nose. Howling, he clutched his face while bright red blood streamed between his fingers. Lucy screamed and dropped her dog onto the ground.

At the same moment when I reached out, hoping to stop my sister from a second punch, the Morkie snapped at my outstretched hand. Several times, biting my fingers and thumb. In shock, I stumbled backwards.

"How dare you assault my husband!" Lucy hauled on the leash, tearing her pet away.

I reeled, staring at the drops of red on the ground, and the blood streaming from the ragged wounds on my hand. Mom tore off her light jacket, wrapped my hand, and rushed me to the registration table. I was oblivious to whether Teddy or Lucy Hartman had retreated, or if Maddie and my dad drove them off. Pain seared my foggy brain at last. I'd never been bitten by any animal, dog or cat, in my life.

"Are you okay, Sasha?" Dad asked, crowding me. "How bad is it?"

"Give her a little air," Maddie said, tears streaking her cheeks.

"Isabel, please call 9-1-1," Mom said.

"Already did, Mrs. Silverman," she said and waved her cell. "An EMT unit is on the way."

I drew a long breath. Big trouble was certainly brewing now.

Connect with U s

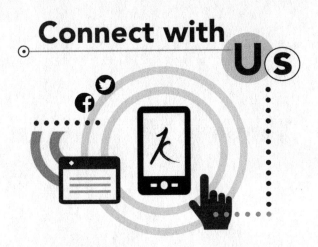

Visit us online at
KensingtonBooks.com
to read more from your favorite authors, see books
by series, view reading group guides, and more.

for sneak peeks, chances to win books and prize packs,
and to share your thoughts with other readers.

facebook.com/kensingtonpublishing
twitter.com/kensingtonbooks

Tell us what you think!

To share your thoughts, submit a review,
or sign up for our eNewsletters, please visit:
KensingtonBooks.com/TellUs.